A LUKE SANZ NOVEL: BOOK 1

UNDER
the
SKY

THE WICKED FEAR THE LIGHT OF DAY

SIG. ALEXANDER

A LUKE SANZ NOVEL: BOOK 1

UNDER
THE
SKY

SIG. ALEXANDER

"Ode to Under the Sky," written by Christina L. Pearson © 2023 and used by permission.

ISBN-13: 979-8-9886367-0-0 - Paperback
ISBN-13: 979-8-9886367-1-7 – eBook
ISBN-13: 979-8-9886367-2-4 - Hardcover

10 9 8 7 6 5 4 3 2 1

First Edition

For Hal Cumpston

For my brothers DJG and RAF.

Under the Sky, An Ode

At some point, we all come here
Under the sky of our Lord
Welcomed or not, for duty
Clinging to the invisible chord

Some here, are His chosen few.
Chosen to wander all of the Earth
Along with their Guardian Angels
So as not to give way, to evil's birth

At some point, we all leave here
To go Above the sky of our Lord
Some here, are His chosen few
To be where the Angels soared

That which is under His sky
The realm that lies in between
That which is above His sky
Remains unchanging, unseen

Christina L. Pearson
© 05-30-2023

PROLOGUE

Although *it* was inhuman, the creature saw *itself* as a man, and was preparing to take another soul to gain the essence of life that gave *it* power. The name he was given when *it* was created was something from the distant past, something he guarded more than anything. Languishing in the home brought him comfort because he was free from enslavement from the catacombs of Hell.

The creature ceaselessly whittled down the man of the house through constant attacks, deteriorating his resolve. The attacks were comparable to an immovable weight upon the man's mind. The man had a son named John, who had opened a wall that concealed the belongings of one of the souls the fiend held captive. That soul, one of his most loyal followers, was sidelined as a greedy zealot seeking to play with his childish property. The soul's audiophile-directed personality was fragmented by the theft of his terrestrial belongings.

The malevolent spirit's true goal, since the family moved into the home, was to control and possess the energy within each family member and not the body itself.

Causing those surrounding the evil spirit to sin was why he existed. He felt a perverse pleasure with the control of the soul. Forcing others to do his bidding by introducing his diseased thoughts and pressuring the father of the home to neglect, instead of protecting his family brought him pleasure He had twisted the man's mind into knots enough that he would be persuaded to allow anything to happen.

The demon's reliance on his servant, a long-term companion of several decades, had become tedious. The rifling and movement of the soul's property minimized the abomination's power over him. The other souls in his possession were sent all at

1

once to begin pressuring the other occupants of the home.

Earlier, John brought a young woman named Barbara with him. Together they ruffled through his captured companion's belongings. She had long, curly blond hair and was incredibly voluptuous. As something inhuman who had never walked physically on the earth, he did not realize what *it* felt was infatuation. He existed as a wisp in the wind, part of the ether and not a corporeal entity, he did not function the way a human being would. He spent most of his time reacting to urges endemic to *its* ilk. The consumption and possession of souls brought a deep sense of satisfaction. Controlling the essence of the soul and watching the family as a unit deteriorate in a home, brought him a horrific pleasure. That deterioration was what he lived with, for decades, if not centuries. As time passed differently for him.

What he feared the most was if somebody discovered his name, which *it* guarded. He refused to think of the name his master gave *it* so long ago. Without his name, he believed he could not be controlled, and *it* could not be returned to his lords' possession.

The introduction of Barbara was different because of her youth and beauty. Something new in his time after having escaped from his master. This infatuation forced him to try and caress or touch the woman. In truth, he wanted to have sex with her. He had never truly felt anything. Maybe it was just another urge. It was confusing.

Barbara slept in the nude, curled up on the edge of the full-size bed. She was small and vulnerable, but he had to have her. All the souls under his control surrounded the bed and formed into one near the girl. The shimmering form took the sheets off her. She did not move, deep in sleep. The form touched her foot. He felt something, not entirely, but enough to create a surge of energy to flow into his form. He grabbed her ankles. Barbara pulled her feet away, which angered him, so he yanked her forcibly. The captured souls yanked her legs apart, so he flowed on top of her like a weighted blanket. She screamed, waking John beside her.

"Are you okay, Barb?" John yelled while trying to grab her foot, but he could not penetrate the shimmering form before him.

The intense pleasure *it* received dissipated when John tried to stop the assault. He sent its minions on the attack, who grabbed John and held him down to the bed. Red bolts of lightning massed around John and pinned him to the wall.

He wanted to be able to touch and feel the woman itself. To do so, he needed to become corporeal. To walk the earth and act on his urges and needs. What he needed was the essence of a strong person. A person of faith, such as a man of God. He had met a priest before but felt that the man's soul had no value to *it*. He needed a man of God who had absolute faith and was not another person stuck in the rut of life. This young man was insufficient.

He was weakened by the loss of essence from his form. Barbara jumped out of bed and ran out of the room. *It* tried to surge out of the room toward the girl, but the tether he had with his enslaved souls prevented his movement. He tried to pull away once more, which severed the tether with the red mass of light containing John who fell to the ground with a thud. His anger intensified as he stared at young man on the floor. His anger was so extreme that he did not consider taking the boy's healthy soul in his customary measured way; instead, he pounced with his full power. The boy's body gave out, and the soul was partially expelled, fragmented. He took what essence he could and turned to the hunt for Barbara. The dismembered soul of the boy did not coalesce within him. He used his remaining energy to chase after the girl and sent his muscle, the farmer's soul, to stop the girl from running from the home.

He was too late. The family had prepared and fled the home. He failed to realize that during the fog induced by Barbara's introduction into his realm, the family had already moved many of their belongings out already. Barbara and the remainder of the family were outside waiting. *How much time had passed since it attacked the boy?* He shrieked in anger and constricted the four souls in its control. *It* fled the house and jolted straight toward Barbara. He fell to the ground like a lead weight. His power was significantly diminished outside of the home. When he attacked the souls he possessed, it affected the essence that gave him strength. He could not recall why he was tied to the house but remembered his power was concentrated near the home. He lay languishing on the asphalt driveway. *I need to find what is keeping me attached to this home,* he thought. He would never allow this to happen again once he consumed the essence he needed.

He turned toward the house, pushing his now gaseous form toward a gap that would allow *it* entry. A man left the house holding John, who appeared conscious. He even failed to retain that boy's soul. Barbara was gone.

He reached toward John, trying to pull more of the boy's essence from his body. Nothing happened. The family was gone. He kept moving slowly toward the home and the open front door. After a tortuous trek on the path to the doorway, he was able to throw some of his remaining essence through the half-open door. He flowed quickly into the home as he slammed the solid wood door shut splintering it down its center. He was consumed in anger, he darted up the numerous levels of the home into the attic where he stayed and tried to heal. Thoughts of Barbara's flesh consumed him. He had never *felt* this way and aimed to remove these unnatural thoughts that drove him to what humans would call insanity. He would never again be so impulsive and must be measured and strategic with his future victims. What he needed was the soul of a person who had devoutness, wisdom, sagacity, and trustworthiness. Such a soul would provide the mass of the spirit he would need to make *it* whole. Eventually, sleep came to him, but he would not sleep forever.

CHAPTER ONE

Vision

A chaotic scene unfolded below as he soared above in the sky. People dressed in black, wearing face coverings, were climbing tall chain link fences, which buckled under the weight of the Ninja-like bodies upon it. It came to him. This was St. Peters Square. The fence blocked the entrance to the square. Soldiers wearing blue uniforms pushed back against the onslaught of the hooligans.

Abruptly, his point of view had changed. All that was visible was a large view screen, unlike any television he had ever seen. He was not controlling what he saw or what happened before him. It was a news broadcast. The television host was a bearded *woman* wearing high-heeled shoes. The host stood on a film stage in front of various screens that showed different views of the insurrection.

"After days of protests, the brave members of the Army of Christ have finally begun to push toward the Vatican grounds," the bearded host said, while moving from screen to screen. "These righteous protesters are wearing face coverings to keep from being doxed by members of the far right."

He was confused with what he was watching. *Where am I?* He moved around the room aimlessly. He peered outside the window that was halfway covered in snow. He turned his attention to the odd videos on the viewing screen. The guards were being stomped into the ground and beaten with large batons. The Italian State Police, or *Polizia di Stato*, were not present. He knew that the country's government had ruled not to protect the Vatican City from being overrun. Over the past five years, the citizens had turned against the Holy See. On one screen was a group of soldiers holding halberds in a narrow pathway between two buildings. The soldiers were called the Pontifical Swiss Guard. They thrust their halberds forward into the soldiers of the Army of Christ, who dropped to the ground, bloodied.

He yelled at the screen, but his voice was silent. He was supposed to stop this but did not. He was powerless and a failure. He allowed this to happen by foundering in passivity.

"As you can see, the violent members of the Swiss Guard are attacking the peaceful protesters who are demanding the pope hear their grievances ... one moment everyone ... switch the camera then." The host walked over to the new view screen filming from above. The Army of Christ had breached the grounds. A large building was on fire. "The Sistine Chapel is on fire." The host's hairy knuckled hand covered the smile forming on *her* face. Smoke poured out of the windows, followed by growing flames. "This is a sad but necessary day." The host moved across the stage to a new view screen.

The rioters dressed in black were piling dozens of the papal guard into one growing mound next to another comprised of priests, bishops, and cardinals.

The host made a motion toward his neck with one hand and moved to another screen where it was evident that hundreds, if not thousands, of black costumed thugs had stormed the Vatican grounds. Smoke and flames poured out of almost all the visible buildings. "Please don't be distressed by what you are seeing. Many of us have called for this so-called Second Fall of Rome. We are seeing the removal of one of the most pernicious and destructive organizations that remain on our good Earth. One moment ... we have an affiliate partner near the Basilica with an exclusive video feed."

A large view screen showed a massive group from the Army of Christ pulling at a man dressed in white. It was the pope. A flash of blades struck the body of the man quickly turning his attire red. The pope was beyond deceased.

The host gasped and squatted down toward *her* heeled feet. *She* steepled *her* hands toward *her* face as if in prayer. To whom *she* prayed, he had no idea. The host stood up slowly with a growing smile. *She* did not cover *her* face this time.

"It's done. What you witnessed today is the removal of the last remnants of an evil organization that has plagued our planet for thousands of years. They poisoned our Earth with lies, racism, and intolerance. That's it, folks." The host's red lips formed into a grin while *her* eyes grew bold and red. Evil had prevailed.

"The demon is a deceiver. It speaks in opposites and without truth. This evil will walk the earth if it's not stopped," a voice said in Spanish. "Wake up … remember … you can stop it."

Luke Sanz woke quickly and jumped up in the school bus aisle. *Where the hell am I?* The man driving the bus pointed down toward the floor, and he sat quickly. He was on his way home from school. The dream began to dissolve and with it any possibility of a resolution.

✠ ✠ ✠

Overboard

Luke sat quietly on the bus next to his brother, Junior. At that very moment, he could not recall what distressed him moments ago. The dream dissipated in a wisp of smoke. The event was too far away.

"Are you okay, Luke?"

He looked at his brother, Junior. *I need to remember something,* he thought. The dream, he was supposed to recall the dream. It was a message. He had to prevent something from happening. Only a lingering thought remained that it was necessary to recall the lost memory. "I had a bad dream, Junior. Just don't ask me what it was about." *I feel as if somebody wiped my memory,* he mused.

"You were twitching in your sleep. I'm surprised you didn't fall on the floor."

This caused Luke to laugh before looking toward the back of the bus, where his brother Daniel was playing rough with his friends. He looked at the bus driver, who shrugged and kept driving. Everyone seemed to let Daniel get away with everything. The remaining drive from Fort Buchanan to Dorado, Puerto Rico, where Luke Sanz lived with his family. Most of the students at the Antilles School District were the children of United States government employees, both federal and military. His father, Angel Sanz, was a special agent with the Department of State and often traveled throughout the Caribbean to different embassies in foreign countries. His mother, Helen Martin-Sanz, was from Sydney, Australia, and had met his father at an embassy dinner when her father was the Lord Mayor of Sydney.

He looked out the window toward a section of coral reef visible from Highway 165. The drive to and from school was scenic, but the churning water was so close to the road that it brought him anxiety, which he typically suffered from. It was like a lead weight on a fishing line, but with fishing, you at least could have a meal. It was common for him to feel as if a plane was about to slam into a bus he occupied.

There were two routes from the Army base that housed the Antilles schools to their coastal home near Villa Pesquera. The bus driver once said he preferred this route because he liked the water. Something he learned when he asked Junior to ask the driver to take a faster route home.

Luke was always shy but since suffering from anxiety he barely spoke to others. When Luke was younger, he began to hear a man's voice. He does not recall what the man said, but his parents and doctors told him it was all in his imagination. One day, his mother was distraught when she learned that her father in Australia was missing. He touched his mother and saw that his grandfather had fallen in a mine shaft on their ranch outside of

Sydney. He told his mother where her father was, and he was rescued. Instead of being happy, she became angered and took Luke to various medical doctors, psychologists, and psychiatrists. His mother worried that Luke would always have strained relationships in life if they thought he was touched by some type of growing madness. Some doctors experimented on him with prescription medication that stopped the man's voice, but not the images he would see if he touched most people. His parents and siblings learned to keep him at a distance possibly so Luke wouldn't learn their innermost secrets. Luke brought an oddity to their lives that was unwanted.

He met a man during one of his hospitalizations as a fourteen-year-old. The man was a quirky fellow who dressed in a costume. Luke had an argument with the man and complained to his case worker. Fortunately, the man was moved from his room or something, but he continued to hear his voice, which opened a new set of problems and new regimens of experimental medications from his doctors. Afterwards, he concentrated hard on telling his nurses, doctors, and even the janitor that he no longer heard the man's voice and denied being able to see anything when he touched someone.

During one of his medical stays a counselor taught him the fundamentals of playing an acoustic guitar. This tended to help him manage some of his anxiety by concentrating on the notes and guitar strings. His grandparents on his mother's side bought him a black 1989 Fender *Stratocaster*, which he played regularly and had taken some lessons. I brought him a necessary joy that was absent in his young life.

Once he returned home, his family kept him at arm's length. It had been years since his last institutionalization, and he had successfully suppressed everything. Sort of. The voice and the visions were replaced by anxiety, but he learned how to deal with that by vigorous exercise, which added muscle to his frame but little else. He did not sleep at night; he would pass out from exhaustion.

As they entered the guarded entrance to their community in Dorado del Mar, Daniel appeared to get louder as he slapped butts with his baseball player teammates. Once they got closer to their drop-off stop, Daniel stood near the now compliant silent driver, who should have been telling his brother to wait until the bus came to a complete stop. Daniel jumped off the bus first, with Junior close behind him.

Luke followed them with his long brown hair covering his face like a security blanket. At six foot three inches in height, and pushing two hundred fifty pounds, he appeared menacing compared to his soulful brown eyes. His mother, Helen, waited for them at the front door of their home.

"Boys, I put some iced tea on the bar for you," his mother said as Daniel and Junior kissed her when they entered the house. As usual, his mother avoided his touch.

Tony, Luke's Jack Russell Terrier, ran up to him, jumping in the air as if trying to reach into his arms. Instead, Tony hit him in the crotch—one of his dog's unique ways of saying hello. The dog was a gift to the family from his grandparents. Tony was *velcroed* to his side when he was home.

"You little rascal, Ton. Get a new trick," Luke said in a feigned act of discipline.

His brother's beat Luke to the iced tea, but Junior served a glass and handed it to him.

"Thanks, Junior."

Out of nowhere, he began to feel a sense of dread creep into him. He anticipated a life-changing event without having cause to do so. He headed into his bedroom, visibly sweating, with the onset of an anxiety attack. He grabbed his dumbbells on the floor and began to curl them quickly.

While Luke was lifting the weights he thought of a dream he had the night before. In the dream, he was a soldier traveling with his father on a ship heading to the Dominican Republic. The soldier was ashamed for something he did and was happy that he was headed towards a battle he may not survive.

He finished his workout, was hungry, and wanted to see what was for dinner. He found his mother at the range in the kitchen holding onto her chest.

"What's wrong, Mom?"

"I haven't heard from your father. He was due back yesterday." His mother was visibly shaken and even wiped a tear from her face.

Luke walked toward his mother and almost touched her, but she stepped backward. He pulled away as well. "I have this odd feeling myself … maybe you should call his office or his friend Carl, Mom." Without saying a word, his mother walked toward the kitchen and grabbed the phone receiver from the wall. Luke followed his mother, deciding to eavesdrop.

"What do you mean you haven't heard from him in days?" his mother yelled. "Well, find out what's going on and come over here and tell his children where he is." His mother slammed the phone so hard on the cradle a nearby calendar fell to the floor. She ran out of the kitchen without saying a word.

Luke picked up the calendar. Somebody circled the 18th and wrote *Santo Domingo* within the square and *HOME* in block writing. It was the 19th, and his father was indeed delayed.

Luke headed back to the patio, where their makeshift gym was located, and began to punch his heavy bag. The exercise served to tamper down his concern for his father. He heard a loud knock at the front door an hour into his workout. He looked toward the front entrance and noticed his mother hesitated to open the door at the foyer. She roughly wiped away moisture from her face and opened the door, revealing their father's friend, Carl.

"Helen, I'm sorry. I just returned from a trip to New York and did not know that Angel had not come home yet," Carl said, loud enough for Luke to overhear as he strolled into the living room.

His mother grabbed the door as if to slam it on Carl but took a step back and allowed him to walk in. Luke walked toward the kitchen, allowing the adults to think they had privacy in the living room, but it would let him hear their discussion.

"Just let it out, please. The suspense is killing me," she said while motioning for Carl to sit on the rattan sofa before she settled on the loveseat.

"Helen, Angel took a team to Santo Domingo to assist in recovering the daughter of one of the ambassador's staff. From my understanding, everything was routine. They were due to report to a Coast Guard cutter waiting for them east of Punta Cana. They never made it to the cutter."

"How long has he been missing?"

Luke heard a loud sigh as if somebody had punctured an inflatable boat. "Two days." Carl paused before saying, "A debris field was found, but Angel, two men, and the child are missing."

Luke walked into the living room. His mother's mouth was open. She covered it with her hand and collapsed into Carl's arms, sobbing uncontrollably. His father must have perished at sea, and their lives here would change. This cannot be real, he thought. He imagined vividly that they would be moving back to Australia. It was where he was born and where he grew up until he was ten years old. It's not that he didn't want to return to Australia, but he had grown accustomed to the shielded life he had on the *island*. An intense burning sensation formed within his body. Anxiety, which was a constant in his life. It smacked Luke down with vengeance. It threatened to remove any type of hope that his father survived at sea for two days. No matter what, life as he knew it had been altered.

Carl walked up to Luke and tapped his shoulder. Everything went dark as if his eyes closed but they had not. It was like a switch had been thrown on an attic light that had been off for eons.

"You've gotten bigger since the last time I saw you, Luke."

Luke recalled meeting Carl years ago with that painful smack to his shoulder, but something else had happened. He looked downward to the man that he towered over. The man stepped back a bit, alarmed. "Find my father, Mr. Vaughn."

Carl smiled, but it quickly turned into a frown. "I'm going to Aguadilla straight from here to meet with a Coast Guard buddy." With that the man left the house quickly.

"Touch your mother now, Luke." A man's voice said in Spanish.

There was a familiarity to the voice he recognized immediately from the past. He felt inclined to follow the man's advice, but his mother always recoiled when he got too close. *I must touch my mother,* he thought. Luke walked over to her. She sat quietly, head pointing to the floor. When he sat, she moved away from him. He hesitated before placing his hand on her shoulder ... *I was splashed with water as I rolled backward into the abyss. A young girl was in my arms with two men near us holding onto flotation devices, possibly seat cushions. We were surrounded by the unending sea. A flash of light coming from high above and into the sky caught my interest. It was a lighthouse. I knew where I was—Isla Mona* ... Luke stood up quickly and almost fell over. A bout of nausea overcame him as he was propelled forward after returning from his vision.

He ran outside and waved down Carl, who was just pulling away. "Mr. Vaughn, Mr. Vaughn." He caught up to the vehicle's passenger side and opened the door.

"What is it, Luke?"

"He's several miles east of the lighthouse on Mona Island."

Carl looked at him oddly. "How would you know that?"

He couldn't answer that himself. *How do I know that?*

"The ocean is vast. If I send the Coast Guard out to Mona, they could miss him altogether. Give me more, son, or the Coast Guard will keep following their grid search."

"Mr. Vaughn, I saw it. He has a young girl in his arms, floating near two men. I saw the beam from the lighthouse high above. I have never been there, but I know there are cliffs, and my father is treading water to the shore."

Carl looked at him from his driver's seat. "The extraction was nowhere near Mona ... Luke, your father told me once that you seemed a bit … intuitive."

"Please take a chance. Save my father," he pleaded.

Carl clenched his teeth noticeably before moving the gear shift into park and leaving the vehicle. "I need to use your phone. I'll have them send a helicopter right now."

At that very moment, Luke realized he had awakened the visions he had suppressed for years. Keeping his family at a distance had improved his relationships with everyone but this event could change things for the worse. His visions were always real and that meant the man's voice he heard in his youth was real. He knew his father would be found alive. Fantastical thoughts that his parents were proud of him and welcomed his abilities into his life brought him to deep sleep that night, comforted in positive thoughts of change while waiting to find out if his father survived at sea. In truth, this day brought something dark into his life, propelling his family onto a murky path.

CHAPTER TWO

House Hunting

As Lulu McCray, the family real estate agent, grabbed the doorknob, she turned toward the family. "The house is in disarray and needs a tender loving hand." She opened the front door slowly for the big reveal at the last home they planned to see that unproductive week.

"More like a pot of gold to fix this up." His father, Angel Sanz, survived his adventure at sea. However, after he was plucked from the ocean, his exploits with having saved a diplomat's child resulted in his promotion and a move to form a Continental United States or CONUS post in Loudon County, Virginia.

They had spent the last week living in a hotel near the Dulles Airport while Lulu showed them homes in Leesburg and Ashburn. Eventually, Lulu talked his parents into looking at this disheveled house on Red Hill Road in the City of Lansburg.

That was the explanation his parents told them, but Luke overheard speaking one night before leaving their house in Puerto Rico. His parents drank too much wine that night and their voices carried. Carl had naively told the story of how Luke's vision had saved his father who was too vain and could not withstand the talk in the office. This included an unwelcome prank with a fake signed copy of a Nostradamus book left on his father's desk. His father was angry and conflicted because he was saved by his *weird* son. His parents cried together that night. They had no plans to move from Puerto Rico but the event that afternoon in April was enough to drive them to this new home in Virginia.

"Be positive. Try to visualize what the house would look like with some love and care," Lulu said.

They walked around the battered furniture and junk left in the house. "What a pigsty," Daniel said. "It stinks in here, too!"

"It smells like a water leak, and the carpet is rotten. I need some air," Junior said, stepping back out the front door with his brothers.

"Let's check out the bedrooms," Luke said after having inhaled some fresh air.

They headed up one flight of stairs and stepped into the first room. "Must be the master bedroom. It has a full bathroom. Let's check outo the other room," Junior said. This bedroom was smaller, but it also had a bathroom.

"I want this room." Daniel was visibly happy with a grin across his smug face.

"It figures you would want a private bathroom. All hail King Daniel," Junior said.

"Let's check the other rooms, Junior, since Daniel is going to be the one who decides if we live here." He motioned for Junior to follow him up another set of stairs. He passed a small room that could be an office and two bedrooms were located at the end of a long hallway with a nearby bathroom.

"I want the room facing the front of the house," Junior said.

"Fine with me. I like the view of the backyard. There's a little waterfall, and I can hear it from here." He stared out the window at the brook. It brought him a sense of calm.

He walked down the hallway and saw his parents in the master bedroom with the real estate agent. All three of them entered the room.

"What are you thinking, boys?" his father asked.

"This is the house, Dad," Daniel said quickly.

Luke hesitated, with the hanging thought that he preferred to be back in Puerto Rico. Something else about the house spooked him. He felt as if he was being watched.

"I'm confident we can fix it up, Dad," Junior said.

"Give us a moment, boys." His father returned to Lulu and

their mother, who were conversing.

"I'm going to check and see if we can put a gym in the garage," Luke said, heading downstairs with his brothers guided by the realization that if they moved to this house, he would need his Fortress of Calmness—what he called his workout area.

They walked into the garage, which was long and wide with enough space to park cars and place a gym. "What's in all these boxes?" Junior asked, opening one. "Record albums—strange that they are not even open. Why would anybody leave this here?"

The brothers spent a few minutes looking into the boxes— albums and magazines from what he saw. "Take a look at this one. An unopened Pink Floyd - *The Wall* original album from 1979. It's pristine, guys." Luke loved many forms of music, especially Pink Floyd since David Gilmour was his favorite guitarist.

"How about this one, Luke? The Beatles - *Yesterday and Today*."

"Wow ... wait, do you hear that, Junior?" Heavy footfalls above them caused a sinking feeling in the pit of his stomach.

"Yes, sounded like footsteps upstairs," Junior said.

"Our parents must be in whatever room is above the garage," Daniel said.

"Then who is that in the backyard?" Luke pointed at the back door that had a window built in. The adults were out on the deck speaking. He walked out to the deck with his brothers and joined their parents. "Dad, we heard footsteps upstairs. Is there somebody else here?"

"This time of year, the houses tend to settle a bit." Lulu appeared concerned or scared.

"A forty-year-old house is still settling?" their father asked.

"The house is near a creek, and it has been raining," Lulu said.

Luke's father shook his head as if doubting Lulu but said the opposite of what Luke expected. "Sounds right, boys. Lulu, let us know what the seller says about the price and paying a reduced rent until the sale closes ... come on. We are headed back to the hotel."

They all walked back toward the driveway. He had the feeling again of being watched. When he turned around, he saw a man standing in the hallway peering at him through the second-floor window. Luke walked closer and stared at the figure. It had white eyes, and its bloody skin was a singed blackened burned mess. The creature stared back and pointed at Luke and then at itself eerily. He backed up and averted his eyes with the creature shyly in fright. He looked at his parents waiting in the car, his father pointed at his watch. *I need to tell them.* Luke took a step toward the car and heard a disembodied voice.

"Don't come back. You'll regret it ..." The low wisp of voice was gravelly yet forceful.

Luke stopped in his tracks and looked at the family car. If he brought up what he saw in the house they would immediately realize they brought their reasons for evacuating from Puerto Rico with them. They will not believe him. More likely they would continue to resent him. *I cannot tell them*, he thought in defeat. Luke convinced himself not to warn his family, thus propelling his family forward into potential harm.

I walked through the house on Red Hill Road, but it was different somehow. It had multiple levels with a confusing layout of stairs. I desperately sought a way out, but no matter how I turned, another set of stairs appeared. A door was visible below, finally arriving at a landing where the door was located. I opened it and stepped out. It was dank, and cold, in the empty room that stretched into the distance. I walked into a corner of the room, now seeing what looked like furniture. As I got closer, I noticed that the furniture was made for a small child. A bed, clothing dresser, table with utensils, plates, and a drinking cup were visible. I reached down to grab the cup.

"That's my cup, you fat freak!" A short creature lunged at me ... Luke screamed before jumping up in bed, trying to claw his way out of the sheets. He was bathed in sweat. Tony stared at him with

concern.

"What the hell, Luke? How can a guy get some sleep around here?" Daniel wrapped his blanket over his head while growling.

"I didn't think I was ever going to get out of there. I was stuck, I was stuck," Luke dried the sweat off his face with the crisp white hotel sheets.

"Get unstuck, and either go back to sleep or hide in the bathroom."

Luke jumped into the shower and thought about his dream, which was vivid in his memory. He knew that he was stuck in the house on Red Hill Road. *It's a warning*, he thought. Something about the house was bad, almost like it was rotten. He could not tell his parents. He must brave a new path and get his parents to be comfortable around him again. If his family cannot see the ghost in the house, then their ignorance would just be his misery. *I'm used to it.* The thought he needed to warn his family circled around in his skull, each time ending with the realization they would recoil at anything he said.

CHAPTER THREE

The Clean-up

The weather was balmy, and the humidity could have been unbearable if he had not been used to it from living on the *island* for as long as he had. The forecast called for scattered showers throughout the day. They arrived at the house and prepared to be busy clearing garbage from the home. Luke was a bit excited, but cleaning the filthy mess made him wish he could press fast-forward until dinner time.

They wore their oldest clothes, including jeans, gloves, hats, and respirator masks. Their father opened the trunk, and Junior immediately grabbed a tool bag and headed to the front door. Luke grabbed an ice chest and a large radio. Daniel stayed in the car, prepared to nap.

Their father stood outside the car, looking through the window at Daniel with a scowl. "Get moving, Daniel."

"It's raining, Dad. Why are we doing this?" Daniel asked, with his chin headed back down toward his chest.

"Are you going to rust if you get wet?" Junior asked while grabbing another bag.

Their father stood outside the car, staring at Daniel, but said nothing else.

Daniel winced at the menacing frown on their father. "I'm moving, Dad," Daniel said before grabbing a box of trash bags from the trunk.

They all huddled near one another at the front door. Luke had not noticed before, but the door had a crack running from the top to the bottom, including the glass.

"We are all getting wet, Helen. What's wrong?" his father asked.

"The door is jammed. Luke, can you push the door?"

He looked through the window and could not see into the house. Something blocked his view. He pushed the door forcibly but felt pressure coming from inside. "Weird, it feels like somebody is pushing back on me." As he tried again, two cue ball white eyes stared at him. He let go of the door and stepped back onto his brother, Junior. The door opened inward on its own. He felt relieved when he saw an empty room before him.

"What happened?" Junior asked.

"Nothing, I lost my balance," he said. He did not mention what he saw fearing it would further the divide with his family.

"The door is swollen because of the rain. Go ahead and move, we are getting wet," Luke's father said impatiently.

They walked into the house, and all sighed while looking at the damp mess in the living room.

"All, please wear masks. It smells like mold. Also, make a note of what's in the boxes. If anything is worth keeping, put it aside to sell or keep. Junior, grab those plastic bins your dad brought inside, take some to the kitchen, and leave the rest here."

"Yes, Mom," Junior said. "Keep what? It's all garbage."

"Daniel and Luke are on large furniture duty. Start moving all this furniture out of the house and put it in front of the dumpster." Their mother said firmly.

"Put on your mask, Daniel. This moldy furniture is going to get you sick." Luke tugged at his mask; afraid it was not sitting correctly.

"Stop mothering me," Daniel said, putting on his mask.

They worked systematically by emptying the first two levels of the house, except the kitchen, by placing all the garbage into the dumpster. They found more boxes of items in a small room down the fourth-floor corridor. Their mother had claimed the room as her art studio. She was a known artist who made money by making posters for marketing companies and some movies.

Something she began to do later in life and thought of herself as a sellout that betrayed her prior artistic works.

"This box is full of comic books, and they are wrapped in plastic," Junior said.

"This one has record albums like the ones in the garage. They are still in the shrink wrap." Luke held up one of the albums. "Like they came from a store … let's stack these in the garage and try to sell them later."

All three brothers went up to the fourth-floor bedrooms. Junior took apart the remaining furniture while he and Daniel moved everything to the dumpster.

Junior walked back and forth throughout the room as if he had lost something. "Whose playing games?"

"What's wrong?" Luke asked.

"Somebody took my tools."

"Wasn't us. We've been moving this crap to the dumpster." Luke grabbed onto a box and left the room. He took a load of garbage outside, noticing the faucet running in the bathroom. When he returned to the house, the front door was locked. He looked through the window on the door and saw the bathroom door was open and wedged against the front doorknob. He re-entered the house through the open garage door. The faucet was running again in the bathroom, so he shut it and closed the bathroom door. A red, intense anger surrounded him. It came from something in the house. Once again, he wiped the intuition from his thoughts.

Junior walked down the stairs. "Luke, my tools were in the sink."

"I didn't move them, Junes."

"I don't think you did. Maybe it's me, but I feel like I'm being watched the longer I am in the house."

He grabbed onto the door and stared at the sink. "It's just an old house." Lying to his brother Junior was not easy, but he thought it best he behaved as if he saw nothing.

"Luke, get up here … Junior, get a ladder, please," their father called out.

Luke met with his father upstairs, who pointed at an access in the ceiling covered with white tape.

"I forgot this house has an attic."

"You need to remove that tape, Dad." Junior joined them with the ladder.

Luke grabbed the platform ladder, climbed, and removed the tape. He tried to open the access to the attic, but it appeared to be nailed shut.

Junior handed Luke a pry bar.

"Why do you always have tools on you?" Luke asked, grabbed the pry bar, and removed the nails. He lowered the door, which revealed a folded wooden ladder.

His father handed Luke a flashlight. "Go up there and check it out."

He climbed into the attic and shined the flashlight into the dark emptiness.

"What's up there?" his father asked.

"It's all dusty and full of garbage. I see lots of boxes and furniture." Luke disappeared into the dark attic. The subfloor surprised him by being remarkably sturdy. He shined the flashlight throughout the room, and it was evident there was broken furniture and numerous boxes. *What a shit show*, he mused.

Junior came up behind him, shined a flashlight on the flooring, and then into the void of the dark attic. "What a mess; at least the floor is 3/4-inch plywood, Dad," Junior called back down to the ladder. "This flooring can even hold Luke."

Their father joined them and walked toward a chain attached to a light bulb and pulled it downward. It brought enough light to enhance their field of view. The attic ran the whole length of the house, with the walls half-finished in plywood. Insulation was visible between some plywood boards.

"This is a few steps away from being a living space." His father shined the flashlight throughout the attic.

Luke headed over to some of the furniture on the other side of the attic, where he found an opening in a framed-out wall. One plywood panel was removed at some point. He walked into the opening and entered a hidden room. An old-style high-end metal cot wrapped in clear plastic stood between dozens of boxes. A dark shadow appeared over the cot as a cold hand grabbed at his shoulder, which caused him to flinch. "Dad, why did the prior people leave so much of their stuff behind?"

"What did you say, Luke?" His father yelled from outside of the hidden room.

Nobody was near him. This realization caused an uncontrollable shudder throughout his body. He turned and saw a man scarred with burns from head to toe. He pretended to not have seen the creature. *I must confront this creature*, he thought, conflicted. He was so scared his knees buckled.

"I know you can see me. Who are you? How can you see me?" the creature asked in its gravelly voice.

He wobbled out of the framed-out area using every bit of self-control not to run from the attic in terror. His brothers were not near him. He peered into the room again, and the creature was gone. He continued to search the room and found boxes with comic books and albums. Luke was trembling uncontrollably. His fear was that his father witnessed the interaction. He should have told him what was in the home.

His father joined him. "This looks like a trap. What were they hiding?" His father grabbed one of the comic books. "Who hides comic books?"

Once again, Luke considered telling his father what was in the house. "Those boxes over there say Bolling Collectibles. How about the sofas and the other furniture? How do you suppose this stuff made its way up here?" Luke motioned outside of the hidden room.

"Guys, come over here and take a look," Junior said, pointing at a depression on the attic floor. "Looks like this used to be stairs leading down to the fourth floor."

"There used to be a door below these steps. The builder meant for the attic to be a living space. It answers how the furniture made its way up here, but not that hidden area over there." His father touched his chin nervously.

Junior headed down the unfinished stairway and punched a hole through the drywall.

"What are you doing, dumb ass?" Daniel was often critical of his brothers while oblivious to his failings.

"Easy, Daniel. I know what he's doing. Junior, head back down and find the exit."

They all stepped down from the attic and met Junior in the hallway.

"This is where the door was. Do you see the frame?" Junior seemed perplexed. "They closed it back up for some reason," Junior said.

"Looks like we bought a larger house than we thought," their father said with a smile.

"What are you thinking, Dad?" he asked.

"We will build this out and make it into a living space as the builder intended … we need my father." Their grandfather was a contractor in Puerto Rico.

"We need to get started. Grab those trash bags and head back up," their father said. "Junior, open up that wall so we can move the furniture out."

The cleanup took hours. They stacked dozens of boxes containing albums, comics, some old books, sealed baseball card sets, and everything else they found in the attic worth keeping. The rest was moved into the dumpster. Luke walked into the garage and saw a child hovering over one of the boxes. He approached the kid who had a comic in his hand. "Do you live nearby?"

The child stared at Luke blankly and did not respond. The child had pale white skin and was wearing a blue shirt with a green turtleneck at the top neckline. The clothing was something from another time. "Do you want some of those comics?" Luke asked, generously.

The boy did not turn toward Luke. "Some of these are mine ... you stole them from me," the boy said and walked out of the garage to one side of the house.

Luke followed the boy, speechless. When he turned the corner, the boy was gone. The comic was on the grass. He reached down and picked it up off the ground. It was *Mad Magazine* number 1.

Luke did not bother to approach his brothers. He had more significant problems. The white eyes, the faucet, the burned man who knew he could see it, and now the kid that he interacted with. *I can only pretend so far.* For the time being, his brothers and parents did not know that he was seeing things, and that is how he would keep it. His obtuse response gave power to the entity within their home. Regardless of how negatively his parents would respond to his intuition he made a mistake by not using his abilities to protect them.

CHAPTER FOUR

The Door and the Sink

I felt intense hatred, anger, and jealousy as I wandered around the once-comfortable home. In the last few days, my rage grew as I starved for the essence from each body within my orbit. As I moved from room to room throughout the levels of its domain, I saw sleeping intruders except one boy who was fiddling around the house. I tried to drive the people away by opening the door and turning on the water. I tried everything I could to scare the new intruders with the energy I had. As the boy moved back into the bathroom, it moved through me. That action brought an influx of energy—sated from this long-endured hunger. I was intoxicated and grabbed onto the neck of the boy, Junior, and squeezed in delight.

Luke woke up, startled by a squeaky sound from the corner of his dark room where he stored his guitars on stands. It was still a bit dark but all he saw was his electric and acoustic guitar.

The dream was so confusing. It wasn't his dream, he realized that at least. He propped up in bed and looked toward the corner with what ambient light came into the curtainless windows. Tony began to bark from the bed as his door opened slowly. He turned to look at the door and saw his brother Junior massaging his head. Tony jumped off the bed and began to bark at the carpeted floor near the window and corner of the room.

"Hey Luke, I saw you walking up here," Junior said as he rubbed his temples.

"What? It wasn't me … just woke up."

"I saw you through the window," Junior said.

"I was having an odd dream, and something woke me up." Luke rubbed his face as if trying to remove the dream he was still in.

Junior walked toward the window and stared at the floor oddly.

"What's up?" Luke asked.

"This does not make sense. I swear … a face was against this window. It's not possible though. Your window touches the floor," Junior stood stunned and grabbed the dog. "Tony was scratching right where the face was."

"Maybe you saw Tony?" Luke asked.

"Tony, I don't think so, Luke … ahh man, I keep getting this terrible headache. I feel like …" Blood gushed out of Junior's nose and mouth, which caused him to dart out of the bedroom.

Luke followed his brother out of the room. Clotted blood was sprayed on the sink, counter, and cabinets. Nausea gripped him, so he tried to avert his eyes. It kept him from vomiting. "Hold your head down and pinch your nose. Sit over here on the toilet." He helped Junior sit, avoiding the sight of the blood. "I will be right back." He filled a blue ice bag in the kitchen with ice. He heard footsteps in the hallway above him as he approached the foyer. He figured his mom had woken up. He darted back upstairs and hoped his mother would not be alarmed at the bloody mess in the bathroom and Junior's state.

"Why do you need that ice pack?" his mother asked as he passed her bedroom doorway.

"I heard you walking upstairs. Did you see the mess in the bathroom?"

"What are you talking about? What mess?"

"Junior had a nosebleed. A real gusher." He walked briskly up the stairs with his mother following close behind him. Luke placed the icepack on his brother's forehead.

"What happened? It looks like somebody was killed in here." Their mother touched the specks and globs of blood on the mirror.

"Wasn't me, Mom. Junior was standing in my room when it started pouring out."

"Can you get some disinfectant and rags from the kitchen?"

He retrieved the cleaning supplies downstairs but stopped to close the faucet and bathroom door. He returned upstairs and cleaned up the bathroom quickly before going to Junior's room, where their mother sat beside Junior in bed, wiping blood from his face. Tony was sitting in the room, looking at Junior, then at Luke in confusion. "You look better, Junes."

"My head hurts, but I must have run out of blood. No more bleeding."

Luke pointed at the ice pack. "It helps constrict the blood vessels."

"I think I'm going back to sleep. Thanks for helping," Junior said, with his eyes closed.

"Come on, Luke." His mother motioned for him to leave the room. "Thanks for cleaning this and taking care of your brother."

"No problem, Mom. I still need to take Tony out," Luke whispered but instead walked back into his room. After laying back down, he began to think. Junior had to be mistaken. The burned man was not near Junior that he saw. It had something to do with the dream somehow but how it related eluded him. It was an error not to tell his family about the spirit attached to the home. His timidity and need to be loved by his parents, along with the house caused him to make a mistake. At least his parents were not angry with him. He covered himself with his sheets. *I forgot to take Tony out.* The dog stared at him as it peed on the carpet. *I'll let that one slide, Tony,* he thought.

The Priest

The town center was a ten-minute drive from their house on Red Hill Road. The local catholic church was constructed on a small hill surrounded by the rest of the town. Luke's parents emphasized that Sunday should be the family's regular day together. School and work tended to dominate everyone's lives so evening meals, and weekends became ritualistic for the Sanz clan. The plan was to attend mass at ten o'clock and lunch afterward. Luke tolerated the Sunday church outings because he felt he did not have a choice. In general, he was not a religious person and questioned his faith and religion often.

Luke's father stopped at the red light at the intersection before the church, Main Street, and Joshua Avenue. Luke noticed a man wearing worn-out coveralls and a brown *Dickie Eisenhower* jacket walking away from the corner and towards the west side of town. He mentally waved off the memory of seeing the man although a nagging feeling crept back into his mind. *The man was important somehow*, he mused.

The church exterior was covered with dark red bricks, which made it stand out from the nearby, white-painted buildings. It was more aptly referred to as a cathedral where the vault of the roof and the nave towered into the sky.

The family entered the church and sat in the back pews near an exit in the middle. Plenty of empty benches were ahead of them. Their mother and his brothers were trained to sit where their father preferred. As a former military man and current law enforcement officer, his father prepared their family to always think of safety and have a quick egress from any building they entered.

His parents typically sat on one end of the pews with him and Junior on the other side. Junior was typically a buffer between them. The church was full, so Luke and Junior sat behind their father along with their mother and Daniel.

As Luke sat, he took in all that occurred within his proximity, including a conversation his parents were having. The repetitiveness of the Sunday mass annoyed him. He was baptized, endured communion, and was convinced to undergo confirmation when he was being blighted by a voice and visions. He deemed church to be a chore at best and resented it.

"Which one is the priest?" his mother asked his father.

"Father Dwayne, everyone calls him Father D. The big black man with the bald head beyond the altar and over in the corner. He's supposed to be the best."

"Have you met him yet? He looks like a boxer."

"No, a man pointed him out, but he seemed busy."

Father D commenced the sermon and, at one point, read from the book of *Philippians*. "Welcome him then in the Lord with all joy, and honor such people, because he came close to death for the work of Christ, risking his life to make up those services that you could not give me ... Paul was letting the followers of Jesus know that Christ gives one strength to overcome the obstacles brought forward by all adversaries." The priest held onto the lectern firmly. "You will all face adversity, most of you have and will again."

Luke was distracted by the interior of the cathedral. The ceiling, the stained-glass windows, and all the statues were enthralling.

Suddenly, the room darkened, but a light illuminated the pulpit and the tough looking priest. "Even you, young man ... you will face adversity. How will you react? How will you stand up to this hardship?" The priest stared directly at Luke who almost stood up in defiance. The priest looked away from him and the nave brightened. "Go and announce the Gospel of the Lord, go in peace, and be patient and good with one another." The priest walked away from the pulpit.

Luke sat stunned while parishioners began to stand, while others bowed their heads or knelt in prayer. *Maybe the priest was referring to all the young men in the audience,* he thought. He was paralyzed with fear. Sweat formed on his forehead, which he wiped away with the sleeve. He could not move even while most others stood and walked to the exits.

His father remained knelt on the pew and whispered what Luke believed to be the Lord's Prayer in Spanish. He waited for his father to finish. Eventually, his father stood and walked toward the exit, so they followed him as a well-structured team.

31

Father D was at the bottom steps of the church, thanking parishioners and shaking hands as they left. The priest introduced himself to his parents and motioned toward him and his brothers. "Are these your boys, Angel?"

"Yes, my sons Daniel, Luke, and Junior, also named Angel."

"Boys, welcome to our Parish. Please call me Father D. I look forward to getting to know each of you." Father D offered his hand to each of the brothers. Father D slapped his shoulder somewhat hard when they shook hands ... *I fell backward, suddenly transported decades earlier. I stood in front of a young Father D and an older priest; both spoke in Latin. They hovered over a woman sitting in a chair in what appeared to be a disheveled kitchen. The priests sprayed the woman with holy water, which caused her to screech wildly. This jolted me out of it sharply forward* ... he felt dizzy and a bit unstable.

"You're a big guy, and it looks like you are built like an athlete," Father D said.

Luke stared at Father D, and then at his father who motioned for him to answer. He felt out of place after seeing the vision. "I just work out a lot, Father." He was barely audible. He lacked self-confidence, and his introverted nature burdened him more than he told his parents or siblings. *I wondered if he was going to remind me to stand up to adversity.*

"It was great meeting you, Luke. I am sure I will see you soon."

Luke simply bowed his head down and nodded slightly. Catholicism was a part of his family dynamic and not a way of life he intended to follow. Luke had never sought the answers to his problems at church, school, or a doctor's office. The possibility that a priest or anybody in authority could assist him was absent from his thoughts.

After the family ate lunch, they approached the intersection of Main and Joshua on the route home. He saw the man wearing coveralls again and a boy walking in and out of the crosswalk as if he were playing a game. "Do you all see that boy over in the crosswalk?"

"Are you seeing things, again?" Daniel asked sarcastically.

Luke stared at Daniel, angered, and then back into the now-cleared intersection. *I know what I saw,* he thought.

The family planned to go to several car dealerships in the afternoon, but he wanted to work out, so his father dropped him off at their house on Red Hill Road. Tony darted into the trees when let out onto the deck. Luke looked intently at the waterfall in the backyard, which brought him serenity. Tony ran back and scored a stealthy direct hit on his crotch.

"You little brat, no snack for you," he said, as he walked awkwardly back into the garage for his workout. He grabbed the doorknob and pulled it open, but it was removed from his hand violently and slammed shut with the sound of cracked and splintered wood. "Junior, is that you?"

"Not welcome here." A disembodied guttural voice spoke, followed by a growl.

Tony ran toward the trees, yelping.

"Who are you? We live here now." He walked backward, peered into all the windows, and saw nothing. "Come here, Tony, come here, boy. I'll protect you." He found Tony hiding in the bushes and took him to a boulder near the driveway. Fear enveloped his very core. Entering the house was not an option. He felt a burning sensation throughout his body and felt a cold dampness of sweat on his forehead, which ran into his eyes burning them. Luke was embarrassed that he let the spirit know he could hear it. He closed his eyes and lowered his head. He began to shake uncontrollably while grabbing onto his knees.

After about an hour the family Taurus, driven by Daniel, made its way down the driveway, followed by a gold Dodge *Grand Caravan.* Junior exited the minivan and walked toward him.

"I think Dad paid full price for this thing. What's wrong with you?" Junior asked with concern.

"Something growled at me and told me I was not welcome here."

"You kidding? We are back now, so let's go inside. We live here now and not whatever it is that's bugging us," Junior said inaccurately.

"I think you are wrong, Junior. This thing lives here and doesn't think we belong."

His parents entered the house, oblivious as to what was within. Daniel shot a middle finger toward his brothers before following his parents into the home.

Eventually, Junior coaxed Luke into the house long enough to change into his running gear. A brisk summer run may burn out the panic that had settled in him.

CHAPTER FIVE

Drop Kick

That weekend, Luke prepared for an early work-out. As he dressed near his closet, loud voices arose from the shared wall with Daniel's room where he typically slept in on Saturdays. He walked downstairs with Tony scampering behind him. Daniel's gear bag was in the foyer, which reminded him that his brother had another baseball camp. His mother and brother sat in the kitchen. "Have a great weekend at baseball camp."

"Thanks, Luke." Daniel played several positions within baseball but had become an excellent first base player. He was one of the best at that position in Puerto Rico within his age group.

He let Tony outside in the back and noticed something brown on one of the benches on the deck. The sound of the gurgling brook in the backyard calmed him. He stood with closed eyes listening to the churning water before grabbing his brother's glove. He returned to the kitchen and tried to hand it to his brother. "You'll need that, Daniel."

"Thanks, Luke." Daniel stared at the glove and then at the table.

Not even his glove was enough to cause Daniel to touch Luke. He let out a sigh and placed it on the table so as not to accidentally touch his sibling. He walked out of the kitchen with a burning sensation in his chest. *Why should I care if my family fears my touch?* He wiped the tears that fell down his cheeks before he allowed them to see his weakness. In truth, it pained him immensely to have a brother who was repulsed by him.

35

"Didn't I tell you to collect all your gear? You took forever to wake up and I had to bring all your bags down for you," his mother told Daniel.

Luke left his brother and mom speaking and entered the garage. He opened the rolling door halfway to let the cool morning air in. While he prepared his father's new universal gym for a triceps workout, he noticed his brother and mom walking toward the family Ford *Taurus*. His mother was holding Daniel's suitcase and gear bag, while his brother appeared to only have the car keys. He walked toward his mother and tried to grab the bags. She placed them on the ground and took a step back. "Open the trunk, bro."

Daniel unlocked the trunk with the key but did not lift the lid. Instead, he walked back toward their mother and hugged her.

I think Daniel will need an assistant if he ever becomes a famous baseball player. He headed over to Daniel, who was seated in the front. "Grab your bags yourself at the hotel, Daniel. They will not have valets."

Daniel smirked at Luke and turned to look at his mommy. "Mom, they should have somebody at the hotel, right?" Daniel asked.

He shook his head and laughed. "Daniel, you truly live in another world."

"I love you, Mom, come over the weekend if you want to," his brother said with a grin before he drove off.

He looked toward his mother and noticed she was crying. "Mom, why are you crying? Why do you do everything for him?"

"You will find out when you are a parent," she said, turning around quickly before she walked back toward the front door.

"Mom, Daniel needs to take care of his own problems so that he does not need to rely on others."

"Go work out, Luke. I'm going to go get ready for my day."

Luke was unsure of why he inserted himself into that interaction. Next time, he would just mind his own business.

After strength training, he ran on the trail near the elementary school. During the run, he thought about his brother Daniel and his relationship with their parents. Something terrible happened to Daniel, and he had no idea what it could be.

Later that afternoon, Luke watched the movie *Superman* on the family's new Sony 42-inch *Videoscope* big-screen television. Tony was tucked away safely in his arms. He propped himself up with a bunch of pillows that were meant for the two sofas in the living room. Something his mother disliked immensely but his parents were not home. What she did not see would not upset her. Junior was in the garage working on one of his projects. It had been a quiet summer day. The VHS tape in the recorder had begun to distort a little after countless views.

"I hope one of these days somebody invents something that looks better than this," he said while tapping on the VHS player. Tony began to snarl and snap a little in Luke's arms. The tone of the room changed. He began to look for the scarred man but did not see him. A sharp pain invaded his head. His vision was distorted but he knew something was in the room with him.

Tony wiggled away forcibly from him and snarled at the air between him and the sofa. Luke felt the dog must be daft because there was nothing in the room.

"What do you see, boy?" Tony appeared to be tracking something through the room. The temperature dropped enough that Luke saw his breath as he exhaled. It was close to eighty degrees outside. *I shouldn't be able to see my breath*, he thought.

Tony continued to track something throughout the room from the sofa in a circle, now pointing to the fireplace. Tony folded into himself abruptly and flew onto the sofa six feet away. Something unseen kicked Tony. The little dog hit the backrest of the sofa and slid slowly onto the bottom sofa cushion. Luke wanted to rush to Tony, but an unnatural force brought him to one knee. Luke took a deep breath and prepared himself mentally by pushing upward as if deadlifting.

All the muscles in his body tensed up. It felt as if a force field kept him from reaching Tony. He tried to say something, but his vocal cords would not work. "Help me," Luke yelled. "Please, God help me." He finally forced his way into the invisible barrier. Each breath was even more visible. He pushed forward with all his might. He felt pressure on his shoulders, that moved him forward through what remained of the barrier like a ship being moved by a tug. He shot forward toward Tony. "Are you okay, boy? Wake up, boy. You're worrying me, Tony."

Tony was breathing but not conscious.

"Get out of here, spirit!" A recognizable voice yelled again in Spanish. The curtain pulsed forcibly onto the sliding glass window as if invisible buckets of water were tossed onto them. After a few seconds, the drapes grew slack as if nothing happened.

He stood up, rushed to the kitchen, placed Tony into the sink, and poured cold water on the dog's head. Tony came to and started barking. He let go of the dog who shook himself dry, spraying the water on Luke's face and shirt. He grabbed Tony and took the little yapper outside. The dog looked up at him before darting off into the tree line. He sat on an outdoor chair, placed his face in his hands, and shook uncontrollably. *What is happening to me?* He jumped when he felt a touch to his shoulders again but quickly relaxed when he sensed what could be described as a veil of protection.

"Luke, it's me, Sebastian, "A voice said in Spanish.

"Who are you?" Luke asked.

"I have been by your side all your life, Luke. I have been patient, but the time has come for you to listen and learn."

Luke stood up quickly and looked around the backyard. Nobody was there. This voice was always in his head and whatever tools he used to suppress the voice were not working. He felt weak and fell to one knee. Internally he knew that the only way to deal with his insanity was to quell it with medications. He saw images of pills and recalled that his mother kept a prescription of *benzos* for him in the kitchen. The thought of a way to stop the voices brought him a perverse pleasure. He went back into the house and began a search for the pills.

"Luke, that will not help. I can guide you through this."

He refused to answer the voice. Ignoring it was not helping but he could not find his prescription bottle. Sitting within eyesight was a bottle of scotch whiskey. His father's favorite brand. He grabbed the bottle and took a quick swig from it. He then grabbed a glass and tossed some ice along with two fingers of the amber liquid. He paused and waited. No more voices. Medication or liquor? One or the other would solve his dilemma temporarily. Neither one would help in the long run but at least he would be able to live with his illness. Something, internal or external, drove him to serve himself another drink. *I'll worry about the consequences later*, he mused.

CHAPTER SIX

Short Shorts

Their parents had gone shopping and were on something they called date night. Luke and his brothers were scattered throughout the house doing their own thing. Luke dressed in workout clothes before escaping from Junior's torturous death metal music that resonated throughout their side of the house. Tony followed him to his Fortress of Calmness where for the next hour, he worked out with free weights and took turns slamming the heavy bag. Tony watched him from the floor, ignoring his chew toy. He looked at himself in the mirror he installed in the garage. Full of sweat, assisted by the muggy August weather and the lack of a fan for air circulation. He decided to forgo his run and shower after drinking a protein shake. He entered the house through the laundry room and closed the always-open bathroom door. He neglected to shut the faucet because, in truth, it was getting old. As he walked up the stairs a burning sensation began to perk up within his chest. He ignored it and took a shower and got dressed.

A feeling of dread returned. His acoustic guitar caught his eye. His guitars were his failsafe if exercise did not work to tamper down his anxiety that felt more like being launched in an uncontrollable rocket. He grabbed his Fender *DG-94*. Just touching the mahogany body of the guitar brought him comfort. He closed his eyes and began playing The Beatles *While My Guitar Gently Weeps*. He played the guitar while walking down the hallway. At first thinking he had to escape Junior's dreadful music but realized Junior had shut down the repetitive track of a man screeching Halloween repeatedly. He smiled and continued walking downstairs with Tony following obediently. He sat on the sofa in the living room and closed his eyes and began to sing the song. Low at first but then increased the volume.

Tony began to bark and rushed to the front door. Luke's sense of dread forced him to stop abruptly. The thought of the aggressive spirit's attack on his dog stifled him.

The doorbell rang, startling him briefly, but it caused the fire to settle. He placed his guitar on the sofa and walked to the window and looked outside. A stunning young woman with black hair and jean shorts stood outside. He was taken aback by the shapely girl wearing short shorts, his favorite.

Junior ran down the stairs with Daniel close behind. He thought it must be Daniel's friend, but his older brother shrugged.

He opened the front door, quickly seeing that the girl was pretty as well. Tony darted out to say hello to the young lady. The young girl smiled and crouched down to pet Tony.

"Hello, I am Steve Hollowell, and this is my sister Joyce."

Joyce was such a vision that she prevented him from noticing she was with somebody else. "I'm Luke, and this is Tony." Junior stepped out of the house, followed by Daniel. "These are my brothers, Junior and Daniel." Something about Steve seemed off; he was assertive, but it seemed fake somehow.

Joyce stood up, offering Luke her hand along with a striking smile ... *I fell backward with a jolt. Loud screams stung my ear drums painfully. Joyce ran past me in the hallway of our house. Her mouth was frozen open in terror* ... he felt the motion of falling forward as he returned from the vision. He let go of her hand and stared up toward the hallway leading to his room. *I saw Joyce in our house, but when did it happen, or will happen,* he thought. "Nice to meet you, Joyce."

"Sorry, we stood at the door listening to you play and sing. You're good," Joyce said.

She then shook hands with Junior and Daniel while she looked toward Luke.

"Our parents owned this house for almost eight years. We stayed in the house a few years ago while my parents built a new house. We wanted to come over when we heard that you guys are our age."

"Come inside, and we can talk about it." Daniel offered the siblings.

"We prefer not to come in," Joyce looked toward her brother before placing her hand on his shoulder.

"We should at least go to the backyard. We have chairs out there," Daniel said.

They all walked around the side of the house into the backyard, with Tony yapping behind them.

"Our parents bought this house when Steve was eight and I was ten. We didn't live here until we were older, but we noticed some unusual stuff." Joyce looked toward them, unsure what to say. "Are you noticing anything yet?"

"Yes, lots of banging on the walls, footsteps, doors opening and closing," Daniel said quickly.

"The faucet at the entrance will not stay shut," Junior said.

"All of this happened to us," Joyce said. "How about you, Luke? You seem to be holding something back?"

"Something kicked Tony. It threw him in the air onto the sofa," he said as Tony jumped on Joyce to show he was fine.

Joyce cradled Tony's head with her hands. "Poor baby, are you okay?" Joyce looked at the brothers. "Whatever is in the house attacked and sent our dog to the vet as well."

"What's wrong with the house?" He stared at the upstairs windows with anxiety building up like a pressure cooker.

"A man died in a car accident behind the house many years ago." Joyce pointed toward the intersection.

"I saw a man wearing a flannel shirt outside banging on the walls." Steve was trembling as he spoke. "He had blond hair and was almost see-through ... it was a ghost!"

Luke took a deep breath. *Am I going to face this head-on?* "The banging we have heard comes from the back door and the kitchen window," Luke said before exhaling.

"I saw him through the kitchen window after I heard the banging." Steve had tears running down his face and shook uncontrollably.

"Have you seen anyone else? A man, a burned man?" Luke asked and moved toward Steve as if to touch him.

Steve shook his head up and down before changing it from side to side. He finally buried his head in his legs and did not answer.

Luke then tried to place his hand on Steve's shoulder.

"Luke … what are you doing?" Daniel asked.

He looked at his brother angrily but knew that he had overstepped with Steve. Daniel would immediately tell their parents that he had mistreated potential new friends. It would be best if he backed off.

"Thanks for coming with me, Steve, but this was a mistake. We should go now." Joyce grabbed Steve's hand as a loving sister would. Steve shook his head up and down, looking fragile, and both stood up. They walked away quickly, within a safe distance, to the front of the house. The Sanz brothers followed them.

"Sorry guys, Steve is usually not emotional like this. It's the house that brings it out of him. I will leave you my number if you need to talk." Joyce looked directly at him, smiling.

Daniel handed her a piece of paper while Luke tugged nervously on his own shirt. Joyce took a pen from her shorts and wrote down her phone number. She tried to hand it to Luke, but Daniel grabbed it.

He looked at Joyce's short shorts while she walked off. Daniel walked beside her down the driveway of the house. Tony and Luke looked at one another, then at the trio walking down the driveway. Tony barked pitifully.

"Sorry, Tony, it looks like this one goes to Daniel." He stood there with his hands up in defeat.

"What a dick, that chick was looking at you like you were an ice cream cone," Junior said before he ran back into the house.

"Come on, Tony." Joyce and Steve had confirmed his concerns.

✛ ✛ ✛

The Hungry Spirit

The months *it* festered in the attic were interrupted by the opening of the access panel on the floor. He watched for months as anger brewed by the day. He was left alone in the attic until the old man used the other men in the family as a brigade whose sole purpose appeared to be to remove his belongings and destroy what peace he had garnered. The family that had infested his home had refused to leave the house after he tried to scare them off. Eventually, he evolved, as it always does, when the scent of the soul within these beings beckoned to him. The sweet odor emanating from each occupier of the house stirred his essence. It would take time, patience, and effort, but he will take what he needs to survive.

The knock at the door did not interest him. Regardless, he poured out of its safety and down to the hallway. He peered at the couple at the doorway, who appeared familiar but looked different. Yes, it was the brother and sister from years ago. Joyce was the one who brought beauty into the house, and Steve was the one who whined and cowered in bed at night, holding his dog.

The group of kids moved to the back of the house. He stirred up in a whirlwind, needing to observe the girl. He wanted the girl; thinking of Barbara clouded his thoughts. This girl had nothing to do with the other, but she had an essence he needed now. He flowed through the levels of the now-empty home. They were on the deck speaking. He settled down as he gained sight of her. They were speaking of it, which infuriated him. What this boy was doing could damage the plans for this family.

He descended to the deck and over Steve. He sprayed his feeding enzyme over Steve, which began dissolving the boy's mind.

The boy began to fold emotionally, and Joyce had to lead him away from the home. He succeeded quickly returning to his resting place, content that he suppressed Luke's ability to see him. He was going to win, and Luke's semi-willful blindness, coupled with the dampening of his power, would be essential to success.

CHAPTER SEVEN

First Day of School

That first day of school back in 1990 was enough to bring back nightmares for the rest of his days. His brothers may recall it differently. He did his best back then to think of his happy place instead of the predicament he was in with being forced to attend a new school. They parked in the senior parking area and walked through the bus drop-off. Daniel trudged through the parking lot impatiently, as if weary that he was not yet in class. Receiving praise for his mere presence at the new school.

Junior and Luke walked tentatively behind Daniel without caring to catch up to him. He stopped in a courtyard with concrete tables and stared at the four-story brick-faced building before him. It evoked thoughts of a prison rather than a center for learning.

As a sophomore, Junior's homeroom would be on the second floor. Daniel was a senior. His homeroom was on the fourth floor. As the younger brothers entered the double doorways, their brother Daniel was no longer visible amongst the herd of students rushing up a stairway.

"Have a great day, Junior."

"You too, Luke." Junior motioned toward the stairway. "He lives fully in Danieland, Luke."

"It's a small-minded world, after all, Junior." He gave Junior a fist bump before they parted ways.

The Lansburg Center High School program had seven

periods and one lunchtime for all four grades. One of these periods could be a study hall class, depending on the need for course credits for the student. Luke entered his homeroom class and saw a bald black man standing near the door. The man was dressed smartly with definable creases to his clothes. He walked up to the teacher and handed the man his schedule.

"Are you new to the LC?" The teacher looked at his schedule and then at Luke. "Football?"

"Yes, I'm new ... no, never got into sports," he said nervously.

The teacher looked at him again. "That makes no sense ... well I'm Mr. Conway, welcome to the LC. The procedure says I need to assign you a tour guide to help you on your first day. Take a seat and wait for the principal to make an announcement."

Luke silently moved to an empty seat in the back corner of the classroom. He sat down nervously, ensuring his long hair covered most of his face. Luke was once again outside of his comfort zone. Mr. Conway seemed nice enough, but after spending the last few months assimilating at their house, he was once again an outsider.

At about 7:30 a.m., the public announcement came to life with a tone. "Good morning, students of the LC. This is Principal Devry giving a fond welcome to all LC students, especially my seniors for the class of 1991. All stand for the pledge of allegiance, and I mean all." Principal Devry said in a slurred voice. Then a prerecorded pledge of allegiance was played.

A young man entered the classroom and shook Mr. Conway's hand. The student wore a blue mechanic's shirt and jeans. The boy was pudgy and about five foot eight inches tall but had pronounced vascular veins, like a bodybuilder.

Mr. Conway motioned for Luke to come up to his desk. "Luke, meet Benji Laio. He will be your tour guide. Benji shares some of your classes including art, music, and history with me."

"What instrument?" Benji asked with a snort.

He stood silently hesitant to respond.

"Let me guess ... with your long hair and size, you play the

Tuba," Benji said with a smile.

"Guitar," Luke said, this time staring at Benji who seemed to wince. "You?"

First bell sounded while they were talking.

"Drums," Benji responded briefly. "Electric?"

"Electric, acoustic, Spanish ... you?"

"Snare, bass, tom, cymbal ..."

"Guys please stop. I'm sure you'll be the best of friends. You have five minutes between the *first bell* and *second bell* to make sure you make your next class. That should be plenty of time." Mr. Conway motioned for them to leave.

"Come on, Luke, follow me to art class. Luke, you seem like a shy guy, and I understand. Are you that cat who becomes a hell-raiser during a full moon?"

"Timid, shy, quiet. All sounds about right, but never been a hell-raiser, though."

"I know what you mean. I would have preferred to have attended high school in 1962 in the Valley in California, but my father is from here, and I lost my time machine last week." Benji made a funny snort and then slapped Luke's back.

He got an odd mental picture of them fishing together knee-deep in a lake surrounded by snowy mountains. Benji grew on him almost instantly. The image quickly faded. "You're all right, Benji."

"I keep telling my dad, but he tells me to return to work. Where did you grow up?" Benji asked.

"Well, I was born in Australia, but moved to Puerto Rico when I was ten years old," Luke said.

"Wow, that makes no freaking sense, man ... total opposites on the globe."

Luke thought about it and figured that Benji could be correct. "I never saw it that way. Long story but my father works for the Department of State and met my mom at some party at the embassy ... that's how they got baby number one, my older brother," Luke said.

"We have music class together also ... kind of boring this year. Next year will be a theory and practice where we play as a group ... this is the class up ahead," Benji said.

A couple embracing outside of the classroom caught his attention. The boy wore a letterman jacket in brown and gold. The jock concealed the girl until he walked into class and saw her being kissed. The girl looked toward Luke, then back into the jock's eyes. She had both hands on the boy's chest, pushing him off with an annoyed look. She had flawless creamy white skin along with a perfect round face. Her long curly brown hair complemented her soul-piercing blue eyes.

"Not here, Todd. Go to your class," the young lady said before following Luke into the classroom.

The class had seating for fourteen students with larger than-normal tables. He sat near Benji.

"My name is Mr. Aames." The teacher looked at his class roster. "I would like all of you to introduce yourself and tell us something about art that's important to you."

The mere possibility of public speaking forced him to burn up in a flash. He does not like public speaking. He paid attention to the first introductions but now wanted to disappear.

"My name is Benji Laio. I have been painting for years and do custom paint work on cars at my father's specialty auto shop."

The introductions continued to drone on until he heard a pleasant feminine voice. "Hello, my name is Alyssa Mars, and I love all art forms."

"It's great to have you back in class, Miss Mars."

He stole a glance toward Alyssa because she was stunning. Alyssa looked at him with a smile, giving him a pleasurable burning sensation. He turned away quickly when he realized she was looking at him.

The rest of the students introduced themselves until Mr. Aames got to Luke and motioned an open hand toward him as if to say continue.

"My name is Luke Sanz. I'm new to this school. My mother is

an artist and taught as a kid."

"Your mother is Helen Martin? From Australia?" Mr. Aames asked.

"Yes, Mr. Aames, that is her maiden name."

"I'm looking forward to working with you Mr. Sanz." Mr. Aames motioned for the other students to continue.

The introduction droned on longer than he thought it should. He tried his best to zone it all out. After class, Benji took Luke to their second-period history class.

"How's everything so far?" Mr. Conway asked.

He shrugged. "All right, I guess."

Mr. Conway motioned toward an empty desk. "Pucker-up. History is the most interesting class in any school."

He smiled because he loved history as much as Art. The *second bell* sounded. Mr. Conway motioned Benji and him up to the front of the class. He tensed up at the sound of his name, thinking he would have to introduce himself until he was asked to distribute textbooks. The relatively large book was titled *Civics, Economics, and the Constitution of the United States*. He handed out a copy to half the class without saying a word.

"Luke here is a transplant from Puerto Rico. He likes Art and spearfishing at night. Benji here likes drawing on car hoods and beating on his bongos." Mr. Conway laughed while clapping his hands.

He looked frazzled and almost dropped the stack of books but finished as quickly as possible. He returned to his seat.

For the next half hour, the class discussion involved looking at the syllabus and schedule for the year, and then the *first bell* rang. Mr. Conway motioned for him to stop.

"Thanks for helping, Luke. See you tomorrow in homeroom. Square those shoulders. We have enough people trying to knock those down without us doing it for them."

"I will, thanks, Mr. Conway." He walked off but turned to look at Mr. Conway, who smiled at him.

Benji pointed at the school map to show Luke where his third-period English Literature class was. They parted ways because Benji's next class was on a different floor. Benji had taught him to read the school map and legend throughout the day as he made his way around. Benji met him outside his English class and walked down to the first floor of his biology class.

Benji showed Luke the classroom. "I'm taking Chemistry. Across the way," Benji said. "Let's meet after class and head to the Beaver Lounge."

"What's the Beaver Lounge?"

"Our cafeteria." Benji snorted, smiled, and slapped his thigh. "Our school team is called the Beavers. Ten years ago, some drunk boosters renamed the cafeteria the Beaver Lounge. A smart ass put in a stripper pole, and the school administrators took down the name. It's like a myth, you know." Benji laughed while walking away.

"Take it easy, Benji, and thanks for showing me around."

Benji turned around and bowed while pointing at the classroom. "Good luck. Mr. Smith is a kind of a dick!"

Benji was wrong. Mr. Smith was a dick. In forty minutes, Mr. Smith put immense effort into picking on as many students as possible. *What can I learn from this man?* he asked himself.

He met Benji in the hallway after class.

"What's the verdict?" Benji asked.

"You were wrong. There was no kind of about it."

Benji shrugged. "Not sure why they hire teachers who hate kids … so there are four cafeterias — one for each grade from ninth to twelfth. The juniors and seniors have the cafeterias facing the quad outside, surrounded by other classrooms. Upperclassmen can eat outside. Follow me."

Alyssa sat at a round table with three attractive girls he could see and another girl with the back of her ashy black hair toward him. Alyssa looked at him, but he turned away, startled, and avoided her gaze. One of Alyssa's friends had curly brown hair with shiny braces he saw from a dozen feet away. One appeared as tall as him and muscular like a gymnast. This girl had dyed blond hair and black eyebrows. The third friend had jet-black hair and black eyes and wore black jeans with a white top.

Luke looked back at Alyssa, and she gave him a welcoming smile. His insides stirred quickly, and his temperature shot up.

"Do you want to meet them?" Benji asked.

"Me, no ... not really," Luke stared at his food.

"Come on, big guy." Benji grabbed Luke's shirt, pulling him.

He complied, but only because he wanted to be in Alyssa's presence. He felt all the girls staring at him as they approached, so he fixated on Benji's shoes. He clumsily bumped into Benji as they stopped before the girl's table.

"Hi Birdy, how's it going?" Benji asked.

"Fine ... who's your friend?"

"Ladies, this is Luke. He just moved here from Puerto Rico."

Luke looked up towards Alyssa, who smiled at him, but she appeared to shy away herself. He got a good look at the girl with the black hair that was strewn with white streaks. She was Asian with pale white skin, as if wearing white makeup. The girl was staring down at the table.

He mustered the courage to stare directly into Alyssa's eyes. "Hi, I'm Luke."

"We know that silly. Tell us something new about yourself," Birdy said.

He was stumped and simply shrugged.

"Ladies, he's a bit shy but will be a hell-raiser in no time," Benji said.

"Well, it's nice to meet you, Luke. Let me introduce you to the rest of us. I'm Alyssa, and I'm in your art class. This is Sandy. She's a bit of an athlete."

Luke looked at Sandy, who crossed her arms and stared at him as if waiting. "Hello, Sandy. What sport?"

"Volleyball and softball, but I like lifting weights, as I can tell you do too."

Luke tried to answer but instead burned up in fear and simply looked at the young lady with the blond hair and waited.

"This is Linnet. Some of the boys call her Blondie, but we call her Lin," Alyssa said.

Linnet appeared more interested in playing with her food with her fork but looked up at him quickly. "I hope you like Lansburg. It's nice, but I cannot wait to attend college out of state."

"It's alright so far, Linnet," Luke said, looking at the girl with graying black hair. She was still looking down at the empty table in front of her. Alyssa did not introduce him to her. "How about her? Is she one of your friends, too?"

"Who? You already met Birdy," Alyssa said.

She may be a jokester or just put her friends in time-out. He pointed quickly at the Asian girl, hoping for time to think of something to say. "Your friend here with the black and white hair."

Alyssa appeared stunned, placed her hand over her mouth, and looked at the empty seat at their table.

"Benji, what gives? Are you playing games?" Birdy asked as she stood angrily in front of Benji.

"I didn't say anything, guys, I swear," Benji said.

The girl stared at Luke with an intensity he had never seen before. She raised her arm, pointed at him, opened her mouth, and tried to speak. No voice came out. Only darkness was visible down her throat until she faded away completely. She was a figment of his imagination, and the girls would think he was some kind of nut. "I'm sorry," he said, looking at Benji and moving his head from side to side. He ran off quickly without a clue where to go. He had music class next and without Benji he would not know where to go. Running from his problems was his new thing apparently, as he failed to realize that wherever you run, there you are.

When Luke finally found his Music classroom, he found Benji in the hallway looking for him. What surprised him even more was that Alyssa was in the classroom. He sat in the opposite corner and every time he looked toward her, she stared back at him. She did not appear angry, just interested. He let his hair hang down covering his face again like curtains and practically disappeared into his head.

CHAPTER EIGHT

Claire

The following day, Luke stewed alone in shame in his homeroom. He expected that Benji would avoid him along with the girls, who would most likely treat him as an outworlder. When he left his homeroom quietly, he felt a tug on his loose-fitting shirt. It was Benji.

"You okay, Luke?" Benji asked.

Luke noticed that Benji did not touch him in any way. It bothered him because of the way most of his family treated him. It could just be in his head. "I'm fine, Benji … sorry about yesterday," he said while walking to art class. "Sometimes, I'm a bit sensitive … about things," he said making air quotes. He felt embarrassed as he did it.

They walked in silence briefly until they approached their classroom. "Well, the girls aren't upset. They just want to speak with you," Benji stammered.

Alyssa and her all-girl crew blocked the classroom doorway. He was alarmed when he noticed Alyssa in the group's center. He attempted to move past them into the class, but Sandy blocked the door.

"Luke, what did you see yesterday?" Alyssa asked. She appeared menacing with her crew of girls surrounding her. This included the pale-faced Asian spirit who now smiled at him.

He took a deep breath and sighed. His first thought was to push past Sandy. He almost did just that when he took a step toward the group. Instead, he lowered his head and said, "I saw a short Asian girl with long black hair with gray streaks."

"Claire, it's Claire guys," Birdy said with tears running down her face.

"Where is she now?" Sandy asked, stepping out of the doorway to him.

"She's right here," he said, pointing.

The whole group of girls huddled together, surrounding Claire's ghost. They all began talking at the same time; mostly apologies and well wishes that were eclipsed by the teacher. It was all a little much to handle for his senses. The *second bell* sounded, alerting everyone the period had commenced.

"Alyssa, please take your seat," Mr. Aames yelled from inside the class.

Luke stepped inside the class, content to walk away from the emotions being expressed outside the classroom door. He expected to be made fun of and shunned today. He turned and saw Claire one last time as she waved at him from the doorway and vanished. Alyssa came into the classroom as she wiped tears from her face. She walked past his desk and caressed his shoulder, and he felt as if he had fallen backward into darkness *… I was somewhere else at a different time. I sat in the passenger seat of a car that had a black and gray interior. Alyssa leaned toward him with her eyes closed and mouth slightly open. She had small perfect white teeth. They kissed, their first, and it was unforgettable …* he came out of the darkness but was consumed with nausea. Fortunately, it was brief. He turned around and saw Alyssa take her seat. She smiled at him, and he saw her small white teeth, again, as she wiped the tears from her face.

Mr. Aames created seven groups of partners for art projects. He was paired with Alyssa. Forty percent of the course grade relied on group projects. The teacher explained it was so that students would learn how to complete art projects together. He sat quietly with her.

"Has that happened to you often, Luke?" she asked.

Luke was afraid to answer honestly at first. What he saw in his house was different. *Was it? I don't know.* Claire was sitting at the cafeteria table and not lingering at his home. "Sometimes … I cannot control when it happens," he said. The truth was out; from now on, he had to be honest with Alyssa.

She stared at him. Her eyes appeared to turn red and water, again. "We lost her last summer. She was the wild one amongst us. She died in an accident overseas visiting family in Vietnam." She grimaced in pain. "Why do you think she was here tagging along with us?"

He was moved by Alyssa's strength to explain her feelings. "I don't know. Maybe she wanted you all to know she was still with you. I'm just surprised you can talk about this."

"Maybe this isn't the correct place. Can we meet after school and talk?"

Luke turned red hot. Beads of sweat arose on his forehead that he wiped away with his long gray sleeve. "Sure, sure we can," he said quietly.

Benji walked up toward them from his desk. "You seem to have gotten close to our resident grease monkey." Alyssa smacked Benji's arm as he leaned in on their table.

Luke was grateful for the interruption. The thought of meeting in private with Alyssa after school was thrilling but also caused anxiousness within himself that he did not know if he could handle.

"I see you and Alyssa are getting along. We have been in school together since kindergarten. I work on her father's '69 Ford *Mustang Boss 429*. That sucker is fast."

"How would you know, Benji? You're supposed to work on the car. Not drive it."

"It's called a test drive, and it's fun, Alyssa! You remember having fun, right?" Benji asked while pretending to drive a car.

"You're never driving my car," Alyssa smirked and shook her head in emphasis.

"I don't mess with that foreign stuff anyway. She has a BMW *M3*." Benji looked toward Mr. Aames, who pointed toward Benji's seat. Benji walked away but turned and gave Luke a thumbs up.

Alyssa and Luke both smiled and proceeded to work out tasks to complete the project. He needed to gain some confidence and formulate how he felt and behaved around Alyssa.

Benji and Luke walked over to history class. "Have you asked Alyssa out yet?" Benji asked.

He whacked Benji softly on the arm, which caused the teen to stumble and almost fall.

"Damn, dude, that was hard," Benji said rubbing his shoulder.

"Sorry. I guess ... I move slowly ... she wants to meet after school."

"Are you going to meet up with her?" Benji asked.

"I don't know ... she's beautiful but doesn't seem to know it, and besides she's with Todd Ordley. She scares me more than Todd ... the championship quarterback," Luke prattled on.

"I'm not too sure how serious that relationship is. I've seen Todd scamming with other chicks." Benji brought some hope into the equation.

As they entered the classroom, Mr. Conway began to sing *School Days* by Chuck Berry, causing them to laugh before they took their seats. *Mr. Conway will be a memorable teacher in my life.*

"Luke, what are you doing tonight?" Benji asked, leaning into him from his desk.

"No plans, Benji."

"I have to work at my father's garage, but I will pop by your house at about seven if you want to hang out."

"Sure, I'll be ready." He was still bothered by the twisting thoughts concerning Alyssa. Still, he was content with the possibility of gaining a meaningful friendship with Benji.

☩ ☩ ☩

Besties

Luke did not meet up with Alyssa after school. Something he regretted but his timid nature still created a weight on his shoulders. He contemplated how he felt for some time, twisting himself into knots until eight o'clock that night. He heard a loud engine rev up and down outside, and then the engine shut off. He looked out the window in the hallway near his bedroom and saw Benji stepping out of an older car with a pearl white paint job. He met Benji outside.

"How goes it, Luke? Do you mind if I step inside to wash up a bit?" Benji had black grease stains on his face, arms, and shirt.

"Sure thing, first door on the right." He jumped ahead of Benji, opened the door, and turned on the hot and cold water for him. "Just trying to avoid having to clean everything."

"You should see my steering wheel." Benji boldly stepped into the bathroom and washed his hands with pumice soap he pulled from the pocket of his work pants. "Sorry, I rushed out the door and forgot to clean up." Benji left the door open while washing his face and forearms before flinching and jumping out. "Cut it out."

"What's wrong?" Luke asked from the hallway.

Benji stepped out of the bathroom, looking confused. "I thought you were behind me ... something grabbed my ear." Benji moved his hands around his face as if trying to swat away a cobweb.

Luke did not think it would harm anything with honesty. "I think the house is haunted."

"Seriously? Let's get out ... wait a sec." Benji grabbed a towel from his pants. He doused it in water and rubbed the pumice soap into the rag. "For my steering wheel."

They got into the car, and Benji turned around in the driveway and headed onto Red Hill Road and into the center of town.

"What's with your house?" Benji asked.

"I'm not sure what it is ..."

"Have you seen it? Like you saw Claire?"

Luke thought for some time before responding. With what happened earlier in school, he could not lie to Benji or dismiss his abilities. "It's not the same. It's different somehow. Nice car." Changing the subject should help.

"Thanks, it's a 1972 Plymouth *Gran Fury* with a 440 cubic inch engine. Do you like the pearl paint?"

"Yes, I do. It looks like a yacht. Did you do all the work yourself?"

"Yes, this one was a state trooper patrol unit." Benji drove to the local convenience store and stepped out of the car. "Have you ever had cream ale?"

"I have no idea what cream ale is."

Benji returned with the beer and a bag of ice and placed them in the trunk. "We are going to a park down the road." The engine roared to life. "You're wondering if I have a fake ID or something ... I work on his car and don't charge him labor." Benji pulled into an entrance surrounded by large trees and passed a sign that said Lansburg Memorial Park. Benji parked the car near the circular parking lot. "Luke, grab the ice chest from the trunk and follow me."

They walked to a part of the park with a giant bronze statue of a man on a horse. The statue was the park's centerpiece, surrounded by concrete benches and a barbecue area. Benji grabbed two cans out of the cooler and handed one to Luke.

Luke popped open his can and said, "Cheers, mate."

"*Sláinte*." They tapped cans, and each took a drink.

"Not bad. What does *Sláinte* mean?"

"Good health, from Irish and Scottish Gaelic, but I'm not from there. My ancestors are Italian."

"Italian, I would not have guessed that."

"Why don't you talk much about Australia?" Benji asked.

Luke considered what to divulge about that but either the beer or his growing friendship with Benji made him let it out.

"My parents and grandparents in Australia had a falling out. I don't know the adult stuff, but my father won the argument by moving us to Puerto Rico." He drank almost the rest of his beer. "My grandparents came to visit and gifted us our dog Tony, but they got into another screaming match. It's been two years."

Benji let out a loud burp and laughed.

Luke punched Benji's leg.

"Sorry brother, you were getting too real," Benji said, grabbing two more beers passing Luke one.

A car parked nearby in one of the spaces. It was a large black coupe with a bump on the hood. It looked like a Buick *Regal* but had a slick look to it.

"What kind of car is that?" Luke asked.

"You have a great eye, my friend. That's a Buick *Grand National GNX*, the fastest production car in the US market in 1987."

"Is that what we are, friends?"

"Why not? You are late to the game since we will graduate in a couple of years but why the hell not."

The driver of the *GNX* got out of the car and walked toward them. He looked like a guy in his late twenties. A young woman sat in the passenger seat.

"Hey, Tom. Are you taking the *GNX* for a stroll?"

"Hey, Benji, what's shaking? Yeah, breaking out the big guns with my new girl. Who's this young man?" Tom asked, offering him his hand.

"Tom Genaro, this is my friend, Luke Sanz," Benji said.

Luke stared at Tom's hand and thought for half a second before shaking it … *I fell backward and was being held upside down in muddy water. I was choking and could not breathe* … he stood up sharply and let go of Tom. He reeled forward, falling into Tom and belched. *I almost vomited just then,* he thought.

"Are you okay, young man?" Tom asked confused.

"Sorry, Tom … I'm just not used to this beer," Luke said, embarrassed. "I like your car."

"I barely drive it. It's a real beauty. It's part of my collection."
Tom had a large grin. "Benji works on my daily car, a 1969 *Hurst-Olds 442.*"

"She's a beauty. I did the paint job."

"I have this one and an '87 *Grand National* with T-tops. I crashed it a few months ago and could not go through my insurance company to get it fixed. Bad circumstances with the crash. It needs like six grand worth of work, says Benji here." Tom said, a bit soured.

"You need to stop crashing your rides, Tom," Benji said.

"True ... nice to meet you, Luke. I need to find a private area to talk with my girl."

"Tom, are you and Stacy having trouble again?" Benji asked.

"No, we are okay ... I just have needs, Benji," Tom said confidently but then looked toward the car. "Watch it with those *screamers*, gentlemen." Tom returned to his *GNX* and moved the car into a darker part of the parking lot.

"Who's Stacey? Tom's wife?" Luke asked.

Benji seemed embarrassed. "Yes ... I'm just a kid, but I've told him to cut it out before. His wife's a good woman, and they have two kids."

"She hasn't left him?" Luke asked.

"She has but she loves him, and he's kind of rich," Benji said.

Adults can do hurtful things to one another. He hasn't even gone out on a first date with a girl but has heard stories about affairs. His father's parents went through some trouble when they were younger. "Wait, what's a *screamer*?" he asked.

"That's what people call this beer. Some people in Buffalo came up with the nickname after claiming it gives you diarrhea."

"Great, Benji, I could have eaten salad instead."

Benji snorted again and stared at the can. "It's one of my favorites. It tastes great going down, Luke."

Benji motioned his beer at the statue. "What do you think?"

He looked at the statue of the man on the horse, then at the plaque. He walked over and read it. *Colonel Lancel Samuel Mars,*

The Savior of Lansburg. "Is this Alyssa's ancestor?"

"Don't take her here to make out. She's embarrassed about it."

"Great advice since she's with Todd." That fact angered him immensely. "Wait, so Lansburg is named after this guy?"

"Exactly, and I've known Alyssa since we were kids. She rarely smiles for any of us." Benji took another gulp from his beer. "From what I hear, Alyssa and Todd are on the outs."

"Really?" Luke asked, happier again.

"Alyssa thinks that Todd does not take their relationship seriously and wants only one thing. When she gives it up, he will work on his next conquest," Benji said.

"That's great news. Where did you hear that?"

"Birdy ... I've had a crush on her since we were younger. You're golden, my friend. You need to make your move." Benji grabbed two more cans of cream ale. "One more before we take off, Luke."

"Sure. How old is Tom?"

"I think he's twenty-five or so." Benji made a face and drank the rest of his beer.

Luke mimicked Benji and followed up by tossing the can in the trash. "Let's get back." They will need a restroom soon, and this park doesn't have one. "I better wait for Alyssa and Todd's relationship to fail. I don't want to get caught in the middle like that lady with Tom right now." He was running again from confrontations and problems. Within him, he knew he should brave it with Alyssa, speak with her, and see how it progressed.

CHAPTER NINE

Non Sei Degno

I sat alone in the backseat of a limousine. The car moved over smooth pavers from years of use. The large black leather seats were cool to the touch. The driver stopped at an open gate manned by two guards wearing colorful blue, gold, and red uniforms. I knew the buildings to be in the Baroque style but did not truly know what that meant. They passed a street sign bearing the name Via Sant'Anna. The limousine came to a stop. A priest wearing a red sash opened my door and beckoned me to follow. I knew the man was a bishop. More guards held their bloodstained spears pointing upward. The uniforms themselves had some dark red blood on the cuffs. The bishop was walking about ten feet in front of me. I followed the priest as if on autopilot. I walked through imposing hallways and entered an area with mosaic flooring and two large iron doorways where two large guards stood on either side. The priest walked through the entrance into the chamber toward a man wearing white papal regalia. The guards closed off their spears, blocking the door. They began to slam their spears on the tile floor loudly. "Non sei degno," they yelled repeatedly, pointing their spears toward me. They rushed forward with a battle cry.

Luke darted up in bed and opened his eyes. He looked over to Daniel, who had a pillow over his head. He rose, sat at his desk, and wrote in his school notebook, *Nan say degno, What's this?* Their grandparents were visiting, and Daniel lost his room to them. Daniel was relocated to Luke's room removing any privacy he had.

Loud footfalls from above reminded him that the family was working in the attic, which was positive because the result would be three more bedrooms upstairs. The red block lettering on his alarm clock read 6:00 a.m. Daniel was still asleep on the other side of the room. He got ready before heading up the new stairs to the attic. The construction materials they moved over the past week blocked the whole center of the attic space. They devised an entire plan for upstairs via phone calls.

Over the past month, subcontractors completed much of the electrical and plumbing. This past week, his family and several tradesmen worked on the house. The plumber completed his work already. Junior had framed out the two new bathrooms and bedrooms. Two of the bedrooms will be what's called a *Jack and Jill* that will share a bathroom enclosed between the two rooms. They have also framed and installed several windows with dormers and skylights throughout the attic.

Rich, the electrician, finished up new wiring for two air conditioning units and the new outlets in the attic. The air conditioning guy, Juanito, installed two mini-split units on either side of the house.

The electrician kept swatting at something while working on the lighting fixtures and ceiling fans. "What's this crap?" Rich asked, losing his balance, and falling headfirst toward the ground.

Luke lunged forward, breaking his fall. They both end up falling to the floor. He felt a presence but could not see the burned man around him.

"Thanks, kid. Something pushed my ladder."

"It was not me," Luke said quickly.

"I know it wasn't you ... something was playing with my ear, before I was pushed." Rich passed his hands over both of his ears. "I'm going to finish up here and head outside."

Rich had run conduit and wiring from the electrical breaker box to the closest foundation, the one furthest away and the electrical for the air conditioning unit that Juanito installed. Luke and Rich headed outside together toward the side of the house.

Juanito stood on a ladder twenty feet up the side of the house. Luke watched Juanito and thought he was happy not to be on that ladder himself. Juanito began to swat away near his ear. Luke saw the ladder move away from the house as if pushed. Rich ran over, grabbed the ladder, and pushed it forward, causing it to slam against the side of the house. This motion caused Juanito to lose his balance and fall down the ladder's rungs. Fortunately, Juanito controlled his descent and did not fall the whole way.

"Something pushed my ladder," Juanito said as he massaged his wrist, laughing nervously.

"The same thing happened to me upstairs, Juan," Rich said.

This event shook Luke's core because two men could have been injured as they worked on his family's house. He needed to tell his parents.

"I only have twenty minutes of work left," Rich said, walking to Juanito. "Try to finish the job but leave if you get attacked again."

Luke went to his dad to explain what happened and stopped himself. *I don't think he'll believe me, but I must do something.* He sought his brother Junior up in the attic. "Junior, both the workers were attacked by something."

"Dad may believe you. Grandpa was complaining of some insects bugging him. Something is happening in this house even if our father doesn't believe it," Junior said.

Once Juanito and Rich left, the rest of them, apart from Daniel, met outside on the deck. Luke's father and grandfather drank some beers.

"Dad, I have to talk to you about something." Luke was cautious but hoped he would have the courage to tell his father.

"What is it, Luke?"

"Juanito and Rich almost ate it today. They both had their ladders pushed by what ..." He hesitated before he let it out. "I think they were attacked by what is haunting this house."

"What's with this crazy talk? This house is not haunted," his father said with confidence. "This better not be this crazy stuff you're dealing with," his father said.

Luke took a deep breath to compose himself. He never should

have kept the burned man to himself. "I was there. I saw what had happened, Dad. Something is wrong." His hopes were deflated as he realized his father did not believe him, again.

"Nothing has happened to me, son."

"Angel, I told you earlier. Something whispered in my ear when we were framing, and I felt like I was walking through webs. Your son could be onto something," Grandpa Julio said.

"I don't recall that ... you too, Dad?" his father asked before standing up and throwing his beer across the yard.

"Just get the house blessed already ... you should have done it as soon as you moved in," his grandfather said.

"Dad, if you were here more often, maybe you would notice something weird with this house," Junior said, pleading for his father to listen.

"I'm going to take a shower. I suggest you all do the same." His father pointed menacingly at him before walking away and tried to avoid getting too close to him.

"Your father is a skeptic; he has to experience it himself," Grandpa Julio said.

That evening Luke found himself staring at the ceiling while lying in bed. He was scared because he did not see the ghost that had attacked the workers. The events of that afternoon consumed him in a way he was unaccustomed to, and sleep eluded him. He tended to be able to dismiss problems as not his concern. His father's constant denial caused him to mature quickly. *What am I feeling right now?* He focused on the lights from passing cars through his windows. The shadows from the trees reminded him of the calm he had from ocean waves breaking on the beach. Sleep was slowly creeping in.

I was submerged at the knees in the watery sand. Some shallow waves caught up to me. I was not in danger of being swept to sea, yet. I looked toward the horizon at a three-masted ship anchored ahead of me. I walked into the water, carried on impulse, instead of my own volition. The water quickly rose to my chest. With one wave, my head was underwater. I gained the ability to control my body. I pushed down on the sandy bottom and rose into the air. Suddenly something grabbed my foot and pulled me deep into a bottomless ocean. I looked downward and saw a blond-haired man had latched onto my foot like a heavy weight pulling me down. I screamed and then swallowed water. Panic set in as I realized I was drowning. I saw the flash of something metallic as it shot toward the blond-haired man.

"Wake up Luke, it's time, wake up!"

Luke opened his eyes and tried to take a breath but could not. He got on his knees, mouth wide open attempting to inhale and then exhale. *Nothing.* He stood up and ran toward his office chair and shoved it into his abdomen. A fountain of water sprayed onto his desk. He could breathe again. He sat on his bed and looked for his sheets that were now ten feet away near his closet. *I was pulled out of bed.* He closed his eyes and placed the palms of his hands over his eyes. Slowly, he looked toward his desk. The water was gone. He could now hear the noises that came from upstairs. Seven days into the project, his grandfather was set to finish that afternoon.

Luke headed upstairs and helped his family finish the project. His father gathered the whole family into the attic before they all ate lunch.

"Oh my God, this feels like a whole new house. It's nice and cool in here, too." Their mother beamed with pride.

"It's the new air conditioning system. It even circulates into the rooms because we placed ducts into the bedrooms through the ceiling, and we have ceiling fans."

"I was wondering what you all were doing up here. It looks great," Grandma Aci said.

"Junior, give your mother and grandmother the tour." Grandpa Julio motioned throughout the room with a bit of flare.

"Sure thing, Mom. Grandma, follow me this way ... this new room here is storage." Junior began but rushed quickly toward other doors. "Let's go check out the bedrooms over on the other side." Junior took them across the hallway into one of the bedrooms. "There are two bedrooms on this side with a full bathroom in the middle."

"A Jack-and-Jill bathroom, only access is through the bedrooms. I like it, but what if somebody else needs to use the bathroom?" Grandma Aci asked.

"Grandma, there is another bathroom on the opposite side. Two new full bathrooms in the house." Junior pointed at the door leading to the other bathroom. They walked through the bathroom, into the additional bedroom, and back out through the door into the loft.

"I will need a housekeeper for all these new bathrooms! What about this door?" she asked.

"This room last, Helen," his father said while guarding the door.

"Mom, this is the game room on the left side and the kitchenette. No oven, but there is a drop-in burner on the countertop, a microwave, and space for a fridge. I almost forgot this section is a wet bar."

"This is a great upgrade, and this game room is perfect." Grandma Aci appeared pleased.

"Angel, what is this room you are guarding?" She knew what was behind his father was meant as a surprise for her.

Luke's father opened the door and let her into the new room. "It's your new art studio." The room was about 12 x 15 feet and had a bench toward a bay window that gave natural light. A giant movie poster in a frame stood out on the wall.

"This room is so beautiful, Angel," she cried. "My first movie poster, so thoughtful, honey." She hugged her husband and kissed him. "Thanks, Angel."

"You're worth it, baby. Thanks for following me throughout the world."

She stepped out of the room and hugged Daniel. She hugged Junior and kissed the top of his head. She never got to Luke but did blow a kiss toward him. "You all did a perfect job and were so thoughtful for including me in your plans."

"Junior is going to move into the bedroom at the end," Daniel said.

"You can always move up here too, Daniel, and share a bathroom." Luke pretended to poke Daniel who jumped back awkwardly. The whole family noticed but said nothing.

For a few minutes, Luke felt like he was part of the family and allowed himself to think that he could be himself. He must learn not to lower his guard. Within a few minutes, his mother and brother avoided his touch. Earlier in the day his father almost jumped to avoid him. He looked at his grandfather and then his grandmother who both avoided his eyes. He shouldn't have mentioned the house was haunted. *I should have kept my mouth shut*, he mused.

CHAPTER TEN

Wrecked

I stepped out of a taxicab in the driveway of a large house. I felt comforted because the style of the front façade of the home reminded them of Puerto Rico. Overall, it was a fusion between a home in the Caribbean and one in Northern Virginia.

"Thanks for your service, Sergeant." The cab driver told him.

"You're welcome. It's my pleasure, truly," I told the driver, as I stared at my reflection in the cab's window. I was not me, not now at least. I had short hair and wore a dress uniform with one arm in a sling. I walked into the house's side gate, past a pool, and knocked on the door. I belonged on this property but not in this house. I knew that I had to knock on the door.

Joyce opened the door. I walked into the house and Joyce gave me a firm hug. She smelled of cinnamon and chocolate as if she was baking.

"Welcome home, Luke. Tristan is over here." I followed Joyce into the living room. "Daniel is at an away game in Montreal. Tristan is on the floor playing with his toys."

I recalled now. I missed by nephew's fourth birthday and had promised him a toy. I leaned down and handed Tristan a gift I bought while I was overseas.

"Hello, Uncle. Were you at war?"

I helped Tristan open the box and handed over several action figures from a popular movie franchise. "It wasn't a war, Tristan. I'm sorry that I missed your birthday party. I came here from the airport and couldn't wait to come to see you."

"Thanks, Uncle. I'm going to call him Luke."

Tristan had a crown-shaped birthmark on his left thigh. I pressed it like it was a button. Something I did since he was a baby, which typically caused him to laugh. Tristan did not laugh. He stopped moving; my nephew turned purple, then white. "Joyce! Joyce! Something is wrong with Tristan!" I reached out to the toddler, grabbing him, but the boy crumbled into powder. "No!"

Luke woke up screaming and jumped out of his bed. He stumbled to the carpet, looking at the empty spot where Daniel was sleeping before he moved to the attic. Luke folded in on himself and started crying uncontrollably. He began convulsing as if in a seizure. He lost control of himself with the sight of his dead nephew in his memory.

"It's okay, Luke. You can change that future. Come out of it." It was his protector speaking in Spanish.

I don't have a nephew, he thought. Luke opened his eyes. The seizure stopped, and he heard Tony barking at him from the bed. "I'm okay, Tony, it's a dream." He stood up and sat on the bed next to Tony. He looked at the alarm clock, which read 0500 in bold red numbers. He grabbed a book and started reading again. It did not take long for him to fall back to sleep.

He woke up a second time. It was ten in the morning. *Darn, I overslept.* He headed downstairs with Tony. The *Monte Carlo* and the *Grand Caravan* were not in the driveway. Tony ran up to the sofa and jumped into the arms of Luke's grandmother.

"Good morning, Luke and Tony ... how are you both this morning?"

"Good morning, Grandma. Where's everybody?"

"They went grocery shopping for the week, and your father wants to have a barbecue this evening." She motioned toward the kitchen with her index finger bearing a long-painted fingernail. "They left you a note."

Luke walked over to the kitchen table and grabbed the note.

Luke, we went shopping for stuff for a barbecue. You can invite a couple of friends if you want, Mom.

He served himself a cup of strong Cuban coffee with cream and sugar and then took Tony outside before he decided to pee on the carpet. He sat outside and drank coffee while his dog ran after squirrels. Suddenly, a loud thud startled him, causing his coffee to spill. He looked around at the window, but nothing was there. He headed upstairs into the attic and turned on the television and gaming console. Another loud thud, and the floor shook. He began to feel light-headed and then heard a growl.

"Bugger off ..." a disembodied voice said.

He bolted in the air and tried to run downstairs but was pushed forward and stumbled on the floor onto his hands and knees. He just missed striking the cabinet with his head. Slowly, he looked behind him. Nobody was there. He ran downstairs into the garage and began pacing back and forth. The garage door was left rolled upward. He received an impulse to pound on the heavy bag bare-handed. He kept at it for minutes with all his energy until the sound of his parents' minivan rattled him out of it. He took his first deep breath before stepping out of the garage.

Luke's father opened the car door. "Help us bring in these groceries." His father grabbed some of the bags before turning. "Wipe the blood from your hands before you grab any bags." His father turned quickly and walked into the house. At that very moment he decided to tell his father about the burned man. He could no longer guard a secret that could harm the family.

He peered into the back of the minivan and saw numerous brown paper bags full of groceries. His mother stood beside him and grabbed a couple of the bags. "Are you shopping for the whole month?"

"No, just for the week. Some people are coming over tonight ... Kamila will be here soon from the airport." His mother's visage brightened after speaking her best friend's name.

"Is that where Grandpa and Junior went?" Luke asked.

"They went to look at the property your grandfather wants to buy."

Later, Luke called Benji and invited him over to the house before taking a scorching hot shower. He made himself comfortable on his bed and began to read. A loud knock on the door startled him. "Who is it?" Odd, nobody ever knocks on my door. Luke tried to get up but was glued to the bed. The door opened, and the burned man walked into his room. He was wearing dark clothing, including a hoodie. The figure stood at his doorway and shuffled from side to side, breathing and rasping hoarsely like an animal trying to scare its prey.

"How can you see me?" the creature growled while shuffling back and forth as if prepared to charge forward. "This is all mine. Where are my albums, my comics?" The creature motioned outward with its arms, claiming everything around it before walking closer to Luke. It peered down at him menacingly.

Luke could not break the hold over him. He flexed his muscles and felt his ligaments and tendons coming close to rupturing.

"Don't fight back. You're powerless over me. I will be here long after I finish with you and your insignificant family."

Luke stared at the abomination defiantly. *I'm so scared.* He felt a firm hand on his chest and heard clanking metal followed by a raspy voice.

"Wake up, soldier—prepare for battle."

He opened his eyes and noticed it was not dark outside, and nobody was in his room. *Was I dreaming?* He sat up, exhausted. His muscles felt like he had just completed a tiring run. It was 5:00 p.m., and the guests were expected in an hour. He stood up and walked toward the window as if on a tightrope. His mother was outside getting the tables ready, so he reluctantly approached her. "Do you need help, Mom?"

"Where have you been?" She closed her eyes and put her palm up. "Just get the barbecue started." His mother waved him away.

His father was in the kitchen seasoning the meat and made a slashing motion across his neck as if Luke was dead meat for not helping. When outside he prepared the barbecue for grilling before he heard the distinct sound of Benji's *Gran Fury*. "Benji, come out to the back," he yelled, cupping his mouth as if yodeling.

Benji walked around to the back of the house. He had his trusty ice chest, coupled with his usual smile. This quickly brought happiness to Luke, who had endured a day of odd dreams and sleep exhaustion. *I hope it's not like this every day*, he mused.

"You better put that cooler on the other side of the house," Luke said, motioning to Benji.

"I put sodas on the top to throw the adults off and brought a few *Koozies*."

That caused Luke to smile, and his day magically brightened up. "What type of beer?"

"This time, some Samuel Adams *Boston Lager*, which I know you like." Benji handed him a bottle wrapped in a *Koozie*.

Junior's friend, David Villa, rode a bicycle to the house. Daniel took off in the Taurus to pick up his friend for the barbecue. Kamila Poder, the godmother to the boys, had arrived in a taxicab. He saw her inside the house through the sliding door window. She told him once that her name meant priest's helper. "Hey, Junes, let's say hello to our godmother." Luke headed into the house through the sliding glass doors.

Kamila smiled proudly at them teary eyed. Her dark brown eyes and black hair complemented her light bronze skin. "My beautiful boys." She hugged Daniel and Junior and blew Luke a kiss. Kamila tried not to touch Luke, but she told him as a child it was so that he would not be forced to see something adult oriented.

"Luke, take her bags up to the guest bedroom. Then, come back down and start grilling," his mother ordered, still bothered by him not helping earlier.

"Yes, Mom." Luke grabbed all the luggage and took it to the attic bedroom near Junior's room.

Luke headed back downstairs and started grilling the meat. His grandparents and father were at a table with some friends of their parents named Jorge and Emily Villanueva. His mother and

Kamila were at a nearby table chatting about something. He started grilling but returned to the kitchen. The front door opened, and Daniel spoke to a young woman with a familiar voice. Daniel came into the kitchen with Joyce Hollowell.

"Hey Luke, do you remember Joyce from a few months ago?" Daniel asked, knowing that Luke had to recall her.

"Her family used to own the home and was afraid of coming into the house," he responded.

"Daniel told me it's not so bad anymore and that we would mostly be outside on the deck," Joyce said.

Luke stared at Daniel who looked meek and pleaded with his eyes to be easy on him. "I need to go check on the grill." He walked off and saw Daniel introduce Joyce to his mother and Kamila and then to everyone at his grandparents' table.

He served all the meats on a buffet table his mother set up.

"Great job upstairs, Luke," Kamila said.

"I was the laborer, and Junior was the foreman on that project," he said proudly of his brother.

"Your mom has high expectations for you and pushes you in return."

He smiled at his godmother. "She pushes me while babying Daniel. She doesn't have any expectations for him?"

"Little more to it than that, sweetie. I know we will speak on that one day."

After they ate, all the youngsters sat together at one of the tables. Daniel and Joyce were transfixed with one another, kissing here and there. It must not be their first kiss. "Joyce, how long have you two been hanging out?" Luke asked.

"We have been 'hanging out' for the past month or so. We bumped into one another in school, and Daniel called me relentlessly," Joyce said, using air quotes jokingly at the hanging-out phrase.

"Don't be jealous, Luke. Be happy for us," Daniel said with a wink.

Junior shook his head in frustration. "Seriously, you're going to take a jab at one of us?" Junior asked protectively.

"We need to talk, Daniel, but it's best to do so privately." Luke wanted to shake Daniel for misleading Joyce about the haunting.

"You're jealous and always want another guy's girl," Daniel said with another stab.

"What's your point, Daniel?"

"Alyssa … you're trying to steal Alyssa from Todd. Who knows what you're up to." Daniel was deliberately trying to push Luke into a confrontation or a reaction.

"Daniel, what are you doing? Please stop already." Joyce placed her hand on Daniel's arm.

"Alyssa and I are in a few classes together. That's it." He stood up. Daniel recoiled in fear. "Don't worry. I need to go to the restroom." Luke walked to the second-floor bathroom.

When he returned outside, he met up with Benji on the edge of the deck. "Did my brother talk any shit while I was gone?"

"No, I think he said what he wanted to earlier," Benji said.

"He can be such a tool. He's lying to Joyce about what's happening in the house, so he pushes me about Alyssa," Luke said.

"Just ignore him. Your brother is a conceited guy," Benji said.

Luke did not have a response to that and simply shrugged. He returned to the table with Benji joining him.

"Luke, how's everything going in the house?" Joyce asked, concerned.

"It's getting worse. I heard some banging, and a voice told me to *bugger off* before it shoved me." Luke responded with Daniel staring at him. Telling her about the burned man was not an option.

"I hope you're joking," Joyce said, leaning into Daniel. You told me it was getting better!"

Daniel did not say a word. He glared at Luke and gave him a cowardly middle finger in a way that Joyce could not see. Daniel stood up. "Come on, let's go to the park."

"Daniel, please don't drive the car … you've been drinking,"

Junior said quickly.

"Shut up, child. I only had a couple of beers." Daniel filled a tote bag with ice before grabbing one of their father's six-pack of beer and tossing it into the bag.

Luke walked up to his brother, but he tried not to get too close to him. "Brother, why don't you just walk to the park? It's just a mile away."

Daniel stared at him intensely. "I need the car to take Joyce home later. Don't worry. She's just a mile away."

"Daniel, we can walk," Joyce said quietly.

"Don't let them spook you. "Come on, let's go," Daniel grabbed her hand, and they were off toward the driveway. All Luke thought was how his failure to warn his family about the burned man led up to this day. He was wrong. He should have spoken up.

"Looks like I'm walking home," Benji said, taking a long pull from his beer.

CHAPTER ELEVEN

The Confrontation

I drifted into an oncoming lane. Fortunately, no other cars seemed to be on the road. I over-corrected and moved into the shoulder of the roadway and sheared off the right side-view mirror with a telephone pole. Music played loudly and unintelligibly from the car speakers. I slurred my voice as I sang between sips from a bottle hidden inside a brown paper bag. I had no control over the body I occupied. I was an observer. I began nodding off and dropped the bottle on the vehicle's floorboard. I woke suddenly when I struck a boulder and launched into the air, hitting a tree. I must have passed out. When I woke up, I was coughing blood and forced myself out of the car through a window. My chest felt broken, like I had a shattered plate under my shirt. A light shined brightly from a door in the distance. It beckoned me like an emergency room sign. I was close to passing out, so I walked to the door and pounded on it. A woman peeked out of her window. The light shut off. I banged on the door as loud as I could …

Luke woke up to see his brother Junior successfully shaking him awake. He wanted to drift back into the nightmare, trying to seek a resolution. His eyes began to shut again.

Junior shook him again. "Wake up. Daniel was in an accident."

Luke put his shoes on and followed Junior down the hallway. He saw a bright light outside from a tow truck. They both headed out and met up with their grandfather.

"Where's Daniel, Grandpa?" The anxiety Luke felt included fear of the potential loss of his brother. He had never experienced the loss of a person he loved and cared for. *I was Daniel in my dream … wait, I couldn't have been Daniel,* he thought.

"He's fine, boys. Daniel is being treated at the hospital. Your parents are with him." His grandfather shook his head from side-to-side, perturbed about more than just the accident.

Junior approached the car and saw the front passenger side fender bent into the tire. The vehicle would need to be repaired before it could be driven again.

"I warned him, but he always does whatever he wants," Junior said before kicking at a loose piece of plastic from the bumper.

"Did he get arrested?" Luke was concerned for his brother's safety, but he also hoped that this accident would lead to a learning experience, by facing the consequences.

"No, your dad met up with the officers, and they cleared some stuff up." Their grandfather looked at Luke and down to the floor as if ashamed.

"Daniel will never learn, Grandpa. He gets away with everything all the time." Junior knew their parents enabled Daniel and was turning him into a monster that would feed off them in perpetuity.

"You prefer he was arrested?"

"No, we want him to learn from his mistakes, and if our parents keep protecting him, he will never learn," Junior said.

"Do you feel the same way, Luke?"

"Yes, Grandpa, but Junior thinks he can reach our parents by speaking up. None of you can see that we are treated differently." Luke had to try to get their grandfather to understand.

"I'm sorry you feel that way, Luke, your father makes intervening difficult for me. I promise I will try and speak to him … one other thing, Luke."

"Yes, Grandpa."

"I have been sleeping on the cot you found in the attic." His grandfather paused. "Daniel's bed hurts my back. I saw something." His grandfather appeared agitated. "I woke and saw a woman in the room. She was dressed in white. Have you ever seen something like that?"

"Not like that, but we have seen other stuff. Tony was attacked once."

"She looked like she was trying to scold me, but I couldn't hear her. I turned on my lamp, and she disappeared," his grandfather said.

"Have you seen or felt anything else before or after?" he asked with interest.

"My things keep moving in the room—my wallet, keys, and watch. They have been moved, and I cannot find them. When I give up, my stuff returns to where I placed them."

"That happened to me, Grandpa. With my tools." Junior knew what it was like to have his stuff moved around on him.

Their grandfather motioned the matter away with his hand. "You two speak with your brother Daniel, and I will talk with your father and try to make life easier for you. For now, try to go back to sleep."

Luke and Junior headed upstairs in silence until they arrived at the doors to their rooms. They both knew speaking to Daniel would go nowhere fast.

"I have this odd feeling that we did something wrong," Luke said.

"What are you talking about? I'm just pissed at Daniel because now we need to take the bus to school."

"Junior, I think we are somehow going to catch the blame," Luke said.

"Go to sleep, you're talking nonsense," Junior waved him off and entered his room.

Later that morning, Luke's parents asked him and Junior to come downstairs for a family meeting. Both sat down on the couch, but Daniel was not with them. Their parents came out of the dining room and stood before them like a firing squad prepared to levy a guilty verdict. *Why are they angry with us?* Their father was visibly agitated, although he appeared to be trying to compose himself. His grandparents, and Kamila, were in the kitchen eating breakfast.

Their father walked behind the sofa, rubbing his trembling hands together. "Boys, I want to start this by saying that your brother is doing fine and only bruised up his left arm, but it's not broken."

"That is good news, Dad." Luke wondered why his father was so agitated when Daniel was doing fine.

"Luke, no talking. Listen, please," his mother said impatiently.

"Daniel has admitted to drinking and claimed that Luke and Benji were also drinking." His father glared at him while pounding a fist into an open hand.

"What does that have to do with anything?"

"Not one word, Junior. I'm losing my patience. We realize you are getting older, and we were your age once, but your brother doesn't need the bad influence from Luke."

"Your brother looks up to you, Luke, and says he felt compelled to drink." His mother looked down to the ground as she spoke.

"Can I say something, please?" Luke asked.

His father took a deep breath with closed, strained eyes. "Go ahead."

"Daniel was openly drinking before me, and you both allowed it. I drank a few beers with Benji out of his sight." Saying that much was difficult for Luke. However, he still was taking the position of a doormat.

Junior appeared compelled to interject. "I told Daniel not to take the Taurus to the park to drink because he could have walked there. What does this have to do with Luke? It sounds like you will discipline the only people you can."

"What did you say to me? I'm not taking it easy on Daniel," their father said.

"Then, tell us our consequences. Then we can tell you how easy you are on, Daniel." Junior looked at his father defiantly.

"You little ass. Would you prefer a belt instead?" Their father walked toward Junior while grabbing the buckle on his belt, prepared to pull it out.

Luke was burning inside about whether he should speak up and protect Junior. *I cannot disrespect my father.*

"Angel, please, don't let him get to you. Let's discuss consequences." She stood between her husband and son, the discussion circling back in front of the sofa.

"I told you, Junes," Luke whispered.

"Boys, it's obvious that the car is out of commission. I took it to the shop already. It will cost almost $1,000, and we cannot go through the insurance. The consequence is that it will cost each of you a portion of your savings to pay for the damage."

"Our savings? You can't go through the insurance because you protected Daniel from the consequences he earned with the police. That sounds fair, Dad. Does that include Daniel's savings or only ours?" Junior's sarcasm was a defense mechanism from all the years of punishment for Daniel's behavior.

"Why would we include Daniel's savings?" Their mother appeared hurt at the suggestion that Daniel did something wrong.

"Daniel did nothing wrong? We did?" Junior had a surprised and confused look on his face.

"You both were culpable because you did not steer him from drinking and driving," his mother said.

"Mom, we tried to stop him from drinking and driving. Daniel called Junior a child when he tried to stop him from driving the car. He does whatever he wants." Luke tried to be diplomatic with their parents, who had an innate instinct to protect one specific son.

"You both bought into his bullshit and are unconcerned with this unfairness and completely ignorant of how you treat the two of us!" Junior held his head in disbelief.

Their father grabbed Junior off the sofa and lifted him into the air. "How dare you speak to us that way and defy me? Say one more word ..."

Luke was growing red with anger, and his indecisiveness was killing him inside. It burst out as he stood up, stared at his father, and walked closer to him. "You will not be beating Junior for something your Godsend did."

Luke's father released Junior and stepped back, wide-eyed with surprise at his son. In truth, he appeared afraid of having a hulking young man approaching him angrily.

Grandpa Julio walked into the room. "Angel, may I speak with you, please?"

"Dad, not now." Their father looked meekly toward their grandfather.

"Outside, son." Their grandfather opened the sliding door and stepped on the deck.

Junior sat frozen in shock on the sofa with his hands raised. His shirt bunched up toward his neck. Their father followed their grandfather outside.

Luke moved closer to Junior, grabbing his hands, and moving them down before straightening his brother's shirt. "Mom, you seriously don't see that you are being unfair to us and favoring Daniel?" He thought speaking patiently, in a low tone, would not anger her.

Tears flowed freely down their mother's face. "I'm not thinking, Luke. We haven't slept and had a bad night."

He saw his father and grandfather hugging outside the door before returning to the house.

His father walked past them without looking in their direction and motioned for their mother to head upstairs. They walked up the steps into the foyer and spoke privately.

"Luke, they are discussing disciplining Daniel, but we are still in the equation." Junior was out of shock and kept his voice relatively low. "We lost money with his crying once and are about to again."

His parents returned to them. They appeared somber but no longer infuriated with them. "It would not be fair to ask both of you to be accountable for your brother's behavior. Daniel will also have to cover his mistake from his savings."

"Daniel needs to learn accountability by holding his brothers responsible for his behavior?" Junior looked at him in disbelief. "The lesson here is that you want us to control the uncontrollable, or else we will be punished." Junior appeared to forget that his father tried to menace him into compliance moments ago.

"Junior, we have spoken, and those are the consequences." This time, their father controlled his anger by not reacting to Junior.

"Let's go tell Daniel. He will not be happy." His mother's principal concern was her firstborn's happiness. Both parents glared at Junior before walking away.

"We would not want to anger Daniel by holding him accountable for his actions." Junior tossed one more snide remark toward his parents.

Their grandparents and Kamila walked toward them. "Junior, you were disrespectful to your parents." His grandmother's lack of self-awareness was as strong as her disappointment toward her younger grandsons.

"Our father was not exactly commanding respect, Grandma," Junior countered.

"Junior, take it easy. We're outnumbered." He grabbed his brother's arm. "If you only understood what it's like to live in a home as a second and third son to Daniel." He sat between his grandmother and Junior. "She looks like she found us under a rock," Luke whispered.

"Aci, let's leave them to cool off for a bit," Grandpa said.

Their grandmother stared coldly before she returned to the kitchen.

Loud voices could be heard coming from upstairs. Luke and Junior walked toward the entrance, trying to listen and overhear the conversation.

"How much do you want to bet that Daniel is telling them how unfair they are to him? He will convince them to screw the lesser life forms." Junior grabbed onto his head, staring at the floor.

"I will not take that bet, Junior."

Kamila walked up to them and placed her arms around them. "No need to eavesdrop, boys. Your parents are parenting a squeaky wheel."

"Titi, do you see the unfairness and how easily Daniel manipulates our parents?" Junior asked through tears that flowed now after first standing his ground against their parents. Junior was a survivor but was still just a young kid.

"I will no longer stand by and watch our parents treat us like Daniel's punching bag," Luke said confidently after finding his voice. Their parents treated Daniel like a precious commodity that could fracture if told it behaved badly.

CHAPTER TWELVE

La Curandera

Kamila stood between her godsons and rubbed Junior's back lovingly. Luke was content that she was with them and witnessed their father's behavior. She had been in their family's lives for decades. She was an open-minded person who their father tended to shy away from.

Although the enforcer of their mother's protective nature with Daniel, their father's behavior was truly surprising. He was not himself. His father was ordinarily extremely diplomatic and against their mother's overt hovering over Daniel.

Kamila was a well-known paranormal author, lecturer, and media personality within those circles. As such she was at times recognized in public, and invited to functions around Latin America.

"Boys, let us go for a little walk. Step outside into the fresh air," Kamila said, turning back into the house for a sweater.

They each grabbed a pullover and followed their godmother out of the front door. It was a cool windy fall day. The forest was brilliant with the colors of Autumn in Northern Virginia. He took a deep breath as he stood outside. The air outside felt alive whereas air inside was stagnant and stale.

Kamila motioned to the driveway. "Is there a path around here?"

"Yes, I ride my bike on a trail about a five-minute walk from here. Luke uses it to go on runs." They walked to the path quietly.

"Luke, Junior, I'm your godmother and Daniels, and I love you all, but I have a story to tell you, and it's going to be a little different than you're used to."

They were confused but nodded their heads as if they said go on already.

"I know you have heard from your mother that Daniel almost died as a baby."

Junior shook his head in the affirmative. "Yes, we hear it whenever we point out how they treat Luke and me differently."

"You don't know the whole story, and I always told your parents you both need to hear it." Kamila looked at the ground and appeared to be searching for words. "It was 1973, and we were all in New York City. Your parents had flown in from Sydney, and your Grandma Aci flew in from the island. I had a place in Manhattan and drove them all around."

She followed Luke quietly when they crossed the street and entered a dirt path surrounded by trees. Possibly created by children who walked to and from the school. Before long they entered a paved path.

Kamila continued her story. "They were seeing specialist after specialist. From hospitals to clinics, each one would say the same. They could do nothing. Even the doctors who seemed positive at first gave up in the end."

"Kamila, we have heard this before," Junior said impatiently.

"Not this part. Let's sit at this table." They arrived at a small park that was accessible on the trail. They took a seat, and Kamila continued her story. "I sat with them in my apartment, where they'd been staying for weeks. I told them about a *curandera* ... do you guys know what that is?"

"A spiritual healer," Luke said.

"Yes, I met her when my mother was sick several years ago before that time. Spiritual healing has been around for hundreds of years before medical doctors. Your parents were initially against visiting the healer, but your father was on the verge of losing his job. At the time, your father had been a special agent for two years, and his boss wanted him back at work, or he would be fired."

"They never told us that part. Right, Junior?" Luke asked.

"Yeah, they told us he had some kind of wasting disease and would not eat, but they have not spoken about our father almost losing his job."

"Daniel was slowly wasting away as if something had a hold of him, and it was something undiagnosed, and that medicine in the 1970s had no chance of curing," Kamila said, as she grabbed both their forearms. "Your parents were desperate. Do you think your father would agree to meet with what he would call a witch doctor?"

"He does not ever talk about this type of stuff." He was willing to hear why Daniel was treated as if he was special but did not like the way the story was progressing.

"They were determined to save their son. They would do anything for you all."

"For Daniel, maybe, their golden child," Junior said.

"Let me finish. You may think differently once I finish." Kamila held onto Junior's chin. "So, we flew to Puerto Rico, and I drove them to Aguas Buenas, where the healer lives. I introduced them. She lived in a remote area that used to be an old banana plantation. Palms, banana, and mango trees surround her old concrete block house."

Luke grew a bit dizzy. He could see the entryway of a courtyard of a block house. He shook it off and could see Kamila move her hand to him which she placed on his forearm … *I fell backward and found myself in a house in a different time.*

Kamila hugged and kissed a woman on the cheek.

"Doña Isidora, my love, how are you?" Kamila asked in Spanish.

"Here with our Lord," Isidora Puente said.

"These are my friends, Angel, Helen, and Acidina. This is baby Daniel. All, this is Doña Isidora."

"It's terrible to meet in this circumstance. Let me see the baby."

My mother handed over the baby to Isidora. They were all so young, but haggard with a noticeable defeated look. My mother's face appeared swollen with her eyes bulging.

"Please save my baby," my mother said, as she cried into my young

father's arms.

I walked closer to Isidora and the baby. She removed the blanket and took off his diaper. The baby was emaciated. It was Daniel but a near dead version.

Isidora closed her eyes and moved closer to the baby. She cringed and moved her head up as she whispered a prayer over the baby who was lying on a table now surrounded by the blanket.

My parents held onto one another tightly. Kamila joined them. My mother grabbed at her. My grandmother, who was not an emotional woman, also joined the huddle. Watching them all cry bothered me. It was ugly to watch. I felt like an interloper, as if I was spying on an event I was not supposed to witness.

"Be hopeful, don't you feel it? He's going to make it through this!" My grandmother said, hopeful but also praying out loud.

"My poor boy, God, please save our son." My father teared up while holding onto his mother.

Isidora came to the doorway. "It's the spirit of one of his ancestors on the father's side. He meant good but is very confused."

"Tell him to leave Daniel alone ... he's killing him." My father punched his thigh in desperation.

"It's going to take time. Kamila, please take them to wait in the living room."

Kamila led them into a living room area with rattan chairs. My father turned as if to go back into the room. "Please, Angel, let her concentrate, and pray over him." My mother joined his grandmother on the sofa before embracing one another.

My parents sat impatiently. I walked closer to Isidora's private room. I heard her praying and singing for some time. The prayers stopped suddenly.

"Is that a man's voice I hear?" My father stood up and began walking toward Isidora's prayer room. Kamila stopped my father. I heard the voice to and began walking toward Isidora.

"Please, Angel, sit and wait here with Helen." My father almost pushed past Kamila, but stopped and bowed his head, defeated. My father returned to my mother ... abruptly, Luke snapped out of the vision.

Failing to see whose voice he heard. He was back in Lansburg with his godmother and brother. He felt nausea come over him, which caused him to buckle forward. This was the first time he had seen a vision with his godmother's touch. She wanted him to be there at that moment with the *curandera*.

"Are you shitting me, Titi?" Junior asked in awe.

"I walked into the room and saw a shadow of what looked like a man holding a staff, and then the shadow disappeared," Kamila said.

"Get the heck out of here. Luke, do you believe this?"

He didn't answer his brother. He was in shock. He stood and looked down the running path and placed his hand on his chest. He found he could not control his breathing and his heart was slamming rapidly.

"Isidora brought Daniel out of her room, and he was smiling at me. Daniel had never smiled at me before. Isidora handed Daniel to me, and I took him to your parents who began to laugh. Your parents were so happy."

"So, he was cured?" Luke asked.

"Yes, he was fine after that. Isidora told me that the spirit was a soldier who killed a wealthy landowner in Puerto Rico. He was returned to earth to guard a descendant."

"So, this spirit's guarding Daniel throughout his life." Luke pushed himself up from the bench.

"Isidora explained that the descendant is a warrior for the Lord and a protector of *su rebaño*, his flock. The spirit was confused. I don't really understand why it happened."

"This is beyond *Twilight Zone*-type stuff, Luke."

"You bet, Junior. Not sure what this means because Daniel only protects Daniel."

"He was stuck at the wrong time and was on a mission assigned to him by an angel."

"How old was Daniel?" Junior asked.

"Daniel was ten months old."

Junior pointed toward Luke. "Our mother was pregnant with

Luke, right?"

"Oh my God, yes, yes she was. We found out that same week in Puerto Rico." She grabbed Luke's hand to look at his palm ... I was in a room at my grandparent's house in Puerto Rico. My parents and family were celebrities along with Kamila.

"You have a long, strong lifeline Luke, and a second line follows your line."

"You're the protector of God's flock, brother." Junior punched Luke's arm to get his attention.

"Please, bro, I'm nobody's protector. I think this spirit needs to wait another generation." He took his hand back, from Kamila. "Titi, are you saying my parents cater to Daniel because he's special?" he asked, attempting to change the conversation.

"No, they remove all the barriers he faces because they almost lost him. They were close to accepting that he would die."

"Thanks for telling us, Titi. We will ease up on Mom," Junior said.

Luke's face turned red. Sweat formed on his forehead. He pushed on his chest, trying to remove the tightness. "I'm sorry ... I'm getting an anxiety attack. I need to get out of here ..." *I need to stop running from my problems*, he thought but could not stop the fire building within him. He felt like a rocket preparing to move upward with all its flames pushing toward the ground.

A large part of how he learned to cope with his anxiety was to use specific behavioral management tools. He needed to push aside the extraneous material and find what disturbed him. While running, rather briskly, within his mind he peeled away each area that bothered him such as the curandera, the ancestor, the near-death of Daniel as a baby, and finally the protector of God's flock. He stopped running abruptly. *I did not like my brother referring to me as anybody's protector let alone one assigned by God.* He stopped running and then thought. *What's happening to me?* The crushing feeling in his chest returned. He looked toward an unpaved running path that shot towards a large hill. He turned his feet and ran toward the hill as fast as he could. By the time he reached the crest of the hill, he felt serenity. *I must be some kind of masochist.*

Luke ran downhill and felt disappointment until he realized he was several miles away from home. He came to a congested area of the trail that stopped at several intersections controlled by traffic signals. He came to a stop to allow a line of cars through. He saw a man wearing a red long-sleeved shirt standing in the trail ahead of him near a tree. He ran into the trail and slowed down when he noticed the man was wearing a helmet and holding an odd-looking spear with an axe on the top, called a halberd. The man wore breastplate armor, a curved helmet, and puffy gray breeches. The sight of this man caused an immediate adrenalin rush which made him tremble. Panic enveloped him. Instead of stopping, he picked up the pace and blindly ran past the Spanish soldier who reached out and grabbed at his shoulder. Luke pushed faster inattentively through the signal-controlled intersection. He stared at the *DONT WALK* sign in bold red.

A loud car horn, screeching tires, and a burned rubber smell attacked his senses. He felt weightless and intense pain emanating throughout his body. He tumbled through the air before landing on the hard asphalt street like a sack of potatoes. Nausea invaded his body as he felt his soul attempting to elude its shell.

"He never stopped or slowed down." A voice rang in the air distantly. "Somebody call an ambulance."

Luke heard heavy footsteps walking toward him. He was frantic and wanted to keep running but was immobilized forever. He was dying.

The soldier from another time reached down toward him, placed a gloved hand over his eyes and shut them. "You must see to be reborn ..." the soldier stated in accented English.

I had the sensation of falling backwards as my eyes rolled into the back of my head and everything went black. My mortal body had been damaged. I took my last breath.

CHAPTER THIRTEEN

The Landed Soldier - 1655

The beauty of the ocean bay in this remotely populated part of the island gave Captain Sebastian Sanz-Basque the feeling of being an explorer. The balmy weather diminished with the ocean breeze blowing inland in the southwest region of Isla de San Juan de Puerto Rico. His faith in Catholicism dictated his life as a daily regimen. At least, that was how he tried to live life. He was on the island as a representative of his father, General Gerardo Sanz-Cruz, who was affiliated with the Swiss Guard while he resided in San Lorenzo near Escorial palace. He traveled in a caravel funded by King Philip IV and Pope Alexander VII. He prayed at Iglesia Porta Coeli in the township of San German. He arrived in Bahia de Boqueron two weeks prior with a contingent of eighty Spanish land soldiers along with his spouse Maria and their two sons Rafael and Esteban. His soldiers set up camp on a nearby hilltop to the southwest with his family living in a church-owned cottage.

Sebastian did not wear a soldier's typical clothing. He obtained several pairs of sturdy gray breeches and red long-sleeved shirts from his father's tailor. A cobbler fabricated his calf-length leather riding boots in Italy. He regularly wore his armored Cuirass breastplate but not the accompanying *Gorget* as it dug into his neck. His helmet, a Spanish *Morion*, was typically on his horse, head, or near him, depending on the situation. Still, he always carried a velvet hat that was given to him by his mother. His long black hair was tied in a knot behind him, and he tried to keep his beard and mustache well-trimmed. A tall man for the time at five foot ten inches, he was fit and muscular, being no stranger to physical labor.

His father, the general, had tasked him with serving two sealed orders to the largest landowner and farmer in San German named Don Roberto Rodriguez-Burgos who had been enslaving the poor and indigenous people. He pressed them to work his land as if he was a captain of a ship. Sebastian approached Don Roberto several days ago and was able to serve him with both sealed documents. One was an order from the Holy See and the other from the King of Spain. Don Roberto was contrite and agreed to the demands. Roberto promised to obey his king and eminence, the pope. Indeed, he was not privileged to review the documents before they were sealed or opened.

He faced a problem compounded by the deviousness and greed that came instinctively to his wife Maria who had been pecking at him like a bird during all this. She was slowly trying to whittle away at his will. Maria wanted him to forcibly remove Don Roberto from the land and send him back to Spain to answer for his crimes. Her constant scheming and insults had lowered his spirits and aggravated his tendency to suffer from depression. The captain was praying to seek divine guidance. He did not have time to seek further advice from his father, who may already be at sea and on his way to the island.

The day before, he had discovered that Don Roberto used several hired brigands to remove six men and women from a town called *Barrio Libre* where *Taíno* of mixed race and impoverished Spanish outcasts lived together. The village was self-governed and comprised prior inhabitants of a Spanish *encomienda* where indigenous populations were pressed into Christianity.

Earlier in the day, he confronted Don Roberto, without his soldiers, who threatened to have his men bludgeon him to death. He retreated to the protection of the church; it brought him solace while seeking divine guidance.

"Sebastian, why are you praying? Take your soldiers and remove him and his family from his land. The man is a heretic and is bedding Taino women," Maria said in Spanish to the kneeling soldier.

He took a long breath and avoided looking at his wife. "How do you know that to be true? Those are not my father's wishes or orders."

"You're not even a man! Why did I marry a woman instead of a man?"

"We are in God's house, Maria. Please leave me to my prayers."

"You're no man at all. I am going to the town tavern to look for a man to handle this problem for your father and see if they can meet my other needs." She grabbed her hips to send him another message about what she sought to handle.

He stood up. "Why do you belittle and whittle away at me like an axe? We are in our Lord's house, and I seek his guidance."

Maria spat on the floor and walked away from him and out of the church.

A priest, Father Bonifacio Dittalia, looked toward him and shook his head in disapproval. Father Dittalia was an associate of Sebastian's father with ties to an anti-slavery movement within the church.

His blood boiled as he ran after Maria with an intense fury. Maria's act of disrespect to the church served to minimize his manhood while also defiling the church. Sebastian left the church without finishing his prayers, which annoyed and infuriated him. Maria's spicy personality often aggravated him, but it made for an exciting time in their bed chamber.

Lieutenant Ricardo Fernandez-Lopez was at the church doorway with several soldiers watching the spectacle. It angered Sebastian that his wife would be disrespectful in front of the priest, let alone one with his father's ear. It was even more emasculating to occur in front of his soldiers, which was Maria's goal in the first place. Once he stepped outside, he grabbed his wife's arm, pulling her to him. "How dare you defile our church, Maria?"

"I'm trying to make a man out of you. Your father sent you here to handle the King's business. You must become a man, even if you are not one."

He loaded his gloved hand as if to smack his wife into submission. Instead, he pushed her to the ground and motioned to his second in command. "Ricardo, assemble five of our best troops with our horses. Bring them to the clearing south of town where we planned." It was clear to him that his actions were driven by his wife, not the guidance he sought within the church. Which was most likely why she interrupted his prayers.

"Yes, Captain ... full gear and arms?"

He looked at his wife with contempt, then at his lieutenant. "Yes, Ricardo, we are going to confront Don Roberto."

"Now go and become a man." Maria stood up without brushing herself off and walked back toward the cottage, taking her impishness with her.

They rode for some time until they arrived at the outskirts of Don Roberto's property. Taino natives were working in the fields alongside other men dressed shabbily. Some men motioned toward him and his soldiers and pushed the captives away toward a hut and out of sight. That's enough evidence of Don Roberto's refusal to stop enslaving indigenous and the poor. They rode until they arrived at the primary residence of the hacienda. He had sworn before his father's benefactor, Cardinal Cadolini, that he would never take slaves as a soldier for Spain. He was ordered to prevent the enslavement of the indigenous of any country Spain explored or governed.

Don Roberto stepped out of his home holding a pickaxe, accompanied by five of his paid thugs. They had macanas, which were Taino native weapons used as bludgeons. "What is the meaning of this, Captain?"

"You've been served by a king's man and representative of the pope. You agreed to comply but instead defied them. You are not worthy of this land. You will be removed and returned to face justice," Sebastian said.

"I will not give up my land. I made this property into the most productive farm on this island. I don't recognize your authority to remove me and will not follow the orders of two tyrants an ocean away ... my men will not allow you to remove me." Don Roberto nodded at the dangerous men, who stood before the soldiers defiantly. Their macanas had bloodstains from all the beatings they had served.

"Ricardo, remove the Don's men from this discussion," he ordered while trying to control his anxious mount.

Ricardo motioned to the soldiers. Two of them moved forward with their halberds pointing toward the enemy. Don Roberto's thugs stood their ground. The soldiers struck them down quickly. One of the thugs jumped, lunged to one side, and struck Sebastian's knee with a macana. The captain's horse reared upward, causing him to drop his halberd and fall off his horse. The thug walked up to him and raised his macana for one final blow. Ricardo rammed the point of spear through the man's side before he finalized the attack on the captain.

Sebastian stood up, steadied himself, and grabbed at his knee, which seared with pain. "You must comply, Don Roberto. You and your family will return to Spain, face the King, and explain your enslavement of his subjects."

"What do you know of this? The King's courtier authorized me to take servants. They were fleecing me. They take almost all I earn on this farm."

"The king and the pope think differently, Don Roberto."

"I refuse to listen to Don Gerardo's upstart and would prefer to die fighting," Don Roberto swung his pickaxe upward.

Sebastian unsheathed his sword and thrust it into Don Roberto's abdomen. A woman's scream rang out into the sky. Don Roberto's newly minted widow, Clara, ran from the home, followed by several older children. He wiped his sword on Don Roberto's pants and placed it back into its sheath. He felt stunned almost immediately, understanding that his actions were wrong and would bring unbearable consequences. This was the opposite of what his father wanted. He looked toward his soldiers, and they appeared equally stunned. "My Lord, what have I done?"

"Why did you do this? You had enough men to seize him and force him to Spain. You did not have to kill a father in front of his children. May God damn you, Sebastian. Roberto is a man of God and a friend of the pope!" Clara shouted in anger.

He recoiled, knowing she was correct. This boulder he unleashed would roll down the mountain with or without him. "Ma'am, collect your things. You must be out of this hacienda and off these lands by morning." He walked toward Ricardo with clenched teeth. "Stay here tonight with most of the men. Free anybody held in captivity and ensure they are returned to their homes. I will return to San German with two soldiers. Make sure that the wife and children are moved to Boqueron tomorrow."

"Yes, Captain. What do I do with the rest of Roberto's men?"

"Tell them to leave. If they refuse, bury them with their friends."

When he returned to town, Maria tore at him again until he placed her as the Doña over the hacienda. She convinced him to transport Don Roberto's family to Higüey on the island of Hispaniola instead of Spain, where the widow could file a complaint with the king's courtiers.

Maria convinced him to become the de facto Don of the hacienda. After several days, he became diseased by his wife's constant scheming, which led to disobeying his father's wishes.

Months passed until the day there was a knock on the door of the hacienda. He had been drinking rum and wine nonstop, gaining weight, and becoming soft. His injured knee had not healed correctly and ached all hours of the day. He was overwhelmed with depression and had not been to church since the day of Don Roberto's death.

"Don Sebastian, your father is here." Ricardo looked toward him and looked down in embarrassment but bowed to Sebastian's father. "My General." Ricardo walked out of the hacienda backward in deference to Sebastian's father. Ricardo shut the door awkwardly with a disgusted look on his face.

"You have turned into a fat slug. I give you clear orders, and you kill one of the pope's friends. Don Roberto was a friend of mine. You were to correct him, not force yourself into his position and lands."

He dropped to his knees before his father and general. "Father, my wife Maria would not stop. She whittled at me until I did what she wanted."

"I warned you about that woman. Are you not a man of God? Don't you have principles? You were to serve my friend Roberto the sealed orders from our king and holy father and bring him to me alive if he did not comply ... you and your family will return to Spain, and I will take command of your troops." The general gave his son a dismissive wave of disappointment.

"Father, Don Roberto told me that the king's courtiers authorized him to take slaves. They were taking his earnings," Sebastian said.

"That is why Cardinal Cadolini sent you. There were other things at play. You must think for yourself, but your evil wife ruined you."

"No, Father! Please, Father, one more chance. Please let me redeem myself. I know I let myself be led astray by a greedy woman." He grabbed at his father's belt while blubbering.

His father glared at him in apparent disgust more than anger. "You disgraced me, but I am here on our King's orders—the English are planning to attack Hispaniola. You will sail with me on my sloop of war as your men follow on your caravel and support Fort San Genaro. It's your last opportunity for redemption."

"Yes, Father, I will ... I'm sorry for killing Don Roberto."

"Sober up. You are an embarrassment. Go to confession and prepare. We begin loading the ship in seven days." His father stepped toward the door before turning around. "We will discuss your scheming wife when we return."

He followed his father and noticed a dozen soldiers sitting

atop horses. His father spoke with Ricardo, who pointed toward the location of his soldier's camp. He walked toward his subordinate, Ricardo. "We will be leaving in one week to Hispaniola for battle. Please go tell the men."

Ricardo looked at him as if with hope and curiosity. "Are you fine, Captain?" Ricardo appeared to doubt that Sebastian was prepared to lead the men.

"I am good, Ricardo. Let the men know we are headed to Hispaniola to repel an attack from the English. Be prepared to travel and ensure the men drill for battle. Begin breaking down the camp before I join you this evening."

"Yes, Captain." Ricardo smiled before running to his horse and galloping away ahead of the general's troops.

Light pierced the darkness of the abyss as I felt the sensation of moving forward. The heavy weight on my eyes made it impossible to force them open. The experience of being struck by the car was awful. The jolting numbness was gone but the aching remained. Consciousness eluded me. The voices were loud and excruciating but slowly dissipated into oblivion ...

CHAPTER FOURTEEN

The Awakened

Luke opened his eyes. The pain was gone, but it was replaced by that same bout of nausea. It was so intense he doubled over and vomited. He was not lying battered and dying on the asphalt. He stood before the Spanish soldier he knew now as Sebastian. He felt different somehow, not just because he was no longer broken. *I feel confident. I feel strong.*

"I know who you are, Sebastian." Luke realized that he had two choices. Continue to run away from his problems, face them, or grow into who he was meant to be.

"Yes, Luke. Sebastian Sanz-Basque, at your service," the man said, holding his fisted right hand at the wrist and giving a slight bow. "You needed to experience that … you need to know who I am."

"Sebastian, Halloween is still a few days away. Why are you wearing armor and girls' pants?"

"Girls don't wear pants … at least they shouldn't." Sebastian had a pleasant warmth about him. "I think you know who I am … I died in battle wearing this." Sebastian motioned toward his chest and helmet.

"You look ridiculous!" Luke said, feeling feisty having experienced death and then an awakening. He knew he was a different person.

Sebastian appeared to grow in height. "I'm a Spaniard, a landed soldier. My father had this armor made for me," Sebastian said with the confidence of a serious man.

"What's this emblem on your armor and helmet? These two keys and a crown?" Luke asked while tracing the keys and crown with his finger.

"It's the symbol of Vatican City. My father was a member of the Roman Curia and protector of the Holy See."

"The Vatican? The pope?" What was all that … did I just die?"

"In a way. I had to pass a message to you clearly and touch you. You have abilities that will grow over time and some that will present themselves when they become a part of you. Your being struck by the carriage was because of your stubbornness, but as you saw, quite necessary."

"Are you shitting me? Necessary. I can still taste the blood."

"Do you feel different?" Sebastian asked.

Somebody just ran down the path and stared at him oddly. "I don't know why that guy is looking at me weird. I'm not the one wearing weird pants."

"Well, he was looking at you because he cannot see me," Sebastian said.

Luke looked down at his shirt and saw where some of the vomit had landed. He knew he was not talking to himself. After the vision, he knew who Sebastian was and that he had been protecting him lately. "Can you run in that costume?"

"Of course … this is my uniform, Luke."

Luke ran down the path and found a private area away from all the intersections and other runners. "Can you explain what happened to me?" Sebastian ran beside him. The clanking sound of his armor had a familiarity about it. He heard that sound countless times beforehand.

"Yes, I had to send you that message, so you understand who I am. Being struck by the carriage had to happen. It triggered who you are to be."

"That makes no sense. Was that you who attacked my brother Daniel? You almost killed him."

"I was clouded and only saw Daniel." Sebastian paced and lowered his head. "I was unsure of what to do and attached myself to Daniel. I was wrong, and my actions almost caused his death."

"The Curandera, Isidora Puente. She reached you and

convinced you to leave Daniel?"

"I was confused and trapped. She helped me escape." Sebastian ran silently for several seconds. "I stood patiently by your mother's side when I realized she was with child. I could feel your thoughts, and once you were born, I followed you and joined with you until you needed me. Until you were in peril."

"I'm in peril? Why didn't I get sick like Daniel?"

"I'm your guardian. We are meant to be together."

"Why me? Why do I need a guardian?" Luke asked.

Sebastian laughed, stopped running, moved closer to him, and looked at him eye to eye. "You are a soldier of the Lord. You are a protector of the Holy See on earth. The angel explained that my descendant would have the gifts from God of sight and the ability to protect his flock on earth."

"You are my guardian angel, and I'm a soldier of God?"

"Non-Sum Dignus. I'm not worthy of being called an angel. I'm your companion and protector during the battles you will engage in while protecting our Lord's interests," Sebastian said.

"I've heard that before in a dream. I was trying to enter a room in a large building, and two guards yelled at me. What did they say ... non sei degno. Does that mean the same thing?"

"Yes, you were not worthy to be presented to the Pontiff."

"How do you know that? Only I would know that. Oh my God, in heaven, this is all in my mind. I'm talking to myself." Luke grabbed his head and crouched down, waiting for the burning sensation, the anxiety, which never came.

"I'm aligned with your soul more than in your mind. I sent you that message, but you're not crazy, Luke. You're learning and preparing and will meet the Holy Father one day."

"I'm standing before a conquistador talking about battles and the Vatican. I'm going nuts!"

"I'm a soldier, not a conquistador. I'm here to prepare you ... dig deep. You know who and what you are. It will come to you."

"Prepare me? I'm only a kid who can barely wake up in the morning."

"You're not a child. Not anymore, and you know that to be true. You're a man many people worldwide will rely on one day," Sebastian said.

"You should have landed in my father. He's the warrior, not me. I'm a shy kid who isn't comfortable in his own skin." He stared at Sebastian defiantly. *Why am I pushing back?*

"Your father is an impressive man, as was my father. However, I'm where I need to be."

Luke stood proudly before Sebastian. "Sebastian, I know you are right. These gifts … these abilities … I need to learn how to use them."

Sebastian beamed at him confidently. "That is why I am here. It will take a lifetime. Your full potential will depend on what you will encounter."

The bouts of anxiety he felt throughout his adolescence were replaced with power. He was done running. His battles were ahead of him. He was done deluding himself that he was not worthy. He was no longer that scared child.

✝ ✝ ✝

Mobsters

I was driving a car around a congested city, making turn after turn. I wore a blue tracksuit with white stripes and wore shiny jewelry, including a heavy gold neck chain I handled with my left hand. I knew I was lost but did not want to stop for directions. I approached a dead-end alley where two groups of men wearing business suits with open collars stood facing one another. The men held Thomson submachine guns and Browning Automatic Rifles from the Prohibition era. The men appeared to be a cross between Colombian drug traffickers and Italian mobsters. One had an open briefcase glowing in amber, and the other case had a greenish-hued light emanating from it. I parked in front of the group before removing my firearm from my shoulder holster and said, "You're under arrest." All the mobsters pointed their rifles at me and began to shoot as I tried to flee by running behind the car. The glass from the car window splintered shards at me as I found cover. I saw a man walk toward me, so I shot him, center mass. Directly behind me was another man who took a well-aimed shot that struck my forearm …

Luke woke up with his arms guarding his face and chest. He stared through the gaping hole in his forearm. He saw the ceiling through the hole. Blood dripped onto his face. He jumped out of bed and fell on the carpet. He looked at his arm again. The hole was gone but not the burning sensation. The dream, the nightmare, had faded, but he knew his father was in jeopardy. Sebastian stared at him from his office chair.

"Weird dream," Sebastian stated.

"No shit. What do you think it meant?" Luke asked.

"Your father is in danger and needs to be warned," Sebastian said quickly.

He stood up and walked toward his parent's room. He sat on the stairway, staring at the door. *Why am I wasting my time?* Moments later, the door opened. His father stepped out, holding a small suitcase with rollers and a leather business satchel. His father stepped back, obviously surprised.

"Why are you sitting there?" his father asked.

"I had a strange dream about you and wanted to talk to you about it." Luke knew he was towing a line with his father but thought it best to avoid a tragedy.

"You know, I don't like talking about this type of stuff," his father said, clearly being diplomatic. "I need to be out of here in five minutes. Follow me."

He followed his father to the kitchen. He was glad for the additional time because he had no idea where to begin. If his father was compliant, it was best to let his father guide the conversation.

"Go ahead, son, I'm listening."

"I dreamt that you were driving around a congested city … you were wearing a tracksuit and a shoulder holster."

His father sighed before taking a deep breath. "I don't wear a shoulder holster, and I certainly don't have a tracksuit." His father poured two cups of coffee and mixed them with milk before placing one cup on the table's edge as far away from Luke as possible. "You have two minutes. Let it out."

Luke reached for the coffee. "Okay, you drove up on a drug deal and pulled your gun. The gangsters shot you down," he said in the last part, standing up pretending to shoot a submachine gun.

"You're worrying me with this type of stuff," his father said before taking a large gulp of his coffee. "Okay, I promise I will walk away from any drug deals I interrupt." His father drank the rest of his coffee. "Okay."

"I'm serious, Dad, don't go for your gun, please." He loved his father unimpeachably, even though he dealt cautiously with him.

His father clenched his jaw. "I promise, son. I want to come home as bad as you want me home." His father grabbed his luggage before walking to the waiting taxicab in front of the house.

Luke walked upstairs while looking at his father out of the hallway window and made the sign of the cross. "May God protect you, father." In truth, Luke hardly believed in the Catholic faith. Since he met Sebastian, he has felt different somehow.

"Your relationship with your father seems problematic," Sebastian said from behind him,

Luke turned to his guardian and considered what to say. "I can hardly remember everything, but when we lived in Australia, I touched my mother's hand and saw her brother dying from falling from a horse on their ranch outside of Sydney. I told my mother that my uncle's horse, Banjo, would hurt him. She ignored me, and my uncle died."

"Accidents with horses happened often in my time. I do remember what happened. I was there with you," Sebastian said.

"We moved to Puerto Rico after that," he said, but his voice cracked. "I haven't seen my grandparents since then. I loved visiting their ranch ... I just learned not to touch my family members." He took a deep breath and wiped the tears from his eyes. "Whenever I saw visions, I just learned to turn it off and ignore them." He slammed his hand against the wall and walked back toward his bedroom. "I convinced myself it was all in my head with the help of some doctors in two countries."

"It was hard for me to see you get weathered by that. I knew I contributed to some of it and tried to console you ... do you remember?"

"Yes, that's when I thought my parents were right. That I was nuts." Luke walked into his room and petted Tony under the sheets. "It's all a fog ... I spent so much of my life pushing all that down. I erased it from my mind." Luke's eyes widened in realization. "It's all real, though." He stared at Sebastian standing before him. A spirit from a time long past.

"It is real ... you must learn how to use your gifts. When you unknowingly touch a person's soul, you can see a way to help them or you with your goal or mission."

"Or like a dream about my father. I see what may happen and can interject myself and try to prevent it from happening," Luke said.

"Yes, exactly," Sebastian said. "Understand that when I touch you, I can amplify your power, but I lose my mana or spiritual life force until I recover." Sebastian approached him and sat down on his office chair. "I have these ideas of what your power will be."

"What do you remember before you were sent back to earth to guard me?" Luke asked.

"I remember the guard at the gate. His name was Miguel. He told me I was to be released from *Limbo,* but I was to move forward in time to prepare you. You would be born with powers but can absorb some of the powers and abilities from others." Sebastian rested his chin on his hand as if in thought. "I recall that I was told the transfer of soul from where I was to here would affect my memory. I only remember some of what I was told."

"How odd ... this whole thing is so surreal," Luke said, shaking his head in disbelief.

"Your abilities will grow in time. Every day will bring you closer to your purpose. I will be here to help you."

"Right now, I see a crystal ball on a table in a dark room as my future," Luke said, laughing.

"You are destined to a much different life than a fortune teller. Only time will tell. Just trust your visions as they are messages from on high."

"I will, Sebastian." Luke knew then that he would no longer shelve his abilities even if it made his family uncomfortable.

CHAPTER FIFTEEN
Confidence

Luke was completing an individual project in his art class. He had sketched out what he knew to be Boqueron Bay to the west of Cabo Rojo in Puerto Rico. The drawing depicted a time over one hundred years before the city was officially founded in 1771. Holding his halberd, Sebastian stood facing the bay where one ship was anchored in the distance, and another was docked. Soldiers and horses were being loaded onto the closest boat.

"What are you drawing?" Alyssa asked.

Luke held up his drawing pad so she could get a better look. "It's 1655 in Boqueron Bay in Cabo Rojo, Puerto Rico. "This is a Captain with the Spanish army watching as his ship is loaded with soldiers. They are heading to the Dominican Republic to battle the English." He made it a point to look directly into Alyssa's eyes. She wore a skirt, and her flawless, shapely legs were distracting.

"That's very detailed, Luke. The assignment was to sketch out a relative where we grew up," Alyssa said, showing her drawing of a girl playing a piano. "This is my mother playing the piano as a child."

"It's flawless, I love the way you sketch." Luke had left other details out on purpose and quickly realized she was preparing him to answer the same questions the teacher would ask. "This is my Great, Great, Great Grandfather, or something like that. His name was Sebastian Sanz, and he was a captain with the Spanish in the 1600's."

"Oh, I didn't think to go back that far, but I wouldn't even know who my relatives were in the 1600s," she said before adding. "How do you? Have you ever been to that seaport?"

"No, I have never even been to Cabo Rojo … it's mostly my imagination," he said, unsure how to respond.

"Ten minutes, everyone. Wrap up your projects and be prepared to present in front of the class," Mr. Aames said.

Luke smiled as he was hoping to be able to explain his drawing. Which was odd since he detested public speaking.

"Can we meet after school?" Alyssa asked. "I would like to finish that conversation we never had."

"Of course, do you want to drive me home?" Luke asked boldly. "My brother Daniel can drive my younger brother Junior."

"Yes, meet me in the Senior parking lot after school," Alyssa said confidently.

Luke spent the remainder of his school day daydreaming about Alyssa, but each thought ended with the picture of Todd Ordley. That's how it continued circularly, and with each thought, he inched closer to thinking that relationships fail every day. Luke should push to win over Alyssa. Eventually, he settled on the realization that it was not his decision. Alyssa was alone in the driver's seat.

During lunch, Luke sought out Daniel in the senior lunchroom. Luke found his brother sitting at a table with several of the school's athletic players, including Todd who was not a senior, yet sat a few seats from his brother. As he approached Daniel, Todd eyed his every move. He considered wandering off, but he was focused and determined to get it over with.

"Daniel, I have a ride today. Can you make sure Junior gets home?" Luke asked.

"Did you forget? He has that trade class at that vocational school on the way home, and I have a thing, too. I was going to ask you to take Junior and pick him up," Daniel said.

Luke had indeed forgotten but considered a resolution. "I can get him to his class. Can you pick him up? The car will be here."

"Sure thing … will do," Daniel said, waving him away.

Sig. Alexander

He stepped away and met eyes with Todd again. He never mentioned Alyssa, but as he walked out, he saw Todd head over to Daniel. All he wanted to do was talk with Alyssa.

Luke walked over to his brother Junior and told him where to wait for him after school.

Later that afternoon, Luke headed to the prearranged spot and grabbed his brother, Junior. "Come with me, Junes," he said, motioning toward the other side of the senior parking lot.

Junior followed him obediently to Alyssa's car. "Where are we going?" Junior asked.

"Alyssa is going to drive you to your class. Daniel will pick you up later," Luke responded quickly.

"Alyssa? Where are you going with Alyssa?" Junior was confused and worried.

"She's going to drive me home so we can talk … as friends," he said.

"Is she still with what's his name?" Junior asked.

"Yes, she is," he said, realizing where this was going. "We're just friends, Junior."

"If you say so … I hope you know what you're doing?" Junior asked.

They walked the remainder of the way in silence. Alyssa waited outside her car and waved at him to ensure he saw her. She smiled intensely as he approached the vehicle. "Alyssa, this is my younger brother, Junior," Luke said.

Alyssa offered her hand to his brother. "Hello, Junior. Nice to meet you. Your brother speaks quite highly of you," Alyssa said.

"Really … he speaks of you all the time, too," Junior said as he poked at his brother.

Alyssa nodded her head. "He does, does he?" Alyssa asked as she unlocked the car with the key fob in her hand.

They got into the car. Minutes later, they were in a line of cars headed toward the exit. "Thanks for doing this, Alyssa," Luke said as he watched Alyssa changing gears quickly with the BMW's gear shifter. Her driving a five-speed was very attractive

112

for some reason.

"No worries, I have a hidden motive," Alyssa said, winking at him. "What classes are you taking, Junior?"

"Well, I'm taking some trade classes as part of a construction management program so I can be a contractor someday," Junior said proudly.

"Wow, that's awesome. Aren't you in the tenth grade?" Alyssa asked, looking at Junior in the rearview mirror.

"I've been working in construction since I was a little kid. Our grandfather was a developer in Puerto Rico and just started a company here," Junior said. "Can you drop me off by that dumpster, please?"

Alyssa parked quickly near the large green dumpster. Luke opened his door and let Junior out of the car.

"Thanks, Alyssa ... see you later, Luke," Junior said, shaking his head in disapproval at his older brother.

Luke sat back inside the car, feeling nervous. *So much for being reborn, tough.* "Do you know where I live?"

"Yes, Birdy pointed it out one day when we were driving around," Alyssa said laughing.

She pulled into his driveway and hesitated briefly. "Where should I park?" Alyssa asked.

"Over there by the shed," he said, pointing. He noticed his mother's car was missing which meant they were alone.

After they entered the house, he gave Alyssa a tour. He didn't step inside with her when he showed her his room. It made him nervous to have her in there. Tony ran out of the closet and threw himself at Alyssa.

"Aren't you a little charmer," Alyssa remarked, Tony licked her face.

He proceeded to go up the last set of stairs into the attic. It was freezing. "My brother must have left a window open. Give me a second, and I'll close it," Luke said. He checked all the windows, but none were opened. When he returned, he saw Alyssa sitting on the sofa with Tony beside her. The round thermostat's red dial hovered between 40 and 50. *I've never seen it that cold in the attic,* he mused. He walked over to Alyssa. "Do you want a blanket or something?"

She patted the sofa cushion beside her. "A blanket, maybe, but sit here with me."

Luke grabbed a throw blanket and handed it over as he sat beside her and took a deep breath. Something was troubling him, but thoughts and urges surged, making it hard to think.

"What's wrong, Luke? You seem distant." Alyssa placed a hand on Luke's thigh, which caused him to stand up.

Luke saw something, but it was fleeting, and told himself it was nothing. He sat back down. "Sorry, I'm a little nervous and worried about Todd.

"Don't be, Luke. We're just talking. Todd and I have been close for many years, but I'm just not interested in him anymore," Alyssa said. "Sit with me." She grabbed his hand and pulled him next to her … *I drifted backward into darkness, once again with Alyssa in the car with the black and gray interior. We kissed passionately, our first kiss but maybe not. It felt perfect, and I had a sense of belonging that I had never had. I was comfortable with her touch and wanted to consume her love with all the intensity I could muster. I grabbed around her waist, lifted her, and placed her on my thigh. We came close to kissing …* Tony was barking incessantly.

"It's a little early to get so handsy," Alyssa shouted.

Luke opened his eyes. The sensation he felt when he received a vision of moving backwards was dizzying, but nothing like the vertigo caused from the forward motion when he returned to the present time. "What happened?" Luke asked, pissed because he wanted to kiss her but knew this was not the correct time.

"Something just grabbed my leg," Alyssa said, standing up. "It couldn't have been you." Luke's hands were holding hers.

Luke stood up and looked around in a panic. He saw nothing. No ghosts. "Let's go talk outside," Luke said. He led her cautiously out of the home.

✝ ✝ ✝

Mania

It slept, mostly hiding from the one called Luke. He could make himself invisible to the boy who could see him now, and deep within his core, and knew he was dangerous. On several occasions, *it* asserted himself, trying to get the boy to warn the family the home was already occupied. He sent his minions to attack the family members, slowly eroding the patriarch's mind. His name was Angel. What an inappropriate name that served to anger him more and made him determined to flip the man's alliance away from his family. The destruction of the family brought him a perverse pleasure. As a creature who had never walked the earth, he mimicked emotions and did not experience them.

The house had been emptied of the family for hours. He liked it that way even if he lost energy whenever the house was empty. He suckled on the essence of living souls as if it was food. The dog Tony was left in the home alone most days unless the mother, Helen, was home painting in her office. At times, he would chase the dog around the house. Terrorizing the creature brought *it* to power.

He saw and felt movement outside the home. A car was coming down the driveway, one he had not seen before. He watched through the window of the third-floor hallway. Luke exited the car from the opposite side. Seeing the large teen leave the vehicle was a bit comical, he caused the car to keep moving as if it were docked on the water. A young woman exited the car next. She looked like Barbara, could it be her? *It* felt a surge of energy flow inward. His minions began all speaking at once.

"Silence," he yelled, causing the house to tremble. Luke was about to bring the young woman into the home. He was flustered, out of control. Luke would be able to see *it*. He must calm down.

He slithered upstairs quickly and tried to focus. He could hear them walking through the home, which caused his red electric static to flow to his extremities. He allowed the power to move and expel into the air. What would he do if it was Barbara from all that time ago? It had to have her, but Luke was in the way.

Luke and the young woman entered the attic—his domain. He could lessen the boy's power in this room. The boy would not be able to see him. Slowly, he slinked closer to the young woman. It wasn't Barbara, but she was beautiful. Hunger enveloped him that needed to be sated.

She sat on the sofa and took off her shoes. She had beautiful white skin that beckoned to be caressed. He moved closer, touched her foot, and moved hiss essence up to her thigh, trying to absorb her flesh. He could not, which caused a frustration that enraged him. When he touched the skin under her skirt, he latched onto the flesh and squeezed.

The girl, whose name was Alyssa, reacted to his touch. The boy still stood in front of her but now pulled her away enraging him. He wanted her, and Luke was in his way. The boy moved Alyssa behind him and appeared to stare at him. He tried to react and attack the boy, who was an impediment, but recalled the power he felt emanating from him. He needed more souls. He hungered for Alyssa and knew what he wanted.

Realization came to him. Once he became corporeal, he strived to consume Alyssa. He needed to approach his target smartly. He would wait; Alyssa was worth it. Something else outside the home caught his attention and he flowed toward the interloper. He moved quickly through the multiple levels of the home into the backyard and secured his prey.

Fighting Irish

Luke practically pulled Alyssa from the home while she mumbled unintelligibly to him. Tony had darted downstairs toward the dining room where he liked to hide under the dining room table. She spoke while they moved out the front door. She held onto her shoes, running barefoot through the cold grass.

"Can I at least put my shoes on?" she asked angrily.

Luke stopped and helped her put on her shoes. "I'm sorry … I think we're alone now."

"What do you mean?" she asked.

"My house is haunted, and I think something in the home … "Luke paused briefly. "Something tried to possess you somehow, like you are a gem or something," Luke said. He did not want to tell her, because she would think he was crazy.

Alyssa looked at him and still smiled. "Are we always going to get interrupted? Come on, let's go to the park down the road?" She ran to the car, and he followed willingly. She should have been asking rapid fire questions about the house, he thought.

It wasn't a park. It was the local elementary school that happened to have swings, slides, and a play area for the younger kids. Once parked, he stared at Alyssa's bare legs. He wanted to touch them but recalled that the spirit did the same. That made him apprehensive. She smiled again when he looked into her eyes and leaned in toward him. She placed her hand behind his neck and brought him toward her. He looked at the car's interior and saw it was all black without any gray trim. *I'm in the wrong car*, he mused. Nevertheless, he was impatient and wanted to kiss her. He reached down, grabbed her knee with his right hand, placed his left hand behind her back, and closed his eyes. They kissed briefly. He saw stars as if he stared to long into the the sun.

Without warning, his door opened, and he was lifted violently out of the car … *I rolled backward until I stood in a field staring at Todd Ordley wearing a green jersey with white lettering. I was in the house that Rockne built, a football stadium in Notre Dame, Indiana. The center snapped the ball backward to Todd, who caught it effortlessly, looking ahead. He launched the football forward to the receiver. The crowd in the bleachers cheered as the flash from cameras blinded me ...* Todd punched Luke's face, stunning him back into real-time. Luke grabbed and blocked the next punch, then placed Todd in a bear hug, moving the quarterback's hand quickly behind his back, prepared to snap the arm ... *I stood inside a disheveled living room of an apartment. Todd sat shirtless on a sofa, drinking beer from a can. Numerous empty cans were scattered on the table. The former football star had a sizeable, jagged scar on his shoulder that ran down his arm. The man had an ashtray on his colossal belly ...* Luke stopped himself from breaking Todd's arm. Instead, he lifted the future star player and placed him in the passenger seat of Alyssa's car.

Luke could not live with himself if he damaged the throwing arm of a young man who would one day be a star football player. "Join the Irish or end up a nobody once I break your arm and bust up your shoulder," Luke said. Todd winced in his arms but stopped moving. The boy's tension in him softened as if it was expelled, and he fell forward powerless. He let go of Todd and met eyes with Alyssa. "Talk things through with him. Believe me, it's for the best."

"Will he hurt me, Luke?" Alyssa asked.

"No, just hear him out ... Todd, I never wanted to get in between the two of you, but you and I know it's over. Don't you?"

Todd shook his head up and down before crying into his own hands. "I'm sorry, Luke. I saw red, and something else was controlling my body. I swear it wasn't me," Todd blubbered. "I'm sorry, Alyssa. I know we need to break things off."

Luke leaned out of the car and closed the door. "You'll be fine, Alyssa. Call me later, I'll be waiting," Luke said and walked off toward home. He thought about what he said and considered that the spirit in their home may have forced Todd to attack him. *How could it have that type of power outside of the home?* He thought. Luke shrugged that off and ran toward home. He turned and looked back toward Alyssa's BMW and saw the couple embracing. It hurt, but it was necessary. He never wanted to be caught between the couple; either way, he had to move forward.

CHAPTER SIXTEEN

The Cave

I ran on a trail downward on a dirt path through a forest that reminded me of Puerto Rico. I was once again an observer in a body I could not control. It was stifling hot, while I ran between numerous Caoba and Ceiba trees. I was not in Virginia. A cacophony of voices enveloped me along with the bodies of unwashed men. I stared at a group of soldiers forming a shield wall. I stabbed downward against the wall with my spear. A projectile shot toward me from the shield wall, striking my neck violently. I fell backward. I tried to run off but could not move. A burning sensation formed within my throat. The sound of the blood spurting from my neck grew louder. The flow increased as I bled out ...

Luke jolted awake and grabbed his throat, trying to cover the gouge on his neck. He jumped out of bed spurting blood from his neck as he moved. The wall was full of blood. He closed his eyes for several seconds before re-opening them while holding his breath. The blood was gone.

The alarm clock started blaring its annoying chime, startling him. He ran over to the alarm and turned it off. He sat back down on the bed and tried to relax. He recalled having promised Junior to help with one of his projects. Their mother hated this large wooden built-in cabinet, a fabricated breakfront, running across the dining room's back wall and pushing three feet into the room itself. Junior planned on removing the cabinet and resurfacing the walls.

He put on his work clothes and let Tony out onto the deck. They removed the countertop and some cabinets, and Luke moved some debris to the driveway. He returned to the living room to find Junior staring at the wall. "What's wrong, Junes?"

"This looks like an access panel under the paneling I took off. It has a hinge, but I cannot open it without breaking it." Junior looked at the panel puzzled. "I guess I can put caulking around the seam."

The access panel measured two feet by two feet. Luke walked up to the panel with a pry bar and broke it open.

Junior stared perplexed at the now open panel. "I guess that works too."

Luke grabbed at a flashlight from Junior's tool bag and shined into the opening. "It looks like a cement tunnel. I can see a void. Look." He handed the flashlight to Junior, giving him some space.

"That would be a tight fit for me to get through that. I best go first though."

Junior moved back. "I'm not going in there and neither should you. You're going to get stuck." Junior laughed nervously, getting a squeak in his voice.

Luke did not hesitate or show concern for getting stuck in the tunnel. "Wait out here and call Dad if I get stuck."

Luke forced himself into the tunnel. Once within, he realized it was not that tight of a fit. He arrived at an immense void with a five-foot-tall ceiling covered in drywall. The floor was coated in dust, and cobwebs. He could not stand up fully. It was a small, enclosed area, but the darkness made the area look larger than it was. "Hey, Junior. Come in there's plenty of room." He shined his light toward the deepest corner of the room. A small bed, table, dresser, and chair were visible. A small plate, bowl, drinking cup, and candle holder were on the table. A blue chamber pot sat on the floor near the bed. He walked over to the table, hunched down, and grabbed a pitcher coated with dust. Junior now stood beside him having braved the trek through the tunnel. "I had a dream about something like this." He shined the light at the exit to access the void they were in.

Junior walked back to the wall while the top of Luke's head skidded on the ceiling. There was an access panel with a latch pointed inward that looked like a lock. Junior made a motion not to close the access panel.

"Don't close it! That looks like a locking mechanism." He took a deep breath of stale air, concerned they would have been locked in the room. Nobody knew they were there.

"I won't, Luke." Junior held his hand on the latch portion of the access panel and moved it up but did not shut it. There are scratches, blood, and tiny fingernails glued with dried blood on the wall and access panel.

"What happened in here?" Luke shined the flashlight on the access panel and wall. The words SAVE ME FROM AVONDALE were visible in dried blood on different parts surrounding the access panel. Junior touched the letters. "This is awful, Luke. They had somebody locked up in this room."

"Probably a child, Junes." He motioned over to the child-size furniture.

A loud growl reverberated throughout the small, enclosed space. "Trespassing," a disembodied voice echoed in the room.

Junior flinched and almost fell to the cement floor. "Something touched me." Junior started spinning in the room trying to grab at something unseen. "My hands, Luke. It burns, it burns, Luke, help, help me … get me out of here now."

Luke saw numerous spiders crawling all over Junior's forearms. The place was infested with spiders. He grabbed Junior's elbows trying to avoid the burn marks. "Can you make it headfirst?"

"No, my hands are on fire. I cannot pull myself," Junior said panicked.

He shined the flashlight on Junior's arms. The spiders were gone but the skin was bubbly as if Junior had dunked his hands and forearms into boiling water.

"I will go feet first and pull you through," Luke said.

"Quick, Luke, I'm going to pass out."

He placed himself into a raised push-up position and pushed his feet through the tunnel one foot at a time. "Grab my hands."

"I can't. My hands are on fire," Junior yelled.

"I will grab your forearms. Now Junior!" Luke grabbed Junior's forearms, who grimaced and let out a blood-curdling scream. He continued pulling his brother through the tunnel, not finding an alternative. "Almost out, Junior, it's fine. You'll be fine." Suddenly he felt something grabbing his legs, and he was yanked out of the tunnel into the living room. Junior fell out of the access to the tunnel face first but tumbled onto his side. Sebastian stood over Luke but appeared winded somehow and suddenly vanished. It was his guardian that pulled them to safety.

Daniel walked into the dining room looking angry. "What are you ladies doing in here?" Daniel asked. "What's that hole in the wall?"

Junior screamed and raised his red and swollen hands upward, his skin sloughing off as if being boiled. Luke moved Junior to the sink and rinsed his hands in cold water. The skin began to fall off and was washed away into the drain.

"I'm fine, I think. It's not hurting anymore." Junior stared at his intact hands.

"What just happened? The skin was falling off your hands and now they're totally fine." Daniel stared at his brothers oddly. "I need to go tell Dad what you idiots are up to."

"Junior found this access panel, and we were checking it out. There's a room, a cave in there." Luke motioned toward the living room. "We made the house angry."

Daniel walked into the living room and examined the void. Luke followed him but did not walk near the access. Daniel began to crawl into the tunnel. Junior was ready to stop their brother, but Luke placed his index finger on his lips and shook his head from side to side.

Daniel was halfway into the tunnel and yelled out. "What was that?" Daniel scooted backward out of the tunnel, falling onto his knees. "I saw two red eyes staring at me."

"There's a bunch of children's furniture inside a large empty room and, and, and ..." Junior stammered on.

"We need to tell Dad." Daniel started to walk out of the dining room quickly.

Luke grabbed at Junior's hands, looking for any injury. "That's not possible." He peered into the cave and saw the burned man staring at him wearing an eerie smile. The eyeballs were white glowing orbs in the darkness. Luke noticed a smile formed on the abomination that also pointed its middle finger at him.

"I am sealing up that darn room." Junior grabbed his hammer and approached from behind.

"We need to wait for Dad," Luke said.

Their father walked into the living room peered into the hole. "Is that the access to the room?" their father asked in disbelief.

"It's like a cave, Dad. There's a room with children's furniture back there." Junior did not sound like his usual confident self. "It looks like they had a kid locked inside."

Their father peered into the void. "Where's the flashlight?"

"I dropped it inside," Luke responded.

"Did you burn yourself, son?" Their father walked over to Junior and looked at his hands. "I don't see any burn marks." Their father looked at them worriedly. "Are you all going nuts?"

"Dad, something in there is mad at us. It growled at us, called us trespassers, and then my hands burned. They saw." Junior said, pointing at Luke and Daniel. "My skin was falling off my hands."

Their father looked like he was becoming impatient. He looked toward the access again and then at each son. "All of you wait here."

"Don't go in there, Dad. It's not safe." Even if his father was skeptical, Luke believed the entity in the house could injure him.

"We all must face our fears. Wait here." His father either courageously or mindlessly entered the tunnel.

Once his father entered the room the access panel closed. A few seconds passed before it began to shake as if his father was trying to open it. He heard a muffled voice and banging, so he entered the tunnel. The panel was secured to the latch. He pushed on the access, but it did not budge. He searched the panel's borders, found the opposite end of the hinge, and pinched it—the panel released so he pushed it open.

"Thanks, Luke, move backward. I'm coming back out."

His father exited the tunnel. They all stood in silence for a few minutes. "I need to make a phone call. Junior, can you please complete the demolition and get everything outside?" His father walked into the kitchen and calmly grabbed a small planner from his pocket before making a call. "Jorge, it's Angel. If you are not busy, please come to my house … and bring your evidence bag."

Junior and Luke completed the demolition and moved all the debris outside as Jorge Villanueva arrived. Surprisingly, Daniel helped.

Jorge crawled into the tunnel wearing a jumpsuit, gloves, and a respirator. Luke waited patiently sitting on the nearby floor in the living room like a fly on the wall. Jorge brought his work gear bag that included all he needed to collect evidence. The detective was inside the room for what seemed like an hour. When Jorge came out, he pushed several evidence bags with some items from the room, including the access panel.

Jorge removed the respirator from his face. "Angel, I collected blood samples and lifted some prints from items like this cup. The prints were under a layer of dust."

"What do you think? Should I call the local PD?"

"No, I can handle it. I will meet with some of my counterparts in the PD, but mostly to look for old police reports … I found this magazine. This gives me a time frame to start on." Jorge lifted an evidence bag and handed it to his father.

It was a Mad magazine bearing the date, June '60 No. 55 and the title *Fair Foul*. "We had other stuff like this upstairs and in the attic." His father returned the evidence bag to Jorge.

"I will have to run down who was living here in that time frame," Jorge said.

"The house was built in the 1950s, but I don't know for sure."

"That should help. I'll let you know. I need to go home to take a shower. It's creepy in there. It felt like spiders were crawling all over me. I felt like someone was watching me." Jorge visibly trembled.

"Thanks, Jorge. I owe you lunch," his father said.

"Sounds good, Angel. Say hello to Helen for me."

"Same here with Emily. Let's have dinner next week."

Luke tried to pay attention to the adult conversation but was truly perplexed. *What did the burned man have to do with a void in his house?* He reflected on the boy he saw in the garage when they first moved in. He was missing something and was concerned. The realization that Sebastian was able to interact physically with him was worrisome at first, but he considered that it was also quite fortuitous.

CHAPTER SEVENTEEN

Stitch

I walked on a congested sidewalk. I knew I was supposed to monitor a money drop at an old Customs House. I muttered to myself, "I'm running late, again." The drone of traffic, with loud car horns and unrecognizable profanity attacked my senses. I passed several streets, before entering a crosswalk with a sign with red lettering demanding pedestrians DON'T WALK, but everyone was walking. A street sign at the intersection said WALL ST and NASSAU ST; I knew I was in New York City, although I had never been there. A set of concrete steps headed up to a building with columns, and to the left was a statue of George Washington. A sign on a concrete pillar had the words "ON THIS SITE IN FEDERAL HALL ...."

I collided with person after person as if in a pinball machine. A large man with blond hair and a red plaid shirt under coveralls rushed toward me, and shoved, causing the sensation of falling backward in the air weightless. I was back on the street, no longer full of pedestrian traffic. An unseen presence enveloped my body.

"Do not fear, for I am with you. The way you're with our Lord under the sky," Sebastian said.

The blond-haired man reappeared and lunged toward my legs. Suddenly, a blur collided with the blond-haired man, forming a vortex of a fight like a battle between cartoon characters. The sound of canines snarling and snapping at one another resonated. I touched the vortex, and my hand snapped backward as if hit with a bat.

Luke awakened with a jolt; his hand slumped down from his forearm. He jumped out of bed, as his hand slammed loosely against his chest. He was bathed in sweat and had trouble breathing as if overexerted or somebody stood on his chest. He rushed into the shower and doused himself with cold water. It did the trick because it woke him quickly. He switched the knob to heat. The warm water calmed him and helped as he massaged his wrist under the hot water. His wrist ached but was no longer broken.

Luke returned to his room and grabbed his underwear from the dresser. He noticed it was still dark out. He looked at his alarm clock and saw that it was 3:30 a.m., *unbelievable*. He dropped his towel onto his chair and put on his underwear and jumped back on the bed.

He tossed himself around in bed for an eternity. He realized that the confusing disjointed dream must be a reminder that Sebastian was his guardian. When the alarm was triggered at 6:00 a.m. he tried to move but the fitted sheet from his mattress was tightly wrapped around his legs. He reached his alarm clock and hit snooze. The cave under the house Junior discovered bothered him. The burned man was in the void. He stared out of his window and focused on the ice that formed on the edge of the window. Sunlight was reflecting on the ice crystals … *I stood in a room that smelled like a gym locker. A man was pounding on a heavy bag in a low-lit room. The man had a bald head and was heavily muscled. He struck the bag so hard that it jumped upward, causing the chain holding it onto the ceiling to rattle. The man turned and looked at me menacingly. It was Father D …*

Luke woke with a start when the alarm went off the second time. *I need to speak with the priest*, he mused. He needed to convince his mom but wanted to wait until his father took off to his office. He found her in the kitchen drinking a cup of coffee and sketching on a large pad.

"You're down earlier than usual," his mother said without looking up.

"I wanted to speak with you about the house and the cave we discovered over the weekend," Luke said, sitting next to his mother.

She moved back, distancing herself from him. "What's going

through your mind?" His mother looked at him awkwardly before focusing once again on her sketch of what looked like a man holding a gun as a plane flew overhead.

He had to be careful how he approached this topic with his mother. If he explained that he dreamed of the void they found beforehand, it would have served to place her on the defensive. It was how he felt around his parents before and after seeing his father treading water off Mona Island. "Mom, with the discovery of the cave, don't you think it's time to finally have the house blessed?"

"Maybe, but your father says it's not necessary." She continued to sketch, disinterested. She motioned him away. "Go get ready. I need to get my thoughts onto this pad … I have a meeting this afternoon in Arlington and need to finish this."

Later that morning, he sat half-listening to Mr. Conway's lecture centered on how John Adams and Thomas Jefferson were overseas as US diplomats. Jefferson advocated for the inclusion of a Bill of Rights. Adams wanted the protection of the absolute power of a government to have checks and balances. He was listening but once again stared at the ice crystals formed at the edges of the windows. His mother practically ignored him, and he was no closer to resolving what boggled him.

"Luke. Luke. Mr. Sanz?" Mr. Conway waved in front of the classroom like a ground air controller.

"Yes, Mr. Conway," Luke responded.

"I asked you a question. Are we boring you?" Mr. Conway asked with a smirk.

Everybody in the classroom laughed at him. A month ago, that would have caused him anxiety. Now, he turned his gaze back to the ice crystals.

"Something you said about checks and balances struck my imagination." At that moment, he realized he needed to try to balance out the problem in the home. He needed to speak with the priest.

"At least you're half listening." The class laughed again. "My question was regarding Jefferson and Adams. How do you think they felt being overseas and not part of the Constitutional Convention?"

"From what it sounds like, Adams was a controlling person and was frustrated he wasn't part of the process. Maybe, out of touch with the only way to communicate were via letters and newspapers."

"We take that for granted nowadays. I imagine how we communicate today will be much different in twenty years."

The first bell rang, and the class left for their next period. Mr. Conway motioned for him to stay behind. He, in turn, motioned to Benji not to wait for him.

"What's wrong? I can tell you have something going on."

Luke hesitated, but he felt extremely comfortable with Mr. Conway. He considered saying that everything was fine but found himself unusually honest. "This is embarrassing, but I think my house is haunted. So far, something has attacked my dog, my brother and more." He took a breath and wiped a tear from his face. "This weekend, we found a void under the house that was used to imprison a child decades ago."

"My God, how dreadful. I wonder if one thing has anything to do with the other," Mr. Conway said, before pausing. "When I was an Army Staff Sergeant in Vietnam, I had a Corporal, his nickname was Stitch." Mr. Conway's face brightened at the mention of the name Stitch.

"Was he a friend, Mr. Conway?" Luke asked.

"He was, but the officers tell you not to fraternize with your soldiers who you will have to discipline." Mr. Conway wiped his face dry. "Stitch was fun-loving and always kept us laughing through all we were dealing with." Mr. Conway placed his hand on Luke's shoulder ... *I fell backward forcibly as if yanked with a tightrope and landed into a forest in the Dong Nai province. I stood watching a group of soldiers on patrol. Mr. Conway walked in the middle of the group of men and placed a fisted arm into air and all the soldiers went to one knee. Mr. Conway had an embarrassed look on his face.*

I walked up to him. "What's wrong Mr. Conway?" Of course, my teacher could not hear me.

"I think we just walked us into an ambush," Mr. Conway said.

The forest lit up in a firefight. The US Army soldiers had indeed walked into an ambush in a clearing in the forest. It was a mistake they would pay for with their lives. They were surrounded.

Mr. Conway was struck in the chest, causing him to fall from his knee to the ground, stunned.

A soldier yelled, "The sarge is down, get behind cover now." It had to be Stitch running to each soldier to ensure they were behind the cover of fallen trees. Stitch then tossed grenades all around them. The remaining soldiers kept firing from cover.

The firefight continued for what seemed to be ages but in truth must have been a minute or two. Mr. Conway propped himself up as the firefight ended. A medic ran over and opened his shirt revealing blood. The medic pulled a book out of Mr. Conway's shirt, it was a Bible. It must have deflected the bullet's movement enough that it hit his side without striking any vital organs.

"Stitch is down," the medic said.

Mr. Conway walked over to Stitch and knelt beside his bullet ridden friend and cried ... Luke was hit by a bout of vertigo as he returned. Nausea overcame him but he kept himself from vomiting.

"He saved us," Mr. Conway said.

The vision was gone, but not the moment. It was so realistic, he felt like he was in a battle. "Stitch was fearless. What does that have to do with me?" he asked confused.

Mr. Conway paused as if considering what to say. "I kept seeing him. Whenever we were in danger, Stitch would point to the enemy location. One day, I felt him next to me, and he told me, to tell his parents that he was brave. This happened a few times."

"What did it mean?" When Luke dreamed, it seemed like messages. Maybe somebody was trying to tell him something. The spirit in the house tried his best to scare the family away from the house. His parents pretended the problem did not exist.

"I talked to some of his friends. His father told him he was a coward and would never amount to anything. The next time I was stateside, I met with his parents and siblings. I told them this same story."

Everything your parents tell you can reverberate years later. "So, did you ever see him again?" Luke asked.

"During the Tet Offensive. I saw Stitch pointing at a wall. I had my soldiers fortify it, before a swarm of VC came at us. We took them all out."

"That must have been scary," Luke said.

"I was scared for two years straight," Mr. Conway said, looking up to his left.

"Was that the last time you saw Stitch?"

"Ten, twenty years maybe, he thanked me for talking with his family back in the States." Mr. Conway then stared at the wall as if elsewhere.

Students poured into his class. Mr. Conway reached for an excuse slip, wrote on it, and handed it to him. "Find out what your spirit wants ... now go and head to your next class."

"Thanks, Mr. Conway." He stopped and turned around to say something else. "Thanks for trusting me with your story."

"Thanks for trusting me with yours." Mr. Conway pointed at the door, telling him to get moving.

As he walked toward his next class, he began to form a plan. He would head to the church and try to meet with Father D himself. It was the only way. If he failed, it would be on him, but his mother and father were not going to acknowledge the cancer that formed within their home.

✝ ✝ ✝

The Priest Wasn't Worth a Farthing

Luke and Benji walked up to the church and stepped inside. He approached a priest who was cleaning wax from the votive candle rack.

"Excuse me, Father, may I speak with you," Luke asked. The man turned his head toward him slowly. He was a tall, fit young black man in his twenties. He had immaculately trimmed hair and chiseled facial features.

"It's Deacon, Deacon Robert … how may I help you?"

"Sorry about that, Deacon. My name is Luke Sanz, and this is my friend Benji. My family goes to this church. I wonder if you could direct me towards Father D."

"I've seen you here before with your family." He looked at Benji. "I don't recall seeing you before at service, Benji."

"Sorry, Deacon. My family has never been into the whole church thing," Benji said, motioning his hands everywhere. The stained-glass windows, statues, and candles could be too much for a non-religious person.

Deacon Robert laughed slightly before giving his attention back to Luke. "Unfortunately, Father D is away, and we are not sure when he'll be back … is there something I can help you with?" Deacon Robert asked.

"I'm not sure, I need to get our house blessed. I was hoping it could be done this afternoon," Luke said, trying to smile.

Deacon Robert raised his hands, exposing his palms covered in wax. "I can ask Father Lee, but he typically insists on an offering."

"That will not be a problem, Deacon," Luke said.

"Wait a moment, gentlemen. I best go wash my hands first." The Deacon walked away but turned and grabbed a candle from a cart. "Luke, please light this candle and pray while you wait."

Luke grabbed the candle and saw that it was Saint Jude Thaddeus. The patron saint of lost causes. The deacon was quite perceptive. He lit the candle and placed it in the large candle rack. He bowed his head and prayed for guidance and strength and a vision to illuminate what was happening in his home.

"I wish I had the foresight to direct you on what is plaguing your home," Sebastian said, standing beside him.

"How come you cannot see what this spirit is?" Luke asked quietly.

"Something is keeping me from seeing. My role is to train you and prepare you for everything else you will face in life. I don't know what is blinding me."

"Big help you are," he said louder this time.

"What's that?" Benji asked.

Sebastian seemed hurt and stayed quiet. He bowed slightly before dissipating away as Deacon Robert walked through his shimmer.

"Father Lee can be at your home this afternoon at about three," Deacon Robert said while handing Luke an envelope. The deacon pointed at a number handwritten on the envelope.

Luke grabbed it and saw a dollar sign and 200. He gasped and stared at the deacon, who shrugged. "Thank you, Deacon. I will see you at three." He turned and walked away with Benji in tow.

"What's with the envelope?" Banji asked, confused.

"It's like a tithe or offering. They want two hundred bucks to bless my house."

Benji appeared pensive. "Maybe I should start my own church ... what will you do?"

"I guess we are going to the bank next. Drive fast because we will be late for our next class."

Father Grant Lee and Deacon Robert showed up a few minutes late. His parents were gone, and his brothers were out as well. Daniel had practice, and Junior was taking a trade class until five. The deacon entered the house first with the priest who ambled behind him with his hand palm up toward Luke who handed him the envelope.

Deacon Robert prepared a censer with incense and began walking around the house, saying prayers in Latin. Father Lee spent little time downstairs and skipped his parent's room altogether. Luke was prepared to say something but hesitated as they approached his bedroom. A young boy stood in the hallway, pointing his middle finger toward the priest. The same boy he saw in his garage holding a comic months ago. The boy ran down the hallway toward Luke's room when the priest walked closer. A large crash reverberated throughout the house. It felt as if a plane hit the home. Luke fell to one knee, and the holy men fell to the ground. The thurible in the deacon's hand fell onto the carpet. Cold air enveloped the hallway. The burned man grabbed Father Lee's hand and leaned in toward his ear. The priest stood quickly and ran past Luke.

"I've been here before," said the defeated priest, rushing down the stairs and outside.

A fire commenced on the carpet near Deacon Robert, who stomped at it. Luke ran to the Deacon and helped him put out the fire. "What happened, Deacon?"

"Other than being slammed to the floor … I'm at a loss," Deacon Robert said sarcastically.

"Why did Father Lee yell that he had been here before?" Luke asked.

"I'll go find out." The Deacon grabbed the censer and headed downstairs before he turned. "I'm sorry, Luke … I'll call Father D and tell him what happened."

Luke was left alone in the house. He walked downstairs, sat on the sofa, and held his bowed head in his hands. He had failed, and that ineffective priest kept his money. *I shouldn't have paid a penny for that man*, he thought.

CHAPTER EIGHTEEN

Wrong Alley Mr. Sanz

Luke sat on the toilet in the downstairs bathroom. He heard voices coming from either the kitchen or dining room. He could not quite make out what was being said with the hum of the circulating fan. His brother Daniel and girlfriend Joyce were in the kitchen earlier with his mother. He heard a car pulling into the driveway. *My father must be home from his trip to New York.*

"I'm home … is everyone packed for the trip?" His father asked while Luke washed his hands quickly in the sink.

He was about to open the door but heard his father walk down the steps quickly.

"What's going on?"

He was going to open the door, but something about his father's muffled tone worried him. They planned on taking their Christmas break at their grandparents' vacation home near Piñones beach in Puerto Rico. He stepped out of the bathroom and stood quietly by the banister.

"Did I interrupt something?" His father asked.

"Angel, Daniel, and Joyce were giving me some news. Do you want to share with your father, Daniel?"

He felt ashamed for eavesdropping but felt he needed to hear what was said.

"What is it, Daniel?

"Joyce is pregnant, Dad. I don't know how it happened."

"I hope you know how it happened because we discussed this when you were younger," his father said rather loudly.

"I meant we used protection, Dad. Joyce and I discussed it and are considering getting an abortion."

After Luke heard the word abortion, he placed the knuckle of his right hand in his mouth and bit down. He walked down the stairs slowly and crept closer to the opposite side of the wall. His anger boiled inside him. It almost overran him to the point of jumping into the dining room. It wasn't his place to insert himself into this specific family conversation. He almost convinced himself to walk back to his room. Instead, he decided to stay put.

"What's your opinion, Joyce?"

"Well, she was thinking ..." Daniel said.

"Daniel, let her talk. I want to hear what she wants. It's ultimately her decision," his father said. "Joyce, please, I want to hear your honest opinion and not that of my son or wife, now."

"Mr. Sanz, I want to keep the child. I want Daniel in its life, but I think Daniel feels like I was trying to trap him," Joyce said, her voice cracking while she cried.

"Daniel, what are you thinking?" his father asked, with anger noticeable in his voice.

"Dad, I have baseball, and I'm going to college out of state next year ... a baby? I don't see where that fits into a baseball player's life."

"Helen, how about you?"

Luke thought his father was rather patient with the situation and the conversation. His father was not typically a patient man.

"Angel, it's too early in their lives for this," his mother said.

"Your concern is that Daniel's life will be derailed if Joyce has this baby?" His father asked testily.

"I didn't say that. Please don't put words in my mouth," their mother said.

"I'm not, Helen. I just see where you are steering this," his father said.

Luke had to intervene. He expected some serious blow-back from his brother and especially from his mother, who appeared to be bent in a direction Luke feared. He entered the dining room confidently. "Joyce, I will help if you need me to. Please don't have an abortion," he pleaded.

"Luke, this is none of your business. You need to butt out!" Daniel stood up and pointed his finger defiantly at him. This was the angriest and most aggressive he had ever seen his brother.

Joyce grabbed onto Daniel's hand and gently sat him back down. "Thanks, Luke. I appreciate that and will keep that in mind."

"Joyce, your baby is a boy, you'll name Tristan," he said, pleading.

"What? How could you even know that? My grandfather was named after the story of Tristan and Isolde." Joyce held her hand to her mouth. He saw a smile peek through.

"Luke, not now, please," his mother said.

"Joyce, I had a dream I was visiting Tristan. It was a message for me to tell you. Tristan will be everything to you!" The room was silent. His parents appeared stunned, but it also brought back memories of previous odd moments whenever he talked about the future.

"Luke, we can talk about this later. I don't want to lose my grandson, either. Please leave this to us," his father said calmly and lovingly, placing his hand on Luke's chest … *I sunk backward once again into darkness, landing into my father's body. I felt out of place, lost, and worried because I would be late for the meeting at Fraunces Tavern in Manhattan with the new agents I recruited. I was an observer within my father. Very weird feeling.*

I drove a car on Mulberry Street and realized I was in Little Italy. I looked at the map and admitted to myself that I was lost but did not want to stop for directions. I mapped out how to get to the restaurant and turned into an alley to find a way out of the one-way streets. I came across an unusual scene. Two groups of men faced one another, each wearing a variety of dark-colored tracksuits and sunglasses. They looked like stereotypical movie mobsters. Some of the men were holding submachine guns at the low ready. Two men in front appeared to be in charge. One had an open briefcase, pointed toward the man with a suitcase, who had an open mid-sized bag before him. I shuddered, realizing I had interrupted a drug deal. The man with the suitcase motioned to a large man with a submachine gun with his head pointing his lips and chin toward me. The man moved quickly forward. My hand moved reflexively to the handle of my snub nose .357 revolver, and the other hand grabbed at my door handle.

"Don't be a hero. This is why I warned you," I yelled.

The man walked up to my rental car and tapped the barrel of his firearm on the driver's side window which I lowered. "Hey, boss, can you tell me where Fraunces Tavern is? I got lost with all the one-way roads".

"Are you serious, buddy? Get out of here before you get a lead bath," the man said in an accent.

I saw that the man had a globe and an anchor tattoo on his forearm. "Help a brother Marine out, man," I said quickly, although I was in the Navy.

The man looked at him intensely. "Get off Mulberry up ahead and go to Mott and head down to St James and take it until you get to Broad St. You're like ten minutes away ... Semper Fi."

"Hoo-uhh, Semper Fi," I said, placing my car in reverse. I made the sign of the cross, pushed through the tension, and laughed ... Luke was back inside of his own body. "Yes, Dad. Thanks for listening to me about that mobster thing in New York," he said before backing up.

His father looked at him curiously, his mouth wide-open mouth. Instead of speaking, his father shook his head and looked downward stunned.

Luke turned toward his brother. "Daniel, I'm your brother, and I love you. I'm here for you and will help you with whatever you need so that you can have your dream of playing for the Orioles," he said, holding his palms out to his brother. Luke wanted his brother to know he was being honest, but he also wanted to make sure Daniel understood he was not trying to touch him.

Tears rolled down Daniel's face, and he shook his head. "I love you too, brother. Thanks, I'm sorry I jumped at you ... wait, Oriole? I want to be a Yankee."

"I don't know what to tell you. I will be upstairs if you want to talk." He walked out of the dining room backward but kept eye contact with Joyce. He knew he had to ensure his nephew would be in all their lives. He hesitated but moved toward Joyce and placed his hand on her shoulder ... *I stood in the living room of my brother's residence sometime in the future. Tristan sat on the floor, playing with a toy soldier. I walked toward my nephew and waved at the toddler.*

"Whose that, Uncle?" Tristan pointed to his side.

I stared into a mirror on the wall. I saw a short-haired man wearing a US Army dress uniform. Sebastian stood beside the man who had multiple ribbon bars on his chest and one arm in a sling. I stared at the intense-looking man, who stared back intimidatingly. It was me ... he succeeded; Tristan will be in their lives.

He took a shower after his run and came into his room, thinking that he would pack quickly for the trip to Puerto Rico. His father was waiting in his room on his desk chair. "Hey, Dad ... I'm sorry I interrupted that private conversation," Luke said. His father motioned for him to sit down on his bed. *Luckily, I dressed in the bathroom after my shower.*

"It's your family, too. After learning about Joyce being pregnant, your mother wanted me to talk with you and Junior. She wants to make sure you are not having unprotected sex."

Luke was stunned because he was a virgin and had yet to truly kiss a girl. "You can tell Mom that I'm still a virgin."

His father stood up and walked to the door and grabbed the doorknob. "Did you see what happened to me in Manhattan?"

Luke was concerned with how to answer. His parents seemed disgusted when he brought up anything omniscient, he experienced. Instead, he thought it best not to shine his father on or pretend he did not understand what his father asked of him. "Yes, Dad. Thanks for listening to me."

His father walked back to Luke and leaned toward him as if to hug him but stopped himself. "I should be thanking you ... I don't know what's happening here, but this stuff is hard to discuss." He walked back toward the door. "Please, don't tell your mother." His father left the room, shutting the door behind him.

Luke laid back on the bed and sighed loudly. *That worked out better than I envisioned.* He knew he needed to be more vocal when problems arose and that hiding was not the best way to resolve issues. They needed to be faced head-on.

CHAPTER NINETEEN

Who Was the Child in the Cave

It was a cold Saturday morning, but Luke had worked out for the past hour in the garage and was sweating. Once he finished his garage workout, he prepped for a run. He was unconcerned that it was close to forty degrees out but the dead batteries on his Sony Walkman did phase him. He headed to the kitchen to look for new ones. The doorbell rang as Luke walked past. Wildomar Rivera and Jorge Villanueva were at the front door. Jorge was holding a brown accordion file folder. "Hello, Mr. Rivera, Mr. Villanueva." Luke let them both into the house. "My Dad is either in the kitchen or on the back porch." Both men were friends of his fathers from work. He had met them before at family gatherings. Jorge was the detective his father had called when they discovered the cave under the house. Wildomar was a Resident Agent in Charge with the US Customs Service.

"It's Wil, Luke. Don't call me Mr. Rivera when your father is not around." Wil looked around cautiously. *I think Wil fears my father.* Wil did not look like a man to trifle with either.

"Same here, Luke. I'm fine with Villanueva or Jorge. Your father is something else with this mister stuff." Jorge appeared more confident than Wil.

"I will try, but my dad is a stickler for such things, guys." He tried to use a bit of subtle humor.

Wil laughed and slapped him on the back ... *I fell backward and dropped into a dark humid room where a man was confined in a small wooden cage on the floor. I felt claustrophobic just observing the caged man. It was Wil and another man was urinating on him* ... he felt unsteady as he walked down the steps into the living room. He stopped at the sofa and turned. "Jorge, any luck with this void we found in the dining room?"

"I brought this folder for your father. It has copies of all I have found thus far. I sent the blood off for testing, but that may go nowhere."

His parents came out of the kitchen, coffee cups in hand. "Hey, guys, how are you both?" His mother kissed each man on the cheek but hesitated, getting too close to Luke.

It hurt noticing his mother recoil as she got close to him, but Luke was beyond that pain. He felt pity for the woman who had raised him but thought he was weird and feared his touch.

"Hello, Helen. We're doing good, trying to get your man out on the greens to get him some relaxation," Wil said.

"Emily wanted me to remind you of next month's fundraiser at the library. She needs your help with designing flyer."

"I already started it, Jorge. I will call her and ask her to come over."

"Great Helen, she loves hanging out with you."

"Same here, but I especially love shopping with her. It's an education." Her eyes brightened as she mentioned shopping and Emily.

"Our bank account can certainly tell when you shop together," his father said and laughed.

Jorge's wife, Emily Villanueva, was the head librarian at the Lansburg Public Library. Emily was a striking, bookish woman. Jorge motioned his father over to him while Wil spoke with his mother.

"Here's my research, Angel, on that void Junior found. I'm waiting for the blood test, but as I told you last week, I caught a murder that could take months to solve."

"Thanks for all you did, Jorge. It's much appreciated." His father opened the folder.

He began to walk away to start on his run. "Why don't you let Luke take it on? Let's see what he's got." Wil motioned toward him.

"Wil, he's a kid. Not an investigator."

"Give him a chance, brother. I'll tell you what. I believe he can solve this better than any of us."

"Wil … Mr. Rivera, I would not know where to start." He was confused and concerned about how his father would take this.

"Hold up." Wil took off and headed out the front door in a jog.

"Luke, what are you up to?" his father asked with a concerned look.

"No idea, Dad. I was about to go on a run."

"Wil is always trying to find his next trainee," Jorge said prophetically.

Wil returned to the house, holding a small paperback book titled *How to Conduct a Historical Investigation: A Step-by-Step Guide* by Rafael Parker. "Read this and follow the steps. My phone number is inside if you need help."

"Wil, my son is more of an artist like his mother. He doesn't want to follow the old man into what we do."

Wil appeared hurt and at a loss for words. Until that moment, he wanted nothing to do with law enforcement. Seeing Wil and realizing that the man saw something in him added to Luke somehow. He wanted to solve the problem plaguing their home, and maybe a friendship with one of his father's friends would be fruitful. "Let me give it a try, Dad. I am interested in what you all do."

"Fine, son." His father handed him the file. "You can ask any of us for help, but I don't want you relying on us."

"I understand, Dad." He returned to his room and placed the file and book on his bed. He returned downstairs and saw Wil's black 1990 Cadillac *Seville STS* headed out of the driveway. He grabbed the batteries for his cassette player from the kitchen.

"Wil is recruiting you to be an investigator," his mother said as a statement of fact.

His mother stood several feet away from him. "Mom, I want to find out what is happening in the house. I am years away from ever doing what they do."

"Art is more of a hobby. It's not a job. At least, that's how my painting feels. If it were not for your father, we would be struggling."

"You're respected, Mom. My Art teacher says so. Many people know you."

"As long as my boys know and love me, I'll be fine. Go on your run," she said and walked away.

At that very moment, Luke felt that they should have hugged. He missed the intimacy. At least he felt love coming from his mother. *I'm so confused.* His mother treated his brother Daniel as the center of her universe, but he was sure she loved Luke and his brother Junior. It was just a different type of love.

✝ ✝ ✝

Divine Intervention

The Sanz family spent all of Sunday together. Luke spent the whole day with his family. Due to Junior's constant pleading, they watched the movie *Home Alone* after church. Despite all the family endured, they laughed and were in great spirits. They passed the church in the center of town. The large, red-bricked building looked majestic, with the sun setting to the west. *May the Lord protect our family while we are troubled by the spirit infesting our house*, he thought as they passed the intersection at Main and Joshua. The lone child was back, walking into the crosswalk by himself. The man in coveralls stood on the opposite side.

"Please tell me you all see this kid in the crosswalk," he said, scared the kid would be hit by a car.

"Not the kid again." Daniel shook his head as if overly frustrated.

"I don't see a kid, but I see that homeless guy standing at the crosswalk. He's motioning to somebody," Junior said.

"He's motioning to the kid, Junes." Luke realized he needed to try to interact with the kid's spirit and find out what was keeping it in the intersection.

Their father drove past the intersection and turned right onto Red Hill Road, approaching Campbell Bridge, which traveled over the Lansburg River.

"Pay attention and look at the path ahead," Sebastian shouted.

Skid marks painted the asphalt straight into the curb, easement, and grass. A car must have careened off the road. His first thought came from outside himself and beckoned him to ignore Sebastian and the skid marks. "Dad, stop the car, quick!" Luke grabbed the sliding door and popped it open with the minivan still moving. *What was that fleeting thought? I must intervene.*

"What's wrong, Luke?" His father came to a screeching stop on the bridge.

"I saw some skid marks on the road."

"I didn't see anything," his father said but still parked the minivan and turned on his hazard lights.

He stepped out of the van and ran back toward the markings on the road. A street sign was down on the ground, and some small tree saplings were bent down as if they were struck. He moved the street sign that said, *BRIDGE ICES BEFORE ROAD.* He followed the path of the skid marks.

"Luke, quick down by the water," Sebastian said.

The damage must have been caused by a car. He followed the path of damage with his eyes to a large blue vehicle upside down and partially submerged at the river's edge. The tires were still spinning, and the engine still rumbled.

"Oh my God, Luke, how did you see that car? Daniel, hurry, take the van, go home, and call for help!" His father yelled before following him down to the car.

"Yes, Dad." Daniel ran away toward the car.

Junior followed them down the hill and joined them near the car submerged in water. Luke opened the door and tried to get ahold of the man hanging, still secured to the seat by a shoulder harness. Sebastian stood beside him. "How long has he been in the water?" he asked.

"I don't know ... not for sure. The vision did not present itself until we approached the river crossing," Sebastian said.

It was freezing out, and this man could have drowned or died from exposure. Luke removed the shoulder belt off the man and pulled him out of the car. It was Tom Genaro, Benji's friend. "Wake up. Wake up, Tom ... Dad, check and see if he has a passenger in the car."

"You know this man?"

"Yes, Dad, he's Benji's friend." Luke and his father carried Tom to the safety of the muddy bank of the river.

His father began to check Tom's breathing and circulation. "He's not breathing, Luke. Starting CPR." His father began compressions and tried to give Tom a breath. "Luke, check his airway, my hands are full of mud."

Luke shoved his cold finger down Tom's throat. He felt something, but his finger was numb. "Something is blocking his airway, Dad. Maybe it's mud or leaves. I can't see ... my fingers are freezing!"

"Push past the cold. It's just nature. Reach into his mouth and scoop anything in there out."

He did as his father said and felt something, and pulled at it, until it came out. He handed it to his dad.

"It's a cigar ... he must have crashed with it in his mouth." His father tossed the cigar into the mud.

He began performing rescue breaths and felt that more air was going through. He took over compressions and finished off two more cycles. He heard distant sirens and stopped compressions to check for a pulse. "I have a pulse, Dad." Tom began to cough up water. Together, they moved Tom to his side, who coughed out another piece of the cigar before vomiting. It smelled of stale beer. The smell almost made Luke vomit.

"What happened? Oh my God, where am I?" Tom asked weakly.

"You were in an accident, Tom. Does anything hurt? Was anybody with you?" Luke asked.

"Oh my God, it's freezing. My ribs, back, arm, argh ... everything hurts." Tom shivered while spitting out mud from his mouth. "I dropped my girl at her house. She wasn't with me."

Several firefighters and paramedics arrived and rushed down the hill. They took over and began checking all of Tom's vitals. Luke walked off with his father and started trying to walk back up the riverbank toward the road.

"Luke. Luke. Thanks, Luke," Tom said in a hoarse voice. He was reaching out to him.

"You're welcome, Tom."

They walked up to the bank and met up with Junior. They were muddy and a wet mess. Daniel arrived back from the house.

"Turn on the heater full blast in the van," their father yelled through rattling teeth.

Daniel ran off to the minivan without responding. There were emergency vehicles surrounding the minivan on the bridge. It looked like a Christmas light show.

A firefighter came up to them and handed them two heavy wool blankets. "You all saved that man's life." The firefighter ran off quickly before he could thank him for the blankets.

"Where are the skid marks, Luke?"

"Right here, Dad ... I saw them right there." The skid marks were gone.

His father followed the path of the car. "Luke, there are no skid marks except tire marks on the curb. You couldn't have seen this from the road with us driving by."

"I saw the skid marks, Dad. I know what I saw. Something told me to pay attention."

His father shook his head. The same way he did when he dismissed Luke's abilities. "This was a miracle, son. You saved that man's life." His father motioned to the minivan. "Your mother will be so pissed if we get mud in her car."

"Take off your shoes and clothes. I already took mine off and put them in one of those trash bags you keep in the back," Junior said.

"It's like 30 degrees out!" He complained but took off his shoes and clothes and placed them in the bag.

"Daniel, take us home quickly." Luke put the blanket on the seats as they entered the van.

"I wish I had a camera. You two look like little kids in their undies." Junior closed the doors, laughing loudly.

Sebastian's presence had complicated his life, but he realized it was for the better. Without his guardian, Tom would have died from that accident. Together, they had a symbiotic relationship that would benefit others for whatever reason powers outside him had decided. He had to learn how to function in this new world he shared with Sebastian. To start, he had to approach the child at the intersection.

CHAPTER TWENTY

Joshua

I drove fast upon an empty road and quickly approached a stop sign. I slammed on the brakes in time to avoid blowing through the intersection. I could not tell what type of car I was driving but knew two things; this was a fast car, and it was mine. I peered into the rearview mirror and saw my reflection. A man with short brown hair and a goatee. I was stuck in a dream and wondered who I was. The intersection was clear. I pushed down on the accelerator pedal. The rear tires spun quickly as if they were gouging holes into the asphalt before the car fishtailed a bit before pulling forward rapidly. The engine was not as loud as other muscle cars.

Suddenly, I was driving in a town with other cars on the road. I looked around the car and saw that the interior was different, all green, including the dashboard, carpets, and seats. Empty bottles were scattered on the passenger side of the bench seat. Mostly beer bottles but I had a bottle of bourbon in my hand. I turned too wide, hit a parked car to my left, and kept driving even with the compulsion to pull over. My vision was blurry, so I rubbed my eyes futilely. I struck something. I could not see what I hit because my windshield was covered in what looked like reddish-brown mud.

I rubbed my eyes again and was parked at an intersection at a red light surrounded by many cars. I was no longer driving the puke-green interior car. I was back in the fast vehicle with a black and gray interior. The light was still red. All the other drivers were waiting patiently. A little boy walked in the crosswalk and wandered in the highway's median. None of the other drivers seemed interested in the little boy.

I stepped out of his car and approached him.

"Where are your parents? You need to get off the road."

"Who are you?"

"I'm Luke. What's your name?"

"I'm Joshua."

"Joshua, come with me and get off the road. It's not safe."

"I can't. That man won't let me." Joshua pointed to the corner of the road, when a man was standing at the corner of the same intersection. The sound of a loud, red-lined accelerating engine forced me to cover my ears. A green car headed toward us. I grabbed Joshua's hand as the car struck the boy. I yelled out ...

Tony was sitting over him, barking repeatedly. "Tony cut it out." Luke covered the dog with his blanket.

He got up off the bed and began to feel two things—nausea and dizziness. He ran to the bathroom, vomited, and sat beside the toilet. His mother walked into the bathroom and gazed at him with disappointment.

"Have you been drinking? It's three in the morning."

"No, Mom, I wasn't drinking," he said.

"It smells like a brewery in here. Oh, my lord, flush that toilet before I vomit too," she said.

He did as his mother ordered. Then washed his hands and face before grabbing the mouthwash and rinsing. His mother stood near him with a look of concern.

"Are you sure you weren't drinking?" his mother asked.

"Mom, I was sleeping. I had a bad dream and woke up sick," he said.

"How do you feel? At least I don't smell the beer anymore."

"Mom, I was with you all at the movies, and we came home after we helped at the accident. Do I look hung over?" he asked.

"To be honest, you did when you were hugging the toilet. Even your eyes were bloodshot. What was your dream about?" His mother asked with interest more than concern.

"I dreamed I was driving a new fast car, and then it turned into an old car. Then, back into a new car. I was drunk in the old car. Then, I dreamed I was talking with Joshua," Luke said, recalling every detail of his odd dream.

"Who's Joshua?" she asked.

"He's the little boy I keep seeing at the intersection of Joshua and Main. In my dream, Joshua was killed in that intersection by a drunk driver."

"How's that possible, Luke? I have never heard that a little boy died there … have you?" his mother asked.

Luke did not know how to answer that question. "The road was named after him."

"Please cut it out with that psychic nonsense. I think we need to take you to the doctor again."

Luke shot up quickly clenching his teeth. "That will not be necessary, Mom."

"You had a nightmare. That's all it was. Go back to sleep … you were screaming, so try to keep it down." His mother walked away without another word.

"How motherly," he whispered to himself. He returned to his bed but turned on the lamp on his bedside table and grabbed a book. "Are you there, Sebastian?"

Sebastian stepped out of the dark shadows of Luke's room and walked toward him. The guardian placed his halberd on the carpet and sat on Luke's chair. "I'm here."

"What was that nightmare about?" he asked.

"It was a vision that was disrupted by the presence in this house," Sebastian responded.

"What do you mean? I think it's clear that I need to confront Joshua, but I could feel myself getting struck by that car and my mother was right, I have never felt that drunk."

Sebastian leaned in toward Luke and grabbed his hand. "There is an evil in this house that has prevented your growth. When we defeat it you will have clear visions." Sebastian let go of Luke's hand and stood up. "I apologize that I am a faulty vessel. Together we will work on improving ourselves."

"Evil … the burned man, the blond-haired man must be ghosts. Not demons," Luke said a bit frazzled.

Sebastian shook his head. "I'm not sure Luke. They are spirits that once roamed the earth. We are missing something but have faith the truth will come to us in time," Sebastian said walking to Luke and removing his glove. He then placed his hand on Luke's forehead. "May God bring you peace and rest."

Luke drifted into a deep sleep. Sebastian was correct, something was with him. Something was hanging over them in the house, trying to exert itself over the good that remained in the home.

✝ ✝ ✝

The Overlook

Luke woke when he felt something sitting on his bed. He flinched and jumped out of bed, believing he would once again be paralyzed by a visit from the burned man. He was not. It was his father sitting on his bed. It felt unnatural because his father typically winced if he was too close to him.

"Get dressed and come with me. We need to talk," Luke's father said.

He dressed quickly, half asleep, and joined his father in his *Monte Carlo*. They sat silent for a long twenty or so minutes while driving in an unfamiliar area. He wondered why his father did not speak to him if that was the purpose of the drive.

His father pulled into a parking area that was empty of other vehicles. "I came across this area when I needed some time to myself. He saw a sign that said *Red Rock Wilderness Overlook Regional Park*. Let's go for a walk," his father said, stepping out of the vehicle.

Luke stepped out of the car and looked at his surroundings. To one side was a bunch of trees. To the other side was the main road and some old-looking, broken-down buildings without roofs. One of the sides of the long building looked more like a wall with open voids where windows once stood.

"There's a trail here to see the Potomac River." His father grabbed a folder and tucked it away in the pit of his arm.

He followed his father in silence on the dirt path between large trees. It was frustrating, but he figured his father would speak when he was ready. His father finally stopped near where the trail opened, and the river was visible. This would be a great place to go on a vigorous run where the reward was the view of the historic Potomac River.

"Luke, I'm not sure what's happening with the house. I don't see what you see ... I know you are gifted somehow. After what happened in Puerto Rico and New York and then with Tom's accident ... I wanted to help you somehow," his father stammered and went silent.

"I'm listening, Dad."

His father held up his hand. "Let me get all this out ... I met with one of my agents who used to be a police officer in Lansburg." His father went silent again. Luke did not interrupt. "We talked about the boy you saw on the street near the church."

"I know, his name is Joshua. I'm unsure why or if I want to know."

"None of this makes sense, son. How could you be seeing a kid that died decades ago?" His father closed his eyes, standing silently. He reopened his eyes and walked towards Luke.

He instinctively recoiled, fearing that his father would feel that Luke had invaded his privacy. It was more than that. It was a precipice. Once his father touched him it would be an acknowledgment and an acceptance that Luke had powers and those powers were for good.

"Wait, son, and see," his father said, placing his hand on Luke's shoulder ... *My eyes rolled into my skull. I was elsewhere in a bar, standing over my father and another man. I knew they were attending a going away party for a retiring agent with the Joint Agency Response Team. It was why my father moved to Virginia. He built a multi-agency team representing agencies that worked at the US* consulates in the Caribbean and Latin America. The team was a prototype group, my father's idea.

My father had personally paid for an open bar for a small group of agents from the team my father ran. The man next to my father was named Vito Pugliese, a DEA agent.

I felt somebody staring at me as I stood behind my father and Vito. The man was wearing a hoody, but I could not see his face. The man raised his glass to me as if he could see me. I knew who it was but pretended not to.

"Buy you a drink?" my father asked Vito.

"Funny boss, you already have," Vito said, lifting a glass.

"I need your help with something."

"What can I do for you?"

"You used to work for the Lansburg PD, right?"

"Sure, for a couple of years in the '80s. I started at twenty-one. I had an uncle who was a lieutenant at the time," Vito said. "What gives?"

"Did something ever happen at the intersection of Joshua and Main Street? A dead child, maybe?"

Vito looked stunned and stared forward at his own reflection in the mirror. "My first memorable call was for a pedestrian hit and run at Main and Church Street intersection."

"Church Street?" Angel asked.

"It used to be called Church." Vito stalled as if trying to push through some severe pain. Then, he cleared his throat and downed his drink in one gulp before motioning to the bartender for another. "A grandmother was walking her five-year-old grandson through the intersection, and a deuce drove through the red light and took the five-year-old right out of her hand."

"That's horrible. What happened to the little boy?" my father asked, motioning to the bartender with his beer bottle for another drink.

The bartender came over and served Vito and his father more drinks. Vito looked like he was in pain but continued. "I interviewed a witness who recognized the Chevy Nova. I went to the owner's house." Vito's voice cracked, so he took another drink while composing himself. "I found the boy on the car's hood and the driver on his sofa... so I put my *gun in the man's mouth and begged him to grab it." Vito looked at his father, possibly rethinking his honesty. "I almost ate my gun myself over this. I still see that kid stuck over the hood on bad nights."*

"Is that why you left the department?" my father asked.

"Eventually, yes … strange you should bring this up. I only remember it when I try to sleep. Whenever I try to think about it, my memory is obstructed somehow. Probably a defense mechanism. I can see it now like I'm supposed to tell you."

"What does this have to do with Joshua Avenue?"

"The street was renamed after Joshua, Joshua Kent," Vito responded.

"Oh, I see … what happened to the driver?"

"He was given twenty years in prison but got out early for good behavior. He's nothing more than a vegetable. He spends most of his days hanging out at that same intersection." Vito finished his drink and tapped it on the counter. Vito held up two fingers to the bartender. "I went there once and tried to speak with him, but all he would say was, he will not let me leave, and pointed into the crosswalk. The darndest thing."

"Thanks for telling me, Vito. I appreciate it."

"You're welcome … it looks like I may need a ride home because I'm only getting started."

"Have a few more on me. I'll put you in a cab myself," my father said … Luke returned to his body with a jolt. He doubled over with a sharp pain in his abdomen. He held steady and began to take deep breaths, keeping them in and then blowing back out. It was a trick he used previously when he was plagued with anxiety. It helped to keep him from vomiting.

"Are you okay, son?" his father asked as he leaned in to help Luke.

Luke motioned for his father to stop. "I'm okay," he said, and he felt much better, but something about the vision disturbed him. Not just what happened to Joshua, because he had already experienced that. The burned man was sitting in the bar raising a drink to him during the vision. It was a message within a

156

message. The burned man somehow resided in his father's mind.

"I'm sorry I have not been paying attention to what's happening in our home. I failed you all by allowing something to put blinders over my eyes," his father said as if in tune with his son.

Luke nodded in affirmation but was hopeful now that his father's eyes had opened. "What matters is that you're ready to deal with what's happening now."

I don't know if I am … one thing at a time." His father handed him the case folder. "I have everything you need here. Not sure what you need to do with it but figured you could use it."

Luke thought about opening the folder immediately but placed it under his arm.

"What do you think?" his father asked while motioning to the overlook area and river.

"It's calming," he responded.

They stood in comfortable silence for a few moments. "Let's head back. I wanted to share this place with you. It's where I go when I am stuck in my head. I'm sorry, I don't wear my heart on my sleeve," his father remarked before walking back toward the car.

Luke made headway with his father but seeing the burned man in his vision alarmed him. He knew that Sebastian was correct. They were dealing with more than a troubled ghost. He would carve away at this problem until all the malevolence was gone allowing the sun to shine brightly in a way that disinfected the rot that hung in the air.

CHAPTER TWENTY-ONE

Ascended

I was driving recklessly in my car, as fast as I could without rolling over. I knew somebody was chasing me. I felt anxious and excited but determined to lose the bully driving the red car behind me. A projectile whizzed past my face and shattered the passenger side window.

He woke up startled when he realized he was sleeping in his car in a parking lot overlooking the intersection of Joshua and Main. Stanley Howard was standing across the street.

"What are you doing, Mister?"

Joshua stood outside his car window. He recalled that he parked at a gas station at the intersection waiting for the boy to appear. "Joshua, what are you doing?"

Joshua pointed at Howard across the street. "Tell him to leave, Mister. He's holding me here, and I want to join my Nana now."

"If I tell him to leave, you'll go to a good place," he said calmly.

"Tell him to leave now!" It was no longer Joshua; it was the young boy he saw in his house. *It* had fangs. *It* lunged into his car headfirst.

Luke woke again, striking the roof of the Ford *Taurus* with his head and the steering wheel with his knees. That's going to leave a bruise on both legs. He grabbed the top of his head sure he could see stars.

Joshua stood at the intersection hanging onto a small street sign in the median of the highway. Stanley was on the other side of the road watching the boy.

He crossed the empty road onto the median and walked slowly to the boy. "Joshua, my name is Luke. Can we talk?"

"We are talking silly," Joshua said, barely visible up close.

"You shouldn't be in the middle of the road. It's not safe," Luke said.

"You're being silly. Nothing can hurt me now. I want to leave, but I can't." Joshua pointed at Stanley Howard who stood across the street shuffling back and forth eerily.

"Is the man holding you here? The man that hurt you?"

"Yes, I want to go to my Nana, but he keeps me here like he tied a rope around me."

"Joshua, I will tell him to go. If I do, will you go to a good place with your Nana?" Luke asked with tears escaping his eyes.

"Yes, Luke. If he leaves, I will finally see my Nana and be good. I promise," Joshua said staring at Luke now.

"God bless you, Joshua. Nobody is going to hurt you again."

"I like you, Luke … tell him I'm not mad at him, please. For me."

"I will, Joshua." Luke grabbed onto his face attempting, but failing, to control his emotions.

Luke ran across the roadway to where Stanley Howard was poised. "Stanley, my name is Luke ..."

"Tell him to get off the road so he does not get hit again." Stanley pointed at Joshua with a trembling hand.

"Stanley, Joshua said it's okay for you to leave. He's not in pain. If you let him go, he will be happy. His grandmother waits for him on the other side."

"Did he speak with you?" Stanley asked.

"He did, Stanley. "You are keeping his spirit here because you are both tethered to that terrible day," he said.

"I don't want to hurt him anymore," Stanley said.

"Go and allow him to ascend to heaven. Go in peace and be assured that Joshua is not angry with you."

Stanley looked at Luke and then at Joshua, who was waving goodbye to them. "I'm sorry, Joshua." Stanley waved at Joshua's spirit.

A light fissure opened above Joshua as his soul ascended to the heavens. The event gave Luke a sense of harmony he had not experienced in his short life. The tears flowed freely from him.

Stanley turned and began to walk away. Luke jogged toward the man and placed a hand on his shoulder ... *I stood in a room with many adults sitting in a circle. A noticeably older Stanley held a clipboard and read something foreign to me yet understood it to be the guidelines for a new code of behavior for the Twelve Step Program. Stanley was running a group and helping those suffering from substance abuse* ... he let go of Stanley, who continued walking away. "You're going to be okay, Stanley." Luke yelled, smiling before returning to the family car.

The feeling of accomplishment gave him strength. It imbued him with an ability he would need for future battles. He looked at his watch and saw that it was almost 3 a.m. He realized his parents would be angry with him for arriving home late but hoped they would not notice.

✝ ✝ ✝

Flight of the Viejos

Luke pulled into the driveway of the house on Red Hill Road and knew something was wrong. His grandparents stood outside of the home, in the freezing cold, beside all their luggage. He stopped beside them and exited the car quickly. "Grandpa, why are you all leaving in the middle of the night?"

His Grandma Acidina moved away from him angrily and sighed. "Something attacked us, and your father pretends it's in our minds!" His grandfather seemed incensed.

Luke felt inclined to walk toward his grandfather who was so angry, and placed a hand on his grandfather's shoulder ... *I was hit backward so hard that I thought I would slam against the car but as always, the feeling was internal.*

I stood by my grandfather, as an observer. A noise from the bathroom made him stir in his cot. I tried to focus but it was very dark. I looked at the alarm clock. It was 3:00. The bathroom door opened, and a low glow emanated from the room. A woman in a white nurse's uniform was at the sink. She appeared to be handing something to someone in the bathtub. I walked closer and tried to focus on the figure. She looked like a projection from a camera.

"Aci, wake up. Aci, wake up." My grandfather reached out to shake her bed, but she did not wake.

I looked toward the bathroom again and saw the woman walking toward my grandfather with a twitchy gait until she stepped out. The apparition morphed into the scarred and burned man with no clothing. The groin area looked like a charred sausage.

My grandfather tried to stand but was pushed down into the cot by something unseen. The burned man approached the cot and sat. My grandfather was frozen in fear and melted into the cot.

"You don't belong here. This is my realm, and these are my flock." The figure said in a disembodied gravelly male voice while motioning into itself.

"Aci, Aci, wake up ... wake up, woman," his grandfather whispered hoarsely.

The entity slinked into the cot and straddled my grandfather. "You die, tonight abuelito."

"Aci, help get this thing off me. It's trying to kill me." A little louder, and Aci began to move in the bed. "Aci, help me!" my grandfather yelled.

My grandmother sat up in bed and looked toward my grandfather. She stepped off the bed and yelled. "Julio, what is that?" She rushed toward my grandfather but was shoved forcibly in the air and landed on the bed. My grandmother screamed and tried to run back to the cot but froze in the air before reaching it and began to convulse.

My parents rushed into the room and turned on the light. A loud audible screeching sound resonated in the room. The blur dissipated into the air before my grandmother crumpled onto the floor.

"Mom, are you alright? What's going on in here?" my father asked stunned at the doorway.

I rushed over toward my grandmother but could not help.

"Angel, Angel, a spirit had me. It was trying to kill me." My grandfather cradled my grandmother gently before placing her on the bed.

"It was a demon, Angel." My grandmother's weak voice was barely audible.

"He was trying to kill me, Angel. It told me I was going to die tonight." My grandfather served my grandmother some water she kept on the nightstand.

"You're exaggerating, Dad. You had a dream."

"You were not here, son, don't insult me like that. Take your head out of the sand!" My grandfather was frustrated at my father.

"I'm sorry, Papa. Go back to sleep." My father's denial had become dangerous.

"Are you deaf and blind?" my grandfather asked.

"What's wrong with you, son? You're in denial. Something is closing your eyes," my grandmother said.

"Angel let's go and give them some space," my mother said, leading my father out of the room without another word.

"What do you want to do, my love?"

"We cannot stay here. We need to pack and go. This spirit wants me out of here or dead." I fell forward … his grandmother was yelling at him, but he heard only ringing. A taxicab approached them. It had high beams on like spotlights. His grandfather immediately began moving their luggage to the taxi.

"You never learned respect, Luke. Keep your distance and respect personal boundaries," his grandmother said.

"Grandma, I was not being disrespectful. I needed to see what happened." Luke pleaded with the one woman who he recalled was the most negative during his youth.

"Luke, we will call you later. Please be careful in this house. It needs an exorcism," his grandpa Julio said while making a second trip to grab some suitcases. "Aci, please leave the kid alone. If our son could see the way Luke does, we would be fighting that abomination together."

His grandmother took a step toward Luke and raised her hand as if to swat him away but lowered it. She opened her mouth but instead of speaking walked briskly to the cab and sat inside it.

Luke helped grab the rest of the suitcases. "I thought the church could only exorcise a person. Not a house."

"The demon has control of the house, and it needs to be exorcised from it before it tries to possess somebody," his grandfather remarked handing the last suitcase to the cab driver.

The cab drove off, taking their grandparents away from the tentacles of the spirits residing within the home. Luke was closer to understanding that he must face the evil within the home and not just ghosts.

CHAPTER TWENTY-TWO

Beaver Lounge

Luke sat in the junior cafeteria in silence. Alyssa and her friends sat several tables away looking at him. He wanted to go speak with her but felt so sour he did not want to channel that energy to their table. He was upset about what happened with his grandparents earlier in the morning. The event with Joshua was positive and uplifting but watching his grandparents flee the home was a stark realization that he was not making headway with the haunting of his home. Just as he faced Joshua, he must face the spirits within the home.

"Are you going to just sit there playing with your food?" Benji asked.

Luke broke out of his thoughts, noticing the empty tray in front of Benji and the cold burger and fries sitting in front of him. "My grandparents were attacked by the ghosts in my home last night," he said.

"Why did it take you so long to share that with me? I thought I made you angry about something." Benji folded his arms as if he disliked what Luke shared.

"Sorry, I didn't think of that … I'm a bit overwhelmed." Luke considered what exactly was happening with the home and what happened with Joshua. "Did I ever tell you about Joshua?"

"No, you haven't."

"Joshua Avenue and Main Street near the church. You know near the gas station?"

"Yes, I lived here all my life. It's named after a kid that died on the street," Benji responded quickly.

Luke realized he was about to admit to Benji that the Claire thing was not unique. "When we first moved here, I saw Joshua on the street all the time with Stanley Howard, the man who killed him standing on the other side of the street," Luke said.

"Seriously, I thought he was a homeless guy," Benji said.

"Stanley stands out there whenever Joshua shows himself." Luke paused for a few seconds. "I saw him over some time but did not know what to do. I finally realized that I needed to help Joshua rise to heaven by getting Stanley to let him go. I approached both this weekend and Joshua ascended … it was moving," Luke said and wiped the tear rolling down his face.

"I wish you would have told me sooner … after what happened to Claire … well, I wouldn't have been surprised or judgmental." Benji looked at him with intensity.

"I don't think my house is haunted by just ghosts. I think there's a demon within my home." Luke left it at that and let it stew in the air.

"Have you seen the demon?" Benji asked.

"I don't think so … there's this burned man I keep seeing. I mean maybe it's him, but I'm confused because it keeps saying that we stole its records and comics."

Benji sat up in his seat. "The stuff you found in the attic, right?"

"Yes, exactly," Luke said.

"I'm not a Catholic, but can a person really become a demon?" Benji asked.

Luke closed his eyes and tried to think about what he knew about religion and demons, but he was a compelled tourist in his parent's religion. It wasn't until recently that he began to identify as a Catholic because of Sebastian. He realized at that point that he needed to speak with Father D and start reading some books. Either he was all in as a believer or he continued as a tourist. "Sorry, Benji, a demon can possess a person … I know people can do evil things, but I'm guessing that they are being controlled by a demon … until this moment I just realized I'm pretty much an amateur at this kind of stuff and need help from a priest." He paused before adding, "I'm glad we had this conversation."

Benji reached over, grabbed Luke's burger, and took a bite. "Glad to be of help."

"Hey, I was going to eat that," Luke said.

"You've been staring at it for twenty minutes ... ah man that's a lot of bacon," Benji said with a full mouth.

Luke was about to yell at Benji, but Todd sat next to him with raised palms as if to show he meant no harm. He noticed that Alyssa stood up and walked toward their table. "What's up, Todd?" Luke asked.

"I need to speak with you in private," Todd said staring at Benji who did not budge from his seat.

"You can speak in front of Benji," Luke said menacingly.

"Todd, what are you doing? Just drop it," Alyssa said, her face flushed red.

"It's okay, let him let it out," Luke said.

Todd lowered his head and placed his hands over his face. "It's weird, and kind of embarrassing."

"I live in weird, and after what happened I think we crossed the embarrassment line."

"Just let it out, Todd. You're the tough quarterback headed to the closest *Super Bowl* near us," Benji said, letting out a snort.

"Look, I'm sorry for what happened but some of it was not my fault," Todd said.

Luke motioned for Todd to continue. He felt embarrassed for the star football player whose only humbling experience was being sacked once in a season. "I'm listening ..."

"Alyssa and I have not been getting along well for a while. Recently she's been talking about you. Like a lot and when I saw you speaking to your brother, I knew that something was up," Todd said before taking a deep breath.

"Get on with it, Todd. Lunch is about to end," Luke said looking at the clock in the shape of a beaver above the serving line. He let out a smile when he recalled he was in the *Beaver Lounge.*

"… I followed you and Alyssa … that day from the school to your house. I parked in the backyard and looked through the windows. I saw the two of you inside and I was furious, man," Todd said.

Luke felt sickened. He should have a sixth sense alarm to warn him that he was being followed, instead he was oblivious. Maybe because he was nervous when he was with Alyssa or maybe it was something else. *I have a guardian, who is not on guard*, he thought.

"I'm sorry, Luke. I am blinded by something in the house," Sebastian said.

Luke pointed at Sebastian. "We didn't do anything," he said looking now toward Todd.

"Listen … I'm not saying you did … I saw someone in the house following you." Todd appeared extremely afraid and looked around the cafeteria. "It was this huge blond-haired dude, the size of a football player but dressed like a farmer."

Luke clenched both his fists and tensed up his whole body — Todd saw the ghost.

"He saw me Luke … he ran at me and went right through one of your glass doors and struck me." Todd let out several tears balled up his fist and struck it on the table. "The next thing I know, I'm in Alyssa's car and you are holding me down."

They all sat in silence for some time. *Can a ghost possess a man that way?* It had to be a demon and he was losing the fight against it. It was stronger than ever and beyond the obvious he did not know what the demon wanted.

"Did you commit with Colorado?" Benji asked and moved chairs closer to Todd and slapped his back.

"No, Benji … I'm going to Notre Dame."

"The Fighting Irish, number twenty-one …" Luke's thoughts drifted back to the house instead of paying attention to what he said.

Todd grew tense and stared at Luke. "What did you just say? That's my father's number."

The *first bell* rang, and everyone began to stand up. Luke did the same and realized he was saved by the bell. "Lucky guess, Todd. See you around." He walked off with Benji, leaving Todd stunned in his chair.

Egged On

It felt closer to his goal than all the centuries he spent hiding from his master. He grew tired of chasing Tony around the house, instead he sent the boy to befriend the dog by tossing a ball at it. Tony would move the ball forward cautiously with his nose but would not get any closer. He felt like Luke's energy was getting closer to home. This caused all the entities to pulse quickly into the boy. Tony, once simply cautious, darted away in terror. Luke approached the home, alone. He was angered at first because Alyssa was not with the boy. When he reacted emotionally it never went well. He was mostly just mimicking emotion. He must calm down ... his time was quickly approaching, and he would attack when it was in his best interest.

Luke entered the house with a strong determined look. Tony jumped into the boy's arms, noticeably trembling in terror. "Sebastian, is it here?"

The Spanish soldier slowly formed in the living room pointing his Halberd spear forward prepared to charge forward and attack.

The iron of the soldier's spearhead scared him immensely. He knew that it could penetrate his essence and cause him harm. Nevertheless, he felt that he could stop the soldier with a full-on attack, and then he could attempt to pierce Luke's soul and injure him. However, this would not fulfill any of his needs and Alyssa would be outside *its* reach just like Barbara was. He had no choice but to retreat into the attic.

"I know you are here, show yourself, coward!" Luke yelled while it retreated.

This caused *it* to pause while flowing up the stairway. He pushed all his essence outward throughout the house. This lowered his energy threshold, and he knew that Luke's poking at him should not cause him to pounce.

"You've attacked my brother, and my dog you piece of shit. I have seen you already. Show yourself and face me now," Luke said.

"It's in here Luke, it is everywhere ..." Sebastian said.

"Why don't you show yourself? You seemed so brave before ... what the hell are you waiting for?" Luke yelled angrily. "Why is my dog so scared? What are you doing to him when we aren't home?"

He was compelled to bring Luke harm and he moved forward. The dog barked at him, empowered.

He must hide and wait for the right time. He would not react in a way to give this youngster power over him. *It* was an impulsive creature. His greatest weakness would not be allowed to crop up and deter his plans. He would take Luke's soul eventually, at the right time. He would become corporeal and feast on Alyssa. He flowed easily into the attic and slept. He would bide his time, looking forward to the opportunity to caress the young girl's perfect white skin with Luke's essence. He would destroy the device that kept him latched to the home. He would walk the earth. Not in the way Lord Ipos demanded by possessing an imperfect body. *It* would become corporeal, in its natural form, in full control. He preferred not to be trapped in the body of a damaged automaton that would fight internally for its soul.

CHAPTER TWENTY-THREE

Research

Luke was on a mission to identify the boy in the cave, so he took a bus to the Lansburg Municipal Library, where he planned to continue Jorge's research. He reviewed the paperwork Jorge provided and read the book that Wil gave him about historical investigations. He needed to access newspaper articles to compare them to the tax assessor information already developed because it showed the specific dates the owners paid taxes.

Jorge provided a photocopy of the inside of the Mad Magazine recovered in the cave where somebody wrote: *PROPERTY OF ANDY B*. The most likely last name of the family was Bolling, but it was nothing more than an informed guess. He needed to find out where the periodicals or newspapers were kept. Emily Villanueva waved at him from behind a counter. He approached her, hoping she had time to help him. "Mrs. Villanueva, how are you?"

"Hello, Luke. What are you up to?"

"I need your help. I'm following up on something Mr. Villanueva completed for my father."

"The room under the house—what can I help you with?" she asked.

"I need to know where to find the old newspapers," he said.

Emily took him to an area in the research section of the library. "Set up here at one of these tables. These machines are used to view newspapers and periodicals. These cabinets contain microfilm holding the data from the newspaper. If you need anything printed, you hit this button. Come get me if you need help."

"Thanks Mrs. Villanueva."

The first entry had the house as being built in 1952, and the first taxpayer was Richard and Jewel Braxton. The Braxton family paid taxes from February 1952 until June 1956. From October 1956 to June 1960, it was Werner Dodge. From July 1960 to April 1964, it was Andrew and Sandra Bolling. From May of 1964 until mid-1980, it was Robert and Esta Bridger, but a different address was listed. Jorge had written on the margin, *likely a rental property*. After that, Stephen Dameron was listed for 1981, David Dew for 1982, and George Cocke for 1983. In the margin, Jorge wrote, *why would they sell each year?* Howard and Judy Hollowell from 1983 to 1990.

"The boxes in the home said *Bolling Collectibles*," he whispered. *I'm sure the Bollings are important to this story*, he thought.

Emily returned, taking the photocopy of the notes that Jorge had left him. "He completed much for you already. He circled the names Andrew Bolling and Robert and Esta Bridger between 1960 and 1980. However, you do not need to worry about the Bridgers. They are property owners and rent out numerous homes in Lansburg." She paused and placed her finger on her lips. "Based upon Andy B and the given name Andrew, I think the last name Bolling is what you are looking for."

"Bolling. Andy B. I get it. Do you recognize the name?" Luke asked, but in truth he recognized the names from the boxes the prior renters left behind.

"The Bolling family are some of the first settlers of Virginia. Three hundred years later … I do not know. The census was in 1960, and it may not help you. Next step, Luke?" She looked at him, waiting for an answer like a teacher would.

"Newspapers. I need to look at newspapers from 1963 and 1964."

"Correct, let me show you where to look. This will take a long time, and it's tedious." She walked up to a sizable, tan-colored cabinet. The sign on the top of the cabinet said, *LANSBURG*

GAZETTE 1960-1970.

"This is where you need to concentrate. Begin with this drawer labeled June 1960. Keep looking until you find what you need ... let me see, April of 1964. It looks like they spent four years in the house."

"I'm guessing that will take a long time." He was concerned he would not have enough time to search these archives.

"It will, several hours at least. I am going to grab the first roll of the film. Come over here, and I will show you how to use this so you can learn for yourself." He followed her to the cabinet, where she pointed at three sets of microfilm stock. "You need these three rolls of film. Have you seen the dates? I am also showing you how to do this for the future, Luke."

"Yes, I see the dates. I appreciate that you're taking the time to help me."

"My pleasure. Come here, and I will introduce you to the Minolta *Microfilm Viewer*." She took a seat and left him standing over her. "You take this cartridge and load it into the spool and push this green button, and then press this guide, and it will run the film through the lens. Bring down this lever and feed the film by pressing the button on the right. Then use this knob to control the speed forward."

"Thanks, Mrs. Villanueva." Luke thought of asking her to help him look but decided it was best he learn how to do this himself.

"Use this knob over here to view the film." She moved the knob, and the film moved quickly through the machine. "Make sure you forward through until you get to May and then June and begin viewing." She stood up, grabbed his hand, and helped him sit down. "Come get me if you need help. I will be over by the front desk."

He took a deep breath and began the search. It was tedious and took a while to get to February of 1964. *I don't even know what I'm looking for.* It took time to go through the rest of the film, and he found nothing of interest. He rewound and then loaded the next canister. He was deep into that roll of film when he saw something interesting. The headline, *Lansburg Child Reported Missing Near Great Falls of the Potomac*. The date of the article was dated February 4th, 1964. He glanced over the piece and came upon the family names. The report has an image of a man holding a jacket and a portrait of a young boy.

Andrew and Sandra Bolling spent the day walking the trails of Great Falls when their eight-year-old son Andy wandered off. The child's mother said he was out of sight for under five minutes. They searched for their son near Bootleggers Trail, closer to the water and rapids. Andrew Bolling claimed he followed the river downstream and found Andy's jacket caught up on a log at the water's edge. Both Maryland and Virginia authorities initiated a search to no avail. The temperature during the day was about 54 degrees Fahrenheit, but the overnight temperature was below freezing. A public affairs representative with the local search and rescue unit has told the Lansburg Gazette that they switched to recovery mode and have personnel staged near Snake Island watching the water flow in the Potomac River.

He printed the article before looking for Mrs. Villanueva at the front desk. He felt a tug on his shirt and saw a smiling Emily behind him.

"Mrs. Villanueva, look at this article," he said with nervous excitement.

"I think you found it. Have you looked for any updates?" she asked.

"Not yet. I will try to find a follow-up article. This looks like it's dated the day after the child was reported missing."

He returned to the viewer and continued searching the third roll of film when he came upon an article dated February 5th, 1964, titled *Missing Bolling Boy Declared Deceased by Authorities*. He printed this article and then placed all three cartridges in the cabinet. The title of the piece indeed said it all. Emily walked over to him.

"It's 5 o'clock, and my shift is over. I need to go home and make dinner. Did you find anything else?"

He handed her the article. "Looks like we know why they moved, sort of. It still doesn't explain if he was the child in the cave."

"So that is what you all call the void under the house? Do you need a ride home?"

"Sure, why not." He gathered all his research material and shoved them sloppily in his backpack.

He got into the passenger side door of her car. She backed out of her parking spot and drove out of the parking lot. He stared out of the window silently.

She parked the car at his house. "Say hello to your parents for me, Luke."

"Thanks for the ride. Goodnight, Mrs. Villanueva." He jumped out of the car and closed the door quickly. "I need to work out," he said. Luke walked inside and caught the scent of his mother's cooking, realizing he was famished but knowing he needed to work out before anything else. He began his workout on the universal machine, then put on his bag gloves, and pounded on his 100-pound banana bag between sets. The workout itself did exactly what it was meant to do. It focused him into the whole reason he went to the library. *I was there to help solve the problem with the house.* The Bolling boy was not lost in a river. He was locked in the void of his house decades earlier. *I will never complain about my parents again*, he thought.

CHAPTER TWENTY-FOUR

The Spiraling Hallway

The whole family was at church listening to Father D's sermon. Earlier that weekend, he convinced his parents to allow him to speak with Father D about blessing the home, failing to mention that he had already tried with Father Lee. He thought he convinced them. Oddly, when he reminded his father that morning, he pretended it was the first time he heard of it. He spoke with his mother afterward, and she agreed to talk to Father D and promised to take Luke along. He wanted to be present, hoping to steer the conversation away from talk that Father Lee had been to the house. It was dishonest, but too much information could set his mother off.

Father D's sermonized from Psalms 103, "Bless the Lord, O my soul, and forget not all his benefits. He pardons all your iniquities. He heals all your ills. He redeems your life from destruction. He crowns you with kindness and compassion." Father D leaned forward in his pulpit. "I want to apologize for being away from the parish for some time. As some of you know, I was in Rome assisting priests to help a troubled family. Several families within our parish have needs that I have neglected. I'm back and ready to help."

Luke hoped Father D was referring to his family. Without the priest's help, his family may be splintered.

His mother asked his father to warm up the minivan because she had to use the restroom. Luke claimed he needed to go as well. Both approached Father D once he was available.

"Hello, Father, I'm relieved you are back from Rome," his mother said.

175

"Thanks, Helen. Let me apologize in advance, and I beg for your forgiveness. Hence, the sermon today. You're not the only family I have wronged by being gone for a month."

Luke approached the priest and tried to subtly close the topic. "Father, would you be able to bless our home? We've been having trouble."

"It's already on my schedule. Deacon Robert and I plan to come to the house this Friday."

"Thanks, Father. I feel hope and relief that you are back." A tear ran down her face, but she smiled.

They walked back to the minivan. Their father drove off, and they arrived at the intersection of Joshua and Main. Joshua and Stanley were not present, it brought a smile to Luke.

His father stopped at Laio's Customs to drop him off. Luke forgot he had agreed to help Benji while the family prepared the barbecue.

"We are at Benji's," Junior said.

"Sorry, Dad, I spaced out." Luke stepped out of the car.

"No worries, son. Don't forget the barbecue later. We all love and appreciate you."

"I know, Dad. I will see you all later," he said with a bowed head.

Daniel stared at him intensely. "What you did last month was heroic. I'm proud of you."

Junior smiled at him and motioned upward with his thumb. His brother seemed to be holding back somehow. Luke nodded at his brother but was perplexed. He waved at them but wondered whether somebody had changed his family out. Benji stepped out of the shop and walked up to him.

"What's up?" Benji asked.

"My family is acting weird … what do you need help with? Do you need me to move an engine around again?" he asked, changing the subject.

"No, we are headed to another car shop for some parts."

Benji got into the *Gran Fury*. Luke shook his head in

bewilderment before jumping into the passenger seat. Benji drove to a shop called *Gen Motorsports*, a few minutes away. He followed his friend into a waiting room where several children were playing on the floor, and a woman approached them. "Luke, this is Stacy Genaro, Tom's wife. She wanted to meet you."

"Nice to meet you, Stacy," he said with a hand reaching out to her, but she moved past his hand and hugged him. She began to cry in his arms ... *I was propelled into an unfamiliar living room of a well-furnished home. Stacy was sitting on the sofa crying again, but her makeup ran down her face this time. She looked to be so pregnant that she was overdue. A young toddler played next to her ...* she released him, the vision vanished. "Thanks for saving my idiot husband's life." She motioned for the kids to come over. "This is our daughter Tommy and our son Rudy. This man saved your father, kids."

He got on one knee to remain at eye level with the children, who came over and hugged him. He braced for a vision, but nothing came.

"Thank you, Mr. Luke." Tommy handed him a drawing.

"Mr. Luke, thanks for saving my father," Rudy said while pointing at the drawing. "This is you, my daddy, and this is the knight in shiny armor."

He felt tension, but the presence of the children made him feel grounded. "I love the drawing, Rudy. You are a great artist, but nobody wore armor that day." Luke failed to realize they could be referring to Sebastian.

Rudy seemed disappointed and leaned on his sister. "Tommy, I thought you said there was a knight."

"It's okay, Rudy ... thanks, Luke," Stacey said.

"You're welcome, kids, but anybody would have helped your father. My family happened to be there."

"Come on, kids. Your father wants to speak with Luke." Stacy moved closer to him. "You saved my husband, the father of my children. You brought him back to us. For some reason, Tom wanted me to tell you that he has changed. I will always be in your debt."

He didn't know what to say. He was still that shy kid and felt out of place. A tear ran down his cheek. He quickly used his hand to swipe it away. He was so embarrassed to show emotion in front of strangers, friends, and especially family.

"I hope we get to meet and speak again soon. You're welcome in our home always. Please go speak with Tom," she said while touching his arm gently … *I was propelled to a hospital birthing room. Tom hovered over Stacy, who was lying on a bed. She was pregnant and preparing for the delivery. Tommy and Rudy sat in chairs nearby. They looked slightly older* … he was back to the present.

"Come with me, Luke." Benji led him out of the waiting room and down a hallway.

Luke felt out of sorts and confused by the visions he saw. He was just having trouble processing all the information and felt overloaded. "Benji, I'm not used to this. I feel out of place," he said.

"You saved the man's life. Relax, Tom is a good guy." Benji directed him into an office where Tom sat at a desk with a brace on his neck and his right arm in a sling. Tom's face had some nasty bruises and looked a bit weathered. Tom stood up as Luke entered the room with Benji and walked toward them with a massive smile.

"Luke, thanks for coming. Please sit down. I had a mental list of all I wanted to say." Tom looked at him and then down to the carpeted floor before canting his head back up quickly. "Thanks for my life. I cannot recall how I crashed, but I saw you working on me in the mud …" Tom stopped talking. "Let me take a breath. My ribs are still bruised … I don't recall the crash. I was hovering above all of you. I walked down a long corridor toward a light. The closer I got to the light, the more it stretched away from me like a rubber band. I heard a voice say, 'You are not worthy,' and saw another corridor with flames at the end. I could hear pleas and yells coming from there." Tom looked away from him. "The corridor was spiraling, and I started falling into it, but I had nothing to grasp. Suddenly, I heard a popping sound and looked up at you."

"Sounds like a near-death experience, and you were hell-bound." Benji laughed loudly but stopped suddenly after looking at the pain in Tom's face.

"That was my impression, Benji." Tom looked at Luke again. "That man standing near you looked like he was from a different time. He was wearing an unusual, armored breastplate and one of those Spanish Conquistador helmets. This man told me that I was closer to hell than he ever was." Tom reached for the drawing his son had given Luke. "That's him right there."

"That must be my father, Tom. He was there and helped me pull you out of the car and revive you."

Tom motioned at another figure. "That's your father right there."

"He's a soldier, not a conquistador," he said without thinking.

"Luke, please don't worry. I'm not trying to rattle you ... I wanted to thank you in person and with something important to us both." Benji helped Tom stand up. "Benji, lead the way."

Benji took them out of the office into the garage, where mechanics worked on various cars. They entered an adjacent large showroom with numerous muscle cars. It was imposing, and he got the impression of a grown man's toy room.

"These are my babies on this side. These others are cars for sale. This is the GNX you saw a few months ago. Buick made 547 of these beauties."

Numerous cars were corralled into a roped-off area. Luke approached a Ford *Mustang* with lime green paint and white stripes.

"That's a 1969 *Shelby GT500*. It was my father's car, but he gave it to me before he passed away." Tom placed his fist up to his mouth. "The two of us rarely saw eye-to-eye, but we always met face-to-face when it came to cars."

He walked to each car, and Tom told him what each vehicle was. One of them caught his eye because it had a unique rear window.

"That's a 1963 Chevrolet *Stingray*. This model had a split window … Benji, can you open the garage door?"

Benji walked over to the garage door and opened it. Another Buick Grand National was parked outside.

"This is my other 1987 *Grand National* with T-tops, but not a GNX. Buick produced a little over 20,000 of these ones in 1987, and a handful got the T-Top option." Tom reached into his pocket, grabbed a set of keys, and tossed them to him.

"Seriously, I can take it for a ride?" he asked with a huge smile. He had wanted to drive a *Grand National* since he saw Tom's *GNX*.

"Sure thing. Take her home after that ride. It's yours." Tom seemed healthier than he did minutes ago. Happy and proud, it appeared.

"What do you mean? I cannot keep it. My father would never allow it."

"I crashed this car months ago, and it was sitting in the lot. Benji here fixed her up for you. You can still smell the paint. We worked it out with your parents. This is your car, and it's already in your name … it's a done deal." Tom reached into the glove box and handed him the paperwork.

"I'm stunned. Thanks, Tom. I'm indebted to you," Luke said.

Tom looked at Benji. "Your boy is humble but not too bright. Don't you get it? I am indebted to you and always will be. Take it for a ride with Benji and come over any time. I need to take my pills and take a nap." Tom walked away but turned around. "Tell your Conquista … I mean soldier that I'm a changed man. I will never walk down the wrong hallway again."

He stood looking at the paperwork and the keys, stunned into silence. "You arranged all this, Benji?" Luke asked.

"Yes, working on a car meant for a friend because he saved another friend was meaningful." Benji patted Luke's shoulder. "Whose this soldier?"

"Ask me again someday," Luke responded.

Luke stepped into the familiar black and gray interior of the car he was meant to own. He started the engine. It was not loud and throaty like his father's *Monte Carlo SS* or Benji's *Gran Fury*.

"Do you want to go for a drive together?" Benji asked.

"I do, but I need to speak with my parents," Luke said.

"Luke, your parents wanted this for you because you deserve it. They insisted on paying to fix the damage so that it would be a group gift," Benji said.

"Thanks, Benji. My parents were planning a barbecue. Do you want to come over?" Luke asked.

"I was invited before you, so yes," Benji said, running toward his car.

How did they hide this from a person like me? he asked himself. When he entered the house, his parents stood up from the sofa. "Dad, how pricey was the fix on the car?"

"Don't worry about that. I sold more of the comics and albums," his father said.

"This is so surreal."

"What are you going to name her, Luke?" His father asked with a huge grin.

"Name a car? You mean like the movie *Christine*?" he asked sarcastically.

"She's a real beauty ... you need to name her," his father said.

"Don't, Angel, don't tell him." His mother covered her face in embarrassment.

"My car is the Intimidator," his father said with a satisfied look.

"Dad, that is kind of corny," he laughed.

"I told you not to tell him." His mother walked toward the kitchen. "Come on, guys, let's get that barbecue started."

Luke had not felt like part of the family for some time. It wasn't the car. It was the thought and effort they took to pull together and execute the plan. How his brothers, Benji and his new friend Tom, gathered to obtain and fix the car was quite thoughtful. He truly felt like his life was progressing. He felt more pressure than ever to resolve the problem with their home. However, he also thought that they had the strength to prevail together.

✠ ✠ ✠

House Blessing

Father D had been an exorcist for the Vatican for decades. He performed many exorcisms in the United States early in his career having been mentored by Father William who passed away during an exorcism of a young girl in Suffern, New York. He refused to teach other priests the craft he learned from his mentor but since meeting Robert several years ago he took it upon himself to build the young man's career. Maybe it was the young deacon's past in bad neighborhoods of Ohio. He wanted to believe it was the man's inner light that drove him to take an interest in Robert's career. In truth, it could have been the cancer diagnosis and advice of his cardinal who reminded him that once he was called on high, he could no longer pass the information that William had spent so much time teaching him.

Father D and Deacon Robert met with Helen Sanz at her residence on Red Hill Road. They were at the dining room table, speaking with Helen, the only person at the home who appeared to have forgotten to brush her hair. He hoped he wasn't too late. "Helen, I will go from room to room, beginning in the kitchen. Deacon Robert told me the home has five levels."

"Yes, Father, the house has four separate sets of stairs. This is the void here on the wall of the dining room. Junior reopened the access panel for you."

"Interesting." He got onto his knees and peered into the void. "Helen, do you have a flashlight?"

"Yes, one moment," she said, walking into the kitchen. She

returned a few seconds later with a flashlight and handed it to him.

"Thanks, Helen." Father D shined the light into the tunnel. "So, there's a room back there with children's furniture?" He had never come across anything like this. This family was tormented by something that conjured this prison by slowly *obsessing* someone into building it to hold the child.

"Unbelievable. What happened here?" Deacon Robert asked.

"Luke deduced that in 1963, the Bolling's reported their boy named Andy missing. He thinks Andy's parents locked the boy in this void and concocted the missing child story to cover his death."

Father D placed his violet stole around his neck as part of his vestments. Deacon Robert prepared the thurible, or censer, with Frankincense and Myrrh. Father D handed Helen the prayer cards. "We will read the *Magnificat* and the *Epiphany* throughout the blessings."

"Yes, Father."

"Robert, can you start in the kitchen and then come to the dining room and slowly enter the tunnel here with the censer?"

"Yes, Father." Deacon Robert began in the kitchen and entered the tunnel carefully while holding the censer, moving his hand into the open space while swinging the censer. Robert left the room, exhaling deeply because he must have been holding his breath.

He started in the kitchen and began the *Epiphany*. "Bless, O Lord, God almighty ... and may this blessing remain on this home and all who dwell herein." He recited the prayers while sprinkling holy water in each room, including the void, accessed via the living room tunnel. They headed into the living room and reached each level, including the garage. Deacon Robert led the way, with Father D in the middle and Helen following closely behind. All repeated the prayer as they moved into the master bedroom and then entered Daniel's room. The mood of this room appeared different. The incense was swirling around the room like a tornado.

"There must be an open window, Father." She walked to the window, moved the still curtains, and dropped the prayer card as if stunned into silence.

"What's wrong, Helen?" he asked.

"I thought I saw someone on the floor in the bathroom, Father. It must have been the shower curtain." She reached down to pick up the prayer card. "This window is closed. I don't know where the wind is coming from."

"Stay out here, Helen, please. Deacon with me." They stepped into the bathroom while praying. He sprinkled holy water while Deacon Robert swayed the censer with incense throughout the area.

"Let's continue upstairs." He followed Robert out of the room and up one more flight of stairs. They blessed one another then each bedroom without incident. Robert began to walk up the steps into the attic. Father D stopped suddenly when a sharp pain inside his head forced his eyes shut. A man with blond hair was suspended onto the wall like he was on an old-fashioned torture device called the rack. A darkened figure walked up, caressing the man's chest.

"This soul belongs to me, Padre," said the evil spirit in a gravelly voice as *it* pointed *its* clawed-fingered hands at him and the tortured soul.

"Father, are you okay?" Robert walked back down the stairs. "Why are you holding your head like that?"

The pain was so intense in his head that he thought he was bludgeoned. The pain subsided when he reopened his eyes. "I'm fine. Let's continue." They walked upstairs into the attic cautiously.

Robert helped him up the last set of stairs; he seemed exhausted or expended. He moved Helen behind him on the stairs without saying a word. They were in what appeared to be a game room with a kitchenette. Robert walked deep into the room recklessly. He felt darkness and anger had descended into the room. He placed a protective arm against Helen.

"Father, what are you doing?" she asked.

"Silence, please." He was uncharacteristically short with Helen. Robert continued moving immaturely into the room without looking behind him. Robert was oblivious to the realm he entered. "Helen, stay still, don't say a word, please."

"Father, you have God on your side," Helen said.

The priest took a deep breath and appeared shaken. "You have a demonic presence in your house. Stay very still ... Robert, Robert. Turn around, son!"

A bright red fire shined darkly, bursting in anger! A form with burned scars rushed toward them, shoving Robert, and shooting toward Father D. The beast flew into the air toward him. He pushed Helen before the figure struck his shoulders with *its* knees. He fell backward, slamming his head on the floor.

"Open wide, Dwayne," The creature said in Italian, which he understood and then something else in what sounded like Vietnamese, that he did not understand.

He grabbed the crucifix from the chain on his neck and stabbed the abomination. It burst into a black mist and screeched into silence. He stood up slowly, looking at Helen.

"Father, I hope you can explain what happened."

'I don't think I can, Helen. Not yet." He straightened up his clothing quickly. "Robert, rise now, repeat the prayers, and take the thurible through each room twice."

Robert looked stunned but stood immediately and began walking into each room with the censer spreading holy incense.

Father D picked up all the items he dropped and read his prayers out loud again. "I'm sorry, Helen. The presence is strongest on this floor. I hurt my head when I tripped." He knew this demon was powerful enough to attack living people and it could pierce the thoughts of the living.

"Father, it looked like you were struck by something ... we should get some ice on your head." After completing the prayers on the fifth floor, they headed to the kitchen. Helen prepared an ice pack and handed it to Father D, who placed it on his head.

"Thanks, Helen. I will get this bag back to you."

"No need, Father. Anything else, a drink, maybe."

"Yes, I will take a scotch on ice if you have any."

"Me too, Helen," Deacon Robert said.

"Sure, I think I will join you both." She served them each ice in a glass and then poured the whiskey. Both motioned for her to keep pouring. They sat and drank in complete silence for a few minutes.

"Your home should improve, God willing. The Deacon and I must go back to church. Please let us know if anything reoccurs." They stepped outside, and Father D wrote *19+C+M+B+91*, over the front door with chalk. The 19 and the 91 pertain to 1991. The C.M.B. was an abbreviation for *Christus Mansionem Bendicat*, or may Christ bless this home. He made the sign of the cross. "Helen, let's talk after Sunday Mass. We want to perform a healing mass for the whole family." He looked exhausted and injured. He grabbed the Deacon's shoulder as they walked to the car.

"Thanks for coming, Father ... Deacon, please take care of him," Helen said. She tried to hand him an envelope containing a donation to the church.

The deacon waved her donation away. "Luke already gave a donation. I will take care of him."

"Luke?" Helen asked appearing confused.

Father D went to the front door of his car and opened the door slowly. "You better drive, Robert. I'm still not quite myself.

"Sure, Father."

After several minutes on the road, he broke the silence of his thoughts. "Robert, we need to research something back in our library."

"Sure, Father. What are you thinking?"

"I'm not quite sure but I need to look for some books in the archive and the library," Father D said.

CHAPTER TWENTY-FIVE

Confession with Father D

When Luke was in his youth, Sebastian's presence brought him to the point where his parents and himself questioned his sanity. Once Sebastian touched his arm that day on his run, he saw and felt himself die and was reborn. He wanted to speak to Father D about his problems but after arriving he realized the priest was holding confession. He knelt in prayer seeking insight into his current plight. His current situation necessitated some guidance from a person of faith.

A parishioner stepped out of confession, followed by Father D. "Luke, shouldn't you be in school?"

"I needed some guidance, Father. I didn't know you were in the middle of confession."

"Wrapping up and was about to take a break. Follow me." The priest motioned for him to join.

Luke and Sebastian followed the priest into his office. "Thanks for taking the time to see me, Father."

"My pleasure, but wait here for a sec … I will be back in a squirt and a shake, so to speak." Father D walked off quickly.

Luke shook his head, trying to make the visual disappear; however, it removed some of his tension as he managed to smile. This was the first time he had been inside a priest's office. He scanned everything in the room, noticing all the books on Father D's shelves and even one on his desk that caught his eye. Whitley Streiber's *Communion*. Not something one would expect a Catholic priest would read. The painting on the wall behind the priest's desk caught his attention. It depicted an angel holding a spear standing on another angel, which had wings and horns.

"I have seen this before," Sebastian said.

"The painting is by the artist Raphael. It depicts the war in heaven and God's triumph over Satan. It's called *St. Michael Vanquishing Satan*." Father D sat in his chair and joined him, staring at the work of art.

"It's disturbing … is that an angel under his foot?" Luke asked.

"Yes, it's a depiction from *Revelation* when the angels fought Satan, who rebelled against God."

"I could stare at this painting all day. It conjures up other stuff in my mind." In truth, he felt that it depicted the future rather than something that happened in the heavens.

"What can I do for you, Luke? Do I need to call your mother?" Father D sat up in his chair as if alarmed.

He considered how to explain himself and settled for honesty. "For some time now, I've been having dreams that come true." He hesitated but continued. "I know this is weird, and I'm not saying I'm a prophet or something."

"God may send messages to his chosen ones through dreams, but most people ignore these voices," Father D said.

He winced at words, *chosen one* because it reminded him of his godmother's story.

"Luke, why don't you start by explaining one of your dreams."

He thought of one of the oddest dreams. "I'm walking on a street in New York City near an old Customs House sometime in the future. A blond-haired man pushed me into the street traffic, but then an invisible force grabbed me, put me back on the sidewalk, and spoke Spanish. This force had a battle with the man."

"How do you know it's in the future in New York?" Father D asked.

"I was older, and it was an important day. I cannot recall the exact day, but I know it's 2001 in September. I met somebody for a money drop … I don't even know what that is." He was trying to explain something he did not quite understand. "I feel this horrible loss. I lost something that day because of a tragedy in New York." He repositioned himself in the chair. "I've had this dream several times of walking in a city I've never been to, but then one day, this blond-haired man inserts himself into my dream."

Father D looked at him attentively. "Let's stick to that dream. What did this invisible force tell you?"

"Do not fear. I'm with you as you are with our God."

"That's a compelling message and one you should heed. You aren't ready to see who your guardian is, Luke, but I believe it's your guardian angel. Have you seen this man before?"

Luke wanted to point at Sebastian who stood behind him but realized the priest meant the blond-haired man. "Maybe, but one of my friends may have."

Father D paused, likely contemplating what was happening at the Sanz household, and leaned back in his seat. "When was this dream, Luke?"

"The dream started months ago. Its only recently where the blond-haired man began to intrude into my dream. Maybe the night your priest ran from our house."

"First of all, he's not my priest. He happens to have served this Diocese almost as long as I have, and he didn't run. He walked quickly." Father D laughed and banged on the table.

"Remarkably quick, Father," he said, laughing a little.

"Are you sure you haven't seen this blond-haired man before?" Father D asked cautiously.

"I have in dreams … and others I know have seen him."

Father D stood up and paced the floor while looking out a window. "I saw him. He was wearing a red plaid shirt and overalls. He looked like a farmer and was dangling from the wall in your hall almost like he was being crucified."

"Crucified. In my house?" Luke's voice squealed, overwhelmed with tension.

"I'm trying to figure it out myself, but I think it was a warning from the dark presence in your home," Father D said.

"This man is being held by something in the house. Something evil. It's becoming clearer."

"The man looked familiar, Luke … I think I may know who it is." Father D said.

"Who, Father? Whom could he be?"

Father D walked toward a small closet, looked around, and eventually grabbed a box and brought it to his desk. "I think what I am looking for is in here."

Luke waited patiently staring at Sebastian.

"Here it is." Father D grabbed a framed picture and handed it to him. "Does anybody look familiar?"

The black and white picture showed a family with Father D. The older white man was shaking hands with the priest. Another man with light hair stood behind a woman, and a young girl stood beside a boy.

"This man, this is the man from my dream." He traced the man's image with his finger.

"That's Kyle Campbell. He died soon after that photo was taken. He was in a car accident behind your house. The rumor is that he was driving drunk, hit a tree, and bled out overnight."

He placed his hands on his face and shook it from side-to-side. "Our house is haunted but it's worse than that."

"I felt something else in your house. Something in the house hated me intensely … it also attacked me," Father D said.

"Attacked you how?" Luke asked.

"We can discuss specifics later. It was a scarred abomination that ran at me and knocked me down. It said some vulgarity I would prefer not to repeat."

"You saw it this time? With your eyes and not your mind?" Luke asked.

"Yes, I saw the abomination," Father D said.

"I call him the burned man … I've seen him many times but not lately," Luke said.

"You've seen both spirits? Interesting, anything else?"

Father, listen to this. Several months ago, I dreamed I was driving a car down a long road hitting mailboxes, a light pole, a rock, and finally, a tree. I was coughing blood while pulling myself from the car. I walked up to this white house and banged on the door repeatedly. A woman looked through the window and ignored me."

"Your house used to be painted white. One prior owner painted over the brick years ago. Another owner must have removed the white paint. I think it looks better," Father D said.

"That accident was at my house, and it was Kyle Campbell. The knocking, the banging on the door. It's him, but he's in our house. How did he get stuck in the house, and why is he so angry? Why doesn't he cross over?" Luke asked.

"He's trapped. Something is holding him in your house."

He felt agitated but strong, realizing the battle must be won. "What can we do?"

"I blessed the house already, Luke. It can be exorcised, but your parents would need to agree."

"Who can do that, exorcise a house?"

The priest leaned back in his chair, visibly tense. "I've been an exorcist for many years for the Vatican, amongst other duties. I would need to seek approval."

Luke contemplated his next move and whether his parents would support him. "Can we talk with my parents?"

"It would be part of the process. It's their home."

"Thanks, Father. Maybe we can do it after Sunday mass," Luke said.

"One more thing. When we started speaking, you seemed bothered by the reference to a chosen one. Why was that?"

"One dilemma at a time, Father."

"I will leave that up to you." Father D made the sign of the cross. "We should meet soon, Luke."

"Yes, Father. Thanks for listening to me," he said. As he left the church, he felt content that he was headed in the correct direction to help solve his family's problems. *I should have told him the whole truth,* he thought.

CHAPTER TWENTY-SIX

The Campbell Family

It was a dark and smoky night in the Argonne Forest. I crawled through the cold mud riddled with roots from upended and destroyed trees. I was trying to reach a fortification of the Germans. I preferred to be doing this as a sapper instead of the idleness I endured waiting for an attack or digging holes and trenches. As a teenager in Northern Virginia, I spent most of my time working on the family farm. Once I turned seventeen, I worked in a local mine until the war broke out. I was strong as an ox and crazy brave. I had been in several battles since my first in Cantigny.

I had sat compliantly with the rest of my unit, digging trenches, or undermining German fortifications as my typical rut. My current goal was simply to undermine twenty feet of wall with the correct placement of explosives. Once I reached the target, I commenced placing the explosives as quietly as possible. I stopped when I heard soldiers speaking in German. Sentries were watching out for allied shenanigans as I was attempting. It was my idea to place TNT in the German defensive line to try and undermine their trenches. The explosion would create a gap they could send troops through. I set the last device and connected them. I turned slowly and began moving back toward my trench. I released the wire from the spool as I moved back to the allied lines, peering as I moved toward my goal. A tall pole with his hat tied to the top. I placed it there as a beacon to strive to return to. I saw it. It brought me comfort to know that my hat waited for me. That was enough of a marker to aim for. I moved with a smile. A successfully orchestrated mission always raised my heart rate and spirits.

Everything became bright, like it was daytime. It was a flare. It would have been terrible if I was spotted by the Germans in the open. This flare came from the Allied side. The Germans were yelling from behind me. I peered back and saw a soldier motioning toward me. I turned and crawled quicker, almost on all fours. Gunfire erupted violently from the German trench, then from the Allied side. Some of it was directed toward me. I dropped the spool of wire while scampering away from the German line. I turned to grab the spool and felt a snap on my leg as if I was slapped. It burned but he kept a tight on the spool. I kept moving faster through the pain. Yells from the allied soldiers charging out of their trenches and advancing stupidly toward where I had just placed the explosives. I raised my hand in the air, trying to tell them to stop, and then part of my hand vanished in a spray of blood. I turned and sat up in reflex and grabbed what remained of my hand.

I was ten feet away from the blasting machine. The plunger was clearly visible. I ran carelessly and threw myself at it, placing the wires into the terminals while staring back to the German line. One of my hands was practically worthless. I pushed the plunger downward. The blast threw me violently in the air backward toward the Allied trenches. A piece of metal was embedded in my chest …

Luke woke up, grabbing his chest. He pulled at the metal, but his fingers were missing. He laid back in bed, trying to convince himself it was a dream. He peered down at the metal protruding from his chest, oozing with blood. A sharp, aching pain came from his left thigh. He reached down blindly with his other hand and felt a hole. He pushed his finger into the hole and shot back up in bed.

"Luke, it is over," Sebastian said, kneeling beside him with his gloved hand on Luke's chest. Tony stared at them oddly several times before jumping off the bed.

"What was that, Sebastian? I have no idea who I was," Luke said, massaging his chest.

"I don't know, but it is important. I think it is somebody you will meet soon."

He immediately decided to go for a run. A half-hour into it, he came across the Campbell Farms sign. A large barn was visible in the distance. The Campbell family was a mystery, but he thought the dream may have something to do with them. He returned to the house and arrived a little after six o'clock, crossing paths with Kamila, who was visiting.

"You run early. I'm only getting started," Kamila said.

"I had trouble sleeping," he said.

Kamila placed her headphones over her ears. "Take a shower. You smell like you're melting."

Later in his day at school, he tried to decipher his dream. He was coming to terms with the fact that the message would be delivered in God's time.

"Do you have time to get some coffee, Luke?" Benji asked.

"No, I arranged to have a meeting with Lulu McCray. She was the real estate agent that sold my parents the house. Do you want to come?" Luke asked.

"I know who she is. She'll have coffee," Benji said.

"Follow me if you don't know where her office is."

"Let's see who gets there first," Benji said.

"I don't want to get a ticket or cause an accident," Luke said worried.

"You must learn how to drive that bad boy, Luke," Benji said relaxed, thinking that his friend was not up to a little race.

"Last one there is a rotten egg." Luke jumped in his car, leaving a plume of smoke for Benji to negotiate. Benji quickly began to catch up to him after zooming through the smoke like a soldier running through a fog in battle. He pressed down on the accelerator and flew forward. Benji started catching up to him at the intersection, where he sat at the red light, waiting to make a right-hand turn. Benji turned into a bank's entrance and disappeared behind a building. Several minutes later, he arrived at the real estate office to find Benji leaning against his car, looking at his watch. "You didn't cheat, but it sure felt like you did," Luke said, annoyed at his friend.

"True, knowing how to drive helps a little, though," Benji said, holding his fists on a phantom steering wheel.

He laughed but grabbed Benji's hand and squeezed it.

Benji squealed in pain. "Easy, tough guy. I need my hand for work and eating."

"Don't be a baby. Come on. We are running a little late." Lulu's office was one of many within a business complex. They walked into her front door, causing a door chime to ring. Lulu walked out of the office and greeted them.

"Hello, Luke ... hello, Benji. You didn't tell me you were bringing in the family mechanic. Are you two looking to buy a house? Great investment homes are available in town," Lulu said.

"I wanted to ask you some questions," he answered.

"Wait a sec, Luke. I may want a flat in the older part of town." Benji cannot help but be sarcastic.

"Benji, please cut it out," Luke said, elbowing Benji on his side.

Benji gasped. "Maybe later, Lulu."

"Come to my conference room where we can sit and talk." They followed Lulu into her conference room. "Would either of you like a coffee or a soda?"

"I'll have a coffee, Lulu. I'll serve myself." Benji moved toward the coffee pot and served himself coffee with cream and lots of sugar. "Do you want one?" Benji asked.

"Sure, cream no sugar."

"How do you and your brothers like the area?" Lulu asked, watching Benji pour way to much sugar into his coffee.

"We like the area, but Daniel is already looking at colleges on the west coast," Luke said.

"You are coming to that age where you need to leave the safety of home. How can I help you?" Lulu asked.

Luke hesitated, although he had previously gamed out what to speak to Lulu about. He decided to take the most delicate route possible. He wanted information but thought he could also trigger her to call his parents or could upset her when it concerned her uncle. "Lulu, we have had some issues with the house, and I wanted to ask you some questions to see if you can help."

"Issues … do you mean problems? Your parents have not said anything. You've been in the house for months." Lulu appeared defensive.

Luke held up his hand, trying to reduce the impact of what he said, hoping to keep Lulu talking. "My parents would not ask you about the kind of problems we have," Luke said.

"Lulu, the house is haunted, and we need to know if you know anything that may have happened there." Benji blurted out while serving Luke his cup of coffee.

"I understand now." Lulu stood up and placed her index finger to her face as if in thoughtful silence, turning to look at them. "The house had some problems. I used to manage the house rentals for the Hollowell Trust. The last family in the house abandoned it and their belongings, as you know. Nobody would go back to clean it. The Hollowell's left it that way for almost a year."

"What kind of problems, Lulu?" Luke asked.

She sat back down and grabbed a pad of paper, doodling nervously. "The family members claimed the house was haunted and that spirits terrorized them. Doors randomly opened and closed on their own, banging on the walls, and even the kids were attacked in bed the night they escaped."

"Why didn't you warn us, Lulu?" he asked, allowing his anger to flow thinking he was in the right.

She looked concerned and covered her face with her hands. "Your parents got the house for a bargain. They paid way below market value. Less than a year later, it's worth a small fortune with all the work you all put into the house," she said behind her hands.

"It may be worth more now, but how can we sell the place if it's haunted?" Luke asked.

Lulu covered her face and sat back down. "I told your parents. They knew the prior renters claimed the house was haunted."

This stunned him deeply. His parents knew and said nothing.

"I heard you tell my parents that the prior renters left the house, but not because it was haunted." They also made money from what the renters left behind in the house. He needed to have a serious conversation with his parents next.

"The renters were trying to get away with not paying their rent for over six months. The last I heard they took off to Canada. I had some early complaints, and their phone was disconnected towards the end. They would not answer their door or any correspondence."

"Lulu, I'm trying to find out what happened before in the house. By looking at the past. We can figure out what is going on now?" Luke asked.

"I can try, Luke. I have lived in Lansburg all my life," Lulu said.

"Do you know if anybody has died in the house?" he asked.

Lulu paused and looked up and to her right. "Let me think about this ... I recall a sick young man in his twenties. It was the Bridger family. They owned the home for more than ten years. One of the sons was sick and had home hospice care. He passed away in the second-floor bathroom tub."

"Do you know when Lulu?" He looked for his notes and found that Bridger owned the house between 1964 and 1980.

"I'm not sure. Late 70's, maybe? He was a nice young man, handsome. His parents loved him dearly. Now that I recall, his nurse doted after him."

"Do you recall her name? Did you know her personally?" he asked.

"Her name was Andrea Walker. I knew her, but I'm sorry to say she's gone. It was ruled an accidental overdose. She became addicted to drugs and drinking. Much of it while the Bridger boy was sick ... it came to me the boy's name was Nathan."

He wrote down the name but thought Nathan's spirit was not in the house. "Where did the nurse die?"

Lulu's face turned white. "She was found in her car on the road overlooking the backyard of your house." She seemed worried about her response and placed her hand over her eyes as if averting the sun.

"She must be the nurse who attacked your grandfather in Daniel's room." Benji was paying attention to the conversation and nursing his coffee.

"You've seen a nurse in the house?" Lulu asked.

"Not only a nurse. I need to show you a picture." He took Father D's photo and placed it before Lulu.

Tears began to fall freely down her face. "I'm sorry for being emotional ... that's my family. This is my cousin, Kyle. He died in a car accident in January of 1963, I think. Kyle was always good to me, and I loved him very much."

"Where did he die, Lulu?" Luke asked.

"I think you already know that Kyle died behind your house ... do you think he is haunting your home?" Lulu's voice cracked as she looked away from him.

"I do, but why would he, Lulu? Why doesn't he move on?" he asked, pointing at the picture.

"Kyle was distraught, Luke. He had a terrible relationship with our grandfather. He drank constantly, and his wife left him before this photo was taken. My grandfather wanted him to have a son, an heir to the Campbell name. His ex-wife kept his son from him and even gave the boy the new husband's last name." She looked at the picture somberly. "This is me, my brother, my mother, and this man with the priest is my grandfather, Archie Campbell."

"So, does your grandfather have an heir?"

She stood again, looking defiantly at him as if he had dug too deep. "My McCray name is by marriage, and my maiden name is Brown, from my father. I'm a Campbell through my mother, but not enough of a Campbell to appease my grandfather. Kyle's son would be his heir, but my grandfather discounted that years ago because he did not carry his name." Lulu's reddened, flushed face appeared as if it was ready to burst.

"Thank you for your help, Lulu. I feel like I overstepped,

mistreated you somehow."

She sat silently and dabbed her eyes with a handkerchief from her purse. "Don't feel that way. I'm sorry you and your family are going through this. Please let me know if I can help somehow."

He stood up, prepared to leave. "One other thing, Lulu. A family named Bolling lived in the house in 1960, right after the Dodge family."

"The missing boy. I didn't know they lived in that house."

"They did, but the kid went missing in Maryland."

"I cannot help you with that, Luke. I'm sorry," Lulu said.

"Much appreciated. We will let you get back to work."

"Thanks, Lulu. About those flats …" Benji said.

"Come on, Benji. You need to head to work." He grabbed Benji and pulled him to the door. Once they stepped out, Benji headed toward his car. "Thanks for coming. That was productive, but I am still at a loss for what's next."

"You made headway in there, but you're missing something. Why would the spirits still be in the house?" Benji asked.

"Why are they still there?" he asked himself. He stopped in his tracks and started thinking.

"What is it, Luke?" Benji asked.

"It's the boy, the boy in the cave. I've seen a little kid in the house. I think he's the key or at least my next step," Luke said, thinking he was close to solving the problem.

"You'll figure it out," Benji said and laughed as his engine began to roar and the Plymouth *Fury's* rear tires began to spin in place. A cloud of smoke built around the rear of the vehicle as it propelled forward with the engine once again going quiet. "See you later big guy."

Funny guy, but I may have deserved that one. As he motioned the smoke away, he ran back to his car for clean air. He realized he had to drive toward a resolution to the problem but knew he would need help from a higher power. He needed to speak with Father D, again. Praying wouldn't hurt either.

CHAPTER TWENTY-SEVEN

It's Still Here

During his lengthy run, Luke basked in the peace radiating from the trails. After several miles, he approached a cutoff where he could either head back toward Red Hill Road or run further and add another couple of miles to his run. He turned quickly off the trail and headed home. As he stepped on the narrow sidewalk covered by overgrown grass, he noticed his father drive past him in his government vehicle. Luke immediately launched forward at a gallop, trying to catch up to his father, and nearly arrived at the front door the same time as his father got out of his G-ride. He stopped and took several deep breaths as his father walked to him.

"I would hug you, but I wasn't planning on showering tonight," his father said, opening the unlocked front door.

"Funny, Dad … we can hug after I shower," Luke whispered. He calmed quickly when he remembered that his father was not a hugger.

When they entered the house, the tension was palpable. His mother and Junior were in the living room with Kamila, who stayed with the family while managing a psychic and paranormal fair.

"Lots of banging on the back door now," Junior said. For emphasis, something banged on the rear windows repeatedly.

"What the hell?" His father unholstered his revolver and moved quickly onto the deck. He looked around before placing his gun back into his holster. He returned to the living room.

"There's nobody out there, Angel," his mother said.

"How long has this been going on?"

"For the past twenty minutes, Dad," Junior said.

Their father walked up to Junior and grabbed his chin. "What's that on your face? Were you in a fight?"

"No, Dad, I was working on the guest room in the hallway, and something whispered in my ear and shoved me into the wall."

"Seriously, what did it say?" his father asked.

Junior hesitated and looked at Kamila, who had stopped praying. "Tell him, Junior. He needs to know since he is such a skeptic," Kamila said.

"It asked me where its comics and *vinyls* were. I think it meant the record albums ... then it said, then it said ..." Junior lowered his head, ashamed.

"Tell him, Junior, he needs to hear this." Kamila said, holding her hands to her hips.

"It said you're mine before shoving me into the wall. I could not move." Junior was shaking and holding himself tightly while rocking.

"I'm sorry you think that happened to you, Junior ... that sounded terrible," his father backed off, holding the side of his head.

"Skeptical, Dad? I spoke with Lulu. She told me both of you knew the house was haunted." Luke blurted out, angered.

"I don't recall that, Luke," his father said.

"Angel, Lulu told us the renters claimed the house was haunted. Listen and help us. We've told you everything that's happened." His mother's frustration with his father was at its peak.

"I know something is wrong, but this makes no sense. Father D blessed the house. It's been quiet since then."

"Maybe it never left. It's back now. I think it's angry at Junior because of the construction and everything you all found," Kamila said.

"Do you feel anything?" Luke knew that his godmother was sensitive to the supernatural.

"Well, I feel it's an immature child, but I also feel the rage of an adult." Kamila tried to take hold of Luke's hand. The house was struck by what felt like a strong earthquake, but it stopped quickly.

Luke steadied himself but almost fell. They all congregated around the sofa. Luke's mother stood up and ran to the kitchen. She returned holding a prayer card. That she handed to his father. "Read this," she said.

His father read the prayer card, and a quiet descended on the house. Luke felt a burning sensation on the back of his neck. He looked toward the front door, and the burned man stood beside Kyle Campbell. They both shimmered in gaseous smoke.

Sebastian appeared and walked toward the two spirits and pointed his halberd at them prepared to strike. The spirits dissipated and shot upstairs in a streak of red light.

"It's gone for now, Angel," Kamila said, correctly.

Luke was surprised at Kamila's timing with the spirits being chased away. It was a useful intuition for the battles ahead.

"What's for dinner, Mom?" Daniel asked as if nothing had happened. They all walked into the dining room except for Kamila and Luke.

He knelt next to his godmother. "Kamila, can we call the Curandera and ask her for advice?" Luke asked although he wanted to tell her what he knew.

"She may have some ideas and thoughts. The problem is your father. He accepted her help all those years ago, but he may not appreciate having her involved now," Kamila said.

"My father seems out of touch with what is going on. All he thinks about is work, not what's happening here." Luke bowed his head, disappointed.

"It's something else, Luke. I think the house itself is blinding your father."

"I want to help and resolve this before something terrible happens. I feel that this is building into something we cannot stop." Luke struck with one hand, shoving his fist into his palm.

"I don't want anything terrible to happen. I'll give you Isidora's number," Kamila said.

"Thanks, Titi."

She wrote the name and phone number down on a page from her planner. "She prefers to speak Spanish but does understand English," Kamila said, handing him the sheet. Tell her that Poder gave you the number. She's always liked my name."

Luke stared at the phone number and simply nodded. He thought he could help the ghosts leave the home if he had the correct guidance.

✝ ✝ ✝

Dialing for Help

Later that evening, Luke planned everything, or so he thought. He set his alarm for three in the morning and placed a piece of paper with the information near his alarm clock. Luke read a book until he fell asleep.

The alarm clock startled him, but he was not fully awake. He sat in bed, confused.

Sebastian appeared on his office chair and pointed at the paper. "You need to call the curandera, Isidora. Remember?"

Luke grabbed the paper and collected his thoughts. *What did I need to remember?* It was eating at him. *I'm missing something.* He had to take control of this situation and call the curandera. He held onto the phone receiver, took a deep breath, and dialed. It only rang once.

"Hello, Luke. How are you?" Isidora Puente answered in Spanish.

Luke was taken aback and dropped the speech he had planned. "Did Kamila Poder tell you I was calling?"

"No, she didn't. We don't have much time. You can do this.

You have God on your side and the ability to help your family."
Isidora spoke English with a heavy accent.

Somebody picked up the phone receiver. "Who's using the
phone so late at night?" It was his father.

Luke was stunned but not surprised. His parent's antique
rotary phone made audible tones if any other phone line
connected to the line dialed out. Fear overcame him, and he
didn't answer his father.

"Angel, this is Isidora Puente. I helped you many years ago
with your son. You need help again."

"Who called you, Isidora? I don't believe in this stuff," his
father voiced, ignoring the curandera altogether.

Luke mustered up the courage he needed. "Dad, I'm sorry I
woke you … I needed to ask her for advice."

"This is Kamila. I cannot believe she would do this … Luke,
come downstairs now," his father hung up.

"Sorry, Mrs. Puente. I shouldn't have called," he said weakly.

"You can do this, Luke. The priest that looks like a boxer can
help you." The phone line produced a sharp sound of static before
the line disconnected. When he hung up the phone, he winced in
pain, realizing that he was about to get his ass kicked. He walked
down his hallway as if being led to the gallows. His father rushed
out of the bedroom.

"What were you thinking, calling that woman?" his father
asked while tying his robe.

Luke's mother followed his father out of the room. "Angel,
wait. Angel, please don't wake Kamila." His mother grabbed his
father's arm forcibly. Causing him to grimace in pain.

His father appeared to be trying to suppress his anger.
"Downstairs, now." His father made a fist in front of Luke and
somehow appeared to be squeezing the life out of something and
tossing it away.

Luke understood the symbolism. His father mimicked,
squashing him like a bug and tossing him to the floor.

They all sat calmly at the dining room table, looking at one another as if prepared for a gunfight, but his mother broke the silence.

"You have missed much of what has happened in the house, Angel. It has been intolerable. It has attacked Junior three times," she said, holding up three fingers. She began to stab them toward his father's chest. "Luke is trying to help."

His father looked at him with a softened gaze. "Attacked how? When?"

"It attacked Junior in Luke's room and put him into shock. I had to snap him out of it and thought we would have to take him to an emergency room. Not to mention what happened yesterday. The other time, he was working on the dining room here, and his hands were burned in the cave, as they call it."

"His hands were burned … what happened yesterday?" his father asked ignorantly.

"The spirit attacked Junior yesterday and told him that Junior belonged to him," Luke said.

"Yesterday, nothing happened yesterday," his father said, confused.

"Honey, it just happened yesterday. Junior has a bruise on his face from this thing!" His mother seemed about ready to pop in anger herself.

"There is something in this house, and the blessing was not enough. I'm trying to help, Dad, but something is closing your eyes and mind."

"Why haven't I been told?" his father asked, grabbing his head as if in pain. He doubled over onto his knees and began to shriek. It was disturbing.

"Dad, are you okay?" Luke knelt beside his father and grabbed him protectively around his shoulders … *I fell backward into darkness staring at a goat. A goat's head, to be exact. It stared at me while chewing on gray matter, which sloppily slipped down its hairy chin. It kept chewing, moving downward through a rupture in my father's skull, ate more of his brains, and continued chewing hungrily.*

"I see what you are doing. Get away from my father you asshole," I

yelled, trying to reach the goat's head.

It moved backward and out of reach, but it stopped chewing. It transformed into what appeared to be countless folds of flesh, breathing an angry mist. This was no ghost; it was the demon, and I felt an urge to destroy it. I lunged at it, knowing that if I could grab hold of it, it could be destroyed … although not quite himself he helped his father stand up.

"What was that, Luke?" his father asked, massaging his temples. His mother grabbed at his father and helped him to the sofa.

"A demon, Dad. It was a demon. It's not a ghost," Luke said.

His mother hugged his father and broke down crying in his arms. She reached out toward Luke, beckoning him to join them. He did reluctantly, but once he joined them, he felt happy, but still let out a tear. He did not drift off into a vision for which he was thankful.

"Tell me everything," his father said with confidence.

Luke now realized he had a formidable partner to help him through this fight. Sebastian stood beside them and shrugged as if trying to point out that he already had a partner. Luke gave Sebastian a thumbs up. He was building a team to destroy this demon, and he knew it was afraid of him.

CHAPTER TWENTY-EIGHT

Coming Clean

The botched phone call with Isidora was unfortunate and it threatened Luke's relationship with his godmother. The result was positive because his father's blindness to the spiritual attack was lifted, and he was now prepared to face what plagued them in the house.

Earlier, Luke had difficulty concentrating at school and oddly found himself at the church seeking Father D's advice. Parishioners were lighting candles and praying. He walked past Father Lee who let out a sigh. The priest briskly walked away and accidentally collided with Deacon Robert. The priest silently scampered away without trying to help the deacon off the floor.

Luke ran toward the man. "Deacon, are you okay?" he asked, reaching out to the deacon, and grabbing his hand, everything went black ... *"It is the Lord himself who has the power over this Demon devouring the soul of this young man," Father D told the deacon. "The demon's name is what it is, but God and his instruments have the power to bring this abomination to its knees."*

"Yes, Father ... I just thought we could control the demon if we knew its name," Deacon Robert said. The man sitting between the priests appeared battered with slime oozing down his face.

"This isn't a movie, Robert. This thing is a deceiver, and we have the power from above to drive it from this man. We need to erode it down, so it does not destroy the body along with the soul," Father D thundered ... Luke almost let go of the deacon's hand but instead pulled him up. He felt nausea but weathered it well. He realized he witnessed an exorcism and understood immediately that instead

of cryptically seeking guidance from Father D he would tell him the truth.

"Thanks, Luke. Father Lee must be in a hurry," Deacon Robert said, dusting himself off.

"I think that he was shocked to see me, Deacon ... something about my house scared the man," Luke said staring down the hallway where the priest had run off. "I understand the feeling." Luke let out a sigh. "Deacon, would it be possible to see Father D today?"

"Luke, he is really busy this time of the month." Deacon Robert paused and turned his head. "Follow me and I will check."

Luke followed the Deacon toward Father D's office. The Deacon knocked on the door and stepped inside.

Sebastian stood beside Luke. "You're going to tell him about your gifts?"

"I don't agree that this is a gift, Sebastian. but yes, I need to come clean to Father D," Luke said.

"It's your decision Luke, but I suggest caution. He may tell your parents and it will only assist what afflicts your home," Sebastian said.

Luke stared at Sebastian sternly. "I know now that this is the right move ... counsel me while I speak to the priest if you must."

Deacon Robert opened the door and motioned for Luke to enter. He stepped inside to the office near the bookshelves and conference table. The deacon was about to step out of the office. "Deacon, could you stay, please?"

"Of course, Luke," Deacon Robert said, stepping back into the room.

Luke walked toward the priest who sat in front of a stack of ledgers and books. Father D was buried in paperwork. The priest motioned for him to sit down, which he did, and stared at the painting of *Archangel Michael Vanquishing Satan*.

"Luke, tell him," Sebastian said.

"Father, I need your help to get rid of it," Luke said.

Father D continued writing in a ledger and looking at

paperwork in front of him. "Are you ready to tell me the rest of your story?"

Luke peered at Deacon Robert and then at Sebastian who motioned his head down in affirmation. "This may sound crazy, but a Spanish soldier is standing right here," he pointed at Sebastian. "He's my guardian and is trying to help with what's drowning us out of our house."

The priest dropped his pen and looked at the empty space where Luke pointed. Father D looked at the deacon and back at the space. "Who does the soldier say he is? Is he a guardian angel?" Father D asked.

"No, he claims an angel named Miguel sent him to help my family. His name is Sebastian Sanz-Basque and he's a soldier and my ancestor who died in 1655 in the Dominican Republic."

Father D wrote the name and date on a notepad then stood up and walked from behind his desk to the chair next to Luke. "Have you told your parents this?"

"No, father … they cannot know this. I wasn't sure I could tell you until I saw you and the deacon involved in an exorcism last year," Luke said looking to Sebastian for strength.

"Keep talking … the priest believes you," Sebastian said walking back toward a coat rack and staring at the priest's violet stole hanging on one of the hooks.

"You know I'm an exorcist … what does this have to do with the guardian?" Father D asked.

Luke tried to place everything into perspective. "I was born with the ability to see visions or dreams of the past and future, but I cannot control what I see."

"This is all hard to take in," Father D said.

"It's the story, *The Protector and the Guardian*," Deacon Robert said.

"Robert, please," Father D said motioning for the deacon to stop speaking. The priest lowered his head and stared at the floor. It was obvious the priest did not want to talk about what the deacon brought up.

"Luke, come over here," Sebastian said pointing at a pin that Father D had on the stole. The pin had two keys and a crown over a purple background. "Look at the symbol on his stole, and then look at the symbols on my armor and helmet."

"It's the same, Sebastian?" he spoke out loud without concern.

"Say Santa Alleanza, Luke!" Sebastian roared.

"What does Santa Alleanza mean?" Luke was confused because he had no idea what language that was or what it meant.

"Tell him, Luke. Say Santa Alleanza now!"

"Santa Alleanza ... I said it okay," Luke yelled.

"Don't talk about such things," Father D walked toward Luke but motioned for the deacon to leave them.

"Father, he needs to hear this," Luke said.

"He's not ready for this, Luke ... he's not a priest and prohibited from knowing this ancient information."

Luke did not know why, but he knew with certainty that the deacon had to hear this conversation. "He must be here, Father. That I know for sure."

Father D motioned for the deacon to get closer as he prepared to explain himself. "Santa Alleanza is also known as the Entity, or one aspect of the Vatican Secret Service. I am a part of it, but I work directly for the Secretary and the Holy Father ... Robert, explain what you know about the protector and the guardian."

"We are told to be on the lookout for a young man who claims he has a guardian and is here to stop some sort of a calamity," Deacon Robert said.

Luke walked toward Sebastian. "What calamity? I have not seen anything."

"You probably have, Luke. Your visions, your dreams. The closer you get to the calamity the more you will remember," Sebastian said.

"That's not an answer. What am I supposed to prevent?" Luke asked.

"I just don't know. My role is to prepare you and help you

prevent, whatever it is," Sebastian said with a bowed head.

Father D approached Luke. "A World War, maybe ... one guardian was placed on earth to prevent the assassination of Archduke Franz Ferdinand of Austria. He failed."

This alarmed Luke. Failed sounded rather ominous. "How did he fail?"

Father D shook his head not wanting to explain further.

"He died during an exorcism in Sarajevo by Eastern Orthodox priests in 1912. A year before the assassination," Deacon Robert said. "He too claimed to have a guardian at first and eventually saw the assassination and war."

This alarmed him but something was still missing. "How old was he?" Luke asked.

"Seventeen ... the boy claimed that a young teenager from his school was going to kill the emperor's heir, but nobody believed him," Deacon Robert said.

"Why didn't they believe him?" Luke asked. Everyone was silent. Even Sebastian looked away. "It's because they thought he was possessed, and crazy ... am I right?"

"We will not let that happen to you," Father D said.

I will not let that happen to me either, he thought. What bothered him most was not knowing what he was supposed to prevent and what he was meant for. For now, he needed to cleanse his home and then maybe he could find what he was supposed to stop. "What am I supposed to be protecting?"

Father D stared at Luke with a ferocious intensity. "Our Holy Father believes that the protector is meant to safeguard and defend the church itself. The protector and his ancestor, the guardian, are placed on earth at the same time to save believers."

"I cannot even stop what's happening in my house, let alone something that causes a war!" Luke said walking toward the exit.

"We will terminate this demon first," Father D said.

Luke kept walking and left the church. He contemplated that his role in life now was to die, and if the archduke protector was an example, he would die soon. Not decades from now.

✝ ✝ ✝

The Oppression of Junior

Luke came home after he visited with Father D. It was about six o'clock and he was looking forward to this all day because Alyssa had planned on stopping by in an hour so they could go for a walk and talk. He knew he should work out but instead felt like taking a nap to forget about his troubles. He did not have the time for either.

As he walked toward the entrance of the house, he saw a little boy run past the window in the third-floor hallway. He opened the door quickly and saw Junior lying on the sofa. "Hey, what's going on? You look like dog shit."

"I don't know. I was working in the garage and started feeling dizzy and barfed. Mom is making dinner, but I can't eat. Can you tell her I'm going to sleep?" Junior stood up and stumbled a bit.

Luke tried to help steady him, but Junior motioned him away, similarly to how his parents and Daniel do when he was too close. This surprised him because Junior never worried about touching him. "Fine, Junior. I will let her know." He went into the kitchen and saw his mother at the range. "Hello, Mom."

"Dinner will be ready in about half an hour. Can you let Daniel and Junior know?" she asked.

"Junior is feeling sick," Luke said.

"He didn't tell me."

"I just saw him head up. I will let Daniel know and check on Junior." Luke walked upstairs to his room but decided to go one more flight up when he heard heavy metal playing loudly in the attic. Daniel was sitting on the sofa playing a console game. "What's with the heavy metal music?"

"I don't know, Luke. I heard his door slam, and the music started blaring."

Luke knocked on Junior's door and checked the doorknob, but it was locked, so he pounded on the door. No response. He walked into the adjoining bedroom into the shared bathroom. The door was unlocked, so he opened it and saw a glowing red light emanating from what looked like red lightning. Junior was dangling from the wall, with a red electrical charge surrounding him. He ran up to his brother, grabbed his torso, and received a shock throwing him across the room into the wall. "Daniel! Daniel!" He yelled loudly, but the music was drowning his shouts. He picked up a shoe from the floor and threw it at Junior's stereo. The music shut off. He crawled out of the room after unlocking the door and pushed himself out as a red bolt of energy shot forward and struck him. He collapsed to the floor unable to move.

Daniel came running over to Luke and prepared to charge into the room. Luke grabbed Daniel's calf.

"Pick me up, Daniel," he said.

Daniel reached down and grabbed his brother, getting a shock. "What was that?" Daniel reached for him again and helped him up.

"We are going in together. We each grab a leg and pull. Count of three. One, two, three. Go," Luke said.

They both jumped into the room, grabbed Junior's legs, and were enveloped in the red electric charge. "I cannot get a good hold on him," Daniel said through chattering teeth.

They both were thrown back into the room, hitting the walls and the floor.

"Get the holy water and pray," Sebastian said, bringing hope to their dilemma.

He pushed Daniel toward the stairs, and they left the attic. "Go get Mom now!" He retrieved his rosary and a bottle of holy water from his room. Daniel ran back up the stairs from the second to the third level, and their mom was behind him. They quickly ran up the stairs to the attic as a red glow emanated from Junior's bedroom. He sprinkled holy water onto Junior. The red light dissipated but came back.

"Repeat after me, Luke. Satan, I command you to leave our presence in the name of our Lord Jesus Christ and God on high. I command you and all your demons to leave this boy alone. I bring the strength of my Lord and command you to leave now!" Sebastian slammed his halberd on the floor in emphasis. "Say it now!"

Luke repeated the declaration and sprinkled holy water on Junior. The glow from the red energy disappeared. Junior fell, striking the dresser then crumpled to the floor.

Luke ran into the room and grabbed Junior. His mother and Daniel ran in as well. "He's not breathing, Mom, he's not breathing. Call an ambulance!" They had been under siege for months, but never like this.

Their mother ran downstairs to call for help from the telephone in her room. Luke placed Junior on his side, ensuring his airway was clear.

"What are you doing?" Sebastian asked, not recognizing CPR.

"I have a pulse, which means he has circulation, but I don't think he's breathing," Luke said and then gave Junior several rescue breaths. He checked his brother for a pulse and once again felt it slightly. He placed his ear to Junior's mouth and heard him exhale. At this point, he was at a loss for what to do. *Should I begin compressions if he has a pulse, or should I continue rescue breaths?* He kept his brother on his side with one hand checking his artery and the other on his brother's chest. He felt movement but nothing major.

The doorbell rang. "Daniel, go downstairs," their mother ordered.

Fortunately, within minutes two paramedics with their equipment came running in.

One paramedic began to assess Junior, while the other sat nearby with an open first responder bag before him. "I have a pulse and breath, but it's weak ... hand me the BVM mask." The other paramedic held a manual resuscitator bag over Junior's face and began depressing it while the other placed a stretcher next to Junior. One jabbed Junior's arm with a needle. "Let's get him to the hospital immediately." They held the stretcher and moved Junior down each set of stairs.

His mother followed the paramedics outside. "Which hospital are you taking him to?"

"Lansburg, ma'am. You can come with us, though."

"Daniel, call your dad. Luke, turn off the range and then meet me at the hospital," his mother ordered. Daniel took off, presumably, to call their father. His mother boarded the ambulance with the paramedics.

This was surreal. His brother Junior was near death just as he was preparing to bring the fight to the demon in the house. His father and the priests were prepared to join the fight. It seemed like the demon attacked when their strength had grown.

"I know why you did this!" Luke thundered. "You're not getting away with it. I'm going to end you." The house shook enough to make him stumble. "That's not enough to stop me … your end is near."

"I'm only getting started … go follow your mother now and say your goodbyes to your brother who belongs to me," the demon said in that gravelly low voice.

"Don't listen to it. It's a deceiver," Sebastian said.

Luke was shocked. This abomination acted as if it was winning, and maybe it was. He was deluded into thinking he had a chance. His brother was near death and the demon was stronger than ever.

CHAPTER TWENTY-NINE

Stabilized

Luke ran downstairs to the kitchen. The meal was ruined, but the house did not burn down. *I should have let it burn down*, he thought. Daniel entered the kitchen holding the dog.

"What should I do with Tony," Daniel, said entering the kitchen.

"Give him to me," Luke said thinking that his dog would be safer in the garage than wandering in the house. "Call Dad … then meet me by my car." He placed Tony in the garage with some food.

He ran to the entrance and his mother's purse caught his eye. He grabbed it before jumping in his car.

When they entered the emergency room entrance, their mother was inside, arguing with the receptionist.

"I was already back there with my son. Why did they tell me to come out here?" his mother asked.

"Ma'am, we need information about your son. We will be right with you," The receptionist said calmly.

"Let me in now! My son and I arrived in an ambulance, and I need to be with him."

"Ma'am, I am not allowed to let you in. A doctor will come to speak with you shortly. Let them do their job stabilizing your son."

"What's this bloody ma'am *shite*? Let me back there now!"

Luke went over to his mother and gently guided her to some seats. "Mom, let's wait for Dad and have him figure it out with them."

"This bloody *galah* needs her head examined!" His mother

stared at the receptionist, who visibly winced.

He managed to laugh and looked at Daniel, nodding his head toward her knowing that Daniel could calm her down.

"Mom, if you keep acting like that, they will never let you back there. Come sit over here, please." Daniel said calmly. She began to cry when she placed her head on Daniel's chest.

He walked outside the hospital to wait for his father to arrive. He heard a siren and noticed blue and red lights flashing from his father's approaching *K-car*. He laughed at the sight of the car masking as an emergency vehicle. Only government bureaucrats would think a K car was suitable for federal agents to drive.

His father ran into the ER, forgetting to turn off his flashing lights and siren.

"Dad, the siren," he yelled with cupped hands over his mouth.

"Shut it off and park the car, Luke," his father said, tossing the keys at him while running past.

He took care of the car. When he returned, his parents were no longer in the waiting room. "Did they let them in?" he asked Daniel.

"Yes, they did ... Luke, what happened? What was that at the house?"

"Not sure, Daniel. I don't think it was a ghost. I think a demon has been oppressing us this whole time."

"It has been building up to this, Luke. Are we going to lose our little brother?" Daniel asked.

"I don't know," he said placing his head into his hands as he shrank into his knees.

"You need to get in there, Luke," Sebastian said.

"I'll be back, Daniel," he said and walked toward a window. He saw and heard an ambulance pulling into the hospital. This must be the entrance for the paramedics. He saw an exit door nearby and walked outside toward the opposite side of the ambulance, near the entrance to the trauma room. He followed the last paramedic to the door and entered the threshold before the doors closed behind him. He buried himself in a curtain and waited for the voices near him to lessen. Then, he walked down a hallway where he saw doctors working on a patient through a glass partition. A sign above the doorway said *TRAUMA #1*.

Fortunately, the paramedics went down the opposite hallway. He found a position to observe the room from the opposite empty Trauma room. He saw Junior had a bag between his legs. One of the nurses grabbed the bag and placed it below the gurney. It seemed each medical staff member spoke in unison as if they were an orchestrated chorus. His mother was frozen at the door of the trauma room. Two nurses approached her as she tried to run into the room, but they stopped her in time.

His mother saw him watching from the window and rushed toward him. "Junior's heart stopped. We lost him. We lost my baby!" She ran down the hallway screaming hysterically. Presumably, to find his father.

Several of the doctors came out of the room. "We are losing him. Find Doctor Rapha quickly ... try over in cardio." The other doctor ran off.

His knees buckled underneath him, causing him to kneel in surrender. He was prostrating himself before God, in hopes it would sustain the family through this horror. He made the sign of the cross, placing his hands in prayer. "Even though I walk through the darkest valley ..."

Sebastian knelt beside Luke laying his halberd on the floor. "The Lord sustains them on their sickbed ..."

A new doctor came running into the room with a medical case, with the mustachioed doctor tailing him. This must be Rapha. He had dark skin and appeared Middle Eastern. The other doctors working on Junior gave Rapha room as he began treating his brother.

Unexpectedly, he saw Junior standing naked near the trauma stretcher and out of his physical body. It's too late; Junior has passed away, and this was his spirit. The puzzled look on Junior's face was haunting.

Dr. Rapha was relocating some pads on Junior's chest and began working on a machine. The doctor grabbed some paddles, placed them on Junior, and yelled, "Clear."

Junior pointed at Sebastian and began to walk toward them, waving, but quickly shot back into his body as if on rewind. A mist formed and shot out and down the hall away from them.

"Your brother is a soldier and will live to fight again." Sebastian stood up. "We have work to do. We must prepare for battle, Luke." Sebastian slowly dissipated into the ether.

His father walked down the hallway toward him and helped him up. "Your mother fainted and is being treated in one of the ER rooms."

One of the doctors walked out of the room, approaching his father. "Are you Mr. Sanz?"

"Yes, I'm Junior's father. How is he?"

"We had a bit of a scare. Your son's heart stopped for a few seconds, but one of our specialists was able to resuscitate him. He's stable right now."

"Can we see him?" his father asked.

"Not yet, Mr. Sanz. We will monitor him for about an hour, then move him to the intensive care unit upstairs … you should not be here now. It's best to go to the third-floor ICU waiting room, and I will look for you in about an hour."

"Thanks for saving my son, Doctor."

Some of the doctors left the trauma room. "Doctor Rapha, can you come over here, please?" The doctor walked over to them. "Doctor Rapha, this is Mr. Sanz. He's the patient's father."

"Hello, Mr. Sanz. I'm sorry for what you and your family are suffering through."

"Thank you, Doctor Rapha, for saving my son." His father was visibly upset in a way he could not recall seeing before.

"He's stable now, but I don't want to give you false hope. Junior must be monitored, and we must pray for his quick recovery. He was out for about five minutes, and permanent damage could have occurred. Only time will tell," Doctor Rapha said.

✜ ✜ ✜

The Reaping

It watched as Luke and Daniel left the house. He typically left some of the soul behind with the carcass. That remaining fragment was how it enslaved those unwilling souls to do its bidding. It was an unfulfilled promise that they could be back in their body someday. Others like the nurse, Andrew Bolling or Kyle Campbell were so broken they would respond to all his demands.

He stood at the third-floor hallway window and waited with his tentacles fanned out. A set of headlights from a car approached the driveway leading to the front door. A young woman stepped out of the passenger side of the vehicle. It was her, Alyssa. He grew and became visible as he darted to the front door, intoxicated with what he believed to be love and lust combined. He could smell the young woman as she approached the door. The car drove off down the driveway.

The doorbell rang several times. It was Alyssa. She knocked on the door as well. The annoying dog barked from the garage.

"Luke, are you home?" She walked toward the side of the house and tried to peer through the garage window but was too short. "Hey, Tony … where's Luke?" She looked at her watch but then returned to the car.

He had to do something, but he did not want to scare Alyssa off. This was the opportunity he sought. He could take her somehow if she entered the house. The young lady was coming back to the door.

Alyssa placed a note in between the door and the frame.

He must take her now. Absorb her somehow into the home, into his realm upstairs. It was all very clear. Once she was placed into suspended animation, Luke would come looking for her. He would attack the young man and take what it wanted.

He unlocked and opened the front door. "Alyssa, I'm here," *it* called out mimicking Luke's voice.

"Luke, is that you? Where's your car?" Alyssa walked into the house naively. "Why is it so dark?"

He pounced and wrapped itself over Alyssa. He took her as it slithered upstairs into the attic into Junior's room and used his newfound energy to place her into the same portal it used to escape to earth from Hell. "Dream, Alyssa. Dream of how it will be when we are together as one and I taste from your flesh."

CHAPTER THIRTY
The Siege of Santo Domingo

I ran on a narrow muddy path amongst palm trees and other foliage. My knee was throbbing in pain. I had wrapped it earlier with a dressing before my run. I removed some of my armor but kept my short-staff halberd and short sword.

A lookout had warned the sentries at the fort that several English ships had docked near the Nizao River to the east of Bahia Ocoa. With the setting sun darkness would come and slaughter. We must push faster. I heard heavy breathing and the noise and clatter of metal armor. I was amongst many men on this path and saw an ocean ahead of me on the horizon beyond some bushes and trees. It was sweltering and humid, and I was bathed in sweat. We were attempting to reach an overlook on a path to repel the English soldiers. I saw the sail of a ship in the distance. We arrived at the crest below a wash carved out from the rains. My soldiers were positioned on higher ground surrounding the deep wash we expected the English to use as a path. It was the most accessible way to the fort.

"Silence. Silence or you will warn the English. Wait for them to get into the cut," I ordered. Once we were positioned, all I heard was heavy breathing as we tried to catch our breaths. Within moments men's voices speaking recklessly in English as they approached.

The enemy used a wash created by runoff from the hilltop all the way down to the beach. The area we chose could be used as an ambush point because it was narrow, and the overlook offered concealment in the trees and shrubs.

"Here they come. Wait until they pass the threshold and then begin striking the soldiers from above. Start with the front and the rear. Then kill all in the middle," I whispered to my lieutenant who passed my

orders to each of the men.

A large group of English soldiers entered the entrance to the cut. We are outnumbered. It was hundreds of English soldiers. My soldiers above surrounded the English, but we were no more than fifty since not all made the run down the hill. We were going to be overrun. I grasped onto my halberd tightly and stared at Ricardo and motioned with my thumb across my neck signifying kill them all. I wanted a fight to the death.

"Attack!" I reached through the brush with my halberd and stabbed a soldier in the neck, then another and another. Men screamed in English and cried out in pain. My soldiers attacked the enemy soldiers in the front who clumsily tried running for the safety of the path above. Other English soldiers who tried to retreat were struck by us from above. A large pile of corpses blocked the way back to the English ship, forcing the soldiers to create a protective circle in the middle of the path with their shields.

"Keep it up. We have blocked the Englishmen from escaping." I moved my spear back and then struck downward again. I killed countless enemies in a matter of minutes. "Attack all in the center!" We repositioned and continued to strike down each soldier, trying to leave the protective shield wall. I repositioned myself to strike into the shield wall and took out another soldier and then another.

"Cladhaire, take him out now, or we'll be slaughtered!" A voice yelled out in English from the mass of men.

A crossbow pushed through the shield wall and fired a bolt toward me, striking my unprotected neck. I lost control of my legs and fell helplessly onto my back, my leg caught up under me awkwardly.

"They hit the captain," a Spanish soldier yelled out. "The captain is down. Finish them off."

"No quarter," yelled out his lieutenant, Ricardo.

I looked upward and could see the sun. "Men, hold the door. Don't let them pass," I yelled, spraying frothy blood into the air, unsure whether I spoke loud enough. I grabbed the shaft of the bolt stuck into my neck and pulled on it, but it would not budge. It was stuck in bone. I was dying. Ongoing fighting and cheers from my men shot energy into my body, but my soul was weakening. I knew we had repelled the

English for now. I looked into the sky and saw stars, bringing me peace. The aching pain in my knee was gone. "Take me, my Lord. Please forgive me for my sins ..."

"Luke, wake up. Dude, wake up. You spilled coffee all over yourself."

Daniel was standing over Luke. Sebastian was on his other side with a gloved hand on his shoulder. He realized that he had a vision that took place in 1655 when Sebastian perished in battle. He looked down and saw coffee had spilled all over his chest and down to his crotch. "Freaking lattes, man."

"Mom mentioned you had been drinking coffee all day."

"Yes, at least I did not pee on myself." He looked around the room. "Where did Mom and Kamila go?"

"They went to the hotel to clean up, remember? Mom has a project for work."

That evening, they were planning on spending the night at their grandparents' house. They still did not have their clothes and their father was planning on making a trip to the house for them. "I remember now." Sebastian moved into the shadows in a corner of the room. "I need to go to the restroom to clean up," Luke said to Daniel but motioned for Sebastian to follow him. "Was that the day of your death?"

"Yes," Sebastian said as he followed Luke to the restroom.

Luke cleaned up the coffee the best he could and washed his hands for what seemed like an eternity. "Sorry, I was trying to wash the blood away from my vision. The dream carried through into real life."

"My understanding is that the dream travels into the real world so that you recall the message," Sebastian said.

"How many soldiers did you kill?" Luke asked.

"We killed hundreds. I don't know for sure."

"Where were you?" Luke asked.

"Hispaniola, what you call Santo Domingo now. Some jungle near Fort San Genaro. Near the Nizao River. It was April of 1655."

"You were a captain? In the Spanish Army?" Luke asked.

"Yes, my father and I led a force of 300 men from Isla de San Juan to help the governor against followers of Cromwell."

"It was so real. The smells, the exhaustion, the fear. You were afraid?"

"I was terrified. I thought my men would fall, and I feared that I would fail my father," Sebastian said.

"You died. But you died bravely with courage. It was an odd feeling. You were tired from running in your armor with your halberd. Yet, in my mind, I felt unstoppable."

"One can be afraid. Freezing would be cowardly. I had to redeem myself after killing that landowner … Luke, killing Don Roberto was bad, but I come from a family of enslavers. It's shameful, and I swore allegiance to a Cardinal who was my father's benefactor. We were to combat slavery by force if necessary." Sebastian appeared depressed somehow.

"Don Roberto was enslaving people, and you stopped him. Why were you punished by being sent to Limbo?"

"The man was conflicted somehow. Somebody in the King's court may have authorized the peonage for a percentage of the profits. At least, that is what Don Roberto claimed."

"With this dream, I could also sense your thoughts. You felt something … shame … you felt shame because you were not wearing something around your neck," Luke said, confused.

"My *Gorget*. I never liked that thing, but it may have saved me. I am not wearing all my armor ... we took some of our armor off for the run."

"You killed so many men, Sebastian. It felt so real. It troubles me still." Luke flicked his wet hands into the sink. In his mind, his hands were still drenched in blood.

"It's not a civilized world," Sebastian said.

"It is, Sebastian. There is no more killing like that here."

Sebastian shook his head in apparent disbelief. "Don't be naive. This happens throughout the world. You will see it and fight your own battles. You will spill blood."

Luke recalled one more thing. "The pain in your knee was

intense. Is that why you limp when you walk?"

"Yes, I was struck on the knee by a man with a club months before I died. It never healed properly," Sebastian said.

"I need to speak with my brother. We can talk later." He tapped Sebastian's armor with the bottom of his fist while he passed his guardian. He stopped abruptly, door in hand. "I'm scared."

"Good. You should be. This thing in your home wants your soul more than your life," Sebastian said cryptically.

"I'm afraid like you were, but I must protect my family at all costs, even if it takes my soul in the process," Luke said before walking back to Junior's room. His guardian showed him the day he died for a reason. Luke needed to be brave even if facing a fate worse than death. The loss of his family and soul.

CHAPTER THIRTY-ONE
Enlightenment

Daniel and Luke stayed overnight at their grandparents' new house that was closer to Leesburg. The house was enormous, and some construction was still going on around the property. They came in late the night before and had not seen the whole house.

Daniel stared out of the kitchen window at the construction. "Abuela, what's with the construction still happening in the back?"

"Daniel, that is between you and your grandfather," their grandmother answered cryptically.

"The hammering started at five o'clock in the morning." Luke was complaining, yawning in between guzzling his *café con leche*.

Their grandmother smirked and did not add to the conversation. Luke had been hardened lately, but he thought his grandparents would go to their graves, not seeing the divide they placed between Daniel and the lesser beings—meaning him and Junior. The way that his parents and grandparents kept him at arm's length was hurtful and he knew one day he should confront them. Luke served himself a second cup of coffee from the carafe.

"Be careful with that coffee, Luke. It's stronger than what you're used to," his grandfather said while he walked into the kitchen and kissed his wife on her cheek.

At least his grandfather spoke with him and did not ignore him like his grandmother. "I'm used to it, Grandpa. Dad makes it this way ... we woke up early with all the hammering, and I needed the boost," Luke said.

"Sorry about that, boys. I want that addition completed as soon as possible."

"Enough of that Julio, Daniel is curious about what you are building in the back of the house," she said while plating her husband's breakfast, which included some *Mallorca* bread, and *revoltillo*, or mixed eggs with green pepper and sausage.

"Grandson, give me a second," their grandfather said in Spanish as he walked into the den, returned with an engineering blueprint, and unrolled it before Daniel. "This driveway here will head to an 1,800 square foot, three-bedroom, two-bath guest house. Over here will be a landscaped area with a fenced-in pool. Julio said, pointing towards the construction. "They are pouring the concrete today for the pool and the patio."

"Is the house for household staff?" Daniel asked with curiosity.

"No, we have an apartment built into the house with a full kitchen upstairs for a housekeeper and a babysitter. We are building this house for you and Joyce to prepare for the baby."

"Really?" Daniel looked toward the construction and covered his mouth. "Thanks, Grandpa." Daniel's voice cracked a bit and melted as he should.

"You will go to college and play baseball as planned. Just not in California," their grandfather said, sipping his coffee.

Their grandmother delivered breakfast plates to his brother and grandfather while Luke served himself what remained in the kitchen. He was the third wheel in this conversation. He was happy for Daniel for many reasons, but mostly because his nephew would be in their lives.

"When Joyce is ready, we want her to help design the house interior and hire the nanny for the baby. One of the bedrooms upstairs is for the nanny," his grandmother said before she began eating breakfast. She must have planned this strategically to secure a place in her great-grandchild's life.

"I thought the babysitter was for Daniel." He smiled happily, realizing he had scored a direct hit on Daniel. He saw the frown on his grandmother's face, which brought him joy.

Daniel threw his cloth napkin at Luke. "Thanks for thinking

of us, but why do we need a nanny?"

"After speaking to your parents, we decided to make it much easier for you and Joyce to go to the university knowing that the baby is being cared for. Seeing our great-grandchild whenever we want is also purely out of self-interest." Their grandmother cried, which was unnatural for an emotionless woman.

Daniel stood up, knelt beside both grandparents and hugged them as he began to cry. Grandpa Julio grabbed onto his grandson. "Papito, let this be one of your last cries. It would be best if you toughen up for your son. That means being your own man and succeeding in all you do. We built a foundation for you, but in a short time, you will stand and be the man your father raised," his grandfather said, grabbing Daniel's face. "Do you understand me?" his grandfather asked in Spanish.

"Yes, Grandpa. I understand, and thanks for everything."

Daniel stood and looked at his younger brother. "We need to go to school." His brother wiped away his tears and appeared to change into his war face.

Luke took one last bite of the eggs and drank the rest of his coffee. "Finish your breakfast, Daniel. I need to go to the bathroom before we take off." He waved at his grandfather and looked away when he saw his grandmother looking sharply at him. He brought that on himself by pushing her buttons. In truth, he made sure that Daniel and Joyce were going to keep the baby, and his grandmother was oblivious that he made sure she had a great-grandchild to spoil.

He started his morning angrily and grew angrier when he saw that Alyssa was not in art class. He sat drawing but was thinking of Alyssa.

"Luke, can you come with me, please." Principal Devry stood in the middle of the class with Mr. Aames.

Luke stood up and gathered his belongings. He looked toward Benji.

"What gives?" Benji asked.

Luke shrugged, perplexed. Once he was in the hallway with

the teacher, he saw Sebastian following behind him.

"Be careful what you say from now on," Sebastian said cautiously.

Luke shook his head in ignorance. "What's going on, Mr. Devry."

"Some officers want to speak with you. Your father is here."

"Okay, Mr. Devry." He entered the principal's office to find three serious-looking men wearing business attire. One of them was his father, and he looked unhappy.

"Dad, what's going on?" Luke asked.

"These detectives claim that Alyssa did not come home last night," his father said.

"Mr. Sanz, if you don't mind, we would like to speak with your son in private," a detective who looked like a linebacker in a sports coat said.

"Not going to happen, gentlemen. I stay, or we both go."

The thinner detective leaned in toward the linebacker. "That will not be necessary, Mr. Sanz. Luke, Alyssa's friend Birdy, claimed she dropped her off at your home at about 8 o'clock last night. Does that sound right?"

"That could not have ..."

"Mr. Sanz, please let Luke answer," the linebacker said.

Luke immediately recalled that Alyssa was coming over to talk the previous night. He completely forgot because of what happened to Junior. "My brother was taken to the hospital a little after six o'clock last night ... none of us have been home since it happened."

"What happened?" the thinner detective asked.

Luke looked at his father and shook his head in disbelief. "We live in a haunted house. Whatever was in the house attacked my brother and sent him to the hospital. Have you been to our house?"

"We'll be asking the questions here, fella." The linebacker remarked.

"Luke, go back to class," his father said before motioning to the detectives. "We'll go to the house together and you can conduct a search," his father said to the detectives.

Luke knew he should do as his father said and stood up. "Please find Alyssa," he said and took off. The only thing Luke wanted to do at that moment was go directly to the house to search for Alyssa, but he knew it would only cause static because his father would be there. He was still a kid and not an action hero who could come and go as he pleased. Sebastian formed before him in the hallway.

"Where's Alyssa?" he asked Sebastian.

"I don't know. I'm blind to it." Sebastian began to flicker as if trying to dissipate.

"What's happening?"

"I enter your house. Something is keeping me away," Sebastian said.

"What do I do? My father told me to go to class, and he does not want us anywhere near the house."

"Respect your father's wishes ... I will try to see what is happening." Sebastian dissipated into the ether, and with him, hope that all would go well.

☩ ☩ ☩

Retribution

The father of the house, Angel, was near. The man's car was in the driveway. He was not alone. Several men stood near Angel. He could tell they were police officers. Angel approached the home; *it* grew angered at him. This man limited his reach into the house and the family. The man's ability to block the weights he had placed on his mind aggravated him. Angel had a strong soul, but it was weathered from the attacks over these past few months.

Angel entered the house and reached for a purse on the foyer's floor. It belonged to the lovely Alyssa, and Angel could not be allowed to see that, not now. He had not thought it all through as he had thought.

Angel placed the purse inside the drawer of a console table in the foyer. "Tony, where are you?" The dog barked from the garage. Angel let Tony into the house, and the dog ran out the front door. Angel ran back out. "Guys, can you please get that dog?"

"Sure, Mr. Sanz," said the thinner cop.

Angel walked back to the purse and removed the wallet. He stared intensely at the driver's license. "Alyssa Mars?" Angel asked.

"I'm up here, Mr. Sanz. Help me," he projected the voice of Alyssa in Daniel's room.

Angel dropped the purse and ran upstairs chasing the disembodied voice.

There was no better time for this. Angel had to be dispatched. It would take the man's soul and let the body degrade and die. It sent the nurse this time. She could compel this man to drop his guard.

"Angel, are you home?" Helen's voice spoke now.

Angel rushed into Daniel's bedroom. "Alyssa, Helen?"

It forced the nurse to project herself in Daniel's bathroom.

The bathroom door slammed open against the bathtub. The nurse dressed all in white ran out with her hands raised towards Angel. The spirit collided with him, throwing him backward into the wall with such force he broke through the drywall, splitting one of the wall studs in two. A blood trail dripped down the wall as the man fell to the floor. He stood over Angel and began to drain the rest of his essence. A red plume of energy formed around Angel. This would not take long.

The detectives rushed into the house. "Mr. Sanz where are you?" the thinner man asked.

The linebacker ran into the room, where Angel sat in between the studs. "What in God's name is that?" The man dropped a piece of paper onto the floor. It was Alyssa's note to Luke proving she missed him at the house the day before.

The other detective entered the room. *It* had to stop; if he kept going, he would cause even more people to invade the house. Before he knew it, a team of law enforcement officers would land in the home as *it* had seen before. That would interfere with his plan. He forced himself to stop and flowed into the bathroom.

The man stood over Angel, checking for a pulse. "Call an ambulance. He has a pretty bad head injury."

"What was that red light?"

"I don't know. He probably got an electrical shock. Go, call a bus quickly. Mr. Sanz, wake up."

He shot upward into the attic and called for the burned man. He needed the rest of Angel's soul. He believed his plan to be intact. Luke, the boy must return to the home so he can finish his transformation into the corporeal so he could be able to lay with Alyssa. It was working and he would be successful.

CHAPTER THIRTY-TWO

Blinders Off

Luke stared into his food during lunch. Alyssa was missing. Her friends sat at their table away from them. Birdy stared at him but did not attempt to confront him.

"Go talk to her," Benji said.

"I don't know what to say." Luke moved his food tray away from him.

"Tell them the truth … after Claire, they'll believe you."

Luke realized Benji was correct. He had to tell them what happened. "Bring them outside," he said, walking out to the quad.

Benji and all the girls came out toward Luke, but only Birdy walked right up to him.

"Where is she, Luke? Don't bullshit me and tell me you have no idea. I dropped her off at your house myself," Birdy said with her hands on her hips.

"I wasn't home, Birdy. My brother was attacked by a spirit that has been infesting our house," Luke said.

Birdy motioned for the rest of the crew to come up to her. "Tell us what happened now," Birdy ordered.

"Ever since we moved into the house, some spirits have slowly attacked us. One of them is this burned man. That night, it attacked my brother, and now he's in a coma. I was supposed to meet with Alyssa last night but a few hours before you dropped her off, I was at the hospital." Luke did not take a breath once during that statement.

"Bullshit, where's our friend, Luke? Did you hurt her?" Birdy spoke gently but then poked him hard in the chest.

Not now, he thought … *Birdy and Benji were yelling at one another. Birdy had a baby in her arms and appeared to be pregnant. "I don't want him in my house, Benji. Not ever."*

"Birdy, please stop. The police never charged him. He's a good guy. He has nobody in his life after Alyssa disappeared and his father and brother died," Benji pleaded to his wife.

"So what … so what, you stupid man. He killed my friend. I loved her, don't you get it? We were supposed to be friends for the rest of our days." Birdy placed her baby into a highchair. *"I'll leave you if you bring him here. You go to him, or I'm gone."* Birdy pushed Benji away and ran off … he was back to the present with another bout of nausea. Not just for seeing the vision but for the content. He would fail to find out what happened to Alyssa, which meant he would fail to save his family.

Sandy and Linnet mustered the courage to walk up to Luke and all three grabbed at him … *I fell backward with such force my soul was ripped from my body. I was stuck in a type of darkened foggy basin. I was chest-deep in murky, and swampy water.*

"Help me, somebody, help me. Luke, where are you?" Alyssa pleaded in the darkness.

"Alyssa, where are you? I cannot see you."

"Luke, I'm scared … please help me," she pleaded weakly.

I rushed forward in the thick bog but could barely see inches in front of me. "I cannot find you … it's too dark," I roared.

"Luke, find me … I cannot hold on much longer," Alyssa yelled, this time.

"Where are you? I can't find you."

"Your house, I'm stuck in your house."

"My house." I rushed forward into the water trying to jump out … he fell forward onto his knees painfully. The nausea overtook him. *I was in a swamp with Alyssa,* he thought. He traveled into whatever realm the demon kept her.

"I'm going to fail … I cannot stop it," Luke said.

"What's wrong, Luke? Stop what?" Benji asked.

"The demon, it's winning. I'm blind and cannot see what it's doing. I need help." Luke grabbed onto his head, which rang like a drum uncontrollably.

Benji approached, trying to comfort him. Luke waved him away not wanting to get attacked by another vision. "I need to stop this somehow. I don't know what to do."

"Luke, go to the hospital. The demon attacked your father," Sebastian said quickly and vanished.

"My father? The demon attacked my father, Benji." Now recalling the vision were Benji claimed that both his brother and father had died. "Meet me at the hospital." He ran off toward the car hoping he could stop it.

Benji waved at him before huddling with Alyssa's friends.

Luke had a severe wake-up call from his vision from Birdy's touch. Yes, he was losing, but he could also change that outcome. He had to push forward nonstop and save his family, which he hoped, on some level, included Alyssa.

✝ ✝ ✝

Illuminated

Luke jumped into his Grand National and smoked the tires as he departed. Sebastian was at his side in the passenger seat, slamming his gloved fist on the dashboard.

"Am I too late?" Luke asked.

"No, you need help from the priest."

"I'll go to the church first," Luke said, pegging the accelerator to the floor.

"Slow down. The priest is already at the hospital."

When he arrived at the ER entrance, he saw the two detectives entering the swinging double doors near the rear of the ambulance. Father D was with them.

Luke parked his car and ran to the ambulance entrance.

Luckily, the doors were open, and he moved slowly into the hallway. He found the priest outside a trauma room. The detectives walked the opposite way. "Father D, are you here for my dad?"

"Luke … yes, yes. I was upstairs praying over your brother earlier. When I was leaving, one of the detectives stopped me. He's a parishioner and knows your father attends our church."

"He's down the hallway, Luke," Sebastian said.

"Follow me, Father." Luke cautiously followed the guardian to Trauma Room #3, where a chorus of medical personnel were working on his father. It brought recent memories of his brother's attack, but he pushed it aside quickly. The burned man stood over his dad. "Do you see it, Father?"

"See what?"

Luke touched the priest's shoulder and motioned to Sebastian, who walked over and touched Luke's back.

The priest gasped audibly, covering his mouth belatedly as if in denial for a few seconds. "My God in heaven!"

The burned man stood over his dad's gurney. The man growled at them like a feral cat.

Father D broke free from them and attempted to walk into the trauma room. One of the nurses held her hands up, preventing his entry.

"Sorry, Father, that's as close as you get."

"That's my parishioner, Angel Sanz, and I must read him his last rites. Step out of my way, Miss."

The nurse looked toward the surgeons who were working on his father. A doctor preparing a drill motioned the priest over. "We need all the help we can get. He has a brain bleed, and his vitals are low." The surgeon said through his mask.

Father D walked up to the abomination and sprinkled it with holy water. "In the name of our Lord God, off with you, Satan." The demon screeched, disappearing into the wall. Father D continued to pray over Luke's father for several minutes.

"You see, his vitals are improving. Thanks, Father. I believe in the power of prayer." The doctor made the sign of the cross.

Luke placed a hand on a nearby wall and steadied himself. He had arrived in time, and his father was safe for now.

✝ ✝ ✝

Stages

Father D led Luke by the shoulders out of the trauma room for some time before he was placed on a bench. He was not himself. He felt like he was walking through vapour.

Luke did not understand what was going through his body at the time. In retrospect, he was shocked by all he had experienced in the last week and failed to see a vision when the priest touched him.

He sat alone in the hospital chapel. At this very moment, he realized that he believed in God. He knelt in submission and prayed for his father, brother, and Alyssa. His father was attacked when he took the detectives to look for signs of Alyssa. *Where could she be?* The demon must have her, but it was all so confusing. He prayed for her safety and for a vision to show him what happened to her. Sebastian joined him at the pew.

"Where is she, Sebastian?" Luke asked.

"I don't know … I feel as if a fog has descended upon me. I did not want to alarm you …" Sebastian stammered.

"Spit it out! What's wrong?"

"I still cannot return to the house," Sebastian said.

"The demon is doing this. It's stronger than ever," Luke said.

Father D walked into the chapel and sat beside him.

"Hello, Father. How's my dad?" Luke asked.

"The doctors say the surgery was successful. He will likely recover, but only time will tell," Father D said.

"Was the burned man, the demon?" Luke asked.

Father D sighed. "I just don't know. It was controlled by the demon. I am most sure of that."

What world am I living in? "Is this a possession?" Luke asked.

"I don't think so." The priest sighed and grabbed at the crucifix around his neck, seeking comfort. "Well, possession happens in four stages. The first is the *infestation*. That's the knocking on the walls, the hair pulls, and physical attacks, like pushing."

"All of that happened to us," Luke said, embarrassed that he never discussed this with the priests.

"The second stage is *oppression*, which can be personal attacks such as bad thoughts and emotions and external oppression involving items in the house being moved or slamming against the house. Items or people being thrown across the room."

"You're describing what has happened in our house," Luke said.

"It's all there, yes ... the next stage is *obsession*. That's when the demon tries to influence a person. The spirit tries to control somebody in the house or some occupants."

"Like the blindness my father experienced. Whenever we told our father what was happening, he would forget. It seemed like he was not listening or comprehending what was happening."

"The demon successfully forced your father's interest away from what was occurring. It had to be from an obsessive attack. It was angry at your father and attacked him when he woke out of his slumber."

Luke recalled the dream of the goat's head feasting on his father's brains. "Father, I had a vision that this creature in the shape of a goat's head ate my father's brains. It was disturbing."

"It sounds disturbing ... what you did over there earlier." The priest paused. "You touched me, and then I saw the spirit. Tell me about that."

"Something Sebastian taught me. I can absorb others' powers or pass some of mine to others ... Sebastian also touched me. He can amplify my abilities, but it diminishes his power."

"What kind of powers?"

Luke glanced at Sebastian, who shrugged. "I don't know yet." Luke tried to consider what other abilities he had but pushed the thought away. "What's the final stage?"

"It's the *possession*, Luke. That's what's confusing me. I don't see the possession here. Your brother is in a coma down the hall. Your father is in the critical care unit. The typical demon wants to possess the body. To destroy the soul and the family. To bring misery into the world. Why would a demon attack your brother and abandon the body as if it was trash?" Father D asked.

"We're missing something. This demon is stronger and wiser that all of us put together. We must be cautious."

"Let's both pray on this together. God will open our eyes in time." Father D knelt at the pew and began to pray. Luke did the same, along with Sebastian. With his prayers came a strength to see the unseen. It was like that day years ago when his father taught him how to drive and grabbed his steering wheel, forcing him on the correct path.

CHAPTER THIRTY-THREE

The Secret

Luke returned to Junior's room after praying with Father D. Daniel sat alone, working on his homework. His brother looked up toward Luke as he walked in and motioned toward the overbed table near Junior.

"Emily Villanueva was here earlier and left you an envelope," Daniel said.

A large brown manila envelope sat on the table. Luke walked over to Junior's bed and touched his brother's foot. He hoped for a vision, but nothing happened. He opened the large envelope, and on a piece of paper was a note with handwriting.

Luke, look at what I found. You might find it interesting, and it closes the loop on what could have happened to the Bolling boy. Be vital for your family. They need you more than ever. Warmest regards, Emily.

He removed all the papers from the envelope and placed them on the table. The first page was an article dated February 2, 1964, from the local paper titled *Comatose Child Abandoned at Hospital in Leesburg*. The following article was dated February 15, 1964, titled *Father of Bolling Boy Burns to Death a Year After Loss in Great Falls*.

"What does it mean, Luke?" Daniel asked, hovering behind him.

"Emily thinks this boy left at the hospital is Andy Bolling." He grabbed the next article. It was an advertisement for selling a house on Red Hill Road. "This one shows the house was placed for sale in April 1964." The next piece of paper was the report of the sale of the house to the Bridger family, and the following

242

paper was a rental notice for the house. "So, once Andrew Bolling burns to death, the house is sold to the Bridgers' who use the house as a rental property."

"It makes sense. The father died in a fire, and they sold the house," Daniel said.

"True, but this is a leap on the abandoned boy being Andy." The last piece of paper is an obituary for Sandra Bolling. It's dated August 20, 1985, and it reports that she passed away at 50 and is survived by her daughter, Patricia Bolling. Emily wrote a phone number below and repeated Patricia's name. *Luke, Patricia is waiting for your phone call. She has her mother's diary and will allow you to read it. P.S. Librarians can be investigators, too!*

"She figured it out, Daniel. I need to give Patricia Bolling a call to close this out." Luke said, his brother was back to completing his homework.

Daniel waved him off, disinterested.

Luke walked toward the phone on the side table and dialed Patricia's phone number.

A woman answered on the fourth ring. "Hello?"

"Hello, is this Patricia Bolling? This is Luke Sanz. Emily Villanueva told you I would be calling."

"This is Patricia. I was expecting your call, Luke."

"I just saw Mrs. Villanueva's message. Would we be able to meet tomorrow?" Luke asked.

"I want to get this over with as fast as possible ... could you meet me halfway today? *Landmark Center*, maybe?"

"Yes, I could be there in a little over an hour."

"Meet me in the Dairy Queen parking lot. What are you driving?"

"A black Buick *Grand National*," Luke said.

"What's that?" Patricia asked.

"It's a black Buick *Regal*."

"See you soon, Luke. It will take me almost an hour as well."

"Daniel, I need to go meet with Miss Bolling. Do you want to come with me?" Luke wanted somebody with him that knew what they were going through. Daniel seemed like the right person. He tried to tell his brother that his abilities could be harnessed to save Junior.

"I'm supposed to stay with Junior. Mom and Kamila will not be back for about four hours," Daniel said.

Luke looked at Junior. "He's not going anywhere," he whispered. I must do this. He called Benji at the shop. "Hey, Benji."

"How's your dad and brother?" Benji asked.

"My fathers in the ICU, and my brother's the same ... hey, I need to go to Alexandria."

"Do you need company?" Benji asked.

"Yes, can I swing by and pick you up?" Luke asked.

"Don't you think you should take Daniel? Seems like a good brother bonding moment?"

Luke looked toward his brother, who looked at him with annoyance and pointed at his homework. "One would think ... do you want to go?"

"Yeah, come over, I'll clean up and close down," Benji said and hung up.

Luke drove to Benji's shop, and they headed east toward Alexandria. Benji appeared presentable and did not smell of grease. "Did you take a shower?"

"Yes, I was a mess ... we have a shower in the shop," Benji said.

"How long do we have left to get to the Landmark Center?" Luke asked.

"In my car about twenty minutes. The way you drive, at least an hour."

Luke laughed but grew tense and pressed down on the accelerator. He wanted to tell Benji one of his secrets, but he had been afraid of approaching the topic for the past half hour. "Benji, I need to tell you something." Initially, he thought Daniel would be the correct person to share his secrets with. Still, his brother rejected him for years, and he was absent as an older brother.

"Well, go ahead. We have plenty of time," Benji said.

Luke was silent, trying to muster the courage to tell his friend what he was enduring. "If I touch someone ... I get a vision from their recent past or future."

"That's nice. So, you live in a haunted house but didn't warn your parents. Nice superpower, bro," Benji said and snorted.

His friend was right. "They rarely touch me, but I saw the ghost when I first came into the house."

Benji looked at him strangely. "So, you didn't warn them?"

He contemplated how to respond for a few seconds. "I was weird as a kid and would tell my parents stuff they didn't want to hear. They took me to many head shrinks and doctors who put me on all sorts of medication like I was a rat in a cage."

"That explains a lot ... so what kind of weird stuff have you seen? Benji asked.

"You and Birdy will be married in a few years and have at least two kids."

Benji smiled and rubbed his hands together. "Great news, man, so it finally happens. How long will we be married?"

"It doesn't work that way. I see what I need to see, not what I want to see," Luke said.

"Does she get fat?"

"Fat ... no, she gets pregnant but still looks good," Luke said.

"Pregnant is good, but Birdy's mom is enormous." Benji shook his head while blowing air. "I don't think I could handle that," Benji said.

They both laughed and began to push each other in the car. "You did have a bit of a receding hairline."

"No, not the hair. Please, anything but the hair," Benji took out his brush from his pocket and brushed out his thick curls. "So, are we still friends?"

A tear ran down his face, and he wiped it away. He did not answer.

"What happens?" Benji asked.

"We grow apart. My father and brother die, and Alyssa is still missing. Birdy thinks I killed her."

"Now I see the rush to meet with this woman tonight."

"We are almost there. There's the Dairy Queen," Luke said.

"That woman is waving us down."

"It must be her." He drove to the woman, attractive in a mad scientist kind of way. Her brownish blond hair and blue eyes didn't detract from the weighted look on her face.

"Are you Luke?"

"Yes, I am. Patricia, this is my friend Benji."

She handed him a leather-bound book with a band that had a clasp with a small combination lock. "The lock's broken. I almost made copies for you but decided it was best to rid myself of the diary. I placed little tabs where you should read."

"Can I ask you a couple of questions, Patricia?"

"Luke, Benji, you seem like nice young men, but I don't want to relive those times. I was young and I'm trying to wipe away what happened at our home." The whites from Patricia's eyes turned crimson, her eyes bulged full of tears.

"I understand. I will call you when I'm finished …"

"Keep it, Luke." Patricia looked away and pointed her foot in the direction of her car. "I'm sorry, I need to go. I hope all your problems get resolved." Patricia walked away.

"May God bless you, Patricia," Luke said.

She looked puzzled at him and placed her right hand on her chest. "Thanks, Luke. May God bless and protect you and your family." Her face brightened before she left. The burden she kept with the diary seemed to have lifted. That burden was now his.

CHAPTER THIRTY-FOUR

The Diary

Luke needed to read and decipher the diary as soon as possible. He knew the key to unlock the mystery in the home resided in the leatherbound book. His goal was to read it and then decide what to do next.

"Do you feel like getting a hamburger?" he asked Benji. He held the diary protectively toward his chest.

"Sure do. Make it two."

He ordered four deluxe hamburgers, fries, and chocolate shakes. The diary's cover had *June 1960* written on the outside without an end date. Patricia did not place any tabs for the first half of the journal.

He thumbed over to the first tab. *JUNE 8, 1962 — Andrew changed when he stopped going to church. Something else happened that I cannot dare write about in this journal. He spends much of his time in his shed and has become highly distant. He treats the children as belonging to another man. He refuses to spend quality time with Andy, who now has an imaginary friend called Dale.*

He moved to the next tab. *JULY 4, 1962 — Andrew spent the day drinking whiskey in the shed from morning until night. He stepped into the house to use the restroom, which is rare because he mostly pees in the yard. Andrew stinks of sweat and rotting onions. Andy and Patricia begged him to take them to the fireworks show, and he pushed them both away from him. I confronted him, and he backhanded me across the face. I saw stars and ended up passing out. I want him out of the house!*

The next tab fell on *JULY 19, 1962 — Andrew has not opened his shop every day as he should. Our savings are dwindling except for the sale of his high-end comic books. He refuses to sell any of his records. He stinks, and I don't want him in my bed anymore.*

"I can almost smell him myself," he spoke out loud without intending to.

"What's that? I hope it's what you are reading." Benji sniffed his underarms.

"I meant something in the diary … are you done so we can hit the road?"

"You left one burger. Are you going to eat it?"

He handed the burger over to his buddy. "You eat it. I lost my appetite. Eat it here because you are not eating it in the car."

Benji started to eat the burger ravenously as if he had been pulled off a deserted island.

He turned his attention to the diary and read the following entry: *July 25, 1962 — I was wrong. Andy's imaginary friend is named Avondale, and apparently, he gets pissed when I tell Andy to go to sleep. The door in the downstairs bathroom opens and closes whenever it wants to. I placed a pillow on the ground so the door would not slam shut anymore.*

"Darn, I wish we would have thought of that," he whispered.

August 15, 1962 — Andrew is drunk day and night. He speaks out loud to himself often and strikes his face repeatedly as if trying to take back a mistake. I caught our son Andy amongst the trees on the property slamming a rock on a squirrel. When I attempted to stop him, he told me Avondale said to shut your trap and walk away, or you will regret it. I grabbed him and was about to give him a hot butt when something pushed me so hard that I fell over. I looked around and saw nobody except Andy, who was smiling with an evil grin. I ran to the house and tried to talk to Andrew. Do you know what he said? Go away, or you are the one that will get a hot butt. How could he know what happened or what was said?

They got back into the car and headed back toward Lansburg.

"Anything helpful?" Benji asked.

"Looks like they had trouble in the house beginning in 1962."

Benji merged onto the on-ramp, goosed the engine a bit, and

the tires chirped when it hit second gear. "This car has way too much power, Luke."

"Faster than your car?"

"No way, just different. Go ahead, keep reading."

Luke kept reading the compact diary. Luckily, Mrs. Bolling's handwriting was quite legible compared to his handwriting.

AUGUST 25, 1962—I have not been writing in the diary. I'm depressed. The power and water were shut off for over a week. It was so hot in the house that I was sweaty when I tried to sleep. I no longer sleep in the same room as Andrew. We both stink. I broke down today and sold a box of his comic books. I am sure I was robbed, but I got the electricity and water back on. The phone has been disconnected for months. I have nobody to speak with anyway. I caught Andy killing the neighbor's cat. Not that anybody cares.

AUGUST 26, 1962—I took Patricia to church today. It was so peaceful, and Patricia seemed so happy. I asked Andrew to come, but he refused and slapped me when I went to grab Andy. He told me, we follow Satan and will not damage our ears by listening to a hypocritical child rapist in a fool's house! What a disgusting man. I don't know what I ever saw in him.

SEPTEMBER 8, 1962—I caught Andy torturing the dog by breaking its leg and nailing it to the wall in his room. It's not the first time. He has killed at least five of our neighbor's dogs. I found a quilt my mom made full of battered, broken dog carcasses. My son is gone. I caught Andrew on a good day, and he agreed to try and reach Andy.

SEPTEMBER 9, 1962—I went to church with Patricia and begged Father Grant Lee to pray over our house. He refused because we had lived in the house for over two years. I offered him $500 for the church, and he finally gave in.

SEPTEMBER 12, 1962—Father Lee came to the house. Andrew was in the shed with Andy, and I asked Patricia to visit a friend's house. Everything seemed normal at first. He said some prayers and walked into every room. When he entered Andy's room, he screamed in terror and ran out and down the hallway. I looked in the room, and there was a pentagram painted in blood on the wall, and several animals were nailed within the symbol. Andy called them offerings. I followed the priest down the hall, and he was stopped by my husband who yelled, the only true Lord is Satan. Off with you, child molester! The priest ran past him and out the front door, and I heard Andy say, Dad, can I cut him open and put him on my wall? Not much more to say. I was beaten, then sodomized, and forbidden from eating that night.

SEPTEMBER 20, 1962—Andrew has been working under the house and claims he found a void. He told me he dreamed the gap under the house existed and decided to work on it. Andy has not been hurting any more animals that I can find. He has been going to school like a good little boy. I was allowed to eat today.

Her handwriting was getting progressively worse and more challenging to understand. She did not eat for eight days. That had to be brutal.

OCTOBER 31, 1962—I have lost over 30 pounds. I was not much, to begin with, and I am even less than nothing now. Andy tried to kill Patricia by hitting her head with a hammer. Andrew became angry and locked Andy into the void in the basement. I did not attempt to stop him; I was more concerned with keeping Patricia safe. It took days for Andy to stop banging on the rafters above him. The screaming was unbearable, but it was quiet now. Andrew assured me that our son Andy was alive. I still prepare his meals for him. The truancy office from Andy's school was beginning to aggravate Andrew. He told me to go to the school and tell them he was being home-schooled. I refused, and he struck me. I still refused, so he sodomized me again. I went to the school like a good girl and convinced them Andy was being home-schooled, even though Patricia was not. I should get an acting award.

DECEMBER 20, 1963—Andrew devised a plan to keep anybody from ever asking about Andy again. He took us to the Great Falls area and faked Andy's disappearance in the river. We were all on our best behavior. Andy promised to sodomize me if I disobeyed and whispered that he would do the same to Patricia. He patted her little behind as a threat to me. I have been having odd dreams and keep hearing voices. I chalk it up to the lack of eating. I weigh about one hundred pounds now. It does not look good on me.

JANUARY 10, 1964—Happy New Year. About five days ago, I heard a large crash from the backyard. I had been sleeping for months in Andy's old room. I saw some lights in the backyard from the bedroom window. I walked downstairs into the living room and saw somebody in the backyard. I looked out the window, and somebody or something banged on it, and the glass cracked. I tried opening the door and saw Andrew standing at the top of the garage stairway. I told him there was a car crash in the back and wanted to help. Andrew elbowed me across the face, spraying blood and teeth on the door's glass. My fault for not eating well. My teeth were loose in my mouth. I tried to get away from him by running up the steps into the garage, but he grabbed my foot, and I fell onto my face painfully. I woke up with him on top of me, sodomizing me again. I passed out and woke up later in Andy's bed. I was bathed, bandaged, and wearing Andrew's shorts and a shirt. I am having difficulty sitting because I have tears on my backside. Even lying in warm bath water does not help.

FEBRUARY 3, 1964—Andrew pulled our boy from the void under the house yesterday. He passed out, but he was breathing with a steady pulse. I had been feeding him thrice daily by crawling into the hole and leaving the tray with food on the floor. Most times, he would be sitting there staring at me. At first, he would tell me, 'I can be a good boy now,' but once he tried to stab my arm with a sharp piece of wood he made from his furniture. Yesterday, when I brought Andy his food, he told me, 'Avondale is happy that you gave me to him as a gift.' Andrew cried over his son after he pulled him from the void. There was something fake about it. He was worried enough that he took him away to the hospital. He returned after several hours, and I repeatedly asked him what had happened. He slapped me and told me he took Andy to a hospital in Leesburg and left him with the doctors to care for him.

FEBRUARY 4, 1964—Andrew woke me and forced me and Patricia to go on a trip to Great Falls. He rented a cheap motel room where we all took showers and put on clean clothing. Afterwards, he told me that we were going to pretend that Andy was lost in the river. I obeyed.

FEBRUARY 15, 1964—I woke up to the smell of smoke. There was a fire in the shed, and Andrew perished in it. I hope he rots in hell. He was a good man once, with dreams. He was weighed down by beliefs in Satan and invited evil into our house.

APRIL 1, 1964—I am in the process of selling our home. I left most of Andrews's comics and record collection in boxes in the attic behind a false wall. I could not muster up the willpower to sell everything and felt everything he touched was damned. I paid somebody to build the false wall and to cover the door leading to the attic. Andrew was a shit husband, but he had good insurance. I am taking the money with us from selling the house and the insurance and starting anew in California. I want nothing to do with this place and will use my maiden name.

He saw one last tab after several empty pages. The handwriting had improved, but it was still shaky.

AUGUST 20, 1985—I had a heart attack earlier today and did not die, unfortunately. For the past twenty years, I have made it a point to live a completely different life with Patricia. I hope she has forgotten. We have lived a quiet life, and Patricia has become an academic and received her doctorate. I have never forgiven myself for my weakness in allowing my Satan-loving husband to destroy our lovely HOME and family. I should have fought my husband and not allowed him to drive my son into the darkness with him. I blame myself for letting him lock our son away like he did. It's just as much my fault, and I deserve to rot in hell for my actions. I have lived a peaceful life and begged for contrition. I sent a letter to the Lansburg Police Department today and told them that my husband was involved in a hit-and-run in June of 1962. He hit a man in Lansburg, drove away, and did not call for help and began worshiping the Devil. I did not tell the police what we did to Andy. I fear that it would affect Patricia in any way. I am still afraid. Although I have prayed to God for forgiveness, I know what I deserve. I deserve to die in a burning building like my husband. I feel that I will die today. My dead parents came into my room for a visit. Andy is at a nursing home called Virts Convalescence and Rehab in Leesburg, VA, under an assumed name as a ward of the state. May God forgive me for my weakness.

Luke closed the diary. It was a horrible way to live, and it happened in their house. No wonder the home was haunted, and they were being terrorized. He prayed silently with eyes closed, hoping for enlightenment and guidance from beyond. From the back seat, Sebastian placed a guiding hand on Luke's head and joined in prayer.

CHAPTER THIRTY-FIVE

Prayer at the LTC

The diary was a disturbing read for Luke. The content included the private thoughts and torment a woman suffered decades ago. It was critical to solve the harm caused by Andrew Bolling. That misery and strife tried to pierce through time into the home his family now occupied. Ending the suffering of the Bolling family might stop what was now destroying the Sanzes. Isidora was right; he could rely on Father D.

It was almost seven o'clock at night. He had no choice but to speak to the priest. "Benji, stop at the parish. I need to speak with Father D."

Benji parked in front of the church. "It's kind of late," Benji said.

"Luke, the priest is coming out of the Clergy House," Sebastian said.

"Drive down to that building. That's Father D over there walking," Luke said.

"Good eye. It's getting kind of dark already," Benji said.

"I had a little preternatural help," Luke said, wanting to tell his friend that Sebastian guided him. *I will tell him one day*, he thought.

Benji drove up to Father D, who had a black satchel in his hand. The priest paused outside the car, presumably noticing Luke's *Grand National* moving toward him.

Luke jumped out of the passenger seat. "Father, we need to talk."

"I was about to head to the hospital and visit some families, yours included. What's wrong?"

"I think I found something. The boy in the cave in my house is named Andy Bolling, and I know where he is."

"He's alive?"

"Yes, can you come with us and pray over the Bolling boy and see if it helps? I can explain myself on the way."

"Yes, I'll come with you," Father D said

"Benji, I'll drive."

"Sure thing," Benji said, jumping out of the driver's seat and entering the back seat. Father D got into the front passenger seat.

Luke found Virts Corner on the map and wrote out the route. Father D got into the car with his bag. "Father, have you ever been to the Virts Convalescence home?"

"I've been there. Get to the Virts area, and I can point it out," Father D said.

He drove out of the area and explained to Father D what he learned from reading the diary. "Father, from what I can see, in June of 1962, Andrew Bolling was involved in a hit and run. The man died. Soon after, he began to worship the Devil, which consumed him and his family. He neglected his business and his family, which cost them everything. His son Andy began to hurt animals and his sister. I think the father gave the boy to Satan."

"Satanism? Dear Lord, in Lansburg?" Father D asked.

"Yes, Father. Andy almost killed his sister. His father, Andrew, locked him in the cave under our house. They reported him missing when they found him unresponsive in the cave. They abandoned his lifeless body at a hospital. Eventually, Andy was moved to this place."

"Tragic, Luke. It's extremely unfair and unjust that someone's evil actions thirty years ago affect your family today."

Life was indeed unfair. He simply shrugged.

"You can say that again, Father," Benji said.

"In January of 1964, Kyle Campbell crashed in the back of our house on Red Hill Road. His spirit walked to the house and banged on the door and kitchen window. Mrs. Bolling heard the car crash and tried to help, but her husband stopped and brutally raped her. Kyle's soul somehow is trapped in the house."

"This is horrible. It's a demon." Father D appeared to be in thought. "It still doesn't make sense as a typical possession."

"We are in the Virts area. Does it look familiar, Father?" Luke asked.

"Yes, make this turn over here on the left. It's down this road amongst those Dogwood trees."

"There it is." Luke parked the car in between two empty spots, "What do you think?" Luke asked.

"Let me do the talking, boys … it's late we are kind of teetering on the edge of visiting hours." Father D walked to the front desk reception area. "Hello, I am looking for a patient of yours. He would be here under the name John Doe or another assumed name."

"Hello, Father. I don't think we have a patient like that, but I'm fairly new. Let me make a quick call." The receptionist picked up her phone and dialed a number. "Jude, do we have a John Doe patient in the facility?" She paused, listened, and then looked at Father D. "Could it be a long-term patient abandoned thirty years ago at the hospital?"

"Yes, that's him. Could we visit with him, please?" Father D asked.

"Jude, a priest is here and would like to visit with him." She listened in again and then hung up the receiver. "Jude will be right with you, Father. Visiting hours are almost over. You may wait over by the door."

"Thanks for your help, young lady. God bless you."

"You're ever so welcome, Father." She smiled at Luke, and he returned it with a wave.

They waited by the door for several minutes, and a nurse came out from the door with a sign that read *PATIENT SUITES*. The nurse was overweight and walked as if her knees were giving out. She could be walking with a cane or walker soon after.

"Father, are you here to see our John Doe?"

"Yes, are you Jude?" Father D offered his hand to her, who

256

took it with a smile.

"He had one visitor, but it was a mistake. A young woman in the late 80s came looking for her lost brother. She claimed that our John was not him … are these young men with you?"

"Yes, they are. This is Luke and Benji," Father D said, pointing at them.

"Follow me. I wasn't sure I was going to let you in. He's never had a visitor." Jude turned and walked back to the door slowly and let them into the ward. Jude ambled down the hall as they followed. "Sorry, Father, I am having a bad knee day. I need to get surgery soon or will land in a wheelchair." They continued walking for a few silent minutes. "I'm retiring soon anyway. I'm almost seventy now."

"Have you been here long, Jude?"

"Yes, Father, for about fifty years now … I was here when they brought him in from the hospital." Jude entered the last room down a hallway. "John, you have visitors, honey."

A man in his thirties or so sat in a wheelchair near a window in the room. He turned his head, opened his mouth wide, and began to move. "Dada da da. Dada da da."

"I think he is trying to say daddy, but what do I know," Benji said.

"He's not in a coma?" Father D asked.

"No, when he was left at the hospital, he was comatose, but a year later, he woke out of it and has been like this. He eats and walks at times, but everything is without a purpose," Jude said and paused briefly. "You've already heard almost all his vocabulary."

"What else does he say, Jude?" Luke asked, speaking for the first time. Something about Andy reminded him of his dream concerning his brother Junior. It had not clicked yet, but he began to feel as if the room temperature had increased. He was sweating as if superheated.

"Let me see if I can recall. Mudda da da, Padda da da, and Avo da da," Jude said.

"So, he's trying to say daddy, mother, Patricia, and Avondale," he said counting with his fingers.

"Do you know this man, Luke?" Jude asked, pointing at John.

"This is Andy Bolling," Luke answered.

"Why is that name familiar? I have heard that name somewhere," Jude said.

"The missing boy in Great Falls." The truth needed to come out after all these years.

"Impossible, the Bolling Boy died in the Potomac River."

"It was faked. This is Andy Bolling," Luke said.

Andy looked toward him as he drooled. "Anda da da."

"There's not much left … maybe he did drown all those years ago," Benji said.

"My Lord. I need to go tell the administrator!" Jude seemed healed as she ran out of the room.

Father D removed his stole from his bag, placed it over his shoulders, and began to pray over Andy. He sprinkled holy water on the man, who did not react.

"I thought he was supposed to start yelling or spit up pea soup," Benji said.

"He should react, but something is wrong." Father D's eyes opened wide as if in realization. "There's no soul, Luke."

Sebastian walked alongside Luke and looked at Andy. "His soul was stolen by the demon long ago. I could not see it until this very moment."

Luke looked at Sebastian and Father D. "Where's his soul? I don't understand."

"It's trapped along with the other souls in your house," Sebastian said as he slammed his spear on the floor. "This is only a shell."

It came to him. Junior was soulless, or close to it, and will be this automaton in thirty years. "Oh my God, no. The demon has Junior's soul, just like Andy."

"What are you saying, Luke? Your brother is going to turn into this meat puppet?" Benji asked.

"It's an empty vessel," Father D said in disappointment. "I cannot help here."

An older man in a suit that was new decades ago walked into the room with Jude. "Is this correct? You have identified our patient as Andy Bolling?"

"Yes, this is Andy Bolling." Father D placed everything back into his bag.

"What do we do? I need to call the police, I think."

Father D handed the administrator a business card. "Have the police call me if they need to speak further."

"Thanks, Father. I will call them now." The administrator walked out of the room.

"Thank you, Father. Thanks, boys. It was good to see him identified before I retire," Jude said.

"We need to leave Jude, but we may be back soon. Go with God. I will pray that your knee improves." Father D shook her hand.

They left the facility and drove back toward Lansburg and the church. "Father, there's something that keeps circling in my mind. Andy had an imaginary friend named Avondale. Does it mean anything to you?"

"Luke, there was an angel named Abdiel whom Satan tried to convince to go against God in heaven, but instead told God. Maybe the demon used the name Abdiel to deceive … take me back to the church. I must request permission to perform the Rites of Exorcism at your home. We need to study and find the demon's real name."

"I want to help if I could." He also wanted to call Lulu McCray and see if she could help him get a meeting with Mr. Campbell.

"Come over in about an hour. I need to prepare Robert."

"Thanks, Father," Luke said. Everything, all the problems in the home, converged into a funnel. Battles were ahead, and dread was building. *I don't think everyone will survive the confrontation*, he mused.

✝ ✝ ✝

Secretary-General

After Luke dropped him off, Father D grabbed a bottle of single malt scotch from a cabinet in his office and served himself a stiff drink. He took a large gulp before reaching for a black-and-white photograph of himself with an older priest, Father William. His friend and mentor died many years ago during an exorcism. It wasn't botched, necessarily. They saved the afflicted person who was being torn apart by a demon, but his mentor died from a heart attack. Tears rolled down his face freely while he touched the image of the older white man.

Father D had to contact the Vatican to seek permission for the exorcism. It was more of a formality because he would not be performing the rite on a person. Still, he had to face the problem of the protector and the guardian. It may have been years before Luke had to face what he was. He considered waiting until after the exorcism was successful. No, he must do it now. At his age and with his illness, he must let the Vatican know that a Guardian may have been awakened and that a tragedy would occur in the Protector's lifetime.

He stood up quickly and placed the picture on his desk. Pushing the frame of his print of the St. Michael Vanquishing Satan painting on the wall, it popped forward, revealing a combination lock safe behind it. He moved the tumbler around, and the access door popped open. He grabbed a red leather-bound book that had a sigil with two keys and a crown on the cover. He sat down, unlocked the book with a key, and unzipped the address book. He found the "S" tab, opened it, looked for Sec Svc General, and saw the phone number. He dialed +379 and the phone number.

"Ready," the Secretary-General answered the phone in Italian.

"General, I think we have a potential protector in my parish. He has a guardian companion."

"Who is he?"

"His name is Luke Sanz. He is a high school student and son of a State Department federal agent."

"Has the guardian been identified?"

"Sebastian Sanz-Basque or Sebastian Sanz de Basque. An ancestor to the boy. The Guardian mentioned the Siege of Santo Domingo ... that took place in 1655," Father D said.

"That helps. Did the protector mention Santa Alleanza or the Protettorato Controspionaggio?"

"He mentioned Santa Alleanza but not the Protectorate."

"Anything else, my old friend?" the Secretary-General asked.

"We must exorcise a demon from his home ... I will transmit our research shortly," Father D said.

"Of course, Dwayne ... we will study the potential Guardian's name. It's always a pleasure to hear your voice, and I hope you are doing fine."

"Thanks, Cardinal." Father D replaced the handset on the cradle and made the sign of the cross. He returned the book to the safe before setting the lock. *I will help Luke remove the demon from his home and prepare him for the life he is meant to live,* he thought.

CHAPTER THIRTY-SIX

Hitting the Books

Luke felt uncomfortable but prepared as he entered the church and knocked on the door to Father D's office. He was ready to work all night, but he wanted to go straight to his house and fight the demon. Deacon Robert opened the door and motioned for Luke to enter. At that moment, he did not want to enter the office. *You're wasting your time*, he thought. The thought came from without—not from him or his orbit. It had to be from the demon. It feared this very moment.

"Hello, Deacon. It is good to see you again," Luke said.

"It's Father now. I was ordained today," Father Robert said with a smile.

"Congratulations, Father ... I'm sorry but I don't understand why we are meeting."

Father Robert motioned Luke toward the table surrounded by bookshelves. Father D sat at the table, already buried in books with notepads in front of him.

"Crash course in exorcism and demons ... take a seat," Father D said.

Luke saw numerous books of varying ages on the desk. The titles were new to him, which concerned him. *On the Incantation* by Saint Athanasius, Saint Cyprian of Carthage, numerous books by someone named Tertullian, and another he noticed was *Against Heresies* by Irenaeus. "Do I have to read all these books tonight?" Luke asked, taking a deep breath.

"Of course, Father Robert just read them. He's a speed reader," Father D said, slapping the table.

"The Father fancies himself a comedian ... no, we are just

taking notes from these extant writings.

"What does extant mean?" Luke asked.

"Old manuscripts that are still in existence. Most of these are copies, of course," Father D said. "Luke, I need you to look through this text." Father D handed a sizeable leatherbound book to him.

Luke opened the hefty tome and turned to the title page. *On Demons* by Prior Alphonse Canton. Everything was handwritten. It was eerie as the book was cold to the touch as well. He turned page after page and saw that the book contained drawings of demons with their corresponding names. "Is this an original?"

"Yes, it belonged to my mentor. It was written over a lifetime by a prior in England. Sometime in the 1600s ... browse through the book and see if anything looks familiar to you," Father D said.

"Familiar ... what do you mean? Luke asked, confused because most of the demons seemed to have characteristics of animals and not humans.

"Father D explained to me that you have visions and dreams, correct?" Father Robert asked.

"Yes, Father. So just look and see if I recognize anything I've seen?" Luke asked.

"Luke, yes ... turn the pages, and I will watch as well," Sebastian said.

Luke stood up and changed seats. "Sebastian is here. He will help," Luke said.

Father Robert looked around the room. "Sebastian is with you now?"

Luke shrugged and pointed at Sebastian, who proceeded to reposition himself behind him.

"Sebastian, I would like some time to ask you some questions ... if Luke would care to translate or, well, let me know how you respond," Father Robert said, talking to the air.

"Who are you talking to? He's behind me," Luke began to turn pages, smiling sarcastically.

He failed to notice the annoyed look on Father Robert, who

did not like being the butt of some joke.

"Tell the priest we can sit and talk later on," Sebastian said.

"After this is done, we can sit and talk with Sebastian," Luke said.

"Okay, Sebastian. I would like that," Father Robert said, glaring at Luke.

For the next hour, Luke, with Sebastian's help, made it through half the book. The named demons were not in alphabetical order, as the work was completed over a lifetime of research. He arrived at a page with the name Ipos, a prince of Hell with the power of divination of the future. It had a lion's head with the feet of a goose and wings. It was feasting on a naked man.

Sebastian leaned in over the drawing. "I have never seen this creature, but it's familiar, as the priest said."

"It can see the past and future. Sort of like me," Luke said.

"That is where the similarity ends … you are trying to help others. This abomination feeds on the dreams of men and takes away their freedom of thought and purpose."

"Just write down the name and page number, Luke." Father D said.

Luke jotted down the information and changed the page. Numerous demons were depicted on both pages under the banner Ipos, Legion of Demons. He stared at the one in the center of the second page. It was the flailed and shredded goat's head breathing smoke as it feasted on his father's brains in one of his visions. Its name was Avandeil, after the name was some writing that was most likely Latin.

"Father, what does this say?" Luke asked.

"A defiant deceiver who dreamed of being human," Father D said.

Luke stood up and stared at the picture confidently. "This is the demon in my house … I'm going to kill it," Luke said.

✠ ✠ ✠

Archie Campbell

Lulu arranged for Luke to meet with her grandfather, Archibald Campbell. She warned him that her grandfather insisted they meet at 7:00 a.m. because he liked to disrupt people and place them at a disadvantage. He met Lulu at the front gate of the entrance to Campbell Farms, where he joined her as a passenger in her car.

"Sorry, Luke, Archie would have his security guys tear your car apart before he lets you drive onto his property. He lets me visit him a couple of times a year."

"Do you think Mr. Campbell will talk honestly with me?" Luke asked.

"He seemed interested when I mentioned it was about Kyle. He doesn't even let me call him grandfather and can flip like a switch."

Lulu drove down a long driveway and passed numerous buildings, barns, and sheds. Several houses with fenced-in yards are scattered throughout the unpaved roads.

"We have ten residences on the property. Some are for adult family members, but now most are for staff and caretakers. That home we passed belonged to Kyle before his wife left him," Lulu said.

He was expecting a large mansion like the one in the gated community called Campbell Estates nearby. Instead, they drove up to a white one-story ranch-style home, which seemed humble, yet well-kept.

"Not what you expected?" Lulu asked.

"I thought it would be this southern-style plantation home." He did not mean for it to come out in a derogatory way. "That's not true. I expected it would be like the estates on the other side of the hill."

"My grandfather sold one hundred acres to the developers that built the estates ... are you ready? This is probably the most

265

difficult person you have ever dealt with, Luke." She parked the car and took a deep breath. "Be honest, speak directly, and don't dance around a topic. It will set him off."

Instead of anxiety, he felt focused. The rush of adrenaline into his system caused his hands to shake. He took a deep breath and exhaled.

Sebastian formed beside Luke. "I'm here with you, Luke. You have a mission, be honest with the man."

He nodded at Sebastian and followed Lulu to the front door. Having Sebastian close brought him strength.

A woman wearing a light blue knee-length day dress opened the door. "Hello, Nancy. How is he this morning?"

"Archie woke up early and looks forward to meeting this young man. Luke, it's a pleasure to meet you. I heard you saved my cousin Tom Genaro after his car accident." They shook hands *… I stood outside a cabin overlooking a lake. It was a beautiful, serene place …* It was fleeting and it meant nothing to him.

Lansburg was truly a small town. Nancy had a warm and inviting nature.

"Nice to meet you, Nancy. How's Tom recuperating?"

"Tom is doing fine, thanks to you. He told me to let you know that the family wants you to come to their house for dinner," Nancy said.

"Thanks, Nancy. I will visit with him soon and work it out."

"Tom will welcome a surprise visit from you. Archie is in his den. I left some coffee with cream on the table inside. Go ahead and go in. He's waiting." She motioned Luke into the faraway room like a game show host.

He looked at the women who stepped away from the room as if in fear. This caused him to want to turn and walk out the front door. He began walking toward the threshold and paused. *Don't go in,* he thought, a bit anxious.

Sebastian walked beside him with his usual staggered gait and placed a hand on his shoulder. "You must go in."

Luke walked into the large den. Archibald Campbell, the

patriarch of the Campbell family, sat with a rifle leaning against his chair. He stared out a window toward a hill in the distance. The sight of the rifle brought a vision of Archie crawling through the mud and planting a bomb. Months ago, he dreamed of the day Archie was injured in the war.

An old ratty olive drab hat hung on the wall near the window. It was the hat from Luke's dream, that Archie used as a guide to return to the correct trench after bombing the German line.

"Hello, Mr. Campbell. I'm Luke Sanz. I was hoping I could have a moment of your time."

Mr. Campbell turned toward him. "That's how you introduce yourself? By stating the obvious."

"I apologize, Mr. Campbell ..."

"Nancy didn't tell me you were a hippie with long hair. Go ahead, Rock Star and sit down already. You're giving me a kink in my neck." Mr. Campbell straightened himself in his chair and motioned toward the coffee on the table. "Help yourself ... do you talk? Right now, you're taking entirely too much space in my den," Mr. Campbell said while flailing his arms like a bird trying to fly from its perch.

Luke noticed the cantankerous older man was missing several fingers on his right hand and had swollen knuckles from arthritis. Otherwise, he looked fit for a man of ninety-five and appeared well-muscled around his upper body. He surmised the man was angered at aging alone in the den of his home without family. "I will not have long hair for long. I may be in the Army someday," Luke said.

"You may be in the Army?" Mr. Campbell asked and shook his head. "You'll probably be one of those wienies safe in the tent away from the front," Mr. Campbell said staring at his hand which was trembling uncontrollably. "It's called an essential tremor. Not sure what's so essential about it."

Archie didn't seem the wrong sort, so he purposely avoided the man's dark humor. "I think I'm going to be an Army Ranger," Luke said cryptically. Mr. Campbell did not appear interested.

Archie looked through the window again. "I was in the Army. I was a Sapper." Mr. Campbell held up his hand and then grabbed onto his chest, where he had a visible scar from his chest up to his neck. "Do you know what a Sapper is?"

"A Combat Engineer. World War II?"

Archie looked at him sharply, rising somewhat in his seat by grabbing his rifle for stability as if he were about to yell at him, but he settled down. "No, the first one. Too old for the second, even if I think I could have done it, but I had the farm to worry about. No, it was the first one for me." Archie looked out the window on his left again and patted the rifle. "I'm not trying to intimidate you with this rifle. I carried my Springfield in the war, and now it carries me."

Luke ignored the rifle altogether. "Mr. Campbell, why do you keep looking out your window?"

Archie did not look at him. "It's the family cemetery. My son, wife, daughter, parents, grandson, and others are there now. More family members are up there than down here." Archie gave him a stern look, although unintended. "Over the last ten years, I have seen many of my deceased family in this room." Archie pointed at the floor effectively. "I have never seen my grandson, Kyle. Why do you think that is?"

"Your grandson cannot visit you." He needed to be direct with Archie. "His soul is trapped in my house. I'm here because I need help getting him to move on."

Archie placed his damaged hand on his face and stayed motionless for ages.

"Poor man, he reminds me of my father." Sebastian moved beside Mr. Campbell.

Tears began to flow down Archie's wrinkled face. "It's my fault. We argued that day. Kyle caught his pregnant wife with another man and promptly forgave her, the silly sap. He wanted to move on and give her a divorce. Presumably, to let another man raise his child—another man raised my grandson!" Archie closed his eyes as if he had succumbed to a terrible headache. "I forbade it and told him he would have to stay married for his child to be my heir. He went back to his residence on the farm and got drunk. I'm not sure why he drove off, but he did. He crashed and died on Red Hill Road." Archie covered his face with one hand for a moment. "Do you know why they called the street Red Hill Road?"

"No, Mr. Campbell," he said.

"It was that Colonel Mars who came across a group of Union soldiers who had orders to assassinate General Lee. The general was visiting a tavern on Main Street before the city was called Lansburg. Mars and his men engaged and killed the assassins in a clearing near your home. As a kid, one of the town elders told me that Mars killed the ringleader with his bare hands even after being shot. The townspeople were so grateful that they named the town after him. They named the street Red Hill for all the blood that flowed down it."

"Lancel Mars, the Savior of Lansburg," Luke said.

"I thought I would tell you that story since you are dating the descendant of the man. I wanted to meet you because I must make peace with Kyle." Archie grabbed a manila envelope he had tucked away in his chair. "Tell Kyle that my great-grandson is one of my legal heirs, as is his cousin, Lulu. I have come to terms with the fact that I will die and regret how I treated him."

Luke glanced inside. There was a cassette tape and a will. "What are you thinking, Mr. Campbell?"

"Play that tape in the house. It's best if Kyle hears my voice. Then, read my will."

"Thanks, Mr. Campbell. I hope this helps." He stood up and walked toward the door, but Archie grabbed his arm with a three-fingered hand ... *Archie laid on his back staring into the dark sky with lighting illuminating the sky as rain and blood dripped from his missing fingers onto his face* ... the vision vanished.

"If it doesn't work, please come tell me. I want the chance to think of something else," Mr. Campbell said.

"Do you want me to come over if it works?" Luke asked.

"I will know if it works." Mr. Campbell sat silently now grabbing his rifle. "Tell Lulu to come back once she takes you to the gate."

"I will," Luke said. "Your hat brought you both home eventually, even if that bomb went off prematurely."

Archie sat up in his chair and stared at the hat and smiled. "It did, didn't it. That's why I've held on to it."

"Take care, Mr. Campbell. It was an honor to meet you."

Mr. Campbell waved to him dismissively. "Try not to jump out of too many perfectly good airplanes, Rock Star." Mr. Campbell said oddly having heard Luke's reference about the Army.

He approached Nancy and Lulu, somewhat stunned after the interaction with Archie. "Thanks, Nancy, for letting me see him."

"You're welcome, Luke. Was it worth your time?" Nancy asked.

"It was fruitful." He turned to Lulu. "Archie wants you to come back after you drop me off in the front … it was nice to meet you, Nancy."

"We best go then. I'll be right back, Nancy," Lulu said, before they left the house. "What did he give you?"

"He wants to speak with you about what's in this envelope. Best he tells you." Afterward, he drove toward his house on Red Hill Road prepared to meet with the team he had assembled the night before. He was not alone in this world, and neither was Avandeil.

CHAPTER THIRTY-SEVEN

"The fight between good and evil in the spiritual realm is not visible to most by the naked eye," Anonymous.

The Gathering – May 3, 1991

Overnight, Luke made several phone calls to those who could help in the battle against Avandeil. He arrived at the house on Red Hill Road near the large brick sign that showed the house number. He took out the worn prayer cards Father D provided him with the night before. A calm enveloped him, realizing this was a turning point in his life. The consequences of failure were high, and he knew he must succeed. He considered rushing the remaining hundred feet to the house to fight the demon alone. A creature stared at him from the bay window of the third-floor hallway above the front door.

"I see it, Luke. It's Avandeil with all the souls inside of him. It's more powerful than ever and waiting for us." Sebastian appeared ready for battle, wearing all his gear.

"It's waiting for us," Luke said, grabbing his boom box from the trunk.

Kamila drove up, and Luke motioned for her to park off to the side. She stepped out of the car, walked up, and hugged him.

Nothing; he saw no visions. He hoped he would have seen how to defeat Avandeil by touching those helping to defeat the abomination that awaited them. It had weakened Luke somehow. Like a dampening field. Regardless, at least his fear that the team he assembled would not show up was misplaced.

"Are you sure she's in there?" Kamila asked.

"She's hidden in some type of portal," Luke said.

Benji drove up in his car and parked behind Kamila. He got out of the car, leaned against the fender, and gave him the thumbs up. Birdy, Sandy, and Linnet poured out of his car and stood near Benji.

Luke bowed his head toward his friend, thankful for his presence.

The priests arrived, and parked closer to the house. Father D and Robert left the vehicle and placed their bags in the car's trunk. Whispering a prayer, they placed their vestments on. Father Robert prepared a thurible, one of his weapons for the upcoming battle like Sebastian's halberd.

Luke motioned for everyone to follow him, including the priests. He positioned his back toward the abomination, which was staring down at them through the bedroom window. "Everyone, please form a circle and hold hands." Everyone did as Luke asked. Sebastian stood in the center of the circle.

"I asked each one of you here for a reason. The priests and I are here to fight the demon that's latched onto our home. Birdy, Sandy, and Linnet are here for Alyssa. My godmother, Kamila, is here because she is a sensitive, and I need her guidance. Benji is here because he is meant to be by my side. I have been unable to explain everything to all of you, but you must now know what we are facing." Luke had gathered his team for battle, but he wanted their eyes open for what they faced. "Benji, do you see anything at the window?"

"No, buddy," Benji said, smiling. Of course, everyone looked.

"Father D," Luke said.

"God, please protect those gathered today to face a beast struck down from your realm. This God—his way being perfect. The word of our Lord proves true as he is a shield for all those who take refuge in him. For whom is God, but our Lord who is a rock, except our God. The God who equipped me with strength and made my way blameless," Father D said.

"For we do not wrestle against flesh and blood, but against the rulers, the authorities, the cosmic powers over this present darkness, and the spiritual faces of evil in the heavenly places." Father Robert bowed his head once more.

"For you equipped me with strength for the battle. You made those who now rise against us sink under us," Luke said. "Now, look at the window."

They all collectively gasped.

"What is that thing?" Benji asked.

"It has different faces," Birdy said. "Gross."

"That thing has Alyssa. My God," Sandy said.

"Don't respond to it. It is trying to cause fear and divide us. It is a deceiver and a liar. If it talks to you, don't bend to its will," Father D said.

The demon shimmered as if four or more faces were in one body. The body was that of Kyle. The apparition had the signature plaid shirt under the overalls. Luke gave the demon the middle finger. "I want my brother back, Avandeil."

The abomination stared, shook, vibrated, and then slithered away like a serpent. He felt his pocket for the envelope Archie gave him. He added several statements he had written the night before to the envelope containing the will and the cassette.

"We are all gathered, but it may not be enough. The energy in the house feels different. It feels solid somehow if that makes sense. You need to tear it apart!" Sebastian slammed the staff of his halberd on the ground and began pounding on his armor with his gloved fist.

"There is a process, a procedure we must follow, Luke. We will enter and begin the blessing in the living room. There is no need to worry," Father D said, grabbing the front door. The priest froze in place, was surrounded by red sparks, and was thrown backward into Father Robert. Some type of supernatural booby trap. They both collapsed onto the ground.

Luke helped both men up ... *darkness and screams* ... The vision was suppressed. "The three of us should go down first. When it's safe, we let the others in."

Father D dusted himself off and repositioned his stole. "Yes, of course."

Luke stepped onto the threshold of the open door. The air was heavy, and the inside of the house was dark. Both priests followed Luke into the house and closed the door behind them.

✠ ✠ ✠

Avandeil

The priests spoke in Latin. Father Robert walked behind him swinging the thurible. The smell of the incense permeated the living room. They walked into the kitchen.

Sebastian and Luke stood together near the fireplace. The initial tension in the home seemed lessened, at least where the priests had just prayed over.

"Do you feel it?" Sebastian asked.

"I feel a weight on me like something was stuffed down my throat," Luke responded. "It must be hiding somewhere in the house. My guess is the attic."

"We need to draw it out from where it feels safe," Sebastian said.

He walked into the dining room and saw Father D pouring the smoke from the censer into the access to the cave. "Anything, Father?" He expected that Alyssa would be tied and bound in the cave.

"I don't see anything ... do you want to go check?" Father Robert asked with a scared look on his face.

"Not especially ... Sebastian, can you check, please?" Luke asked.

Sebastian dissipated into smoke and poured into the tunnel. He returned and reformed before Luke. "It's empty."

"It's empty. Let's bring everyone in for now," Luke said, opening the front door. Benji and Kamila walked in. The girls seemed scared enough and took a step back. "It's okay, it's not downstairs right now." He motioned for them to enter, and they complied reluctantly.

"Luke, we can continue blessing the home unless you want to try something else," Father D said.

"Let's all get back into a circle. I want to read the will and play this tape that Archibald Campbell gave me while you begin your rites." They all formed a school circle once again. His boom box stood in front of him. He loaded the cassette tape into it. "I need to get Kyle's attention and hoping that the prayer will drive Kyle toward the light." Luke removed the envelope and its contents from his coat. Three large raps against the wall of the house reverberated like a tuning fork.

"You have Avandeil's attention, Luke. The demon is afraid. You must grab Kyle's attention while the demon is angry and expending its energy." Sebastian stood on guard in the circle's center, looking in every direction.

Luke grabbed the statement he had written the night before. "Kyle, I'm here for you. I am here to help. I have a message from your grandfather. He is sorry for what happened to you on the night you argued over your son. He has included your son in his will."

Luke pulled out the will and began to read. "At the time of executing this last will and testament, I am unmarried and have no living children at the time of my death. My living relatives and sole heirs include my granddaughter, Lulu McCray and my great-grandson, Archie Kyle Lockwood, the natural-born son of Kyle Campbell, my grandson. All my property, savings, and belongings shall be divided amongst my living relatives except items mentioned elsewhere in this document." He walked up to the foyer and placed the will on the entry table. He took the boom box and placed it on the mantle of the fireplace.

"Keep going, Luke. You have his attention." Sebastian moved to the stairway in the living room. "The demon is moving around, but I don't know where it is."

Luke pressed play on the boom box.

"Kyle, it's your grandfather. I am thirty years older and broken down, but it's me. I am sorry for what happened that night so long ago. I was angry and have changed my mind over the last three decades. I should never have told you I would remove your son from my will. He is one of my heirs, even if he does not carry my name. He carries my blood, which is more important than my last name. I have met and love him. I'm so distraught that your spirit may be stuck here on earth when you should be with your parents and grandmother. Kyle, I love you and have missed you dearly all these years. Please forgive me, and at last, be at peace."

"Watch out. I am feeling some intense anger." A blur of an apparition rapidly came from the third-floor stairway down to the first floor. Sebastian placed his spear laterally against the floor, charged at the demon, and struck it away. "Play it again now!" Sebastian collapsed and fell to one knee.

He pressed rewind on the tape. "Father D, pray now."

"Luke, it's working, but the demon is angry. It's coming back," Sebastian screamed.

Luke saw Kyle in the dining room wearing overalls and a plaid shirt; his head was a jumble of faces. "There," he yelled. He pointed towards the dining room.

The priests sprinkled holy water at the apparition. "Luke, read your prayer while we read the Litany," Father D shouted.

He began to read aloud. *My Lord and God, I pray for your protection ...*"

The demon rushed toward Luke. Sebastian lunged to block it with his halberd. He struck the spirit of Kyle, who separated slightly from the form but tackled Sebastian and him, propelling them into the wall before falling to the floor. The house shook. Dust from the cracked drywall fell from the ceiling, sprinkled down through the spirit but collected over Luke. The circle broke, and everyone scattered.

"Stand up, you fat ass freak. You who are an unworthy second son of a murderer dare to enter my realm and order me around." To emphasize, Avandeil, in the shape of Kyle, urinated on him.

The urine scalded Luke's skin. "He got me, Sebastian. It hurts … please help me, I'm scared."

Sebastian tried to rise but fell. "I cannot move," Sebastian yelled.

The priests, Benji and Kamila, rushed to him and helped him up. The girls ran to the corner holding one another.

Father Robert anointed Luke with oil and sprinkled him with holy water while praying. Kamila and Benji ran to the teen girls in the corner of the living room and stood in front of them.

"Help me to the radio," Luke said.

Father Robert helped him to the boom box. "Kyle, listen to your grandfather and follow the light. You're free from this demon. Don't stay and let it steal your soul. Leave now, Kyle!" Luke yelled and then pressed play on the cassette player. The audio of Archie repeated, filling the room.

Avandeil rushed toward him, but Sebastian struck the demon with his halberd, forcing the upper body of Kyle's soul outward. Kyle grabbed Sebastian's gloved hand, who pulled the soul away from the mass.

"Thank you, Grandfather …" Kyle's disembodied voice said as the soul shot through the side of the house toward Campbell Farms. It was followed by a large screech. The apparition shot up the stairs toward the second floor.

"He's gone, Luke. Kyle's spirit has crossed over." Sebastian pointed toward the stairs. "Avandeil went to your brother's room."

"I cannot go any further." Luke dropped onto the sofa in exhaustion. Within seconds, his head flopped down onto his chest, and he grew sleepy.

"Luke, help me," the disembodied voice of Alyssa pleaded.

"Luke, did you hear the voice?" Father D stood by him. "Read your prayer. Get up, it's on the run, and we must do the same for each spirit. Rise and rest later."

"Seriously!" Luke stood reluctantly and almost stumbled to the floor. "My Lord and God, I pray for your protection around …" The demon was screeching upstairs while striking the house repeatedly. "We need to go to Daniel's room. The rest of you, come up to the second floor when he calls it clear."

Kamila shook her head and motioned for them to move on.

"Which ghost is in your brother's room?" Father D walked up to the entrance.

"The nurse, Andrea Walker, has been seen along with the burned man, Andrew Bolling." When Luke reached the second set of stairs, he felt a downward pressure immobilizing him. He tried to push forward, but it felt impenetrable. "Something is forcing me down. I cannot push through."

Father Robert began to pray while sprinkling holy water on the stairs and on Luke. "Dig deep inside, Luke. Fight it, now!"

"I can do it, Father. Keep praying," Luke said.

"Holy Lord, almighty Father, everlasting God, and Father of our Lord Jesus Christ. You who sent that fallen tyrant to the flames of Hell. Must come forth and remove Avandeil from the earth and this home once and for all …"

The screech again. It sounded like something scratching fingernails on a chalkboard but amplified with a speaker. He fell forward onto one knee on the stairway. The temperature in the house had dropped considerably, yet his brow and shirt were full of sweat. Their breaths were visible. "I'm gassed." His shoulders drop down as if in defeat.

"Move, Luke, or get out of the way. We need to take the battle to this abomination now!" Father D yelled.

Darkness had descended, forcing him to give up. He knew he must fight on but was truly weathered. The priest asking him to get out of the way damaged his ego. He felt defeated.

Birdy, Linnet and Sandy grabbed Luke and helped stand him up.

"Don't give up … keep fighting," Linnet said.

Father D pushed him forward. "Robert, push forward."

"Dig deep, Luke … don't let it keep Alyssa," Birdy said.

Sebastian moved behind Luke, grabbing his shoulders. "Move, soldier. The enemy must be confronted by the worthy!" The Guardian pushed forward. Luke climbed the stairs pushing forward.

Luke rose under Sebastian's hands up the stairs into Daniel's room. Sebastian fell to one knee and vanished.

Luke entered his older brother's room and was confronted by the apparition of the nurse trying to pull out of the abomination, of the burned man. The nurse looked toward him and tried to mouth something, which seemed like a plea for help. Then, the burned man pulled Andrea's spirit back into itself. The demon jumped at him and landed with his feet on Luke's shoulders, throwing him down onto his back as it roared at him. "Hey, sunshine. Your handyman brother cries for you while I have my way with him," said the folded skin goat's head, pouring steam from its horrid mouth. Avandeil hovered over him, dropping its spittle on his face as the beast salivated and took a bite into his soul … *I rolled backward as I floated into the dark and saw a toolbox. Inside it was something important the demon sought, that which was lost* … he came to once the demon released its teeth, prepared to bite back into him.

Benji ran into the room and grabbed at Luke. Avandeil hurled Benji into the wall. The house shook. Benji fell lifeless on the floor. Blood poured from his nose.

"Father. Help Benji!" Luke stayed helpless on the floor. His anger toward Avandeil overshadowed the embarrassment of placing Benji in this situation. He needed to fight this thing. Sebastian reappeared and grabbed Luke's shoulders and pulled him out of the demon's grasp.

Father Robert rushed toward Benji.

"Avandeil, God orders you be stripped from this earth and sent back down to the bowels of hell!" Father D and Father Robert sprinkled holy water on the apparition, now the shape of the burned man.

It shrieked at Father D and slithered into the bathroom, slamming the door shut behind him, causing it to splinter from top to bottom.

Father D helped him up. "What is this thing?"

"It's Avandeil, but it's composed of all the souls it has devoured. I saw the nurse trying to pull herself away," Luke said.

"That means your brother is in there too." Father D helped Luke over to Benji.

The priest had wiped away the blood from Benji's face. "Wake up, buddy," Luke said while he shook his friend.

Benji's eyes opened wide, and he shot up, grabbing his nose. "I think that freak broke my nose."

"It's an improvement," Luke said, laughing. "If you can walk, go downstairs and ensure the girls are okay."

"Sure, buddy." Benji walked out of the room, stumbling.

"Robert, we will continue our prayers. Luke, do you have a statement for the nurse like you did for Kyle?" Father D asked.

"I do, Father." Luke reached into his coat for his notes.

Father D began to recite his prayer. "My Lord, come forth and remove Avandeil from this home once and for all. God, you who sent your only begotten son into the world to crush the evil that walks the earth under your sky. We call for your help to remove Andrea Walker from the clutches of this inconsequential servant of the devil."

A horrendous blood-curdling cry emanated from the bathroom. The floor shook and then pulsed upward as if a giant poked at the subfloor from below, causing all three holy warriors to fall. They rose, and Father D sprinkled holy water forcibly through the cracked door. The demon roared again, but it was a weak effort.

"Now, Luke," Sebastian said, pointing his halberd toward the door.

Luke began to read. "Andrea Walker! Andrea, I know you loved Nathan Bridger and died accidentally in despair. Nathan is not present in this house or inside the demon Avandeil. Nathan is waiting for you in Heaven and seated beside our Almighty God. Because of his illness, Nathan's soul is not trapped by the demon who thought your beloved's soul had no value. Make your way out of this scourge and join Nathan with God in Heaven, Amen."

Sebastian roared and pushed onward to the door, which he hit, and it burst apart, striking the burned man with his spear. Sebastian pulled the spear back toward him, and the spirit of Andrea Walker rushed out of the bathroom and toward him.

Luke saw a smile on Andrea's face as her spirit rushed into the ceiling and onto Heaven.

The burned man rushed out of the room in a mist that pushed all of them, including Sebastian, to the floor. They all stood slowly. A sight to behold because each looked more disheveled than the next. Each had blood on their face, body, and clothing.

"It has lost two souls, but it's still strong," Luke said.

"It has to lose strength, Luke—we need to keep moving," Father D said, grabbing Father Robert ... *darkness enveloped me at the priest's touch. A vision of diseased bones and blood permeated my thoughts. Father D was sick with cancer and dying* ... pushed them forward like a tactical team out of the room and up the stairs. Luke saw that the priest was ill, but they had to move on. He wanted a pause. Removing two souls from the demon had brought him to exhaustion. It embarrassed him slightly because Father D was an older man, and his ailment did not appear to hinder him. He pushed forward, knowing now their time was limited. Alyssa needed out of that swamp.

CHAPTER THIRTY-EIGHT

Climbing the Pagoda

Sebastian moved to the front of the trio as they left the room, pointing his halberd forward. Luke was directly behind the Guardian, breathing heavily. He took a deep breath and received a sharp, unwelcome pain in his right side. Luke felt his side and recoiled in pain. He winced loudly. *I think Avandeil broke my ribs,* he mused. "It has to be in my room."

Father D stopped in between the attic stairwell access and his bedroom. "Father Robert, we will go in first. We will repeat the Litany. You will repeat the challenge against Avandeil. Luke, do you know how to confront the burned man?"

"Yes, Father. I wrote something that should get his attention and draw Andy out, and hopefully Andrew." He stepped aside with Sebastian and allowed both priests to enter.

Both priests flowed into the room. Father Robert swung the censer madly. Luke followed Sebastian. The demon was not visible.

"Can you see the demon, Luke?" Father D asked.

"No, it must be hiding," Luke responded.

"I have an idea," Father D said, grabbing for something within his black suit pocket. He pulled out a purple bag and poured something at the threshold of the room, windows, bed, and then around the desk.

The burned man screeched loudly, hiding under his desk. Luke saw a little boy's head peering from behind its shoulders. Andy's soul was trying to grab at Luke's desk and pull himself out of the burned man.

"Can you see it? It's under my desk," Luke said.

"No, Luke ... it must be low on energy. It will be gone soon enough," Father D said.

"What did you pour from that bag?" Luke asked.

"It's blessed salt," Father Robert said. "We use it in baptisms and to create protective barriers in a room or the altar. The act of blessing the salt is an exorcism."

"Why didn't you break it out earlier?" Luke asked, grabbing a pinch of salt from the windowsill, and throwing it at the cowering creature under his table.

Avandeil screeched in pain and began to scratch itself, trying to remove the grains of salt from its skin.

"We didn't realize the extent of the problem. We should have sprayed the salt on all of us for protection," Father D responded. "Robert, please continue your prayers."

"Strike terror, my Lord, into this beast and thief of souls named Avandeil, who is now laying waste to this Godly home and your humble servants. Fill us, your servants, with the courage to fight this enslaver of souls forcibly. Your mighty hand must cast Andy, Andrew, Alyssa, and Junior from the clutches of this evil spirit, Avandeil. On your command, Avandeil may no longer hold any soul captive in this house ..."

Father D sprinkled holy water on the desk and floor surrounding the area. "Our Father, who is in Heaven, hallowed be Thy name ..."

Luke grabbed the statement he wrote to get Andy's attention. "Andy Bolling. Andy Bolling!" He yelled and appeared to gain the attention of the little spirit. "Andy, you're not your father. Your mommy misses you and is sorry she did not protect you from your daddy and Avandeil. Your sister Patricia loves you. Avandeil and your daddy have been harmful to you. You deserved better. Your sister still lives and misses you. Leave this demon and rejoin your body."

Sebastian walked toward the spirit and turned toward Luke. "It's not ready, Luke. The demon is pretending to be scared."

The burned man sprung at Sebastian through the barrier of salt. Its skin burned as it flew in the air. It forced the Guardian into the wall.

Sebastian tried to push the burned man from him. Sebastian's halberd fell to the carpet without a sound.

"Pray over the bed," he yelled unnecessarily as the bed sheets were now pressed downward.

Both priests stood over the bed and sprinkled holy water and salt. Father Robert began his prayer to release the souls from the evil spirit. Father D read the Litany.

He began to re-read the statement. "Andy, you are not your father ..." Andy began to pour out of the burned man by pushing on the burned man's head. Sebastian secured Andy's head and pulled the spirit away. Andy's soul ran out of the burned man and rushed to the exterior wall. Andrew's captured soul forcibly reached out of the burned man and tried to catch Andy's spirit. Sebastian pulled his dagger from its sheath, stabbed Andrew's chest, yanked the rest of the burned man's soul out of the shrieking demon, and slammed it on the carpeted floor.

"Father, the spirit of Andrew is on the floor. Sprinkle it with holy water!"

"I'll do one better." Father D removed the purple bag from his coat pocket and poured the contents onto the carpet. Then, he sprinkled holy water over the blessed salt. Steam rushed out of the carpeted floor.

A loud and creepy cry rang out. It sounded like somebody was melting in a fire; the spirit of Andrew dissipated in a smoky vapor that shot downward toward Hell, where it belonged.

"Are they gone, Sebastian?" Luke asked.

"Yes. The father and son are freed." Sebastian dissipated slowly. "I'm losing energy and may have to ..." Sebastian vanished.

"The demon is all that remains now," Father Robert said.

Luke considered the priest's words closely. "No, it still has my brother. It must be in the attic." He sat on his bed, touched his side, and winced. The pain was excruciating, and it was difficult to breathe.

"What's wrong, Luke?" Father D asked.

"It broke my ribs when it knocked me down in my room."

"Let's take a break and catch up with the others downstairs," Father D said.

Luke was not going to argue with that. They had to regroup and finalize the battle against Avandeil. His brother Junior's soul was at stake. Not to mention Alyssa, who was trapped in that awful swamp.

✝ ✝ ✝

Poder

They staggered downstairs slowly. Sebastian had not reappeared. The priests held onto one another until they entered the foyer. Benji ran up to him and grabbed onto his arm ... *I fell backward once again, thinking I would strike the stairs. It was another vision. I was in the school lunchroom. Staring at a tall man wearing a leather jacket who was eating off the food tray of an underclassman.*

"My amigo, Jimmy Cladhaire or, as we call him, 'The Bully Cladhair.' His hair is always clad up like that. He's a violent bully." Benji had a disgusted look on his face ... Benji released him on the sofa. He shook away the vision, realizing he had to focus on what was before him. "Thanks, Benji."

"Anytime, buddy but the next time we hang out it better be at one of your barbecues."

Kamila sat next to him and tried to touch him. He waved her off, sat back on the sofa, and promptly nodded off ... *I was at my grandfather's new house. I sat on an outdoor sofa overlooking a pool. I was drunk. A glass in my hand. I heard many voices speaking all at once. This was a reception for a funeral that was just held for my father and brother. I failed, and the demon had won ...* he jumped off the sofa and stood up quickly. He had this impulsion to go pounce on his heavy bag. *No, if I punch anybody it will be Avandeil,* he thought.

"Are you okay, Luke? Benji asked.

"How long was I out?"

"A few minutes ..." Benji did not finish his thought.

Luke walked briskly to the kitchen and began to heat water. He brewed some strong Caribbean coffee with heavy cream. Enough to fill a carafe.

Kamila walked into the room. "How bad was it?"

"It was pretty bad." Luke served himself a cup and another for Kamila. His hand shook uncontrollably. He spilled coffee on the counter clumsily. He took her a cup and tried to hand it to her. She waved him away, so he placed it on the counter near her. He gulped his cup down quickly. "Do you want coffee or not?"

"Did you ask me here to drink a *café con leche*?" she asked angrily. "I thought you needed my help to fight this thing."

"I do need your help. I need to understand something ... I think the demon is afraid of something buried in the house. Are you going to drink the coffee?"

"Stop with the freaking coffee already. Tell me what is going on from A to Z. Go pebble level if you need to."

"We don't have time for A to Z," he said and laughed. He had to hold onto his side with his right arm. He took a painful breath. "In short, this house has been infested since the 1960s by an evil demon named Avandeil. It feeds on souls to give them the strength to possess an area and then oppresses anybody who interferes with it. That is what happened to Junior and my father. It must have felt like my father was a threat and used his power over the souls, and it controlled my father by blinding him. It attacked him when he was ready to protect us."

Kamila stared at him with her mouth wide open. "Get the heck out of here ... you and the priests have removed the souls from Avandeil." Kamila appeared as if she understood.

"You do weird easy, Titi. I need your help."

"With what? You're on a roll," Kamila said.

"Where could Alyssa be?"

Kamila put her finger to her lips. "I thought about this. I think your house has a portal. That must be how the demon entered your home."

"I'm not following you," Luke said.

"I think Avandeil developed the power to force Alyssa through the same portal. He placed her in a spiritual time out."

"I had a vision that she is someplace dark. It feels like a swamp. I can hear her calling out for help."

"Wait, you are still seeing things? she asked. "Like when you were a kid."

"Yes, it was part of who I am all this time," he responded.

"I told your parents to let it develop … you know I had to pry the truth out of your mother when you were kid?" Kamila asked.

"Can you explain it to me some other day?" Luke asked.

"Of course. What else?"

"I know that something in a toolbox is giving the demon a foothold on the house. It's not just the souls. Something happened when it all began in the 1960s."

Kamila's phone rang, and she grabbed it from her purse. "I think it's your mother." Kamila pressed send on her Motorola *Micro TAC Lite Digital Personal Communicato*r telephone. "Hello. I had to step away. I'll head back, okay Helen." Kamila pressed the end button on the phone.

"What's wrong with Junior?" Luke asked.

"Calm down. Calm down. Your brother was waking up but had a seizure. The doctors gave him something to calm him down."

"We need to finish this now, Kamila. We are running out of time." He was desperate to find a way to kill off the demon.

"I don't know everything you do," Kamila said softly.

"What would lock a demon into the house?"

"Santeria, witchcraft, or satanic stuff. A totem, maybe, something that represents the demon itself. A mask, or something like that."

"When it started, the owner practiced Satanism in his shed," Luke said.

"Where's the shed? The one in front?" Kamila asked.

He rushed to the front, passing his friends and the priests. "I made coffee if anyone wants some," he told everyone. They all moved to the kitchen.

He stepped out the door toward the shed. Kamila followed close behind. He entered the structure and looked around. "No, this isn't it. It's just as old, but this isn't it."

"What do you mean, is there another shed?" Kamila looked around the property.

"There had to be a different one. Andrew Bolling burned it down with himself inside of it. He used the shed like an office. I'm thinking it had to be close to the breaker box." He grabbed two rakes. "Come with me." He stepped out of the shed, remembered where the utility box was, and started running.

"What's up?" Kamila tried to keep up with Luke, who was sprinting.

"It must be near the electrical breaker box on the opposite side of the house." He passed the corner of the house, stopped, and looked at the utility box. Turning left and staring at a flat area covered in leaves and tree branches, he believed he had found what he was looking for. He handed Kamila the rake. "Take all the leaves off."

Kamila moved the leaves from the opposite end of the flat area and met in the center.

"There's ash and black scorch marks here right over some cement. This is it. We need to clean off the whole surface." They removed the debris from the area but found nothing remarkable. "Try the edges and look for something that could have been moved or pushed off." They began trying to get through all the branches, but they were too thick, although they were crackling because they were dry.

"I have an idea, Luke." Kamila turned the rake over and began probing into the dry brush.

"Great idea, Titi." They searched for several minutes before Kamila struck something metallic and hollow.

"It's here. We need to clear the brush away," Kamila said.

They both uncovered what looked like a metal toolbox covered in black soot. Luke moved the toolbox away to the dirt, noticing his hands were black when he opened it. It contained a six-inch-long statue carved from a piece of wood. It looked ancient, with one prominent figure surrounded by numerous small figures. He reached in to grab it.

Sebastian slammed the staff of his halberd down. "Don't touch it."

"No, don't touch it. Close the toolbox and take the whole thing to the priests," Kamila said with a stressed voice.

"Did he try to burn it?" Luke asked. The latch was not locked.

"Wait, Luke," Sebastian knelt beside Luke before touching his shoulder.

He began to feel faint, falling backward into another time ... *I stood before Andrew Bolling who was noticeably drunk. It was a cramped area. It had to be the shed. A desk and a few boxes full of comic books surrounded me. Andrew had a toolbox open with a carving inside of it.*

"You destroyed my family. You destroyed my son. Get out of my mind." Andrew took a bottle of whiskey from his desk, took a long swig, and drank almost half the bottle. He then took another mouthful and spat on the statue. "Let's see how you like this." He poured a can of gasoline on himself while drinking some of the fuel.

I walked away realizing what was about to happen. Andrew walked toward the desk but tripped and struck his head against the wall. The toolbox closed. He appeared stunned, reaching for his face where a flap of skin hung from his skull. He went into his pocket and took out a lighter and hit the striker and was engulfed. I stood watching while Andrew burned to death silently ... he stood up quickly and almost fell over but steadied himself before vomiting all the coffee up on the leaves. The stench of the now-soured cream made him vomit again. Fortunately, the caffeine was already in his system.

"What happened? Are you okay?" Kamila asked with concern.

Luke held onto his side and grabbed the toolbox. "Ask me tomorrow. We have a demon to finish off." He could feel it. It was almost over. They were going to win. The demon was all but finished.

CHAPTER THIRTY-NINE

Its Domain

When they entered the home, everyone sat on and around the sofa. They appeared to be napping. Luke brought the toolbox into the house and placed it near the fireplace. "Father D, we found this totem outside, buried near the foundation of an old shed. Andrew Bolling died trying to burn it."

Father D knelt before the toolbox and peered within it. "It's old. I have seen things like this before. They can be powerful against susceptible people. We are going to pray over it and burn it."

"How can I help?" Benji asked.

"Get some kindling and some logs from outside," Luke said.

Benji ran off. The priests dropped the totem out of the toolbox onto the fire grate. It began to emit steam.

"Why is it smoking already?" Birdy asked.

"It's the iron. Demons are repelled by it," Kamila said.

"Superstitious nonsense," Father D mumbled.

Kamila motioned throughout the house. "Really, Father?"

"Sorry, Miss Poder. I regretted it as soon as I spoke. Robert, please, continue the prayer," Farther D said.

"Yes, Father. Lord Jesus Christ, Word of God the Father, and God of all creation, who gave authority to your holy Apostles ..." Father Robert read the Rite of Major Exorcism with his hand over the wooden sculpture. It continued to smoke but not burn.

Benji returned, placed the kindling over the totem, and added several small dry logs. "How does this fireplace light? Does it have gas?"

"No, use these fireplace matches," Luke said, handing Benji the matches while the priests prayed together.

Benji lit the match, and the kindling lit as if gasoline had been poured onto it. All of them fell backward as the totem burned.

A scream from above caused all of them to look up the stairway. Avandeil was dying already. They were winning.

Father D sprinkled blessed salt into the fire. Avandeil screamed again.

"It knows it's going back home," Benji said.

"Kamila and Benji, stay here and make sure that thing turns into ash," Father D said. "Everyone else, come with me."

Father Robert picked up the censer and lit more incense. Father D led the way up the stairs with Robert behind him. The rest followed silently behind the praying priests. With the totem burning, they were prepared to return Avandeil to hell. The air was no longer heavy, and it was bright. Father D opened the door to the attic and walked up the stairs.

Luke stepped on the first step and felt the heaviness in the air again. It seemed darker than the hallway. He took the last step entering the refurbished attic and looked around.

Father Robert walked from one side to the swinging censer and started reading the prayers. Father D sprinkled holy water throughout the room, praying as well.

"Something is wrong." Luke proceeded slowly into the attic. He motioned for the girls over to where the sofa and television were. Luke walked closer to the priests. Sebastian walked backward, protecting Luke's vulnerable back.

The two priests stood in the narrow hallway leading to Junior and Daniel's joined rooms. Junior, or something looking like their brother, walked out of his room and pointed his finger at both priests. A red bolt of lightning shot out toward both priests and struck them. They flew upward together and hit the wall and then the floor.

Sebastian tossed his halberd at Junior and struck the apparition, causing it to vanish.

"Hey, watch it, that's my brother!" Luke yelled.

"That's the abomination pretending to be your brother," Sebastian said, retrieving his spear. "Tend to the priests." Sebastian walked into Junior's room.

"Oh yeah … you're right." Luke grabbed at Father Robert and helped him up.

The girls ran over and helped Father D back to the sofa. They returned and helped him move the other priest to the couch.

"Are you both okay?" Luke asked.

"That really hurt," Father Robert said, massaging his neck.

Father D rubbed his left arm and shoulder. "Turn around, Luke."

The girls screamed as he turned around. Junior rushed to him, thrust both his hands into him, and raised him into the air. Luke was surrounded by a red glow from the electric charge he was enveloped in. He felt weightless and was thrown into the air and fell into the three girls … *the backward motion made me sick. I slipped into the hot, thick, swampy water and could not breathe. I could not move at first and panicked. Eventually, I rose from the fetid water, back in Alyssa's prison. "Alyssa, where are you?"*

"I can see you. I'm over here."

I saw the motion ahead in the water ahead of me and ran to it. Alyssa was here, dirty, and muddy. She stood on something, or she would have drowned. I embraced her and gave her a long kiss. "How long have you been here?"

"Days … it's been miserable," Alyssa responded. "Can you get me out of here?"

"We're trying, but Avandeil is fighting back."

"Is that its name? I haven't seen it yet, but it talks to me," Alyssa said.

"What does it say?" I asked.

"It loves me, wants me, and will lie with me soon."

"Lie with you … how can it lie with you? Pay attention, if you see a way out take it," I said … he was thrust forward violently. He opened his eyes. His angle was sideways because he lay on the

floor.

The demon in the shape of Junior cowered naked in the center of the room. Both priests prayed over him, sprinkling the demon with holy water. It screeched and spit toward Father Robert.

"O God, whose nature is always to forgive and show mercy, receive our prayer for this your servant, Junior, who is bound in chains by the power of the Devil. May your faithful love and compassion mercifully grant him release. Through Christ our Lord, Amen," Father D said.

"Luke, if these jokers don't release me, I'll sodomize your parents every night for eternity!" Avandeil snarled at him like a cornered animal before morphing into its true likeness of a goat's head with octopus tentacles for arms. It then morphed back into the shape of Junior. "Luke, don't hurt me—I'm your brother."

"You're not Junior. You're some creeper who has taken his soul hostage!" *How did this demon gain strength again?*

Sebastian walked over to Avandeil and stabbed the Junior-shaped demon repeatedly with his halberd. Sebastian raised the spear high for one final thrust.

It was almost over. That final strike would remove Junior's soul from the demon. They had won and everything would return to normal.

Sebastian rammed the spear home and pulled it outward. Junior's soul held onto the spear and flowed out of the demon's body, which lay flaccid on the floor. Junior's soul flowed quickly outward toward the hospital.

Luke rose and smiled.

Suddenly, Avandeil, the deceiver, rose, grabbed the staff of the halberd, and wrenched it away from the guardian. It shoved the head of the halberd into Sebastian. Who promptly vanished. Then, it struck both priests with the staff. They were not cut, but Luke saw their souls partially drain from their bodies. Avandeil dropped the halberd, leaned in toward the damaged souls, and consumed some of the essence with its flailed folds of skin. Both priests collapsed noisily to the ground.

Luke rushed to the priests and was again hit with red electrical energy. Avandeil motioned his hand quickly toward the wall, and Luke flew as if tossed. He struck the stairway's banister and fell down the stairs and onto the third-floor carpet. His thigh burned from the blunt force trauma it received.

The girls ran past Luke down the stairs. Luke screamed in pain, but it was pure rage that drove him now. He ran back up the stairs, ignoring the pain, and saw Avandeil holding Father D before him.

Avandeil sprayed the priest with a mist coming from its mouth and then engulfed Father D's head absorbing all the priest's tissue and essence.

Luke heard a loud scream. It came from his own mouth. He ran toward the sinful scene but was pushed backward. He had no choice but to watch Father D's body shrivel, and the demon began to form into a skeleton, organs, ligaments, tendons, and muscles. Father D was most assuredly gone.

Avandeil let go of Father D's body which dropped weightless to the floor. The demon then grabbed Father Robert, who was still unconscious.

Luke positioned himself as if he were a sprinter in starting blocks before a race. He made the sign of the cross. "Strike terror, my Lord, into this beast and this thief of souls named Avandeil, who is now laying waste to this Godly home and your humble servant Dwayne, a pious man of God," Luke roared and thrust toward the demon tackling *it* against the wall. *It* let go of Father Robert ... *I realized immediately that I was wrong. The demon brought me to this very moment. It gave up the damaged souls it had possessed willingly ... It* wanted the priest's souls all along. Andrew Bolling imprisoned Avandeil in the home. The demon wanted the totem burned so it would not be trapped inside the circumference of where the toolbox was buried. He was released from a decades long prison sentence.

"What a child, you fell for my trap," Avandeil said through an unformed mouth.

The creature was a slimy, grotesque, unformed mess. It tried pushing it away, but tentacles poured out and covered Luke. It began to squeeze.

"You cannot have Alyssa. She'll vomit at your very sight," Luke said.

A laugh came from the mass holding him. "Not too smart, are you. You didn't realize all along that I was blinding you as well as your father. The priest was a pious and trusted man of the church." Avandeil laughed again, squeezing Luke as he did. "But you, Luke, are exceptional. I'll take over your life. I will become you, but I will take over this realm instead of protecting the church. I will walk the earth with Alyssa by my side willingly."

Luke tried to break free. It was futile. He was not worthy—*non sei degno*. He laughed now, how could he delude himself into thinking he was a protector. This freaking abomination bested him before he finished high school.

"You're beginning to see it now." Avandeil squeezed harder and formed his face into the folded-skin goat's head. It blew smoke into Luke's face, preparing to devour his soul. "I'll tell you what, I will not kill your parents if you give yourself to me willingly."

"Screw you, deceiver. Alyssa will see right through you. She'll never give herself to you!" Luke yelled and kicked at the slimy mess. His face contorted in pain and sorrow of a man who had given up his life and future.

"Yeah, I shouldn't have brought it up. Ah well, how do you say in Puerto Rico, *buen provecho*?"

Luke screamed loudly, trying to get help, when somebody grabbed his foot ... *I fell backward with such ferocity my brain felt like it detached itself. I felt like someone was with me. I was with Father Robert who was praying in a whisper, the Rite of Exorcism then the word exsufflation repeatedly* ... he stared at the folded flayed skins of flesh before him and took in a lungful of air and exhaled his breath on the abomination. The folds of skin melted away as if struck by acid.

Avandeil released him reflexively. *It* backed up into the wall, spraying tissue everywhere.

Father Robert rose and sprinkled Holy Water on the gore before him. "O God, creator, and defender of humanity, look with favor upon your servant, Father Dwayne, whom you formed in your own image and call to share in your Glory. The ancient enemy is racking him fiercely, crushing him with violent force, tormenting him with wild terror. The forgiveness of sins, the resurrection of the body, and life everlasting."

Avandeil roared incomprehensibly and fell to its knees. "Please stop … I must touch Alyssa at least once?"

"Release her, Avandeil," Luke yelled. He breathed on the abomination again, melting away an arm.

Avandeil screeched in pain. Pointed toward Junior's room, the home shook from its foundation, and a loud thud struck the floor. Then it was silent.

"Luke, are you here?" Alyssa asked, walking toward them. Kamila, the girls, and Benji ran upstairs.

Kamila ran into the attic. "What struck the house?"

"That's freaking gross, man!" Benji said staring at Avandeil's grotesque state.

Luke ran to Alyssa and hugged her. She looked weak. "Get Alyssa to the hospital now, Benji."

Benji and the girls walked Alyssa carefully down the stairs and to safety.

"Kamila, help us finish it off," Luke said, offering his hand to her. She grabbed it, and they walked to the cowering demon. Father Robert grabbed his other hand.

"Together with our brother, let us implore God to deliver us from evil, as our Lord Jesus Christ taught us to pray," Father Robert said.

"Together now," Luke said. "Our Father, who art in heaven, hallowed be thy name. Thy kingdom come; thy will be done on earth as in heaven …" They continued as the gore before them screeched in anger.

"I gave you the girl. Release me. I will not come back," Avandeil pleaded.

"You are in no position to ask for anything. Deceiver!" Luke screamed and breathed on the demon.

Father Robert did the same. The creature continued to melt away.

Luke saw Sebastian's halberd on the ground. "Sebastian, where are you?" His guardian did not respond. He stared at the halberd intensely. He made the sign of the cross. "God, give me the strength to defeat your enemies." He reached down, grabbed the halberd, and struck the demon one final time. *It* boiled into steam that hovered in the air.

The house shook again, and the floor opened below the demon gas. A clawed hand came up from the opening, and another abomination rose from the portal. This demon had the body of a lion with a goose head and feet. *It* reached up to the swirling gas with a *Canopic* jar and collected Avandeil's gaseous remains. *It* replaced the cover, which appeared to have a goat's head on it.

"What in God's name is that?" Kamila asked.

"It's Ipos, a prince of Hell," Father Robert said.

"Thanks, I lost this one," Ipos said, moving to return to the portal. "Next time we meet Luke, I'll bring the rest of the boys. I have seen it. It will be fun." Ipos jumped back into the portal, which closed.

The room was suddenly bright like somebody had opened the shades or a curtain. The evil fog had lifted, and the horrific thief of souls was back where it belonged.

Kamila's digital telephone rang numerous times, but she did not answer.

Luke and Father Robert sat on the sofa together. The pain running through his body was unbelievable. He had been horribly battered, and the throbbing on his leg and the pain on his side was unbearable. *Was it over? After seeing Ipos I fear that it will never be over*, he thought. Father Robert and Luke held onto one another and wept. They both lost a mentor and friend.

CHAPTER FORTY

The Loss

Until now, Luke failed to notice that as Avandeil dissolved, Father D's body had reconstituted but he was not alive. Luke and Father Robert knelt next to the priest, who was most assuredly gone. Tears flowed freely from Luke and onto the priest's chest.

Father Robert placed a rosary in his mentor's hands across his abdomen. "O God, by whose mercy the faithful departed find rest, send your holy Angel to watch over this man."

Kamila knelt near Luke, who had grabbed Father D's hand … *I fell into darkness but landed in a pew at the chapel at the hospital.*

"Luke, you must promise that you will look after Robert. He will be a friend to you and help you through your struggles throughout your life," Father D said.

"Father, you left me too soon. I need you," Luke said, shaking his head and crying. *"How can I face the world naively with a priest who hasn't seen what you've seen."*

"I will be in your dreams, young man, and because of that, I will help lead you both. Have faith as our Lord and I have in you."

"Thanks, Father. Thanks for helping me and my family," I said.

"Your troubles with your home may be over, but your battles ahead are not. Dream and remember the calamity. Whatever it is, you must stop it. Don't be blinded by your future struggles or the battles you'll fight. You must prevent the calamity … he was back in the attic.

Kamila's phone rang again. "Hello? Yes. Helen, is everything better? Did it work? Oh my God. Here, speak with Luke." Kamila handed over her phone to him.

"What's up, Mom?" Luke asked.

"Juniors awake. He's asking for you," his mother said.

"We'll be right over. Yes, Mom, I'm at the house, but I can explain later." He ended the call abruptly while his mother was still talking. "Don't worry, Kamila, no matter what happens, we succeeded." He returned the digital telephone to her.

As he spoke on the phone, he failed to notice that Father Robert sat silently on the sofa. He did not look well and began to cough uncontrollably, grabbing his chest.

"Father, are you okay?" Luke asked.

The priest's eyes rolled into the back of his skull before going limp. Luke checked Father Robert's pulse. It was present but faint.

"Kamila, Father Robert's in bad shape. We may need an ambulance," Luke said, checking to see if the priest was breathing. If he doesn't react, the priest will perish on the sofa. He tossed Father Robert over his shoulder like a doll. "I will take him myself. Call the hospital and tell them to be ready. Then call the police and tell them about Father D."

Luke descended the steep stairs down each level. He ran down the driveway to his car. Luke was a mess, but the priest on his back might as well have been an anchor. He felt himself blacking out but kept running. Luke placed the priest in his passenger seat, put the shoulder belt on, took a deep breath, and retched. He had nothing inside but hot bile. It burned his throat as it was expelled.

He quickly jumped into the driver's seat and drove away toward the hospital. He flew down Red Hill Road and passed two cars in a blur. The streets were more congested in the center of town. He moved in and out of traffic, ignoring the emergency lights of a police car inching toward him a mile behind. He kept pushing through traffic, with vehicles parting to let him through as if they knew he was on a divine mission. He arrived at the hospital, where emergency room staff were waiting outside. The nurses opened the door and took Father Robert into the trauma entrance on a gurney.

Luke had to get to his brother Junior's room in the ICU. He

entered the elevator and leaned up against the side. A young boy and his mother entered the elevator with him.

"What floor, Mister?" the boy asked.

"Oh, I spaced out. Can you hit four for me, Slick?" Luke asked.

The boy pressed the button. "Mister, your head is bleeding."

Luke reached up to his head, and it was a bloody mess. When he lowered his hand, he cast blood on the elevator door and the white shirt the boy's mother wore. "Thanks, kiddo. Sorry about the blood, Ma'am." He walked out of the elevator and found his brother's room.

Junior sat in bed surrounded by his mother, Daniel, grandparents, and medical staff.

"Hey Luke, where's the conquistador?" Junior asked.

"I don't know. He was hurt," Luke responded flippantly.

Luke hugged his brother, almost collapsing on him. At one point, he thought he would never be able to talk with his brother again. Now, he squeezed him as hard as he could.

"Easy, I just woke up ... are you okay? Your clothes are all torn up, and you're bleeding," Junior asked.

"What's he talking about, Luke? Why are you bleeding?"

Luke did not answer his mother's direct questions. "It's been a day, that's why ..." He walked over to a chair and sat down. "Sorry guys, I need to rest a bit now." He promptly nodded off or passed out, unsure, but everything turned dark.

✠ ✠ ✠

Awakening

I stepped out of a limousine parked on Via Sant'Anna and shook hands with a cardinal who beckoned me to follow. Two members of the Swiss Guard opened a door, motioning for me to enter the Palace of Sixtus. I followed the cardinal through several ornate offices. It felt like a labyrinth. I arrived at an office door where two more Swiss Guards holding halberds blocked the door. Sebastian, wearing the felt cap his mother made for him, stood alongside me with pride. The cardinal spoke with the guards, and they shook their heads in the negative, staring toward me. The guards allowed the cardinal to enter but blocked the doorway again, staring menacingly toward me. The cardinal walked toward a man on a desk who wore clothing like the cardinal but more ornate. This was the Secretary General of the Vatican. The cardinal promptly walked to another man wearing white papal regalia who stood near a bookshelf. The man at the desk yelled out, Dignus es! ... the vision was gone. All at once, a bout of nausea attacked him, along with immense pain throughout his body. Everywhere he moved caused pain to a different side of his body.

"Way to go Rockstar," Archie's disembodied voice said.

"He's awake. Hey Luke," Kamila said, with his mother standing beside her.

His mother walked to his bedside with a worried look. She made sure to stand at arm's distance from Luke. "How are you, honey? You gave us a scare. The doctors said you were dehydrated and were suffering from overexertion and the onset of Rhabdomyolysis. Your whole leg is purple, but it's not broken but one of your ribs is ... what happened? Kamila won't answer my questions."

"Where am I? How long have I been here?" Luke asked.

"You're in the ICU. It's been six hours. A police officer wanted to speak with you about your driving, but Jorge got him to back off. What happened?" his mother asked impatiently.

"I had to rush through traffic to get Father Robert to the hospital. How is he?" Luke asked, trying to move up in the bed. Instead, he winced in pain.

"Father D passed away. I'm guessing you know this?" his mother asked.

"Yes, I was with him when he died. We spoke afterward, and we said our goodbyes," Luke said, sharing too much information. "I feel weird. Am I on something?"

"Morphine, I think," Kamila said.

"You two need to answer me now!" his mother's eyes stared at him like daggers.

Kamila shrugged her shoulders and she looked at Luke to respond.

Luke's mind was swirling with thoughts but knew he did not want to be persuaded or ordered to answer his mother.

His mother appeared to calm down. "A woman named Nancy stopped by the hospital with Lulu. Mr. Campbell passed away this morning."

"Do you know what time?" Luke asked.

"How do you even know the man," his mother said frustrated. "I'm sorry, Luke, I don't know. Sometime in the morning. She heard him talking to somebody, and he was gone when she entered the room."

"He lived a full life, Mom, and passed away peacefully. That's all that matters."

"That's true, Luke ... who's Sebastian?" his mother asked.

"Mom, I'm kind of out of it and afraid you wouldn't understand." He stared at Kamila, who took the stare like a stab and moved closer to his mother protectively.

"I need to know, Luke. Kamila is not telling me everything," his mother said.

"He's my imaginary friend." He smiled and giggled. "What kind of medicine did they give me?"

"Morphine, Kamila already answered your question. Answer mine now. Tell me who he is. You don't have a choice—I'm the mother, and you're the son. See how that works."

Luke sat up, looked across the room, and thought about Sebastian, but he didn't manifest. "Sebastian Sanz de Basque, Sebastian Sanz-Basque." The soldier didn't appear. "Sebastian, show yourself now."

"What are you doing, Luke? Who is this, Sebastian?" his mother asked frantically.

"He's dad's ancestor. Sebastian died at the Siege of Santo

Domingo in 1655. He was sent into the future by an angel named Miguel."

"You're nuts!" his mother said, at a loss for words.

"The ancestor? It's true. What Isidora said about the ancestor." Kamila moved closer to him.

"Kamila, what are you two talking about?"

"It's what Isidora told us. A spirit occupied Daniel because he was confused. Junior figures that Daniel became sick when Luke was conceived. When Luke's soul descended from heaven, Sebastian occupied Daniel by mistake. You see, Sebastian was always meant to be Luke's guardian angel."

"Why Luke? I don't understand. He almost killed Daniel." His mother practically squealed that out.

"I am a warrior for God, I guess. They call me a protector of the faith," Luke said, almost nodding off.

"You believe this?" his mother asked.

"I'm beginning to. Look what happened," Kamila responded.

"Where is he? Why did Junior see him?" his mother asked.

"He may have ascended, Mom. He was injured during our battle with the demon ... Junior could see him because his soul was out of his body."

"This is what is going to happen. You're going to talk to a therapist, and you are going to get treated. I'm talking commitment ..."

"No, Mom. I am who I am, and nobody needs to know about this. Neither one of you should know. We will never talk about this again without privacy." He slammed his fist against his thigh and felt intense pain. That's not precisely the emphasis he meant to exert.

His mother looked at him, and her face turned red. She looked like she was about to pop off in anger. Instead, she walked over to him and put her head on his chest ... *I fell backward into another room. I stood near my father's hospital bed. My parents were speaking. My father was conscious ...*

"Thanks for saving my baby," his mother said.

"You're welcome … so Dad's, okay?" Luke asked.

"Yes, he woke after Junior came to … how did you know?"

An attending physician entered the room and grabbed the clipboard at the foot of the gurney. "Mr. Sanz, how do you feel?"

His mother remained on his chest. "I'm awake but still very tired. My whole body and stomach hurt, but I'm not hungry."

His mother moved next to Kamila, wiping the tears from her face.

"The abdominal pain is because it looks like you were extremely dehydrated, and you have one broken rib. You were skating close to a bad case of Rhabdomyolysis. That trauma to your thigh could have something to do with it. It looked like you were hit by a car and overexerted yourself. Your muscles were damaged, and protein was released into your blood, damaging your kidneys. We can tell from your urine that you had a significant case."

"What urine? I don't think I peed yet."

The doctor grabbed a bag and raised it enough for him to see.

"What's that?" Luke was staring at what looked like rotten blood.

"Your urine, you're wearing a catheter."

"Why is it brown?" he asked, alarmed.

"In short, it's the breakdown of your muscles into your kidneys, which comes out in your urine. It's getting better. It was dark red before. When we began pumping you with fluids, we had to put the catheter in while you were unconscious. The good news is that you did not feel it going in," the doctor said.

"That's a blessing."

"The bad news is that you will feel every bit of it coming out," the doctor said with a smile.

"That's great … what's next, Doctor?" Luke asked.

"Your visitors will go home, let you eat, and then rest. If you improve, you go home tomorrow."

"Thanks, Doctor." He preferred to stay at the hospital and get some sleep. He felt like he fell off a building.

"Have a good evening. Thirty minutes, ladies. He needs his rest. I heard he carried a priest down three flights of stairs." The doctor left as quietly as he came in.

"One other thing, Luke, Father Lee called to tell us that Andy Bolling woke up. He's conscious and talking," his mother said.

"Unbelievable, the Bolling boy is awake."

"Yes, but who is this Bolling boy? You're not explaining yourself."

Eventually, his mother and godmother left, and he could eat dinner and sleep. When he woke up, it was dark in the room. He looked at the clock; it was two o'clock in the morning. Somebody was sitting in the chair.

"Who's that sitting over there?" he asked, fearing it was another demon.

"It's me, Luke. I was waiting for you to wake up. I was going to send you a message, but I figured you needed rest." Sebastian whispered as if he did not want to be overheard.

"I overexerted myself. I should be good in the morning. I thought you ascended. I tried calling you," Luke said.

"My soul was healing, I think. This is new to me. I lose energy every time I exert myself in your world. Getting stabbed with my own halberd was most exerting."

"You came here to protect your descendants, and you have. Why have you not ascended yet?" Luke asked.

"I will ascend when the Lord deems me worthy. Until then, I will be here by your side as you fight the evil that walks the Earth."

"How long will that be?" Luke asked.

"The remainder of your natural life will be spent fighting against our Lord's enemies, and I will be beside you," Sebastian responded proudly.

"Sebastian, I'm not going to become a priest."

"That's not in your future. You're a man but also an instrument. You're God's wrath. You'll often be misunderstood and feared, but you must always follow God's will. Be his wrath, but only when our Lord allows it. You have battles ahead. Some worse than what you experienced already, but all will take place under the sky with our Lord, and I will be your guardian."

"Sebastian, you're a strange cat." Luke pushed himself up in bed.

"I'm no cat," Sebastian quipped.

Luke laughed in pain, guarding his abdomen. "Do you know where Father Robert's room is?"

"Yes, I have looked in on both him and your father," Sebastian responded.

Luke stepped out of bed easily. Luckily the catheter had been removed earlier. He walked toward a wheelchair and took a seat. Luke felt a deep need to speak with Father Robert. Sebastian showed him his father's room, but he was asleep. He did not want to bother him but watched him sleep instead. That was enough to make him feel better. Next, Sebastian led him to the priest's room who was awake reading a book.

"Father Robert, how are you?" Luke asked, rolling the wheelchair into the room.

"I'm doing fine, thanks to you, Luke."

"I wanted to make sure you were okay."

"Thanks for rushing me here when you did. The doctors are calling it exhaustion, shock, and heart arrhythmia. I should be out of the hospital soon," Father Robert said. "They had to wire me up to correct my heart rhythm."

"I will let you rest. Hopefully, I will be released soon as well Father."

"Luke, please call me Robert. I'm a kid from a rough neighborhood in Cleveland. I believe you earned the right to call me Robert."

"That would be hard for me, Father. It's the way I was raised."

The priest offered Luke his hand in friendship. "I have a feeling we will have a long friendship, Luke. Please call me Robert."

He stood up and took Robert's hand in friendship. "Robert,

it's a pleasure to make friends amongst one of the Lord's pious and trustworthy servants."

They both smiled at one another. Luke saw something when he touched his friend Robert. It's a story best saved for another day for its a doozy.

✟ ✟ ✟

Under the Sky

The short time that Luke and his family lived in Lansburg, VA, had been challenging. The house on Red Hill Road had a renewed feel; all they hoped for was a bright future.

Junior and their father were back at home. They were prepared to live their lives without the demon that had become an anchor.

Alyssa and Luke planned on spending a romantic evening under the stars at a lookout area outside Leesburg. He parked next to a table at the lookout area and placed the blanket on the picnic table, where they laid looking into the sky.

"How was it sitting in that bog for almost two days?" Luke asked.

"It was horrible ... I just don't understand how you were able to visit me there," Alyssa said.

"I don't know myself." Luke needed to come clean to Alyssa, but he thought it would hurt her to know exactly who he was. "I don't want to scare you ... when I touch somebody, I get a glimpse of something important to them, or to me. Something that will help either one of us."

"But how did you visit me in that ... the swamp?" Alyssa asked.

"Were you ready to give up?" Luke asked.

"As a matter of fact, at that very moment I was thinking of

drowning myself in that filthy water."

They laid silently together for some time. "When I touched your three friends I was brought to you. I think the love your friends have for you sent me."

"Why, would my friend's love drive you to me?"

"It's because I love you, too," he said. Luke leaned in toward Alyssa and they kissed. "We're meant to be in each other's lives."

"When I am with you, I feel seen. I know that I matter," Alyssa said.

"It's because you do matter to me."

Alyssa propped herself up. "What happens when we touch?"

Sebastian stood by the front of Lukes car guarding the bench, looked toward the city, with the halberd at his side. "Tell her, Luke."

Luke closed his eyes and placed both his hands in the air with his palms facing him then he grabbed her hand ... *we sat together with our children and grandchildren. It was too distant in the future to capture the full scope of what I watched. A young girl tugged at my shirt, and I stared into her green eyes—Emerald* ... he returned to Alyssa. "We are together on a home by a lake—I thinks it's in the Ozarks in Missouri."

"What are we doing?" Alyssa asked.

"I see a little girl with green eyes. Her name is Emerald," Luke said. It's all hazy ... it's too far into the future."

"Emerald? Where did you hear that name?" Alyssa asked.

"I saw it. Why? Do you know someone named Emerald?"

"Yes, my parents had another baby after me. She passed away at birth. They named her Emerald because she had these piercing green eyes." Alyssa looked frightened.

Luke hugged her tightly. "I didn't mean to scare you. We should talk about something else."

"How are you seeing this, Luke?" Alyssa asked.

"It's a memory of sorts. A message," Luke said.

"A message from who?"

"From God. I think to keep me focused and looking into

what's possible for the future. I can change outcomes, but I don't want to mess with this one." They kissed again. He still has not recalled the calamity he was supposed to prevent. For now, his goal was to bring light to the evil that walked the earth. He would out the growing demonic influence in the world. Luke and Sebastian were flawed souls who were made whole by that which emanated under His sky.

Epilogue

Luke parked his car and grabbed his pack, which had his surveillance gear. He followed Sebastian for several minutes until reaching the crest of a small berm. He removed his binoculars and positioned them until he saw the white van. "I have a good view."

"Give it some time so you can see what they do," Sebastian said.

"Have you seen them do this before?" Luke asked.

"Yes, but I don't know why they are doing it. Do you see the black container in between the two red ones?"

"Yes, I can also see the wheels and the tracks."

"That is where they will be working and taking out bricks," Sebastian said. "I don't know how to explain what they are doing."

Luke saw movement coming from the warehouse. The red Pontiac *Fiero* was headed toward the white van, followed by a dark-colored pickup truck.

"The sun is going down, Luke. They are about to begin."

He grabbed the phone and called Terry.

"Luke, is this important? We are trying to get an eye on the area. Air is not here."

"I have an eye on the rail yard and can see what they're doing."

"You were supposed to be headed to the office ... ah, forget it. Tell me what you see."

"Moretti moved the white van next to a black container between two red containers. They are in a fenced-in area of the rail yard northwest of the Robertson warehouse. The red Fiero and a black pickup are joining him now."

"Can you take pictures?"

Luke switched to his camera which was equipped with a telephoto lens and zoomed in. "Yes, I have a good view, but it's low light. They are pointing the headlights at the container. Maybe that will help me as much as them."

"Take pictures and tell me when something changes. I will stay on the phone."

Luke took pictures of every player and car in the area, including a nice group photo.

"Surveillance units, we have an eye on the area with our man on the inside. Standby for any movement." Terry's voice was loud enough for Luke to hear from the phone's speaker.

"They are starting, Luke," Sebastian said, sounding anxious. The white van moved closer to the container but did not block his view.

Moretti and Rossi were under the container, working on something. Jose walked back and forth in the area. Looking for law enforcement, presumably. Luke continued to take photos but was mindful that he needed to keep enough film for whatever they pulled from the container. *What could they be doing?*

"Pay attention to how they do this," Sebastian said.

Luke used the camera zoom to look closer at Moretti, who was pulling on something. He must have gotten it loose because packages began to fall. Moretti continued to pull, and more packages fell. Rossi, Francisco, and Jose formed a line from Moretti to the van, throwing large bricks at one another and into the truck. They continued this for some time, Moretti pulled again, and many more packages fell. He captured all of this perfectly on his camera.

"Luke, can you hear me? Luke?"

"Yes, Terry ... they are pulling packages from the bottom of the container. They undid an access panel and removed packages tied to a rope."

"Great news, hold on ... they opened a trap in the container and are removing packages. Looks like a dope load. Standby. Luke, keep watching and let me know when they move out."

"I will, Terry."

"They're done. Watch what these men do," Sebastian said.

One of them grabbed a panel, placing it back on the underside of the container. The men ran back to their vehicles.

"Terry, they're getting ready to take off. All the packages are in the white Chevy van."

"Copy, Luke ... surveillance teams get ready for movement. The white Chevy van is the target. Don't lose that van. Follow it until it lands somewhere. The rest, follow the *Fiero* and pickup."

"Terry, they are all out of the yard. I'm heading out." That was cool, but he was still perplexed about what happened.

"Copy Luke, and thanks. Head back to the office and wait there. Seriously, Wil is going to kill me!" Terry seemed happy, yet angry somehow.

"Yes, on my way, Terry. Good luck," Luke said.

Sebastian ran back toward the car, halberd in hand. Luke ran behind his guardian, holding a backpack and surveillance gear. He laughed at the sight and hoped Father D could see him just then. It was funny.

ACKNOWLEDGEMENT

This novel took over ten years to complete. The first outline was drafted in 2012. In 2020, I was introduced to the acting of Hal Cumpston. I realized that Cumpston's acting was what I thought Luke Sanz would behave like. I would never have finished the story I first thought of in the 1980s without my unwitting muse.

The working title of the novel has always been the Red Hill Haunt. At some point, I realized that Luke Sanz would be a serialized character. His future is to be a warrior for God and the Holy See. I was being guided by a preternatural hand.

I used the *New Revised Standard Version (NRSV)* of the Holy Bible by Harper Catholic Bibles to guide me while writing this novel. I also consulted the *Roman Ritual: Exorcisms and Certain Supplications*. This includes paraphrased prayers during the house blessings, exorcism, and Father D's mass.

Thanks to my proofreader and wife, Dona. Thanks for putting up with what amounted to years of abandonment while I was putting together this work. I genuinely love you.

Thanks to my other proofreader, Christina L. Pearson, who was inspired to write the poem at the beginning of this book.

I want to thank my developmental editors from the Story Ninja. Randy Surles and Laura Graves. It's still imperfect, but without your guidance, the book would have remained a jumbled mess without coherent scenes.

The city of Lansburg is fictional as is Lansburg Center High School.

Luke and Sebastian will be back soon, God willing. Their next battle under the sky will be attempting to stop a bully subjugating the students at Lansburg High in A Dance with the Bully. In a future work, Luke will fight to save a kidnapped Cardinal during the Battle of Mogadishu in *Cardinal Down*. See you soon, *si dios quiere*.

Sig. Alexander

www.ingramcontent.com/pod-product-compliance
Lightning Source LLC
Chambersburg PA
CBHW020909200626
46814CB00001BA/243